Joss Wood loves books, coffee and travelling – especially to the wild places of Southern Africa and, well, anywhere. She's a wife and a mum to two young adults. She's also a servant to two cats and a dog the size of a small cow. After a career in local economic development and business, Joss writes full-time from her home in KwaZulu-Natal, South Africa.

New York Times and *USA Today* bestselling author **Cathryn Fox** is a wife, mum, sister, daughter, aunt and friend. She loves dogs, sunny weather, anything chocolate (she never says no to a brownie), pizza and red wine. Cathryn lives in beautiful Nova Scotia with her husband, who is convinced he can turn her into a mixed martial arts fan. When not writing, Cathryn can be found Skyping with her son, who lives in Seattle (could he have moved *any* further away?), shopping with her daughter in the city, watching a big action flick with her husband, or hanging out and laughing with friends.

USA Today bestselling author **Catherine Mann** has over 100 books in print in more than twenty countries with Mills & Boon. A six-time *RITA* finalist, she has won both a *RITA* and Romantic Times Reviewer's Choice Award. Mother of four, Catherine lives in South Carolina with her husband where they enjoy kayaking, camping with their dogs, and volunteering at a service dog training organisation. FMI, visit: catherinemann.com

Second Chance

Second Chance:

A Love Rekindled

JOSS WOOD

CATHRYN FOX

CATHERINE MANN

MILLS & BOON

First Published in Great Britain 2025
by Mills & Boon, an imprint of HarperCollins*Publishers* Ltd
1 London Bridge Street, London, SE1 9GF

www.harpercollins.co.uk

HarperCollins*Publishers*
Macken House, 39/40 Mayor Street Upper,
Dublin 1, D01 C9W8, Ireland

Special thanks and acknowledgment are given to Joss Wood for her contribution to the *Texas Cattleman's Club: Bachelor Auction* series.

ISBN: 978-0-263-42080-7

LONE STAR REUNION

JOSS WOOD

Prologue

September

Over the decades many wedding receptions had been held at the Texas Cattleman's Club, and there had been a fair amount of scandals, for sure. Alexis Slade remembered talk of a groom being caught in a compromising position with the matron of honor, and a father of the groom passing out under a lavishly decorated bridal party table after streaking across the dance floor, wearing nothing more than a very lacy pink thong. There had been tearful brides, drunk brides, regretful brides and emotional brides, but Shelby Arthur was the first bride who hadn't made it to the altar.

The Goodman-Arthur wedding, or nonwedding, would undoubtedly be talked about for weeks on end. Alex looked across the still-crowded reception room and saw Reginald Goodman, father of the groom, with a tumbler of whiskey in his hand, looking pale but composed. Her eyes tracked left and there was the mother of the bride, a handkerchief clutched in her fist. Alex snorted at her wobbling lower lip, her crocodile tears. Daphne Goodman was a designer-dress-wearing barracuda who'd made no secret of the fact that she despised her son's fiancée and was totally against their marriage. Having been an object of Jared's affections in high school, Alex believed Shelby came to her senses just in time.

Marrying the spineless groom meant marrying his awful family—Brooke Goodman, Jared's sweet-natured sister, was the exception—and really, no woman deserved that. Marriage was tough enough without any added pressure from the in-laws. Jared and Shelby's marriage would've been a marriage of three, with Daphne Goodman calling the shots.

Alex turned when the door next to her right elbow opened and Rose Clayton walked into the reception area via the side entrance. Cool gray assessing eyes met hers and Alex reminded herself that she wasn't eighteen anymore, so the unofficial queen of the Texas Cattleman's Club should no longer intimidate her.

But she did.

Over that long summer ten years ago, Rose waged a war to separate her and Daniel, Rose's beloved grandson and heir. Gus, her own grandfather, had done the same. Because God and every Texan knew, family loyalty and a decades-old feud between Gus Slade and Rose Clayton trumped first love. At the time, she and Daniel had been the Romeo and Juliet of Royal, minus the death by poisoning.

Losing Daniel had felt like another death—she'd missed and mourned him that much. Alex remembered her tears, the desperation and loss she'd endured when Daniel refused to leave Royal with her so she could attend school out of state.

Daniel had said he belonged at The Silver C, but she disagreed, proclaiming they belonged together. They'd yelled; she'd cried. Daniel's stubbornness and intransigence, his unwillingness to choose her—*them*—ultimately killed their relationship.

Yes, they'd been young but, in his own unique way, he'd abandoned her. Unlike her parents, her childhood friend Gemma and, just last year, her beloved grandmother Sarah, Daniel had left her life through choice and not death.

And that somehow hurt more.

Rose approached her and a part of her still wanted to curl up in a ball when faced with Daniel's imperial grandmother. Annoyed with herself, Alex straightened her spine and managed a jerky nod. "Miss Rose."

"Alexis Slade."

Alex rolled her eyes when Rose turned her back on her and glided away, five foot something of sheer haughtiness and holier-than-thou poise. If not for their volatile history, she might even admire the woman for her steely self-assurance, her ability to carve out her rightful place in a world filled with take-charge alpha men.

But Rose was a Clayton and, as such, a sworn Slade enemy. Alex and her brother knew the basics of the Slade-Clayton feud: a half century ago, Gus, her grandfather, left Royal to make his fortune on the rodeo circuit, believing that Rose Clayton would wait for his return. He saved enough to buy a small spread next to the Clayton ranch and went to propose to Rose, excited to start his life with the woman he desperately loved. But Rose had married Ed the year before.

In doing so, Rose fired the first shot and war was declared.

Gus's marrying Rose's best friend—Alex's beloved grandmother Sarah—just escalated the conflict. And her grandfather buying up more portions of the once-mighty Clayton ranch was a nuclear strike. Families took their feuds seriously in Texas, and although sides were most certainly chosen, the Texas Cattleman's Club remained the demilitarized zone.

The Slades and Claytons, both old and young, were all members, and here within these walls, they had to play nice. Or when that wasn't feasible, they opted to ignore each other as much as possible. Just like Gus was ignoring Rose, and Alexis was ignoring Daniel, which was, annoyingly, very damn hard to do.

What woman with a pulse could? Surrendering to temptation, Alex looked toward the bar...and at the devastatingly handsome man who she'd once considered to be the love of her life. She drank in every inch of him. The black curls he hated—but she loved—and those mysterious dark brown eyes he'd inherited—everyone presumed—from his father, because his mother was light skinned with blue eyes. Boring brown, Daniel had once called them, but Alex vehemently disagreed. They could be as rich as expensive coffee, as deep as the night. However, they could also turn as hard as ship-destroying rocks on a jagged, inhospitable coastline.

So much had changed over the years, Alex mused with a wistful sigh. Her once-gangly boyfriend was now taller, broader, every inch a man. He was still lean but with hard muscles and a harder streak. Strong stubble covered his jaw and he looked as good in a tuxedo as he did in worn jeans, but neither was his sexiest look.

A naked Daniel Clayton, as she'd discovered when she was younger, could easily be classified as one of the wonders of the world.

In the past decade, her ex had done quite well for himself. He'd acquired degrees in both agriculture and business, and all the hard work he put into The Silver C had, judging by his designer tuxedo and the German sports car he occasionally drove, paid off. He was smart, wealthy and good-looking, and that trifecta made him one of the most sought-after bachelors in the area. Hell, possibly even the state. Although he hadn't brought a date to this wedding, Daniel Clayton was never, so she'd heard, short of a female companion.

In bed or out of it.

A hand on her arm pulled her eyes off her former lover and she smiled at Rachel Kincaid, her closest friend. Alex didn't make friends easily, but Rachel was someone who'd sneaked under her defenses.

"Why are you standing here by yourself?" her friend asked, handing her a glass of champagne.

"Trying to avoid another conversation about Shelby or what I think of the new president of the TCC," Alex admitted, taking the glass with a grateful smile.

"James Harris is a great guy."

Alex nodded. "I like him, too." She glanced at the tall African American man standing next to the right of them, talking to Rose Clayton. "And, oh my God, he's seriously hot."

In fact, there were many drop-dead gorgeous men in this room, most of them members of the TCC. She knew why she was single—chronic commitment and abandonment issues—but that didn't mean she had to be celibate. Yet she was.

"You keep looking at Daniel Clayton," Rachel remarked. "Not that I blame you. I swear he was birthed by an angel."

An unfortunate choice of words, Alex thought wryly, since Daniel's mom was reputed to be anything but celestial. Daniel never spoke about Stephanie but there were enough gossips in Royal to ascertain a little of what his life with his tempestuous and unstable mother had been like. According to the grapevine, Rose had been the only responsible adult in his life. His loyalty to his grandmother was rock-solid and unshakable.

Their romance had been doomed from the start. Because, as it turned out, Alex had never been able to compete with Rose and Daniel's fierce allegiance to The Silver C ranch.

"Matt Galloway is just as good-looking," Alex commented, partly to be perverse but also to distract Rachel from linking her and Daniel together. There was no "her and Daniel," and there hadn't been in a long, long time. And she wasn't lying, Matt Galloway was a young Clooney: as good-looking, as rich and charming, and as much of a reputed playboy as George used to be.

"He is—was—Billy's best friend." Alex wasn't sure what Matt's looks had to do with him being Rachel's dead husband's friend, but she was familiar with the don't-go-there look on Rachel's face, since it was an expression she often used. Alex liked her own privacy, so she didn't push Rachel.

Rachel wound her arm around Alex's waist and squeezed. "Have I said thank you lately for letting me stay with you at the Lone Wolf Ranch?"

"We love having you and baby Ellie there," Alex responded.

"And I don't take it personally that you frequently run away to Sarah's tree house."

"That's more to avoid Gus's lectures about finding a husband and giving him a great-grandchild than avoiding you, as you well know. Gus is determined to get me bound and breeding. I, on the other hand, need to think about getting back to Houston, to my life there. I came home to be with Grandma Sarah in her last days, but I'm still here, a year after her death. Royal was only meant to be a stopgap. My life isn't here."

"Sure looks like it is," Rachel commented. "As a digital-media strategist, you can work anywhere in the world, and you love the ranch, spending time with Gus."

Of course she did, but being with Gus and working part-time as the Lone Wolf's business manager didn't stop her from missing her grandmother with an intensity that still threatened to drop her to her knees. It didn't stop her from wallowing in the past, from remembering how happy she and Daniel had once been before she learned that love didn't conquer all.

Alex sucked in her breath when his eyes slammed into hers and, as always, she felt caressed by the light of a million stars. Electric tingles skittered across her skin, tightened her nipples, sent heat to that place between her legs. This was just red-hot, carnal lust, and nothing, she silently insisted, like what they'd experienced so long ago.

Back then, they'd been constantly drunk. On love, on each other. They'd hurtled headfirst into love and sex and passion, blithely thinking they could handle the thousand-degree fire they'd created, stoked and fed.

Pfft. She'd emerged with third-degree burns. But

the worst part? Alex still found Daniel physically intoxicating. And judging by the unbanked desire flashing in his eyes, she made him feel equally off balance.

Good. He deserved nothing less.

Rachel accepted a dance from Gus, old flirt that he was, and Alex, wanting fresh air, slipped out the side door. She inhaled the cool, fragrant night air and wrapped her arms around her waist as she walked toward the gardens surrounding the TCC. In daylight it was immediately apparent that the surrounding grounds, flower beds and paths that meandered through the once-glorious garden needed some updating and attention. But at night the gardens were mysterious and welcoming, an old friend. She remembered playing hide-and-seek in these gardens with her brother and her friends, sneaking down to the small pond to steal a kiss from Daniel Clayton, away from their eagle-eyed grandparents.

Fun times, Alex thought with a bittersweet pang.

She heard the crunch of boots on the gravel path, and then a jacket covered her bare shoulders. She inhaled his familiar scent—sandalwood and leather, wood and wildness. Big, manly hands settled on her shoulders and she instinctively leaned back, her head resting against his collarbone, his warm breath on her ear.

Suddenly she was eighteen again. Daniel had his hands on her...and all was right with her world.

"Lexi." Daniel's deep voice rumbled over her skin, as deep and dark as the night.

Alex knew that she should run away. But she was so tired of tamping down her fantasies of what it would be like to have Daniel naked and in her bed. Of dreaming how he would make love. Teenage Daniel had been hesitant, cautious, but adult Daniel would possess her the same way he did everything else, with confidence and raw virility.

And she wanted him. God, how she wanted him!

Alex sighed as his hand brazenly moved over her shoulder, down her chest, to slide under the lapel of his jacket and cup her breast. His thumb swiped her nipple as he pulled her earlobe between his teeth, gently nibbling.

"Still so sexy, Lexi. Love what you are wearing."

She couldn't remember what she'd put on so she glanced down... Right, a loose, off-the-shoulder black top with a full, flower-patterned pale pink skirt.

Alex knew she should push him away, but instead of being sensible, she placed her hand behind her back, her fingers seeking out his erection. There it was, hard and long and thick, and she heard his low, guttural moan as his cock jerked beneath her touch. Then she was making whimpering sounds of her own as his hand pushed aside the fabric of her top so that he could feel her naked flesh and pull her tight nipple between his fingers.

She lifted her head up and to the side, and then his mouth was on hers. Parting her lips to receive his tongue, she moaned her frustration when he smiled against her mouth, silently telling her that he enjoyed teasing her, making her wait. He'd always been more patient, more interested in drawing out every moment of their pleasure.

Daniel's chaste kisses were in direct contrast to his roaming hands. He bunched the fabric of her skirt and pulled it up her legs, and his fingers trailed up her thighs, played with the tiny V shape of her panties. Alex felt him shudder when he discovered her panties were only comprised of one triangle and a few thin cords.

"Naughty underwear, Miss Slade," Daniel growled against her mouth.

"Shut up and touch me, Clayton," Alex demanded, spinning around and slapping her hands on his cotton-covered chest. Ignoring his loose tie and open collar, she gripped his shirt and yanked it from his pants, desperate to find hot, sexy, olive-toned skin. Her fingers danced across a set of impressive washboard abs, and she pushed her fingers between that hard stomach and the band of his pants, seeking and finding the tip of his erection. Daniel released a low hiss, sucked in his stomach and suddenly she had more of him against her fingers, hot and oh-so potent.

"I want you, Lex," Daniel muttered, smacking her bare butt cheek and pulling her into him, squashing her hand between her body and his erection. Needing more, needing everything—she'd missed him, missed this so much—Alex lifted her thigh and wrapped it over his hip, grateful to yoga for making her supple. Then nothing but fabric separated her core from his shaft, and she rocked her hips and lifted her mouth up to his to be kissed.

This time he didn't hold back and his tongue swept between her parted lips, branding, rediscovering, wiping away any doubts that reliving the past was foolish and dangerous.

There was only Daniel, his taste and heat and power, the adult version of the boy she'd known so long ago. Standing in his arms, panting and with soaked panties, her only thoughts were of how much she'd missed his touch, missed his kisses. In this moment they didn't have feuding grandparents, unforgivable betrayals or hurt and pain between them. There was only desire— hot, potent and demanding.

Daniel wrenched his mouth off hers, and in the moonlight his eyes, normally so shuttered, were as deep and dark as a desert night. "Come home with me, Lex."

She had to be rational...and she couldn't be, not when she had her hand in his pants. She couldn't think, breathe. Alex pulled her hand from between their bodies and tried to step back, but Daniel's hands on her hips kept her up close and very personal. "Dan, don't ask me that."

"Why? Because you are scared you're going to say yes?"

It was a typical no-frills Daniel response. He never beat around the bush, and although he was the strong and silent type, when he did speak, people listened. Her ex just had a way of cutting through BS to get to the heart of the matter, and as per usual, he was right. She was terrified that she was going to say yes, but even more scared that she was going to force herself to say no.

"I've been watching you all evening and you've been watching me, too," Daniel murmured, lifting his hand to trace patterns on her jaw. "We've both been wondering what it would feel like to be together again. Especially now that we're older, more experienced...confident in how to satisfy one another in bed."

She was sexually confident? Oh, she was anything but. She might be older and wiser, but she was still more girl next door than femme fatale.

"Come home with me, Lex. Let me peel that ridiculously sexy dress from your gorgeous body and replace it with my lips and hands. I'll make it good for you, I promise."

He'd make it *too* good, and yeah, that worried her. "Daniel, this is *madness*."

"So let's be mad, just for a night. In the morning we can go back to being a Clayton and a Slade, opposing forces in this long, futile war that we never started."

Alex closed her eyes and shook her head. She wanted him but she didn't like wanting him, found herself wishing instead that she could put him in the past, where he belonged. Maybe she *did* need to sleep with him again to flush him out of her system. After all, reality was never as good as fantasy, and then they could both finally move on.

"So, yes or no?"

Alex thought she saw apprehension in his eyes, the fear that she'd reject him, but the emotions flashed across his features too quickly for her to be sure. "Yeah, I'm coming with you."

Daniel stared down at her, his handsome face serious. "Your place or mine?"

Alex thought about their options, knowing that the ranch house at the Lone Wolf was out of the question and, as she'd heard, Daniel had converted an old barn on The Silver C. While his house was a better option than Gus's mansion—Daniel might be met with the working end of her grandpa's shotgun if they were caught—their chances of discovery were still too high.

Which left only one other place available to them…

"Sarah's tree house."

Daniel's hand tightened on her hip and she knew that he was remembering, just as she was.

A long time ago, the tree house had been a boys' fort and a girls' secret club. It had held sleep outs and camping trips and overnight sleepovers. Much later it had been the place where Daniel took her virginity, where they'd spent stolen afternoons and blissful starry nights.

"You remember where it is, right?"

Daniel rubbed his jaw. "Of course I can find it. I just haven't been there since…"

You left, Alex filled in the words for him. The tree house was deep in Slade land and Daniel had no reason or wish to be on Slade land. Land that had once been part of The Silver C spread.

The river-fronted land was one of the first parcels of land Gus bought from Rose when times had got tough, and Alex knew that Daniel mourned the loss of the property. The Silver C had once been the largest spread in four counties, but it was now on par with the Lone Wolf in acreage, a bit of a comedown for the once-mighty Claytons.

"I'll meet you at the tree house," Daniel said, his voice clipped. He lifted his wrist to look at his expensive watch. "In half an hour?" He rubbed his hand over his jaw and shook his head. "I can't believe that I am risking getting splinters in my butt to have you again. Nobody but you, Alex Slade, would tempt me to do this…"

His words shouldn't make her smile but they did. She opened her mouth to explain that the tree house wasn't as bad as it had been… No, she'd let it be a surprise.

"Are you going to walk there?" Daniel asked.

In moonlight or bright sunshine, she always walked to the tree house. "Yes."

"I'm going to go home, pick up my dirt bike and I'll be there as soon as I can," Daniel told her, his eyes steady on her face.

Good, that gave her some time to think about what she was doing, to talk herself out of this madness.

Daniel narrowed his gaze. "Do *not* stand me up, Alexis."

Although it unnerved her how he'd been able to read her thoughts, she couldn't suppress the shiver of excitement that tap-danced up and down her spine. He was gorgeous and determined and he wanted her.

No, she wouldn't stand him up. She couldn't; she wanted this, wanted *him*. "I'll be there."

Daniel nodded, swiped his mouth across hers in a brief but molten-lava-hot kiss. "See that you are."

One

Daniel Clayton released a low curse and buried his head in the soft pillow, cursing his early-morning alarm. Unfortunately, neither cattle nor his ranch hands cared that he'd spent most of the night making love, that he'd had minimal sleep. The Silver C Ranch and his grandmother demanded a daily pound of flesh and since he didn't tolerate excuses or less than 100 percent effort, he knew he should haul his ass out of bed and get to it. He rolled over and pressed his chest to Lexi's back, filling his hand with her perfect, perfect breast. Daniel skimmed his thumb across her nipple and buried his nose in her fragrant hair. Best way to wake up, bar none. His rock-hard erection pushed into her bottom and he skated his hand down her torso, across her stomach, and his fingers flirted with the V shape below. There was nothing like sleepy, lazy sex… His cell phone alarm screeched again.

"Dammit, Clayton," Lex muttered, reaching across him to grab his phone. Mercifully, the strident alarm ceased, and despite wanting Lexi again, Daniel found himself drifting back to sleep. Then Alex's sharp elbow dug into his ribs and he rolled over, frowning.

"What was that for?"

"Sun's up in forty-five minutes, and we both have to leave," Alex told him, whipping off the covers and exposing his naked body to the chilly morning air.

The tree house was heated by a woodstove, which they didn't bother to light because a stream of smoke from the chimney would raise questions—questions neither of them wanted to answer. As it was, he'd already endured a few lectures from Rose, demanding to know the status of his love life. He'd blown her off, as usual, but then she'd upped the ante by expressing her fervent hope that he'd meet a lovely girl through the upcoming bachelor auction—as if!—and that she would be bitterly disappointed if she found out that he was carrying on with "that Slade girl."

Since that Slade girl was currently standing naked by the window, long blond hair tumbling down her oh-so-sexy back, he didn't give a rat's ass what his grandmother or anyone else thought. They'd been hooking up for six weeks—maybe a week or so more—and he'd enjoyed every second he'd spent with Alex. But what they shared was sex and desire and heat and want and nothing his grandmother needed to worry about.

He loved his grandmother—he did—but he just wished she'd stay out of his damn business. Alex, what they had together, was separate from The Silver C—one didn't impact the other. For a decade his entire focus had been on the family spread, trying to restore the somewhat tarnished reputation of the Clayton clan. While Rose held the respect of the residents of the town of Royal and the counties of Maverick and Colonial, his late grandfather, Ed, and his mother, Stephanie, did not. One was a bastard and the other was irresponsible, wild and borderline psycho. Despite his dubious parentage, he'd worked hard to command a little of the respect his grandmother did.

And he thought he was getting there.

While not nearly as big as it had been in its heyday, The Silver C was now regarded as being one of the best-managed spreads in the country, lauded for its breeding program and producing award-winning bulls. He had a waiting list as long as his arm for buyers wanting to purchase his quarter horses, and he ran the entire ranching operation with the utmost professionalism and integrity. And by doing so, he'd recently been inducted as a member of the Texas Cattleman's Club.

Daniel sat up, rested his forearms on his thighs and shoved his hands through his hair before running his palm over his stubble-covered jaw. He watched as Alex picked up a sweatshirt—one of his—and frowned when the voluminous fabric covered her to midthigh. She then pulled her hair out from under the band of the garment and gathered it into a messy knot on top of her head, and he thought that he'd never seen anyone so naturally beautiful, so effortlessly sexy.

"I'm going to make coffee. Do you have time for a cup?"

Daniel glanced at his watch and nodded. "Yeah, I do. Thanks."

He watched Alex leave the room, her hips swaying seductively as she did so. She'd been pretty as a teenager but she was spectacular as a grown woman. Blue eyes the color of the summer sky, high cheekbones and that luscious, made-to-kiss mouth. Yards and yards of fragrant, wavy hair. And… God, that body…lean and slender, finely boned but with curves and dips and flares that made his mouth water.

At eighteen he'd thought he'd loved her, but now, ten years later, he knew that he'd been blinded by lust, had confused love with desire. He didn't believe in romantic love and Daniel sometimes wondered if he ever, deep down, really had. God knew he hadn't been exposed to any marital, or even family, harmony growing up.

He was the unwanted son of Rose's daughter, who had also been raised in a tense household. There had been little love between Rose and his maternal grand-father, and his mother, Stephanie, wasn't able to love anyone but herself. He'd been the unwanted result of one of Stephanie's many bad decisions when it came to men.

Daniel had no idea who his father was and one of Stephanie's favorite games had been to play "Who's Your Daddy?" She'd thrown out names to tease, later telling him that she'd made up names and occupations to amuse herself. It was cold comfort that Stephanie had also played Rose like a fiddle, using him as her bow.

Thanks to his dysfunctional childhood, he was cyni-cal about love. But he did believe in family, in loyalty, in hard work and respect—Rose had shown him the value of those traits, in both word and deed. She'd never lied to him, not even during those worst times, when Stephanie was crazier than a wet hen.

So when his grandmother expressed her reservations about his teenage romance with Alex, calmly pointing out that he'd be throwing away his future at the ranch to follow a girl he *thought* he might love, he'd eventually listened to her advice. And why wouldn't he? She was the one stable adult in his life, the only person he'd ever felt was looking after his best interests.

And yeah, after emotionally and physically divorcing himself from his mother, he vowed that he'd never let anyone emotionally blackmail him again.

Shaking off his disturbing thoughts, Daniel stood up, strode to the small bathroom next to the only bedroom and used the facilities. He returned to the master suite, smiling as he remembered how surprised he'd been when he'd first laid eyes on this renovated tree house.

Gone was the rickety structure from before. Now a sleek, beautifully designed house rested in the massive cypress trees overlooking the river that meandered its way through both The Silver C and the Lone Wolf ranches. Instead of a one-room platform, the tree house consisted of a master bedroom, a sleeping loft above the main living space, this tiny bathroom and a small kitchenette. The abundance of windows and a sliding glass wall allowed for amazing views of the river and Lone Wolf land. He wished he could lie on the sprawling deck, beer in his hand, Stetson over his face, soaking up some winter rays. But there was work to do, and the needs of The Silver C Ranch always came first.

Hearing Alex walking up the stairs to the bedroom, he stepped into his jeans and pulled on his shirt, then his fleece-lined leather jacket. Sitting down on the edge of the bed, he reached for his socks and boots, lifting his head as Alex appeared in the doorway. He took the cup of coffee she held out—hot and black—and sipped gratefully. Another three of these and he might feel vaguely human.

She sat down on the bed next to him, scooted backward and crossed her legs. "Dan…"

There was something odd in the way she said his name, so he whipped his head around to look at her, his eyes narrowing at the frown pulling her arched eyebrows together. "Yeah?"

Alex cradled her mug in both hands and he saw the tremble in her fingers, the way the rim of the cup vibrated. Oh crap, this wasn't good. He removed the cup from her fingers, placed it on the wooden bedside table and turned back to face her. "What's wrong, Lex?"

"Has Rose been giving you grief about me?"

He really didn't want to have this conversation now, didn't have the time for it. "Yeah. She asked me whether we were seeing each other, told me that she wouldn't be happy if I was."

Alex sighed. "I got a similar lecture from Gus, telling me how it would break his heart if he found out we were together." Alex looked miserable and Daniel could relate. Neither of them liked disappointing their grandparents.

"Gus is trying to set me up with guys who are taking part in the bachelor auction."

"That damned auction," Daniel growled, the thought of being sold like a steer raising his blood pressure. Then, to add insult to injury, he would have to pay for the date with the woman who'd paid to spend time with him. Why couldn't he just write a check to cover the costs of the date? Hell, he'd double, even triple, the amount if he could get out of going on a stupid date with someone not of his choosing.

"That *damned* auction is going to raise an awesome amount of money for the Pancreatic Cancer Foundation." Daniel saw the blue fire in Alex's eyes and reminded himself that the charity auction was her pet project. Her beloved grandmother Sarah had died from the disease, and as it was a cause that was near and dear to her heart, Lex had committed herself to raising funds to find a cure.

"I'll be glad when it's over," Alex said. "A few more sleeps and counting. Roll on Saturday and then Gus can stop throwing me into the arms of any man with a pulse."

The thought of Alexis being in another man's arms was enough to have him grinding his teeth together. Daniel reminded himself that he had no right to feel jealous, but the enamel still flew off his teeth. Reaching across him to pick up her cup of coffee, her hair brushed his face and he inhaled her lavender-and-wildflower scent. He immediately felt himself grow hard, and as much as it pained him, he told himself to stand down.

"If I don't leave soon, Lex, I'm going to be late. What's on your mind?"

Alex sipped, sighed and sipped again, before finally getting to the point. "I…um…think we should put this on hold, at least for a while."

"*This* meaning us?"

Alex nodded. "I've got a lot on my mind, so much to do, and while this has been fun, it's taking time and energy I don't currently have."

Daniel felt the prick—hell, stab!—of dismay and pushed the pain away. Sure, he hadn't expected this to last forever, but damn, he and Lex were good together. They enjoyed each other, knew exactly how to make each other writhe and squirm and scream. It would be a good long while, Daniel admitted, before he could even *think* about sleeping with someone else.

Because Alexis—warm and wonderful—was truly one of a kind.

Alex looked like she was waiting for an answer, so he shrugged and uttered the only word he could wrap his tongue around. "Okay."

Disappointment flashed in her eyes. At his one-syllable answer or because he wasn't arguing for them to carry on?

"I'd also like to tell our grandparents that we are wise to them trying to set us up with other people, that they can't interfere in our love lives," Alex stated, her voice determined.

"You want to tackle them together? In the same room?" Daniel heard the skepticism in his voice. "Would Royal survive the fallout?"

"I think it would have more impact," Alex stubbornly replied.

"They've avoided each other for five decades, Lex. You're not going to get them in the same room, at the same time." This feud was exhausting but it wasn't theirs to fight. Gus and Rose had decades of tumultuous history to work through, and Daniel wasn't fool enough to get sucked up in that craziness.

Besides, he had bigger things to deal with, like Alex cutting him off. He didn't want this to end… "You sure this is what you want to do, Lex?"

Alex lifted her shoulders, dropped them and released a long-suffering sigh. "I'm tired of the lectures, the disapproving looks from Gus. I'm tired of sneaking around. I need more sleep and I have a couple of personal decisions I need to make. You're a…complication."

A complication, huh? "It's just sex, Alex."

Was that reminder directed at her or himself?

Annoyance glimmered in Lexi's gorgeous blue

eyes. "Of course it is, but since it's sapping my time and energy, it needs to stop." She looked away from him, shrugged before dragging her eyes back to his. "Maybe once the auction is over, after the holidays, if I'm around, we could maybe pick things up again."

So many maybes, Daniel thought, pulling on his boot. *Wait, what did she say?* "You said, *if* you're around? Are you thinking of leaving?"

Another thought to cool his head. He definitely wasn't getting enough sleep!

"I've had a job offer that might take me back to Houston," Alex said. "I've stayed in Royal longer than I thought I would. My plan was always to return there."

"What's the offer?" Daniel asked, standing up and tucking his shirt into his jeans.

"Managing partner in a social media strategy firm. It's a good offer. I've always wanted to be my own boss."

He quirked a brow. "Isn't that what you are here on the ranch?"

"Gus is still the boss, Dan," she reminded him. "And while I can run the finances, I'm not a rancher. In Royal, everything has a memory associated with it. My parents, Sarah…"

He heard her unsaid *you* and could almost taste the emotion in her voice. They'd both had hard childhoods, had been knocked around by life, but he knew that losing her parents as a little girl had rocked her world. And then to lose Sarah, on top of all that, had truly devastated her. "I am sorry, Lex. Sorry for you, for Gus."

Alex managed a wobbly smile. "Thanks, I appreciate it." Standing up, she placed her hand on his chest, and Daniel felt his heart rate kick up, his throat tightening. Alex just had to touch him and the thoughts of stripping their clothes off and taking her again were front and center. He forcibly held himself still as Alex stood up on her pretty painted toes to kiss the side of his mouth. "Thanks for this, Dan. It was fun. And maybe it exorcised some ghosts."

Yeah, but maybe it also, Daniel couldn't help thinking, *created a whole bunch more.*

She'd said goodbye to him as a teenager but watching him walk away as an adult was surprisingly a great deal harder than she'd imagined it would be. She'd been madly in love with him then, but she wasn't in love with him now, so… Why on earth was she so upset?

You have to let him go. There is no other option. This is not a situation where you can have the cowboy and ride him, as well.

But she still couldn't keep her eyes off him as he strode toward his dirt bike. Sighing appreciatively, she watched as he threw a long, muscular leg over the saddle and gripped the handlebars, dark curls shining in the early-morning light. Man, he was gorgeous, a perfect combination of Anglo and Hispanic. Olive skin, black hair, those smoldering brown eyes and that lean, powerful physique.

Alex leaned her forearms on the railing of the deck and watched her lover—no, her *ex-lover*—ride away, ignoring her wildly beating heart. There was no denying that this man had the ability to liquefy her insides, to shut down her thought processes, to invade her thoughts. But he'd also broken her heart, and she'd never give him the power to do that again.

She'd noticed that Daniel was starting to sneak under her skin, that her thoughts went to him at inopportune times—like every ten seconds—and this morning,

while making coffee, she'd thought about asking him
whether he wanted to attend a country music concert in
Joplin with her the following week. They could stay in
a bed-and-breakfast, try out that new restaurant she'd
heard was fabulous…

Shocked at her thoughts, she'd given herself a mental slap. Daniel wasn't someone to make plans around,
to date, to spend time with. If she was starting to think
of him as a potential partner and not just as a fun, sexy
hookup, then it was time to cut him loose.

So she did.

When the sound of Dan's bike faded away, Alex
walked back into the bedroom and sat on the edge of
the bed, staring at the expensive Persian carpet beneath
her feet. *Only in Texas would you find an exquisite Persian carpet on the floor of a very upscale tree house*,
Alex thought. Only her grandmother Sarah would put
it there. Damn, she still missed her. But Sarah, like her
parents, was gone, and Alex couldn't help feeling that
the people who loved her the most tended to leave her…

Intellectually, Alex understood that death was a part
of life, that people died and hearts got broken. Tough
times came along to make one stronger, that everything
was a lesson…blah, blah, blah.

But losing her parents and her beloved grandmother
long before they were supposed to go was just damn
unfair. It was like some bored god was using her heart
as a football.

Daniel had left her, too, but his desertion had
strangely hurt the most. It was his choice to leave her
and it was obvious, even so many years later, that she'd
loved Daniel so much more than he loved her…

Alex flopped back onto the bed and placed her arm
over her eyes. And that was why she'd cut him loose

today: she couldn't—wouldn't—put herself in the position of being left brokenhearted again.

Wanting to stop wallowing, she started to make a mental list of everything she had to do today. Getting together with Rachel to plan Tessa's makeover was high on her list. As the only bachelorette up for auction, they were going to make her the star of the show. Not that Tess needed much help—the girl was stunningly beautiful, both inside and out.

And as the master of the ceremonies, she had to plan her introductions, find some funny jokes to keep the audience entertained. She also had to psych herself into selling Daniel, the only man she'd seen naked in the longest time, to some woman with a healthy bank account. That was going to be so much fun.

Not.

Alex felt nausea climb up her throat. Really, she was being ridiculous, having a physical reaction to auctioning off Daniel. Yes, sure, the idea of sending her former flame off on a date with another woman wasn't a pleasant prospect, but they'd just shared their bodies, not their hearts and souls. She had no hold on him—she didn't *want* a damned hold on him, and that was why she'd severed their connection! She was being utterly asinine by allowing her emotions to rule her head, and this behavior was unworthy of a Slade.

But still, the nausea wouldn't subside and Alex cursed herself as she bolted for the bathroom and made her acquaintance with the toilet bowl.

Two

Late November

Alex stared down at the long list attached to her clipboard, wondering if she would survive this crazy day. And what had she been thinking, agreeing to be the emcee for The Great Royal Bachelor Auction? It was one thing being the master—mistress?—of ceremonies at friends' weddings and birthday parties, but this auction was a major social event.

What she'd thought would be a small local fundraiser had morphed into something a great deal bigger and was attracting press attention from media outlets in both Austin and Dallas. The tickets to the function had sold out within a day or two, but the loud demands from wealthy single women from the two cities and the neighboring town of Joplin forced her and Rachel to upscale the event, adding another five tables to the already crowded TCC function room.

Who would've thought that this small-town auction for their eligible bachelors would've generated so much buzz? Alex flicked through the program, looking at the faces of her bachelors and lone bachelorette. Who was she kidding? If was the perfect opportunity for wealthy singles with money to burn to buy themselves a hot date. Good, because she intended to make them pay mightily for the privilege.

Alex glanced at her watch, saw that it was just past four and looked down at her messy list. The tables were set, and the flower arrangements had arrived and looked superb. The band was doing a sound check and she heard the haunting sounds of a saxophone drifting from the ballroom to this anteroom that would host the bachelors as they were waiting for their turns to be auctioned. Alex walked over to the fridge, yanked open the door and was relieved to see the bottles of beer that would be needed to calm nervous dispositions. She smiled. Her bachelors were successful businessmen, alpha men every one of them, but every time they were reminded that they'd have to stand in the spotlight and be auctioned off like prize bulls, they all looked terrified.

Hearing the door to the greenroom open, she shut the fridge door and turned to see waiters from the Royal Diner entering the room, carrying platters of food. As she well knew, nothing short of a nuclear holocaust would stop her cowboys from eating.

"Hey, guys." Alex indicated the table where she wanted the platters to be placed. "Those look amazing. What did Amanda send over?"

"The Royal Diner's famous ribs, sliders, quiches. Doughnut and choc chip cookies for dessert."

"Please thank Amanda again for her generous donation. The guys and Tessa will appreciate it." Alex dug in her pocket to pull out a tip. She waved away their thanks, and when she was alone, she placed her clipboard between two of the platters and ran through her list again.

Flowers. Check.

Band. Check.

Food. Check.

Test sound system. That was currently happening.

Tessa's makeover. Alex checked her watch again. She'd allocated forty-five minutes for her and Rachel to give Tessa a makeover. Well, to be honest, to hold Tess's hand while the professionals she and Rachel hired did Tess's hair and makeup. Tess was going to rock the house tonight. Alex smiled. Girl power was a marvelous thing.

Tess reminded Alex of Gemma—she was as humble, as sweet and unaware of her good looks as Gemma had been. Alex pushed her fist into her sternum, thinking of her redheaded, emerald-eyed friend, a band of freckles across her nose. Sixteen years had passed since Gemma's death, but there were times, just like today, when she felt that Gemma was just waiting for her to call, like she was around the corner, about to stride back into her life.

She still missed her best friend; sometimes it felt like she'd lost her a few weeks back instead of so long ago. But grief, as she learned, had no respect for time. She'd lost her parents at ten, her best friend at twelve and Sarah just a year ago. She remembered her parents as well as she did Sarah. And Gemma as well as she remembered Sarah.

She'd heard that memories fade, that lost ones become indistinct. It had yet to happen to her. She could be doing something mundane and she'd hear Gemma's laugh, Sarah's voice or smell her mom's scent, and grief would slam into her, stopping her in her tracks.

When the pain subsided, just a little, she was left feeling abandoned, so damn alone. She was able to wrangle grief back into its cage, but those other feelings always lingered, casually snacking on her soul.

Could anyone blame her for pushing people away? She loved hard and she loved deep, giving all that she had. Sometime in the future, hopefully a long time from now, she'd have to face losing her grandfather Gus. Losing him, she hoped, would be easier than losing her parents, Gemma and Sarah. They'd all died way before their times, but hopefully her healthy and fit grandfather would live until he was a hundred and slip off in his sleep after a life well lived. She could live with that—it was the circle of life—and unlike before, she wouldn't feel abandoned.

Alex flipped the program over and traced Daniel's gorgeous face with the tip of her finger. Although she was right to put some distance between them, she still ached for him for him with every fiber of her being. Warmth pooled through her as she remembered the way he kissed her, the way his clever hands would stroke her body, the rasp of his stubble, the play of hard muscles under her hands.

The growl of his voice against her mouth, painting her skin with sinfully sexy words…

Tonight is all about making you weep as I pleasure you...

Just feeling your eyes on me makes me so hard.

You're going to pass out from satisfaction...

Daniel was a master of the art of talking dirty, using words and phrases that upped the sexy factor by 1000 percent. Then he lived up to his words with his skillful touch and used his mouth like a Jedi Master.

She missed him…

No, her body missed him. Her body missed him a whole bunch…

But stepping away from Daniel had been a wise move and one she'd make again. Her self-protection instinct had been carefully, meticulously honed and was now scalpel sharp. Nobody would slice and dice her again.

Alex shoved the program under the rest of her papers and straightened. Returning to her list, she lifted the plastic cover off the nearest platter and reached for a doughnut. She groaned as the treat touched her tongue, sighing at the prefect combination of fat and sugar.

God, so good. Alex chewed, swallowed and chewed again, polishing off the doughnut in three bites. She reached for another and it was halfway to her mouth when she heard a horrified gasp from the doorway.

"What the hell are you doing, Slade?" Rachel demanded, hands on her slim hips, brown eyes narrowed.

Alex pulled off a piece and chewed. Swallowing, she lifted her eyebrows at the astonished look on Rachel's face. What was her problem? "Um, eating a doughnut? Freshly made, courtesy of Amanda Battle."

"Actually, Jillian from the pie shop made them, but that's neither here nor there." Rachel stepped into the room and closed the door behind her. "Why are you eating them?"

Was that a trick question? "Because they are good?"

Rachel scratched her forehead, still looking confused. "Alex, I haven't seen you eat sugar in four years. You don't eat junk food, *ever*."

Alex looked at the doughnut in her hand, puzzled.

Rachel was right, she never ate junk food and very infrequently ate carbs. So why on earth was she eating one now? And, knowing that, why was she unable to throw it in the trash?

Alex popped the last of the doughnut into her mouth and contemplated her actions. Was she finally losing it? Was the stress of organizing the bachelor auction, breaking up with Daniel and trying to work through the job offer she'd had from Houston finally getting to her?

"Alex, are you okay?"

"It's just a doughnut, Rach. Okay, two little doughnuts," Alex retorted. Then she reached for a paper napkin and wiped the powdered sugar off her fingers. "My sugar levels are probably low. I just needed a boost."

"I'd believe that if I didn't see the way you refused coffee this morning, wrinkling your nose at the smell. And last night you drank some chamomile tea."

"I had indigestion."

"You loathe chamomile tea," Rachel pointed out.

Was her best friend trying to make a point? Because if she was, she was taking a hell of a long time to get to it. "You've obviously got something to say, Rachel, so why don't you spit it out so I can get back to work?"

"Ooh, grumpy," Rachel quipped, stepping forward to grip Alex's biceps with her hands. "Honey, I think you are pregnant."

Alex had never thought it possible that she could feel like she was burning up from the inside, as well as feeling soul-deep cold. "Okay, that's simply not funny."

"Am I laughing?" Rachel asked, her expression serious. "Alex, having been through this myself, I can spot a pregnancy at fifty paces. You, my friend, are pregnant."

"Stop saying that!" Alex hissed, panic closing her throat. "I can't be! I had my period…"

Rachel lifted her eyebrows, patiently waiting for an answer.

"Give me a sec, dammit! I have to think!" Alex pulled her phone from the back pocket of her jeans and clicked on her calendar app. She always kept a record of her cycle and she'd show Rachel that she was talking out of her hat. Alex flipped through dates, didn't see anything and flipped back a month. Oh man, there was no denying it. She was late.

"Apart from eating junk food, has anything else changed? Have you felt nauseous, tired?"

"I threw up a couple of weeks back, felt nauseous once last week and I'm tired because I've been organizing this damn function. I can't be pregnant... Maybe I have a bug! It's far too early for me to have any symptoms of pregnancy anyway."

That was the answer, she had a bug, had picked up a virus. Phew!

"It's not a disease, Alex," Rachel patiently replied. "And everyone is different."

"Oh God. Oh God."

Rachel's grip on her arms tightened. "Breathe, honey. Let's think about this logically. Did Daniel use condoms? Are you on birth control?"

"You know I've been seeing Daniel?" Alex demanded. "Who else knows? Does Gus? Oh crap!"

"It was a guess, which you just confirmed," Rachel replied, her voice low and smooth. "So, condoms?"

"Yes, dammit. We are responsible adults who don't make juvenile errors." Alex bent over, covered her face with her hands and dropped to her haunches. "But there was one time...he pulled out and then put on a condom. God! No! I can't be pregnant, Rach. I can't!"

"I think there's a good possibility that you are."

Rachel ran a gentle hand over Alex's hair. "Alex, just breathe. In and out. Good girl."

Alex sucked in air, using every bit of self-control she had to push away the breath-stealing panic that threatened to engulf her. Still on her haunches, she placed her hand on the floor to steady herself. This couldn't be happening to her. *Why* was this happening to her? She'd had a hot, passionate fling with a man she'd always been attracted to. They'd used protection… She wasn't supposed to end up pregnant! This wasn't how her life was supposed to go.

And in a couple of hours, she had to go onstage, act charming and auction off the father of the baby that might be growing in her womb. *Noooo...*

Rachel pulled her up to standing position and cupped her face, her eyes radiating support and sympathy. "Alex, there's nothing you can do about it now. In the morning, we'll go and buy you a pregnancy test and I'll hold your hand while you do it. For now, try to set it aside. We have a function to host, an evening to orchestrate."

Alex heard a couple of unladylike curses leave her lips. "I won't be able to concentrate until I know, Rach."

"You won't be able to concentrate if you do," Rachel pointed out.

"No, it'll be better if I know. I far prefer to deal with reality than what-ifs." Alex sucked her bottom lip between her teeth and felt the sting of tears. "I have to know, Rach."

Rachel wrinkled her nose. "We need you here, Alex."

Alex pushed her shoulders back and blinked away her tears. "And I will be, Rachel. I promise you, I won't let you down. I'll run to the superstore just out of town and I'll use the facilities there to do the test. I'll be back in thirty minutes, forty at max."

Too many people had let her down, pregnant or not, so she wouldn't do that to her best friend. She'd made a commitment to this evening and she'd honor it, baby or not. But she had to know. It was a burning compulsion, a primal need.

Rachel shrugged. "Okay."

Alex gave her a brief hug, pulling away before she completely lost it and started to ugly cry. She handed Rachel the clipboard, and then she all but ran to the door, yanked it open and slammed into a hard wall.

Another set of hands held her biceps; this time they were far bigger and rougher than Rachel's but oh-so familiar. Alex inhaled Daniel's distinctive scent and lifted her eyes to his chiseled face, sweeping them over his sensual lips and meeting his dark, brooding eyes.

Then, to her mortification, she heard a suppressed sob escape and felt the trickle of tears down her cheeks. Daniel's grip tightened on her biceps as she rested her forehead against his chest. God, she couldn't do this, she couldn't be pregnant.

"Lex, what's wrong?" For a moment, she wished she could lay her fears on him, allow him to enfold her into his strong arms, trust him to hold her up, have her back. But that was foolishness—she couldn't trust anyone. There was only one person she could rely on and that was herself. After all, she couldn't lose herself.

"I… It's nothing for you to worry about."

He remained silent as he lifted one hand to gently stroke her hair,

And, man, even though she knew she should pull away, she couldn't bring herself to. Not yet. Just once, it would be nice not to have to stand alone and be strong, to allow someone else to carry some of her burden.

But that wasn't the way she operated.

Even so, Alex relished the feel of Daniel's hand on the back of her head, his lips against her temple. "Lex, I need to know what's upsetting you."

He almost sounded like he cared. But that was a lie. He loved her body, loved making love to her, but he didn't care enough. Not to stick by her when things got tough, when she asked him to choose her. She'd made the mistake of relying on him when she was a teenager, and she knew not to do that again.

Alex shoved away from Daniel, swiped annoyed fingers across her eyes to wipe away the tears blurring her vision and sent him a hard smile. "I've got to go."

"Wait! What's wrong with you?" Daniel demanded. "Why are you crying? Dammit, Alexis, talk to me!"

She sent him a quick brittle smile. "Talking wasn't part of the deal when we were lovers, Daniel, even less so now. If this turns out to be something you need to know, I'll tell you, but for now, butt out! Okay?"

Alex moved away from Daniel, but she clearly heard the words he threw at her back. "You're crying, Lex! How am I supposed to let you just walk away?"

Alex turned, walked backward and spread out her hands. "It's not like it's the first time we've done this, Daniel. Ten years ago, I walked away from you in tears and you let me go. Let's repeat history, okay?"

Daniel watched Alex stride away from him, bunching his fists as he fought the urge to go after her, to shake her until she spilled her secrets. But, God, she was right. They weren't lovers anymore and even when they were—a handful of hookups over the past two months—they hadn't spent their time talking. That wasn't what they'd wanted from each other...

They'd wanted sex, hot and fast and furious. They'd wanted deep kisses and gliding hands, bone-melting pleasure and mindless nights, an escape from the day-to-day world that they lived here in Royal. They'd always, even when they were kids, had the ability to separate themselves from reality, to pretend that the outside world didn't exist. And they'd done that again, using sex as an escape, as a way to divorce themselves from their lives.

When they were entangled in one another's arms, he wasn't a Clayton and she wasn't a Slade. They were just Dan and Alex, two people who'd once loved each other with all the force and fury that was only possible when you were a teenager, before life showed you the million shades of gray between black and white. He shook his head at his youthful folly; he'd been such a sap for her.

But his days of being a sap for anyone were long over.

"Are you just going to stand there, staring into space?"

Daniel looked into the room that he'd been told was where the bachelors and Tessa were supposed to wait and saw Rachel standing by the refreshment table, her arms crossed and her eyes narrowed.

"Can you tell me what that was about?" he asked. Rachel was Alex's best friend and the two were said to be close. But how close? Like him, Alex had never been one to wear her heart on her sleeve and they rarely, if ever, had deep and meaningful conversations. Did she have those types of conversations with Rachel? Had she had them with another lover?

And why did that thought feel like the tip of a burning cigarette incinerating his stomach? He had no claim on Alex. There was nothing between them but one bliss-ful summer long ago and some recent hot sex.

He had no claim on her. He didn't want to have a claim on anyone and most definitely didn't want some-one to have a claim on him. With attachments came pain and he was happy with his own company, to live his life alone.

People, and their expectations and emotions, drained him.

"Is there anything you can tell me?" Daniel de-manded, shoving his hands into the front pocket of his battered jeans. In an hour or two he would swap his jeans and flannel shirt for a designer tuxedo, but for now he was comfortable. With what he was wearing, at least.

"Nope," Rachel replied, shaking her head. She lifted her clipboard. "I have a ton of work to do."

"And that is why I'm really surprised Alex bolted out of here like her tail was on fire. With her work ethic, normally you'd have to pry her away with a crowbar."

"I don't know what you want me to say, Daniel."

Tell me what's going on! Tell me why Alex was cry-ing. Tell me something, anything to help me understand. Daniel rubbed his hands over his face, before turn-ing to head out the door. He needed a whiskey, possi-bly two. Anything to help him numb his worry about Alex, his annoyance that he'd agreed to be part of this dumb auction. Not to mention the vague apprehension that no one would bid on him, the bastard son of Roy-al's wildest child.

God, now he sounded like a loser wallowing in self-pity. He'd brought The Silver C back from the brink of ruin, was regarded as one of the most talented young ranchers in the state. He was rich, respected. Who the hell cared that his mother was a crazy narcissist who was incapable of love and that his father had walked out on them before he was born?

"Daniel."

He was about to step through the door when he heard Rachel speak his name. He turned around slowly and saw the anxiety in her eyes. Oh crap, this was bad. "Yeah?"

Rachel hesitated and blew air into her cheeks. "Nothing. Ignore me."

Daniel growled his frustration and threw up his hands. "For God's sake, Rachel! What?"

Rachel's hands were white against her clipboard. "Tonight, later, when you run into her, just be gentle, okay?"

And what, in the name of all that was holy, did that mean?

Three

Daniel loved his grandmother—he did—but right now, he didn't like her. Not even one little bit. It was her fault that he was dressed in this stupid suit with a noose around his neck. She'd nagged him until he agreed to take part in this auction, and he'd finally relented, thinking that it was easier to say yes than listen to her harangue him. It was because of her that he'd have to go and stand on that stupid stage while his old ex-girlfriend and his recent ex-lover auctioned him off like a piece of meat.

And his grandmother's latest little surprise? Well, as one of the most eligible bachelors in the area, and one of the wealthiest, she'd informed him about meeting with a lifestyle reporter who was covering the auction. She and the journalist had discussed the possibility of Daniel giving an interview on whether his hopes and expectations of this evening lived up to the reality...

He had only one hope—that he managed to keep control of his seldom-seen-but-explosive temper—and exactly zero expectations.

And his grandmother was doomed to be disappointed. He had no intention of doing any damn interviews.

"Hi, Daniel."

Daniel whipped his head up and saw Tessa Noble standing by the refreshment table, her hand holding a quiche. Judging by the comments his grandmother had recently sent his way, he knew that she hoped that he and Tessa would finally connect, but unfortunately he only had eyes for an annoying blue-eyed blonde. But... *hot damn*. Tessa had always been attractive but tonight she was smokin' hot.

"Tessa? God, you look...incredible." Daniel shoved a hand in the pocket of his pants. "What are you doing here?" As soon as he asked the question, he had his answer. "Wait... Are you the surprise?"

Of course she was. It was classic Alex, when the crowd was expecting one thing, to do the exact opposite. And Tessa, looking like five million dollars, was a hell of a surprise.

"Guilty." Tessa blushed.

"Everyone will definitely be surprised," Daniel said. *Oh, smooth, Clayton. Just tell the woman that her normal look is subpar.* Which it so wasn't. "Not that you don't look good normally."

"It's okay, Daniel. I get it," she mumbled around a mouth full of quiche. "It was quite a surprise to me, too."

Distracted, Daniel leaned his shoulder into the wall, darting a quick look toward the door, hoping to see Alex. He'd sent her a couple of text messages, asking if she was okay, but she'd yet to respond. He needed to know whether, at the very least, she'd stopped crying. If she hadn't, she'd not only go onstage with red eyes, but he might be compelled to kick someone's ass. If she ever deigned to tell him whose ass needed kicking.

Daniel turned his attention back to Tessa. "You must be tired of people telling you how different you look. How did Tripp and Ryan react?"

There was something between her and Ryan, something more than the best friends they professed to be. Any idiot could see it and maybe that was why he'd never asked Tessa out on a date. Subconsciously, he supposed he always felt that if he asked Tessa out, he would be violating the bro code. And since Ryan was a good friend, that wasn't happening.

"Neither of them has seen me yet. I'm a little nervous about their reaction."

She had a right to be. Ryan would take one look at her and, if he was as smart as Daniel knew him to be, would take her to bed and keep her there.

"Don't be. I can't imagine a man alive could find fault with the way you look tonight." Oh crap, that had come out wrong. "Or any night...of course."

Tessa laughed and Daniel smiled at her, feeling at ease in her company.

Tessa walked toward him and laid a hand on his arm. "You know why I feel like a fish out of water. But are you okay? You look out of sorts."

He really had to try to look like he was enjoying this evening, like he was looking forward to meeting his date. He wasn't, but as a Clayton he had a duty to his community and to the event. He wanted Alex to succeed, he wanted this evening to be a resounding success. He just didn't want to stand there, wanting one woman while being auctioned off to another…

Damn you, Gran.

Normally Daniel would deflect the question, change the subject, so he was surprised to find himself giving Tessa an honest answer. He sighed heavily, the frown returning to his face. "For one thing, I'd rather not be in the lineup. I'm doing this at my grandmother's insistence."

"She seems like a perfectly reasonable woman to me." Ha! When his grandmother wanted something, she was as subtle as a combine harvester, or as an F5 tornado. "And she loves you like crazy. I'm pretty sure if you'd turned her down, she would've got over it pretty quickly."

She really didn't know Rose Clayton. His grandmother would make her displeasure known. Quietly but consistently. He shrugged, feeling the need to explain. Damn, Tessa Noble was easy to talk to. Strange that he could talk to her and not want to rip her clothes off, but with Alex, he wanted to do the exact opposite. "I owe my grandmother so much. I don't know where I would've ended up if it wasn't for her. Makes it hard to say no."

As difficult and demanding as she could be, Daniel would do whatever he could to make his grandmother happy. She'd taken a lost boy of mixed heritage and made him the man he was today. He owed her, well, a hell of a lot. Everything.

Daniel thought the subject was closed, but then Tessa spoke again. "You said 'for one thing.' What's the other reason you didn't want to do this?"

Oh damn. The last thing he wanted to do was to get all touchy-feely here. But, God's honest truth, the thought of making small talk with another woman, listening to her flirt, feigning interest in her life while the woman he really wanted to be with wanted nothing to do with him, made him want to put his fist through a door. Or a wall.

As easy to talk to as Tessa was, there were some things he'd never discuss. With anybody. He'd especially never admit to his ongoing, long-term obsession with the girl next door.

"Okay, bachelors and bachelorette."

Daniel heard Alex's command and forced himself to turn around. When he did, he noticed that not only had she entered the room but so had the rest of the bachelors who were up for auction. But his attention was completely captured by Alex. He started at her face, looking for signs of tears, and yep, her eyes were red. But her face was composed, and she had her emotions under control. Daniel released the breath he'd been holding and allowed his eyes to rove. Her hair was pinned up into a sexy knot, and her makeup was expertly yet subtly applied. His eyes widened as he took in the plunging high-slit silver dress she wore like a second skin. It was obvious that she wasn't wearing a bra and he had to wonder whether she'd forgone panties, as well.

Daniel licked his lips.

She looked magnificent, sexy, ravishing, so damn doable. He wanted to go caveman on her by tossing her over his shoulder and taking her straight to bed. Or following her down to the nearest flat surface. Hell, even a door or a wall—he wasn't picky.

Dammit. He'd seen lots of beautiful woman before, and had bedded several of them. But Alex was beyond beautiful. She was… God, what was that word? *Alluring? Captivating? Entrancing?* All three and more?

He wanted her. The thought that he always would terrified him.

"The proceedings will begin in about ten minutes, out in the gardens—which, you have to admit, look amazing. It looks like a real winter wonderland!" Alex said with a wide smile. "So, finish eating, take a quick bathroom break, whatever you need to do so you'll be ready to go on when your number is called."

Alex was in tough-girl mode, and damn, that prissy, bossy voice coming from that sexy mouth sent all his blood rushing south. Daniel resisted the impulse to bang his forehead against the nearest wall and settled for biting the inside of his lip until he tasted blood.

Act like the adult you are, Clayton.

Alex issued another set of instructions, none of which he listened to, his eyes too full of her to take in anything she was saying. How hard could it be? Walk on, try not to scowl, get sold, walk off.

At the end of her lecture, Alex smiled again, and Daniel immediately recognized that fake-as-hell, I'm-trying-to-act-normal expression. The other men in the room might have had all their brains fried by the combination of Tessa Noble looking super hot and Alex Slade looking super sexy, but in the small part of his brain that was still functional, he knew that something was up with Alex. Something life changing, crazy making, worry inducing. He could see the tension in her shoulders, the tight cords of her neck. And that blinding smile didn't come any where near her sky blue eyes.

Daniel started to go to her but then her gaze clashed with his and he easily read her request not to approach her, her guarded expression telling him that she couldn't deal with him. Daniel lifted one eyebrow, a silent appeal, asking her what the hell was going on, and she gave him the tiniest shake of her head.

Daniel tapped his shirt pocket, where the outline of his cell phone was clearly visible, hoping she'd understand that he needed to know, even if it was only by text message.

A tiny nod, but Daniel didn't fool himself into believing that his phone would soon buzz with an incoming message. Alex had only acknowledged his request, not agreed to do what he asked. The woman had her own mind and, God, he liked her that way.

Frankly, he liked her any damn way he could get her.

"Six thousand dollars, ladies, for Lloyd Richardson. Who has seven?"

I'm pregnant.

Alex acknowledged a bid from Gail, Tessa's friend, and that bid was quickly topped by Steena Goodman. Alex briefly wondered what these women saw in Lloyd to make them go that high. Gail, looking sulky but determined to have her date with Lloyd, raised her paddle again. Well, she'd have to pony up because Steena had deep pockets and her wealthy now-dead husband's money to spend.

She was pregnant with Daniel's baby.

It was like two halves of her brain were operating independently. One half was playing the role of the merry, if slightly manic, auctioneer, while in the other half, she was curled up in a fetal position, battling for breath.

Grandpa's first great-grandchild is going to carry Clayton blood.

"Eight thousand dollars, Gail? Wow, that's super generous." *Too generous*, Alex thought, alarm bells ringing in her head. Gail didn't look like she had that sort of money lying around. "Oh, a new bidder at nine thousand dollars! Marvelous."

She had to tell Daniel…and Gus. Daniel would have to tell Rose and, God, what fun that was going to be.

"Fifty thousand dollars."

Alex blinked at Steena's outrageous offer. She couldn't possibly have heard her right. Alex looked at Rachel, who was standing to her right, and judging by Rachel's shocked expression, she knew that her hearing wasn't faulty. Steena Goodman had just bid fifty thousand dollars for a date with Lloyd. Was she out of her ever-lovin' mind?

But knowing her money was good—those weren't fake diamonds hanging from her ears and decorating her fingers—Alex gripped the gavel, preparing to sell Lloyd to the woman before she came to her senses. She flashed a smile at Rachel and lifted her gavel.

"One hundred thousand dollars."

Oh no. Oh hell. Oh crap. Alex widened her eyes at Gail's ridiculous offer, waiting for her to wave the offer away, to tell her it was a joke. But Gail just kept her eyes on Lloyd, one hand on her hip. A low buzz swept through the room as the drama unfolded. Alex knew that she should sell the date, that nobody—not even Steena—would top Gail's ludicrous bid. She also knew that there was no way that the charity would see a hundred thousand dollars from Gail.

Call it a hunch.

Alex looked toward James Harris, the new TCC president, and he lifted his hands in a what-can-you-do gesture. Maybe she was judging a book by its cover; maybe Gail did have a hundred grand to spare. This was, after all, Texas, where anyone could be a billionaire. It had happened before.

Alex dropped the gavel, hiding her trepidation. "Lloyd Richardson has been sold to Gail Walker."

Gail clapped her hands like a little girl getting an award and skipped up to the stage to fling her arms around Lloyd's neck. He responded by laying a hot kiss on her. Gail kicked up her foot and Alex immediately noticed the scuff mark on the back of the heel of her shoe. Oh boy, this wasn't going to end well.

Alex felt a little dizzy as she watched Lloyd and Gail leave the stage. She was exhausted and overwhelmed. Two more to go and then she could go home and collapse.

Tessa wouldn't be a problem; she'd just have to watch the bids roll in. But Daniel? Well, hell, crap and damn. How was she going to sell her baby's father to another woman?

Alex, after spending thirty excruciating minutes accepting congratulations on the success of the evening, slipped out of the festively decorated gardens and headed toward the TCC clubhouse.

She needed some time alone to get her racing heart under control, to reflect on this crazy day, to think, dammit!

Wrapping her arms around her waist, she stepped inside the clubhouse and headed for the small office James had allocated for auction-related business. After closing the door behind her, she flipped on a desk lamp and half sat, half leaned on the wide wooden desk.

Selling a date with Tessa had been a dream, as she'd barely been able to keep up with the flurry of bids for her gorgeous friend. Tessa had looked surprised at the attention she garnered and then relieved when Ryan topped all the other bids with a whopper offer. She'd caught Tessa's pleading look and quickly closed the bidding, accepting Ryan's overly generous bid with a quick snap of her gravel. Maybe there had been a man in the audience who could top Ryan's bid, but Tessa had been a good sport and she deserved a date with Ryan. And maybe, finally, the two of them would figure out what the rest of the community already knew: that they should only date each other. Permanently.

Selling a date with Daniel hadn't been as easy. Rachel, bless her, had offered to take over as auctioneer but that would've caused speculation they could ill afford. So she'd gritted her teeth, pasted on a bright smile and, after fifteen excruciating minutes, she sold Daniel to an oil baron's daughter from Houston: a tall, cool brunette with a predatory look in her eyes.

She'd wish him luck—everyone knew Iona Duckworth had a thing for cowboys. And cowboys who also owned and operated one of the most iconic ranches in the state? Jackpot!

Alex dropped her head, finally able to devote her full attention to the problem at hand. She was pregnant.

With Daniel's baby.

God.

Alex stared down at the exotic wooden floor. How did this happen? Why was life punishing her like this? She wasn't ready to be someone's mom, and couldn't imagine being fully responsible for another life. Moreover, she knew nothing about babies—except how they were made, and apparently she didn't know enough about that! How on earth was she going to raise a child, accept Mike's amazing offer to be a partner in his new start-up and... God!

Through this child growing inside her, she was now connected to Daniel forever. Well, at least until their child became an adult, but that was long enough. Once she told Daniel about the baby, he'd be a permanent and constant part of her life, exactly what she'd been trying to avoid when she told him that they had to stop sleeping together. She didn't want Daniel in her life— she couldn't cope with all the emotions he pulled to the surface, all the memories, the resurgence of the hopes and dreams she'd had as a stupid-with-love teenager.

Being close to Daniel, even if it was just a physical thing, was dangerous enough. But this child, their baby, would require them to find a way to interact, emotionally. Emotional interaction led to attachments and she didn't do attachment.

Though, apparently and according to the three pregnancy tests she'd done earlier, she had no choice but to become attached. That was what happened with moms and babies, wasn't it?

Oh God, she was going to be a mommy.

Alex heard the door to the office open and then she felt Daniel's arms around her. Her bones liquefied, and she fell into him, utterly exhausted and emotionally winded. She didn't think she could take much more tonight.

"Lex. God, honey, what the hell is going on with you?" Daniel demanded, lifting her up and pulling her into his body.

Should she tell him now or later? What was the point of delaying? This news wouldn't be any easier to hear tomorrow or a month from now.

Daniel held her head with one hand and for a moment she felt safe, not so very alone. If she told him now, he'd push her away from him and she'd lose this closeness, this support. Should she tell him? How could she not?

"Lex, you're scaring me," Daniel said with concern

in his voice. "You're as white as a sheet and you're trembling. I'm starting to freak out here."

He was freaking out? And he hadn't even heard the life-altering news yet.

Alex wound her arms around his waist and rested her forehead on his chest. Once she told him, she'd have to build another wall between them, reinforce her barriers. It would be so easy to allow Daniel to take control—he was a take-charge and do-what-I-say type of guy. He was an alpha male, supremely comfortable with making quick decisions, plotting a course and following it.

And she was so tired, feeling so utterly overwhelmed that it was tempting to let him take control, to follow his lead. But at some point, she'd start to rebel and argue. Or worse, she might—although, given her contrary nature, this wasn't likely—start to like him taking charge. No, she was the captain of her own ship.

Even if her ship was currently a leaky rowboat with a broken oar.

Alex gathered her courage and stepped out of Daniel's arms. Pushing her hair off her face, she met those deep, dark worried eyes.

"Dan, I have something to tell you. You're not going to like it."

He lifted one eyebrow. "What can be worse than having to spend *any* time with the cowboy-obsessed Iona Duckworth?"

Oh, she could easily top that. "I have a date for you that's going to last the rest of your life."

Surprise and shock skittered across Daniel's face. Then panic set in. He lifted up his hands and took a step back. "Lex, it was just an affair. We haven't spent enough time together to make those sorts of pronouncements. You don't know me anymore."

If her heart wasn't threatening to jump out of her chest, she might've laughed at his erroneous assumption. "I'm not talking about you and me, Daniel!"

Relief replaced panic and Alex ignored the flare of disappointment. He'd once spent hours with her, painting their future, but now the thought was abhorrent. Yes, they'd grown up, they were adults now, and she'd packed up dreams of her and Daniel a long time ago.

It shouldn't hurt but it did. Far too much.

This, *this*, was why she had to keep her emotional distance, why she had to spend as little time with Daniel as possible. With him, foolish thoughts, remembered dreams and unwelcome emotions crept in and threatened her unattached heart. She'd planned on walking away from him and Royal—leaving all these pesky emotions behind. But if she left now, she'd be taking a part of Daniel with her…

"Seriously, I'm about to shake your news out of you," Daniel muttered.

"I'm pregnant, Daniel."

His guttural bark was short on amusement and long on disbelief. "That's not funny, Alex."

"I know. It really isn't. And I really am pregnant."

Alex walked around her desk, pulled her bag out from the bottom drawer and shoved her hand inside. She pulled out the three pregnancy tests and threw them across the desk. Daniel picked up each one in turn, saw the positive indications and Alex watched a muscle jump in his tight jaw. His sensual mouth was now a slash in his face and his olive skin turned pasty. The news was finally starting to sink in…

"It's mine?"

What the hell? How dare he ask that? She dramatically slapped her hand against her forehead. "Oh, wait, *no*! It could be one of the many other men I was sleeping with at the same time I was sneaking around with you!"

Daniel shoved his hand through his hair, pushing an errant curl off his forehead. He sent her a sour look. "Still as sarcastic as ever."

"It's my default response to stupid comments," Alex shot back. She walked out from behind her desk, sat on the corner and crossed her legs. "I'm newly pregnant, just a few weeks."

Daniel released a couple of f-bombs and followed those with a string of creative curses. When he was done, he stopped pacing, stood in front of her and curled his big hands around her bare upper arms. The heat of his hands burned into her skin as lust burned through her. Her desire for him surprised her; she'd thought that the news of her pregnancy would've killed any thoughts of sex.

But no. She wanted him as much as ever.

"What do you want to do, Alex?"

She lifted one shoulder. "What can I do? It's here."

"You're not considering an—getting rid of it?" Daniel asked, obviously worried.

"You wouldn't want that?"

He shook his head and she noticed his bleak eyes, the desperation. "This sucks. It's not what either of us wanted, but…it's a consequence of the choice we made. We have to deal."

We. Not *you*. On hearing that one small word, Alex relaxed a fraction. She wasn't in this alone…not entirely.

Daniel rested his forehead against hers, released another swear word and sighed. "I'm sorry, Alex. Jesus, this wasn't supposed to happen."

Alex heard the buzz of her phone and looked down at the desk. She frowned at the message that popped up on her screen. It was an SOS from James Harris, of all people. The auction was done and some of the guests had already drifted away. What on earth could've happened that warranted three SOS texts and a terse "We have a major situation"?

She also noticed two missed calls from James and four from Rachel.

"I need to go."

"Uh, *no*. We need to discuss this, Alex!"

"Something has happened—"

"Damn right something's happened. You're pregnant with my child. I want to discuss this, find a way forward."

Yep, alpha male. Alex remembered her grandmother's words, heard Sarah's voice in her head. *Start as you mean to go on, honey. And don't take any horse crap.*

Alex pulled away from his strong grip. "The baby will still be here tomorrow, Daniel, and the next day. We have time." She could see that her answer irritated him, but she didn't much care. Daniel liked having all his ducks in a row, knowing where they were going and how to get there. He'd once confided in her—a moment that was both random and rare—that living with his mom was like standing in a bucket on a raging river, not sure when or how he'd be tossed into the rapids or over the waterfall. He liked planning his own route, being in control of his destination.

She understood that, and they would sit down and have a decent conversation, but right now the bachelor auction had hit a snag and she was needed.

Daniel threw up his hands. "I cannot believe you are walking out on me. You've just told me that we are having a baby, Alex!"

Alex drilled her index finger into his chest. "*I* am

having a baby, Clayton, not *we*. Do not think that you can stomp into my life with your size thirteens and take over. That's not going to happen." She huffed out a breath. "When I am ready to deal with you, with the situation, I will give you a call."

Daniel's eyes widened at her strong statement. Good. The sooner he realized she wasn't a pushover, the better off they'd both be. *This is what happens when you spend your time together making love and not talking*, Alex realized. Assumptions were made.

And babies, too.

She picked up her cell phone, walked toward the door and slipped into the hallway. Pushing away thoughts of that big gorgeous, confused man she'd left behind inside, she walked down the hallway to James's office.

Another fire to extinguish. Hopefully this would be the smallest, as well as the last, of the evening.

Four

In the parking lot of the TCC, Daniel glanced at his watch and grimaced. It was after 1:00 a.m., and he was exhausted. Tired and worried and, yeah, completely freaked out.

He was going to be a dad. Holy crap. He'd never had a father, or even a proper male role model, and as a result he knew next to nothing about being a good father. He was going to be responsible for a tiny human life… a terrifying prospect for someone who didn't have the smallest idea about what to do or how to be a dad. Fatherhood, a state he'd thought he'd only consider far into the future, was a nebulous concept, something as inexplicable as black holes or the binary code.

There was nothing Daniel hated more than the fear of the unknown.

Thanks to his erratic and unsettling childhood, he found security in planning his life, breaking down his future into five-, ten-, fifteen-, twenty-year goals. But to be honest, those plans were all ranch and business related, he hadn't spent a lot of time planning his personal life.

Or any at all.

Leaning back against Alex's sports car, he linked his hands behind his neck and stared up at the vast Texas sky. All his energy—every drop of sweat and blood— went into making The Silver C Ranch the best it could be. He knew and loved every inch of his land and he knew that the ranch was his place, his corner on earth. People came and went, but his grandmother and The Silver C kept him stable as a child and anchored as an adult.

According to Alex's earth-tilting news, the first of the next generation of Claytons was baking inside of her, and what did that mean? For Rose and for the future of The Silver C? And what did it, *should it*, mean to him?

Having children wasn't something he'd thought much about, and when he did, it was only in terms of who would inherit the ranch sometime in the very distant future. Honestly, at this point in his life, he didn't want to be a dad and he had no interest in being tied down—he was perfectly content with brief affairs and one-night stands, keeping emotionally distant. But Alex… Dammit. Well, she'd recently managed to narrow that distance, to pull him closer. She tempted him to unbend a little and to open up a fraction, probably because he subconsciously wanted a way to recapture some of the magic and joy of that heady summer so long ago.

It had been the happiest three months of his life, so why wouldn't he want to experience it again? But she'd been right to call it off, to make them move on. What he hadn't expected was that they'd be left with a lifetime memento of their fling.

They'd made a child. God. He was utterly determined to be a better parent, and the exact opposite of his mother—and to be a stable, responsible and hands-on dad.

His child would know that he loved him, or her, that he would be a constant and consistent part of his child's life. That was nonnegotiable. His child would know his, or her, father's love. *His* love...

He wanted to be there for the big and small things, and that meant having his baby's mother in his life. But Alex... Being with Alex made him feel alive, uncontrolled, impulsive. The way she made him feel terrified him. But he'd just have to deal, find a way to keep her at arm's length, because he planned on being a vital part of his child's upbringing. He wanted to change diapers, do the midnight feedings, pace the floors while he tried to put his child to sleep. He'd do whatever was needed, but in order to be a part of his child's life, he had to be *in* that life. That meant marriage—*God!*—or at the very least, him and Alex living together.

Where could they live? Since Alex lived in the main house at the Lone Wolf Ranch, his house was the most reasonable option. Or they could build a new place, something that suited them both. And they'd have to tell their grandparents—that was going to be a barrel of laughs...

First things first, Clayton. Talk to Alex, offer to marry her, secure his child's future. As for the way Alex made him feel, well, he'd simply have to get over that. He would not allow her to cause him to lose control or focus. They could marry and within that union they'd be friends, even lovers, but he'd always keep himself emotionally detached. It was safer that way.

Daniel heard footsteps and lifted his head to see Alex

walking toward her car and him. Cold air caught in his throat as the rest of his body heated, then sizzled. Man, she looked amazing, so damn sexy. When she noticed him leaning against her car, she released a long sigh. She was past exhausted, he realized, and a wave of protectiveness swept over him. He was right to feel protective over her, he rationalized, because she was the mother of his child. By protecting her, he protected his son. Or daughter.

When Alex reached him, he lifted his hand and ran his knuckles over her pale cheek. "You look done in, honey," he said, his voice gruff.

"It's been a hell of a night," Alex replied, surprising him by resting her butt on the side of her car. She'd pulled a jacket over that sexy dress, but her shapely thigh slid out from under the high slit in the skirt. He wanted to pull the slippery material up and find out for sure whether she was wearing panties or not.

Like that was important! Daniel mentally slapped himself as he moved to stand in front of her. They had a future to discuss, plans to make.

Alex held up a hand and he saw that her eyes were red-rimmed and that she now sported blue stripes under her eyes that her makeup could no longer conceal. "Not tonight, Daniel. I can't take anymore."

He curbed his impulse to push and tipped his head to the side. "What was the great bachelor-auction emergency?"

"Ah, that. Well, that hundred-thousand-dollar bid Gail made for Lloyd was a fake bid—neither have that type of money. To distract a reporter from reporting on that juicy piece of gossip and totally ruining the success of the evening, we've offered the reporter complete access to Ryan and Tessa's super romantic date.

And to distract him further—" Alex's eyes narrowed in the moonlight "—you are, according to Rose, giving an interview to the same reporter on what it feels like to auction yourself off and how it feels to be one of Texas's most eligible bachelors."

Daniel waited for Alex to laugh, to give him any indication that she was joking, but she just sent him a steady look with no hint of amusement. So, ah, this interview was going to happen whether he was on board or not.

Crap.

Daniel closed his eyes and gripped the bridge of his nose. "My damn interfering grandmother."

"Tonight, I am grateful for her interference. The two stories will be a welcome distraction from the fake bid."

"I swear, my grandmother only hears what she wants to! I'm going to kill her. I swear I am!"

"She'll just come back and haunt you," Alex said behind a yawn. "Look, Mr. Most Eligible, I am exhausted, as it's been a hell of a day. I'm going home."

But they hadn't talked about the baby or come up with any concrete solutions. Daniel started to argue but then he saw the sheen of tears in her eyes, noticed that her hands were trembling. *Stop being an ass and think about her for one sec, Clayton. She's been on her feet for fourteen hours, she's just found out she's pregnant and, after hearing that news, she still managed to stand in front of a huge crowd and pull off a super successful event.* Alex had grit and courage in spades—he had to give her that.

Making a quick decision, he took her bag off her shoulder and shoved his hand inside, looking for her car keys. Ignoring her protest, he wound his arm around her waist and lifted her up to walk her around the car, pulling open the passenger door.

JOSS WOOD 67

"What the hell are you doing?" she demanded as he bundled her into the seat.

"Taking you home."

"I can drive," Alex protested.

Daniel crouched down between the car door and its frame and placed his hand on her slim thigh. "Lex, let me do this for you. You are played out and I don't want you making the drive back to the Lone Wolf exhausted and emotional."

Alex licked her lips and sighed. "I was going to go to the tree house, spend the night there. I need some space, to be alone."

"I'll take you anywhere you want to go, honey. I just want to make sure you get there in one piece," Daniel said, keeping his tone noncombative.

"What about your car?"

Daniel shrugged. "It'll be safe enough here." He moved his thumb to stroke her bare thigh. "Let me take you home, Lex."

Alex dropped her head back against the headrest and gave a quick nod. Daniel gathered the rest of her dress, put it inside the car and slammed her door shut. In the five minutes he took to adjust her seat to his longer legs, back out of her space and reach the TCC gates, she was sound asleep.

"No, I'm not going to marry you, and I'm not going to move in with you, either."

With her battered cowboy boots propped onto the railing of Sarah's tree house, Alex held Daniel's hot stare and shook her head to emphasize her point. However, Daniel, dressed in faded, formfitting denims and a green-and-black flannel shirt worn over a black T-shirt, tried to scowl her into submission. But she'd been raised by Gus and had learned at an early age to stand her ground or get run over.

When he started to argue his point—again!—Alex rushed in, "Daniel, we are not living in the 1800s. My honor, your honor, is not at stake. Sure, Rose and my grandpa are probably going to blow a gasket, but they will just have to deal. I am not jumping into a marriage with you or into sharing a house just because I'm pregnant. That's a terrible reason to be together!".

"I want to see my child, Alex." Daniel pushed the words out from between clenched teeth.

"He or she will arrive in only seven months' time. How will us moving in together or getting married help you with that right now?"

Daniel opened his mouth to issue what she knew would be a hot retort only to have the words die on his tongue. Ha! He didn't have an answer to that argument! And there wasn't a reasonable answer because he was being an idiot!

She dropped her feet to the ground and rested her forearms on her thighs. "Daniel, I have no intention of denying you access to our child, but this idea you have of you being a full-time dad—that's not going to happen." Alex caught the flash of pain in his eyes, knew that her words were harsh but it was better to clear this up now before expectations were created that could not be fulfilled.

She was not eighteen anymore and dreaming of this man, fat babies, horses and a life on the ranch, filled with laughter and love. Dreams were for children, for the naive, and she far preferred cold reality. "We're not going to be a couple and we are not going to live together. I've had a business offer. I'm probably going to take it. It's lucrative and it's in my, and the baby's, best interest for me to accept it since my bills are going to quadruple."

Daniel's eyes turned cold. Oh damn. Now she'd properly insulted him.

"I am fully capable and prepared to pay for everything you or the baby need."

Of course he was, the guy was a millionaire fifty times over. That wasn't the point! "And I am an independent, successful woman who can earn her own money and support her own child," Alex stated, her voice dropping ten degrees. Standing up so that she did not feel like Daniel was looming over her, she slapped her hands onto her hips and handed him her most ferocious scowl. He didn't look remotely intimidated, dammit.

"I do not need you, or any other man, to pay my way."

"Goddammit, woman, you are so contrary!"

"Pot. Kettle. Black." Alex threw his words back in his face.

Daniel threw his hands up in the air, whipped around as if to leave and, before she could blink, he'd spun back and he was in her space, his fingers tunneling through her hair and his mouth falling toward hers. Alex knew that she should stop him but instead of pushing him away, she stood on her toes so that she could feel his lips against hers a second sooner. Waiting even a moment longer than she needed to was torture. She wanted him, of course she did, always had. Probably always would.

He drove her nuts. Nobody had the power to annoy her as intensely as Daniel could but, God, when he kissed her, he morphed from Irritant Number One to Sex God to Have-to-Get-Him-Naked-Immediately.

Those amazing lips moved over hers and his hand

on her butt pulled her into him. Denim rubbed against denim and underneath the fabric she could feel the evidence of his desire. They might not know how to be friends and had even less idea of how to co-parent. But, God, this? This they knew how to do.

Daniel's tongue slid into her mouth to tangle with hers, and she groaned deep in her throat. She should stop this; it wasn't sensible. This would just further complicate a crazy situation, but instead of pushing him away, her hand skated up under his T-shirt to find hot, hard skin. Daniel had the same idea, since his hand was down the back of her loose jeans, cupping her bare backside with his big calloused hand.

He yanked his mouth off hers to speak. "I've got to know, were you wearing panties last night? Under that sexy dress?"

It took Alex a moment to make sense of his words. She'd worn the tiniest thong she had and really, she still didn't know why she bothered. But she wasn't about to admit that to Daniel. He wanted to hear that she'd worn nothing more than that silver slip dress. "No."

Alex felt him tighten and harden, saw the fire in his eyes and knew that there was no going back. They were headed for the bedroom, or the sitting room. Hell, they might not even make it inside.

Daniel pulled her long-sleeve T-shirt up and over her head, looking down at the sheer lacy bra she wore. She was in the early stage of her pregnancy, and she'd yet to feel different, but Daniel was looking at her like she was made of spun glass, of delicate platinum strands. His index finger gently traced the outline of her nipple and she sucked in her breath, watching his dark hand against her lighter skin. Even in winter he looked tanned, courtesy of his Hispanic heritage. So sexy, Alex thought as he pushed the lace away to touch her, skin on skin. Daniel bent his knees, wrapped his big, powerful arms around her thighs and lifted her so that her nipple was in line with his mouth. Holding her easily, muscles bunching but not straining, he tongued her, pulling her nipple into his mouth, nibbling her with his teeth. She ran her fingers through the loose curls he hated, tracing the shell of his ear, the strong cords of his neck.

"I want you, Lex. I know I shouldn't but, God, I do," Daniel muttered, pulling away from her to look up, his eyes blazing with lust.

"Dan…"

He rested his forehead between her breasts, still holding her, and she felt his ragged breath against her skin. She knew that he expected her to ask him to let her go, to step away, but she couldn't. She didn't know how to be a mommy, to have Daniel in her life, how to navigate her suddenly complicated future, but she knew how to make love to this sexy, infuriating man.

She loved being naked with him.

"Take me inside, Dan. Love me until I can't think anymore," Alex whispered, brushing her fingers across his lips, his jaw.

Daniel flashed her a grin that was sexy enough to melt glass, and then he carried her inside. Allowing her to slide down his body so that their mouths could meet, he kissed her as he navigated his way to the bedroom at the back of the tree house. With long hot slides of his tongue, and hands possessively skimming her skin, he silently demanded that she match his passion. Alex held on to him as he lowered her to the bed and sighed when he settled into the V shape between her legs. Right place, far too many clothes.

Her shirt was gone, so Alex pulled his over his head

and tossed it to the floor. She sighed when his naked chest touched hers and lifted her head so that she could tongue his flat, masculine nipple. A good start but not enough.

"Please, Dan, I don't want to wait. It's been too long."

Daniel heard her pleas and pulled back to yank her boots off her feet and tug her jeans down over her hips. His eyes moved down, stopping on her breasts before moving over her still-flat stomach to her relatively modest bikini panties.

His eyes widened and he released a low chuckle. God, he had a great smile. It crinkled his eyes, revealed his straight white teeth and hinted at the tiniest dimple in his right cheek. But as much as she liked seeing his smile, she couldn't understand why he was laughing.

Alex pushed herself up to rest her weight on her bent elbows.

Daniel arched an eyebrow. "I'm game if you are."

Ah…what was he talking about? They'd had great sex but nothing weird or kinky, so where was he going with this?

Daniel gestured to her panties and Alex tried to read the slogan upside down. Okay, but Afterward We Get Pizza?

She groaned. She was *not* wearing her sexiest lingerie. "They were a gag gift from Rachel," she explained, blushing. "I haven't had a chance to do laundry."

"Silk or cotton, I can pretty much guarantee that anything you wear will always end up on the floor."

Daniel slowly peeled the panties down her legs, his smile still tugging at the edges of his gorgeous mouth. He dropped the panties to the floor and stood up to undress. Lifting his feet, he pulled his boots off, then pushed his jeans over his hips, taking his underwear with him. Embarrassment forgotten, Alex stared at him and Daniel stood there, allowing her to look her fill. Broad shoulders, muscled arms, that wide chest. He had sexy abs, but she also adored those long hip muscles, his lean, powerful thighs, the arch of his surprisingly elegant feet.

Daniel was a curious combination of masculine grace and rugged good looks, but beneath it all, he was a man of honor. By marrying her, he wanted to do what was right, what he thought was best for their baby. She respected that, respected *him*. But she couldn't marry him or move in with him; she shouldn't even be making love to him.

But this…thing…between them ran too deep and she couldn't resist him. She would always, as long as she breathed, want him but she wouldn't let herself love him. She couldn't afford to do that, to let him hurt her again.

Daniel placed his hands on the bed on either side of her face and placed his mouth on hers, sipping, tasting, exploring. They'd had slow sex, hot sex and crazy sex up against a door, but his kisses seemed different tonight, intense with a hint of gentleness. Alex slipped her tongue into his mouth and tried to dial up the passion. Hot and fast she could deal with, but she didn't know how to handle slow and sexy and profound.

She lifted her hips to make contact with his shaft, wanting to get out of her head and fully into the physicality of the act. Daniel didn't take the hint so she ran her thumb up his dick and when she stroked his tip, he jerked and then groaned.

"Need you, Dan, now." And she did. She needed him to remind her that this was all sex, that she couldn't have the ranch and the horses and the hot baby daddy in her life. Dreams like those put her heart at risk…so she'd just take the sex.

It was simpler that way.

Daniel nudged her legs farther apart with his knee before stroking her secret folds with his fingers. "You're so wet, Lex."

"Because I need you, Dan. I need sex." Alex heard the desperation in her voice and didn't know whether she was trying to convince herself or him.

He pushed inside her and Alex wrapped her legs around his back, pulling him closer. Heat, warmth, completion. The rest of her life was crazy confusion but, as Daniel started to move, Alex realized that this made sense. It was the only thing that did.

As he pushed her higher and higher, the needs of her body stilled her whirling thoughts and all she wanted was more of him. Her hands skated over his back, his butt, down the backs of his thighs. A strand of hair landed in her mouth and she thrashed her head from side to side as he kissed her neck, pulled her earlobe between his teeth. She was so close, teetering on the edge of pleasure, when she heard Daniel's demand to let go, his reassurance that he would catch her.

She wanted to stay here, just for another minute, bathed in that silver light of anticipation. "Dammit, Lex, I can't hold on," Daniel muttered.

Placing his hand between their bodies, he found her clit and stroked it, just once with his thumb. It was the sexual equivalent of a hard hand shoving her between her shoulders and she plunged over the cliff… Falling, falling, shattering. But he fell with her, his body shaking as he came.

Daniel collapsed on her and Alex didn't mind that her breath was shallow, that his body weight pushed her into the soft mattress. When they were lying like this, intimately connected, they were at peace. It was only when they started to talk that things went wrong.

Alex pushed her nose into his neck, kissed his skin and ran her hand down his spine. Beautiful but stubborn. Gorgeous but flawed.

Just as she was, contrary and imperfect.

Daniel pulled himself up and gazed down at her, holding his body weight on one hand as he pulled the strand of hair from her mouth and tucked it behind her ear. Alex saw her confusion reflected in his eyes. Then determination replaced confusion and she knew that he was looking for the right words to use to convince her to come around to his way of thinking.

Okay, she might be stubborn but he was relentless. "I'm not marrying or moving in with you, Clayton. No matter how good you are in the sack."

"Dammit." Daniel slipped out of her, stood up and stalked to the small bathroom attached to the bedroom. "You are a stubborn pain in the ass!"

Sure she was but that didn't make her wrong!

Five

The end of January

Gus heard the door to his study open and looked up to see his still-beautiful Rose, and his heart, old and jaded, thumped against his rib cage. He'd waited for fifty-plus years to see that soft smile on her face, for her to walk into the room and into his arms.

Man, he was riding the gravy train with biscuit wheels.

Rose placed her hands on his chest and her mouth drifted across his.

"Mornin', husband."

He was her husband. And how freakin' great was that? He smiled, allowed his hand to drift down over her ass and grinned. "Mornin', *wife*."

After a little canoodling—the best way to start a morning—Rose rested her head on her chest and sighed. "Have you had any more thoughts on what to do about our grandchildren?"

During their wedding reception last night, Rose dropped the bombshell news that Alex was pregnant and that Daniel was the baby's father. Strangely, instead of feeling angry, he'd felt content. Like this news was right, simply meant to be. He'd initially thought that he was so very relaxed because he'd been floating on a cloud of wedding-induced happiness, but upon waking this morning, it still felt right, like it was preordained.

He wasn't, however, happy that Alex and Daniel were going to try to raise their great-grandchild separately and not as husband and wife. That wasn't acceptable. Not because he cared about convention or how it would look, but because, dammit, those two were meant to be together.

They'd meant to be together ten years ago—shame on him and Rose for making their grandchildren casualties in their stupid, long-held feud—and they were meant to be together now.

"My Alex is 'more stubborn-hard than hammered iron.'"

Rose pulled back and smiled her appreciation. "Shakespeare, Gus Slade? I'm impressed."

Gus felt his ears heat at her admiration and then shrugged it off. They had more important things to worry about. "So, about these darned kids…"

He refused to allow them to repeat his and Rose's foolishness and waste so much time. They had to reunite Alex and Daniel and, after showing his wife exactly how much he loved and wanted her, he'd spent a good part of the night working out how to do just that. "I have a plan, but it might involve a sacrifice on our part."

"Okay. How big a sacrifice?"

Oh man, she wasn't going to like this. "Our honeymoon. I'm sorry, sweetheart. I want to spend some time with you alone and I know you want that, too—"

Rose stepped away from him, pulled a chair from the dining table, sat down and crossed her legs. She didn't look mad but, since they'd been married for less than a minute, what did he know? "Gus Slade, I have waited fifty-two years to be your wife and I don't care about going away for our honeymoon." A soft radiant smile lit up her lovely face. How could she possibly be more beautiful today than she was half a century ago? Yet she was. "Being with you—whether it's here in Royal or at Galloway Cove or on the damned moon—is where I want to be."

"Such language, darlin'." Gus tsk-tsked.

Rose rolled her eyes. "I'm not a fragile flower, Gus. Neither am I sixteen anymore. And I can swear if I *damn* well want to."

Gus hid his smile with his hand. But before he could investigate this saucy new side of his wife—man, that word just slayed him, every single time—he saw the speculation in her eyes.

"Tell me what you have in mind, and I'll gladly sacrifice our week on Matt's island to get those two to see daylight."

Gus outlined his plan and watched as Rose stared out the window at the east paddock, where his old paint horse, Jezebel, was keeping company with his prized Arabians and Daisy, the airheaded goat.

"Do you think it can work?" Rose asked him, worry in her eyes. She no longer wore her mask of aloofness and he was clearly able to read her concern for both Daniel and Alex. He could see her deep desire to see them happy. Rose didn't wear her heart on her sleeve, but that didn't mean she didn't feel things deeply, sometimes too deeply.

Gus sighed. They'd wasted so much time being angry

with each other, but he couldn't regret loving Sarah—they'd had a good marriage. Losing his son so early had been horrible but raising his grandkids had given both him and Sarah a second lease on life.

Rose's life hadn't been so easy. Her daddy had been a hard man and Ed, her husband, had been as cuddly as a hornet and had made her life hell. They'd made so many mistakes, but he was damned if he'd watch Alex and Daniel repeat their history. They might argue like crazy but the room crackled with electricity when the two of them were together. They owed it to themselves and their baby to make it work.

"Gus? Will your plan work?"

He shrugged and, needing to touch her, held the back of her neck. "I hope so, honey."

Rose nodded and leaned her head against his side. "If it doesn't, we'll lock them in the barn until they come to their senses."

Gus laughed, thinking she was joking. When she remained silent, he looked down at her. "You're joking, right?"

Rose stood up and wound her arms around his waist. "We're giving them the chance to come to their senses in a nice way. After all, it's the least we can do after everything we pulled to keep them apart. But if it doesn't work, we'll do it the hard way." He saw her stubborn expression and grinned. His wife was fierce. And he loved her that way.

He loved her, period. Always had.

The first week of February

Alex sat on the leather seat of the private plane Gus hired to fly his bride to Galloway Cove for their honeymoon and wished that she could ask the pilot to close the doors and whisk her away to Matt's stunning private Caribbean island. She couldn't think of anything she'd rather do more than stretch out on white sand beneath a blue sky, read a book and just be.

But no, before he left, her grandfather wanted to give her one last lecture and that was the only reason why he would've asked her to meet him and Rose on the plane. He'd leave her with a reprimand about doing the right thing, raising her baby with its father and not as a single mom in Houston.

She was depriving Daniel of being a full-time dad, depriving Gus and Rose of having quick and easy access to the baby, making life ten times harder for herself without having the support of Daniel, as well as her family and friends.

Yada yada.

She knew that—how could she not? Being on her own in Houston, trying to run a company as a single mom, was going to be the hardest challenge of her life! But Gus didn't understand—she doubted anyone would—that was less scary than remaining in Royal, utterly in lust and half in love with her baby's father. The best chance she had to stop thinking about Daniel Clayton and the life she could never have was for her to move back to Houston. She had a far better chance of pushing him out of her mind there than here in Royal.

If she stayed here, she might just do something crazy.

"Grandpa, Daniel and I had our chance."

"That doesn't mean that you can't have a second one," Gus replied.

It was like talking to a brick wall. In an effort to get through to him, Alex pulled out the big guns. "One of the reasons we missed our chance was because you and your new bride were vehemently opposed to us being together."

Gus hesitated before replying. "We might not have been completely correct in that assumption."

Okay, that was as close to an apology as she was going to get from her taciturn grandfather.

"But in our defense, you were also very young."

"Daniel," Alex reminded him, "chose The Silver C over me. His loyalty to Rose and to the ranch has always been stronger than any love he had for me."

She hadn't been able to explain further, unable to admit to Gus that she couldn't trust that Daniel would be there for her and her baby when life got tough, couldn't tolerate the thought of being second or third on his list of priorities.

"I think you are making a mistake, Alexis," Gus quietly told her.

"But, Grandpa, it's my life and my mistake to make," Alex insisted.

"Except it's not—you have a baby to think of," Gus replied before ending the call.

Why couldn't he understand that she'd lost so much? If she and Daniel lived together, raised their child together, there was a good chance that she would fall in love with him again; of that she had no doubt. Wasn't that the reason she'd broken up with him recently, because she could feel herself sliding downhill into love?

Alex had lost Daniel's love once, and she'd mourned him for years. Their breakup had been another type of death, and she was done with death, of all types.

She wouldn't survive another loss. Her shattered heart would crumble into pieces too fine to be patched back together again. And while she had no intention of denying him access to his child, she needed to start getting used to being on her own, to a life that didn't have Daniel in it. He was her baby's father, not her lover and definitely not her friend.

It was better, safer, this way. Gus might've found love after a half century—and she was truly happy for him—but his path wasn't hers. She didn't want love in her life, it hurt too damn much when it left.

If only she could get Gus, and by extension Rose, to understand that.

Alex heard footsteps and turned to look down the aisle, expecting to see the happy couple. Oh crap. Daniel. Maybe she wasn't in for a lecture; maybe Gus and Rose simply wanted a glass of champagne with their two favorite people before jetting off for a week of sun and sand and sex—*ooh, can't go there*. Sun and sand was descriptive enough.

Daniel took the seat opposite her and looked at the open bottle of champagne sitting in an ice bucket. "We're here for a dressing-down, aren't we? This time they are going to tackle us together?"

Alex wanted to think otherwise but she nodded. "Probably."

Daniel placed his boot on his ankle and Alex noticed that his denims, soft from washing, had a rip at the left knee and that the hems were frayed. She pulled in a deep breath and her womb throbbed at the intoxicating scent of soap, sun and ranch life mixed with pure, primal alpha male. She'd missed him so much. Keeping her distance was torture but so very necessary.

"Thanks for answering my fifty million calls," Daniel bit out, pulling his designer shades off his face and hooking them onto the neck band of his T-shirt.

"Don't exaggerate," Alex retorted.

"Stop evading the subject. You've been avoiding me

for weeks and I don't like it." She had. Leaving Royal for Houston for a couple of weeks helped. She'd needed to meet with Mike, discuss their partnership agreement and get a feel for his business, but the fact that she was half a state away from Daniel had helped with her evasion tactics.

"I saw you at the wedding," Alex pointed out.

"Where you refused to discuss anything to do with the future and the baby. We have plans to make, Alex! We need to know where we are going!"

"Do we really have to go through all this again?" Alex threw up her hands and leaned forward. "I am going back to Houston. I am taking a partnership in a start-up company, and you are staying here. In five months I will give birth."

"What about visitation rights? A nanny to help you? Child support?" Daniel bellowed.

"We can sort that out later when—" Alex broke off when she noticed the attendant approaching them. The young woman stopped, stood in the aisle alongside them and tossed them an easy smile.

"Sorry to interrupt but we've just had word that Mr. and Mrs. Slade are running a little late. But we need to move the plane so that the next aircraft can take our slot."

Alex looked at Daniel and they both shrugged. "Okay?"

That bright, mischievous smile flashed again and Alex saw that her name tag read Michelle. "Safety regulations state that we can't taxi without you both wearing a seat belt. Regulations, you know?"

"For God's sake!" Daniel muttered, reaching for his seat belt and pulling it over his waist. "Do you have an idea when they might be here? I need to get back to the ranch. I have a meeting in an hour." He frowned at Michelle, as if it were her fault their grandparents were late.

Michelle watched Alex buckle up before turning her attention back to Daniel. "They should be here soon, Mr. Clayton."

Alex felt the aircraft move forward as the pilot guided the plane to its new position. The attendant walked away and Alex reached for the bottle of champagne and a crystal glass. Now, this was the way to fly. And if Gus had meant this champagne to be for Rose, then he should've been prompt. Besides, any sane woman needed alcohol while dealing with Daniel Clayton. It was deeply unfair that that much sexy covered a whole bunch of annoying.

Before she could tip the bottle to her glass, the champagne was whisked from her hand and the bottle dropped back into the ice bucket. "Not happening."

Alex glared at Daniel. "When did they make you the no-champagne-for-breakfast police? Last time I checked, I'm an adult and I can have—"

"Cut it out, Alex. I'm the dad who's telling his baby's mom that she can't have alcohol while she's pregnant."

Alex wanted to lash out at him, tell him that he had no right to tell her what to do, but dammit, on this point he was right. She couldn't drink alcohol while she was pregnant. Gah! What had she been *thinking*? Probably that she needed the soothing power of the fermented grape, especially if she had to deal with Mr. Impossible.

Alex risked looking at Daniel and saw the smug smile of his face at winning that minor battle. Annoyed, she kicked out and smiled when the toe of her right boot connected with his shin.

"Ow, dammit!" Daniel howled before bending down to rub his injury.

"Don't be a baby, Clayton." Alex looked out the window, saw that the plane was whizzing past the trees bordering the airport and frowned. "Aren't we going a bit fast?"

"Don't kick me again," Daniel warned and followed her gaze to the window. He released a low curse. "We're not taxiing."

Alex gripped the arms of her seat. "Daniel, what's going on?"

"If I'm not mistaken, we're about to take off." Daniel looked around, saw an electronic panel and jabbed at the button labeled Attendant.

"This is Michelle. What can I do for you, Mr. Clayton? Miss Slade?" Michelle's melodious voice drifted over them.

Daniel didn't waste time looking for explanations. "Stop this plane right now or I'm going to have you all arrested for kidnapping." Alex shivered at the I'm-going-to-kill-someone note in his voice. She'd only heard that voice once, maybe twice, before and she knew that you didn't disobey Daniel Clayton when he used it.

"Sorry, sir, but we can't do that. Besides, Mr. and Mrs. Slade promised to pay all our legal fees if you decide to sue us. Plus a hefty retainer."

"What the hell are you talking about?" Daniel asked, his eyes widening.

Alex immediately understood why. They'd left the ground and they were literally jetting off to God knew where.

"There is an iPad in the side pocket of your seat," the airline attendant continued, and Daniel kept his eyes locked onto Alex's face as he dropped his hand to the side of his seat.

"Switch it on and there's a video clip on the home screen. It should answer all of your questions," Michelle stated, and Alex heard the click as she disconnected the intercom.

Daniel booted up the iPad, glared down at the screen and impatiently jabbed the screen. He leaned forward so that she could see the screen and there, looking far too pleased with themselves, were their respective grandparents.

"Yes, we've kidnapped you. Yes, we are bad people," Gus said, sounding utterly unrepentant.

Rose jabbed him with his elbow and stared into the camera. "Alexis and Daniel, we are sorry for being so intransigent a decade ago. We should not have pulled you into our little dustup and we apologize."

Only in Texas could people call a fifty-year feud a dustup.

Gus leaned forward, his blue eyes serious. "That being said, it must be noted that you two are the most stubborn creatures imaginable and unable to see what's in front of your faces. To help you with your lack of vision, we are sending you to Galloway Cove in our place. Matt's house is the only one on the island, and it is fully stocked with everything you might need. We packed a suitcase for each of you, which Michelle will give to you when you land."

Daniel hit the pause button, looked at Alex and shook his head. "I'm adding breaking and entering to the charges I'm laying against her."

Alex rolled her eyes and tapped the play button so that the video could continue. Gus picked up the conversational train wreck. "The plane will return in a week and, by then, we want a proper, thought-out, reasonable plan on how you two intend to raise this child together. And by together we mean in the same house, preferably the same bedroom."

"Just to be clear, marriage is our first choice," Rose added.

"When hell freezes over," Alex muttered. On-screen, Rose smiled, oblivious to their anger. Which was exactly why they recorded this message and didn't video call them. Alex snorted. Cowards.

"And don't try to bribe the pilot and his crew to turn around. We already told them we'd double whatever you offer." Rose, looking pretty and content, blew them a kiss. "One day you'll thank us for this!"

"Not damn likely," Daniel muttered.

The video faded to black and Daniel tossed the iPad onto the seat next to him. He groaned and covered his eyes with his hand. Alex opened her mouth to speak but no words emerged. She tried again—nothing—and shook her head. Had Rose and Gus lost it completely? "They can't do this," she whispered.

"They just did," Daniel shot back, pulling his phone out from his back pocket. He hit a button, dialed a number and waited impatiently for it to ring. "Voice mail."

"Gran, I am not happy! What the hell gives you the right to meddle in our lives? We're adults and your actions are reprehensible and unacceptable. Have you completely lost your mind?"

Knowing that Gus rarely carried his phone and that when he did he was prone to ignoring it, Alex called her younger brother, Jason. He answered on a rolling laugh.

"Not funny, Jason! I'm on a plane because Grandpa has arranged for us to be kidnapped. Tell him to turn this plane around. Better yet, just let me talk to him."

"He's not here, sis. Or if he is, he's keeping a very low profile, if you get my drift. He is, after all, on his honeymoon."

Ew. The words *Gus* and *honeymoon* did not sit well next to each other. "I don't care what you have to do but find him and tell him to turn this damned plane around!"

Another chuckle. God, when she saw Jace, she was going to throttle him. "Grandpa told me to tell you, if you made contact, to pull on your big-girl panties and suck it up."

"*Find. Him.* Tell him that this isn't funny, that we want to come home!"

"Are you mad? You've been sent off to stay in a luxurious house on a private island in the Caribbean. It's windy, wet and cold here in Texas, and our grandfather is getting more action than I am. My heart bleeds for you! As I said, big-girl panties—"

Screw big-girl panties, she was going to take off her thong and strangle him with it! "Find Grandpa," she muttered, death in her voice. "Tell him what I said."

Alex disconnected the call and rubbed her forehead with her fingertips. "It looks like we're going to Matt's island."

"Looks like?" Daniel snapped back, his expression blank but his body radiating tension.

Alex sent a wistful look at the champagne bottle. "Don't you think this warrants a little champagne? For medicinal use only?"

"No, you're pregnant. No alcohol."

Daniel narrowed his eyes at her, pushed the intercom and ordered a whiskey, straight up. He looked at Alex and his small smile was just shy of evil. "But, as you said, this situation warrants alcohol."

Alex responded to his smirk with one of her own and deliberately, swiftly kicked him again.

After playing Daniel's voice message to Gus, Rose lifted her eyes to meet his. His body, like hers, was older and they didn't have the energy they once had. But his eyes were still those of a young man's, with the power to stop her in her tracks. And underneath the layer of mischief, she saw his grit and determination, his rock-steady calm. Gus did what he needed to do and always stayed the course.

"He is not a happy camper," Gus commented.

"I've seen him lose his temper and it's not pretty," Rose admitted, pushing her phone away. She picked up her coffee and took a sip.

Gus was silent for a good twenty seconds. "Would he hurt her?"

"Hurt Alex?" Rose demanded, horrified. "Good God, no!" When Gus still looked skeptical, she placed her hand on his arm. "No, honey, he would never hurt her. He witnessed his mom being slapped around, beaten up, and he'd never hurt a woman or a child."

Gus's eyes softened with sympathy. "His rough childhood must have done a number on him."

Rose nodded, not bothering to hide her sadness from her man. They were married, so she could share anything, and everything, with him. "Stephanie… God, Gus, she was so wild. I couldn't tell her a damn thing—never could. She hit thirteen and entered self-destruct mode."

"I don't know whether she's alive or dead. When she lost custody of Daniel, she refused to have any contact with us."

"And that happened when he was twelve?"

Rose released a quavering breath. "He spent the summer of that year with me, and when Stephanie came to fetch him, he told her that he wasn't going back with her. Neither would he let me pay her to let him stay."

Rose knew that her chin was wobbling. "He told her that he was staying with me, that he was going to go to school in Royal. That if she made trouble for him or me, he'd go to the police and detail every drug deal he saw, finger every dealer she had, tell the police about every 'uncle' who lifted a hand to him." She released another breath. "She had a choice—she could leave him with me without a fuss or he'd make life very, very difficult for her. Stephanie chose to leave him with me."

"And he never spoke to her again after that?"

Rose shook her head. "Neither of us have."

She ran her finger around the rim of her cup. "I can't help thinking that if I'd done some of this and not that, loved her more, disciplined her more, gave her more time and energy, she would've turned out better."

"Sometimes there is no better, Rosie."

"She's her daddy's daughter—she's Ed through and through. Mean, aggressive, malicious." She saw the concern on his face and quickly shook her head. "Daniel isn't like that. He's a good man, Gus. You'll see that eventually."

Her husband pondered her words. "The TCC members seem to think so. The younger members trust him implicitly and they say he has integrity." Gus smiled at her. "I'm looking forward to knowing him, darlin'. It's time to put the past to bed, and young Daniel has done nothing to me."

"Except get your granddaughter pregnant," Rose replied.

Gus shrugged. "The way those two look and act

around each other, I'm just grateful it didn't happen when they were teenagers."

"He's the best thing—apart from you, recently—that's ever happened to me. I can't lose him, Gus."

Gus took her hands is his and waited until her eyes met his. Then he squeezed her hands. "You're not going to lose him, Rosie. I promise you that."

"He's so mad…"

Gus shrugged. "Let him be mad—he'll get over it. In a little less than an hour, he'll be on a deserted island with a beautiful girl he's crazy about. Trust me, he'll be thanking you soon."

"I doubt it," Rose retorted. "They just might kill each other. Or maybe they'll wait to do that until after they've killed us." She frowned at him. "Why are you looking so chipper? Didn't you get a nasty voice mail?"

Gus's cocky smile belonged to the young man she knew so long ago. "Prob'ly did. Don't carry my phone. No doubt that Alex has sent Jason an annoyed message to give to me."

Rose shook her head in exasperation. "You've got to start carrying a phone, Gus. What if I need to get a hold of you?"

"Not a factor." Gus lifted her knuckles to kiss her fingertips. "I don't plan on being a couple of feet from you anytime soon." His mouth curved as she moved her hand to his cheek. "But I am thinking of getting another phone, one that only you have the number to."

"That would make me feel so much better," Rose told him. "I don't want to be that woman who constantly keeps track of her man, but you know…in case of an emergency."

Gus's smile turned wicked. "To hell with an emergency. I'm only getting it in the hope that you'll call me up for a—what do the kids call it—booty call?"

Rose's shocked laughter bounced off the walls. "Augustus Slade!"

Gus looked at her, his face full of love. Then he waggled his eyebrows to make her laugh. "Anytime you have the urge, I'm your guy."

He really was her guy. And damn if she didn't have one of those urges now. Rose looked out the window and saw that it was ten o'clock on a cold, wet winter morning in February, not the time a woman of a certain age should be slinking upstairs. But to hell with that; this was supposed to be her honeymoon. Rose took his hand, grinned and stood up.

"Come upstairs and rock my world, handsome."

It was Gus's turn to look utterly poleaxed, but that didn't stop him from leaping to his feet with all the energy of a twenty-year-old.

Six

Upon landing at Galloway Cove, Michelle lowered the steps to the private jet, stowed their suitcases in the back of the golf cart parked to the side of the landing strip and tossed them a jovial smile. "Have fun." With that, she ran back up the steps to the plane. Minutes later the jet was in the air and headed back to Houston.

Alex climbed into the golf cart and sat down next to Daniel, her thigh brushing his. Leaning forward, he pulled off his flannel shirt and threw it into the back of the cart, before placing his hand on the wheel and cranking the small engine.

Tired of their silence, Alex darted him a look. "Any idea where we are?"

"West of the Bahamas."

Alex wrinkled her nose at his brief reply. "Can you tell me anything about where we are going, what to expect?"

"Matt is one of the wealthiest guys in Texas. All I

know is that the house is completely secluded, has its own private beach and reef. It will be jaw-droppingly amazing." He gritted his teeth. "The other thing I know is that I need to get the hell off this island. I've got a ranch to run. I can't just take off on a Monday morning with no warning!"

"You've said that before, numerous times," Alex told him testily. "Look, you might as well accept that we are stranded here until that plane returns." She gestured to the awesome view of a flat turquoise-colored sea. Below them, nestled against the cliff and partially covered by the natural vegetation, they could see the tiled roof of what she assumed to be Matt's beach house. She gestured to the well-used track in front of them. "The sun is shining. The sea looks amazing. So, on the bright side—"

"There *is* no bright side," Daniel muttered, and Alex gripped the frame of the cart as he accelerated forward.

"I can't think of anything better than lying on the beach for a week. I'm exhausted and it will give me time to think. We don't even have to talk to each other. Actually, it would be better if we didn't."

Clenching his jaw, Daniel steered the car along the track, and Alex heard the cry of a seagull and the sound of a rushing creek above the cart's rumble. Daniel kept moving his head from the path to look at her and back again. Annoyed, she half turned in her seat and glared at him. "What? Why do you keep looking at me like that?"

"What about sex?"

"Where did that out-of-left-field question come from?" Alex lifted her hands in confusion.

Daniel's dry look suggested she get with the program. "We're together. Alone. On an island. We might be as frustrated as hell with each other and the situation, but you cannot be that naive to think that, with our sexual chemistry, we're not going to end up in bed."

She wanted to deny his words, but she knew she would come across as being disingenuous if she brushed off his comment. Alex lifted her thigh up onto the bench seat, her knee brushing his hard thigh. After marshaling her thoughts, she picked out her words. "Daniel, we've known each other for a long time but we don't *know* each other."

"What do you mean?"

She'd been thinking about this a lot lately. She and Daniel communicated with their bodies, not with their minds. They were both guarded people and they both struggled to let people in. They knew each other's bodies intimately, knew exactly how to behave naked. But fully clothed? They were like drunken cowboys stumbling around in the dark. As her baby's father, Daniel was going to be in her life for a long time, so didn't she owe it to herself and their child to get to know his mind a fraction as well as she knew his body?

"Let's be honest here, we've always been sexually attracted to one another, and even as teenagers, we far preferred to make out than to talk—"

"And it's still my first choice."

Although tempted, Alex ignored his interruption. "That trend continued when we hooked up. I don't know you—not really—and you certainly don't know me."

Daniel sent her an exasperated look. "Of course I do."

Alex snorted. "Rubbish. Let's test that theory, shall we?"

Daniel released a frustrated sigh. "If you're going to ask me a dumb-ass question like what is your favorite color, then I won't know."

Alex thought for a minute. "No, let me start with an easy one. Do I prefer to shower in the morning or at night?"

Daniel hesitated before guessing. "At night."

It was a good guess. "What do I like on my pizza?"

He hesitated and she pounced. "You don't know. Neither do you know whether I have allergies and I don't know if you vote."

"Of course I vote!" Daniel retorted.

Alex ignored him. "Do you believe in God? What are you currently reading? What is your favorite season? Are you on social media? What is your favorite meal? Who is your closest friend?"

"Yes, sort of. A Corben novel. Fall. Hell, no, I don't have time to post crap no one cares about on Facebook. Beef stew. And yes, I have friends… Matt. Ryan. I talk to James Harris pretty often, too."

She'd said *closest* friend, not friends in general, but she'd still found out more about him in thirty seconds than she had in ten years. How much more would she find out about him if they actually conversed instead of kissed?

"We're going to be raising a kid together, separately but together. Should we not use this time to get to know each other better?"

Daniel steered the cart around a corner and Alex was momentarily distracted by the magnificent house in front of them. It hugged the side of a cliff, and trees and natural vegetation cradled the house like a mother holding her child. A massive wooden door broke up the sprawling white expanse and Daniel parked the cart to the right of it. Leaving the cart, she turned to take her bag but noticed that Daniel already had it in his grasp, as well as his own duffel bag.

She smiled her thanks and watched as he walked up to the front door. Alex took a moment to appreciate his long-legged, easy grace, the way his big biceps strained the bands of his T-shirt, the width of his shoulders. It was brutally unfair that he was the walking definition of sex on feet. Alex sighed and watched as Daniel placed his hand on the door. It swung open from a central pivot and he stepped back to motion her inside.

Alex stood in the doorway, unwilling to go inside until she had an answer from Daniel. "So, are we going to try and get to know each other a little better?"

"We can try," Daniel replied. He shrugged and looked down at her with those deep, compelling eyes. "But I guarantee you that, thanks to the combination of sand, sea and you in a tiny bikini, you're going to be under me sooner rather than later."

Arrogant jerk, Alex thought, walking into the beach house. How dare he think that he could just click his fingers and she would lie down, roll over and let him scratch her tummy. Sure their attraction was explosive, but she wasn't so weak that she'd just fall into bed with him—

Oh my God, this place is fantastic.

Alex stopped in her tracks as she drank in their luxurious surroundings. It was open plan, as all beach houses should be, with high vaulted ceilings displaying intricate beams. As soon as they stepped out of the hall and into the living space, the eye was pulled toward the massive floor-to-ceiling windows, across the infinity pool to the view beyond. Alex was momentarily unsure where the pool ended and the sea began. Stepping forward, she spared a glance at the sleek kitchen, the wooden dining table and the chairs that were the same blue as the sea. Under comfortable sofas, an expensive rug covered the floors, but it was the view that captured her attention: it was the only piece of art the room needed. The white beaches, the aqua sea, the lush emerald of an island in the distance.

"Holy crap."

Alex turned to look at Daniel but he was equally entranced by the house and the view. Dropping their bags to the floor, he strode over to the windows and looked at the frame. Within seconds, the windows turned into sliding doors, and warm, fragrant air rushed into the room. Alex walked out onto the covered deck and looked left and then right. "It looks like the deck runs the length of the house. I imagine all the bedrooms open up onto it. We can sleep with the doors open and listen to the sound of the sea."

Daniel looked down at the tranquil sea and lifted an eyebrow. "It's as calm as a lake—I doubt we're going to hear the sound of crashing waves."

"Don't be pedantic—" Alex's eyes widened when she saw Daniel bend over to pull off his boot. When his feet were bare, he pulled off his T-shirt before attacking his belt buckle and ripping open his fly. "What the hell are you doing?" she demanded.

He gave her a wicked smile and gestured to the pool. "Going for a swim."

His hands slipped under the fabric of his jeans and Alex squeaked when she saw that he was stripping them off. "You're swimming naked?"

Daniel shrugged as his clothes pooled at his feet. "We're totally alone and you've seen it all before."

She had and every inch of him was absolutely glorious. "You're not going to help our cause of not sleeping together if you're going to parade around buck naked, Clayton."

Daniel's smile broadened. "That's your cause, Slade, not mine. I intend to get to know you and sleep with you. I also plan to spend a great deal of time trying to convince you not to go to Houston. If you won't marry or move in with me, then I want you as close as I can possibly have you."

"I—you—argh!" Alex, annoyed by his cocky smile and his self-assurance, threw up her hands. She did, however, watch that magnificent body dive into the pool.

After his swim, Daniel pulled on his wet clothes and padded barefoot into the house. Not seeing Alex in the living area, he picked up his bag and walked down the hall, opening doors as he went along. Study-cum-library, gym—nice—and a sauna. He entered the first bedroom he came to and threw his bag onto the massive double bed, taking a minute to appreciate the view. Like he suspected, the floor-to-ceiling windows were in fact another set of doors, and he immediately opened them, welcoming fresh air into the room. This room was super nice but he wouldn't bother to unpack; he would end up sharing whatever bedroom Alex chose.

Which, if he knew her, would definitely be the master suite.

Daniel pulled his phone out of his pocket and checked for a signal, of which there was none. Cursing, he tossed it onto the bed and left the room to head for the study. If he was going to stay on this godforsaken island, he would have to send some emails, leaving instructions for his foreman, his PA and his business manager. And he would drop his grandmother another message, reminding her how out of line she was.

Daniel sat behind Matt's desk, pulled out the first

drawer, and yep, as he thought, inside the drawer rested a state-of-the-art laptop. If Matt had a laptop, then he'd have an internet connection, which was exactly what he needed. Daniel leaned back in his chair as he waited for the laptop to boot, thinking that he could, with a couple of keystrokes, have another plane on the runway in a couple of hours.

He could hire a private plane as easily as Gus had, and this farce could come to a quick end. Except that maybe he didn't want it to...

Daniel stared out at the tranquil ocean. He was here, Alex was here and they were nowhere near Royal. They could escape their grandparents' machinations, the Royal gossips, the crazy normal that was their day-to-day lives. They could both take this week to find a way forward, to have some heart-to-heart conversations, to plot a course.

He still wanted to marry Alex—that was the plan that still made the most sense to him. The Clayton-Slade feud had been buried with Gus and Rose's marriage—something that Royal was still talking about—and after their nuptials, his and Alex's nuptials would barely raise a brow or two. He wanted to raise his child in a conventional family, one with a father and mother close at hand. He'd spent the first twelve years of his life with an unstable mother, constantly wishing he had a father he could run to, live with, a bigger, stronger man he could look to for protection and comfort. He never ever wanted his child to think—not for a second—that he wasn't there for him, that he was anything but a shout away. He wanted to teach his son to ride, shoot, fish. Hell, if he had a bunch of daughters, he'd teach them the same thing. He wanted them to have the run of the farm. And if his kids were Alex's, then they'd have the

Slade ranch as an additional playground. He wanted them outside, on horses and bikes, in the stables, swimming in the river or in the pond. He wanted his kids to have the early childhood he never had, with two involved, loving parents.

For the sake of their kids, he and Alex could make a marriage work. They were super compatible together sexually, and they could, if he took her suggestion to learn more about each other, become friends. Friends who had hot sex—wasn't that a good marriage right there? Love? No. Love—having it, losing it, using it as a carrot or a club—just complicated the hell out of everything.

Marriage was a rational, sensible decision. He just had to convince Alex that this was the best option available to them both. Hell, even if she balked at getting married—and he had no doubt that she would—she could still move into his place. Gus and Rose wouldn't be happy at their nontraditional living arrangements, but it was better than nothing.

Right, he had a plan. He liked having a plan; it made him feel in control.

Alex leaned back against a sun-warmed rock and watched the sky change. Blue morphed into a deep purple, and then an invisible brush painted the sky with streaks of pink and orange. This Caribbean sunset was possibly one of the prettiest she'd ever witnessed, and she couldn't help but sigh her appreciation.

Alex felt warm, strong fingers graze her shoulder and she turned to look up at Dan, who held out a bottle of water. She smiled her thanks, shifted up a bit, and when he sat down next to her, she noticed the bottle of beer in his hand. He'd changed into a pair of swimming shorts and wore a pale yellow T-shirt. She wore a sleeveless tank over her bikini and her hair was a tangled mass of still-damp curls.

"Thanks."

Daniel's bare shoulder nudged hers and Alex ignored the flash of desire that ricocheted down her spine. Taking a sip from the bottle he'd thoughtfully opened for her, she gestured to the sunset. "I wondered if you were watching the sunset."

"It's stunning," Daniel murmured.

She hadn't seen him since before lunch and she wondered what he'd been up to. "So, what have you been doing?"

Daniel took a moment to answer her. "Hanging out, chilling. Seeing if I could find signal for my phone."

"Did you find one?"

"Nope."

She also had no cell phone signal, and it was a problem. She needed to talk to Mike, ask him for some more time to think about his offer, to work out the logistics of moving to Houston. "I need to send my grandpa an irate email, telling him how much I resent his interference and machinations. He doesn't carry a phone but he does read his emails."

Daniel's chest lifted as he pulled in some air. "You can."

"I can what?" Alex asked, digging her toes into the sand.

"Send an email," Daniel admitted. "I found a computer in Matt's study. I should've realized that the guy, with all his business interests, would have to have some contact with the outside world. On further examination, there's also a satellite phone for emergencies."

Alex flew to her feet. "Why didn't you tell me sooner?

Why are we here? Why aren't we at the airfield, waiting for a plane?"

She could go home, confront Gus, talk to her clients, Mike. She could put some distance between her and Daniel, start her life without him. At the thought, her heart stuttered, then stumbled. She had to; she had no choice. She and Daniel didn't have a future, not as anything more than co-parents.

She wasn't marrying him or moving in with him; both options were impossible.

Daniel pulled his legs up and rested his forearms on his knees as he squinted up at her. "You're missing the sunset, Lex."

"We can go home, Daniel! We need to go home."

He gently took her wrist and pulled her back down so that she sat with her back to the sunset. The pink-and-yellow light danced across his face. Daniel's thumb stroked the sensitive flesh on the inside of her wrist.

"Let's not, Lex."

"Let's not what?"

"Go home," Daniel said, and she sent him a shocked look. He'd been furious about leaving, about being manipulated into taking this time away and now he wanted to stay?

"I don't understand," Alex said, pulling her hand out of his grasp. She couldn't talk to him and touch him— she wasn't that strong.

"As loath as I am to give those two meddlers any credit, I think that they are right. We need to work some stuff out, and we can do it here," Daniel suggested. "You're exhausted. Organizing the auction was hard work, and I haven't taken a break for nearly a year. We both can do with some downtime. And while we relax, maybe we can plot a way forward."

"You and your plans, Daniel!" Alex muttered. "You can't plan for every eventuality. Some things you have to allow to evolve, to work themselves out."

"Work themselves out? God!" Daniel released a harsh laugh. "That's such a stupid thing to say. Things very rarely work out, Alexis!"

Wow, that was quite the reaction to an innocent comment. Instead of jumping on him, Alex tipped her head to the side and waited for him to speak.

Daniel picked up a handful of sand, clenched his fist and allowed the particles to slide down the tunnel his hand created. She'd never seen such sad eyes, she decided. Sad and angry and distraught.

"Do you know what it's like to live a life lurching from crisis to crisis? Do you know how unsettling it is not to know where you are going to be, what bed you're going to be sleeping in? Whether your mother will be there when you wake up? It sucks, Alex!"

She stared at him, shocked at his outburst but even more surprised that he'd revealed that much about his childhood to her. When they were younger, she'd pried, tried to get him to open up about his life with the infamous Stephanie, but he'd never so much as mentioned his mother and what his life was like before he came to live at The Silver C. From the pain she saw in his eyes, Alex knew that it was way worse than she'd ever imagined.

"I'm sorry—"

Daniel immediately cut her off. "Forget it. Ignore what I said. My point is that I like to plan. I always will."

Because it made him feel secure, like he was in control. Alex understood that now. She picked up a handful of fine sand and allowed it to trickle through her fingers. Knowing that Daniel had said everything he intended to for now, she contemplated whether to stay on the island or to leave. She could call for a plane and within hours they'd be winging their way back to Royal and nothing, not one damn thing, would be settled between them.

But on the other hand... With a couple of emails, she could clear her schedule, take this time they both desperately needed. Didn't she owe it to herself, to Daniel and her child, to stop, to breathe? To think?

To plan? Dammit.

Alex made herself meet his eyes and reluctantly nodded. "Okay, we can stay here."

His eyes turned smoky and Alex immediately recognized that look. She held up her hand. "Hold on, cowboy. If we do this, then there are going to be some ground rules."

Daniel released a low curse, and a frown pulled those black brows together. It wasn't a surprise to see that Clayton didn't like anyone else calling the shots. Tough—it was something he was going to have to deal with. She wasn't eighteen anymore and so desperately eager to please.

"I'll only do this if we can start fresh."

"What the hell does that mean?" Daniel demanded, grumpy again.

"I am not hopping back into bed with you." Alex drew a heart in the sand and quickly erased it, hoping he hadn't noticed. "As I said, I want us to do something different, be different!"

"Lex..." Daniel muttered.

"Dan, we're having a baby together! We're not going to get married, or even live together, but if we are going to be in each other's lives, see each other every weekend, then there has got be something more between us than some hot sex."

"I'm not good at talking, Lex."

Neither was she. But they had to make an effort. "I know, Dan, and neither am I. We're not good at opening up, at sharing, but, God, the next eighteen years are going to be sheer misery if we don't start to communicate."

Daniel stared past her shoulder and Alex picked up the tension in his body, saw his hard jaw, his thin lips. She needed this, she suddenly realized. She needed to dig beneath the surface to find out what made this amazing man tick, and not only for her baby. She needed to know him. Because even if they couldn't be lovers, they could be friends, and being friends with Dan was infinitely better than being lovers and casual acquaintances. He had fabulous mattress skills but between that gruff exterior was, she suspected, a lonely guy who needed a friend. And to be honest, so did she.

Daniel's cheeks puffed and then he expelled the breath he'd been holding. When he turned to look at her, his expression turned rueful. "I can't promise you anything, but I can try, Lex. That's all I can give you."

"I still want to sleep with you, though," Dan added, being brutally honest.

"I know." Alex picked up her water bottle from the sand and dusted it off. "But we can either have one or the other, not both."

"I vote for sex."

She rolled her eyes. "You're a guy—I wouldn't expect anything else. But no, that's not going to happen. I think we need to be friends."

"Not half as much fun," Daniel grumbled.

Alex smiled at his sulky face. "Man up, Clayton."

Although his expression remained sober, she caught the amusement in his eyes. He leaned toward her, his amazing eyes on her mouth and his mouth hovered over hers. She should pull back—she *would* pull back…but how much could one little kiss hurt?

Alex frowned when she saw his lips twitch and then he resumed his position against the rock.

Oh, that was just mean.

"Jerk."

That twitch widened into a sexy, full smile. "You're easily distracted, Lex. I like it."

She nailed him with a don't-push-it glare.

Daniel's expression turned serious. "You've changed. You're not half as biddable as you used to be."

"Yeah, I grew up." Alex half turned, put her hands behind her and leaned back, stretching out her legs. She looked at the sunset—the light was slowly fading and the colors were deepening in intensity. She turned her head to look up at the house and noticed that it was fully lit. There were also lights along the entire length of the path running from the beach to the house. It looked like a totally different structure, mysterious and sexy.

Just like the man lounging next to her.

Daniel followed her eyes and whistled in appreciation. "Wow. Matt Galloway is one lucky bastard to own this place." He turned his head to look at her. "So, did you choose a room?"

"Yeah, I couldn't resist the master bedroom. When the doors are open, it's like you are sleeping outside, and it has this amazing shower enclosure. It's three walls of glass and utterly breathtaking."

Daniel's mouth twitched with amusement. "That would give anyone on the beach an eyeful."

"I thought the same thing," Alex said with a smile.

"But when I walked down to the beach, I checked. It's made of that fancy glass where you can see out but not in."

Standing up, Daniel held out his hand. Alex put her hand in his and he hauled her to her feet. "I'm starving. Let's go see what's in the fridge. I think I saw some no-alcohol beers if you're interested."

"I'd far prefer a glass of wine," Alex said as she headed to the path with Daniel behind her.

"Well, I'd prefer to be sharing your bed. But apparently we can't always have what we want."

Seven

The next day, Daniel looked up and saw Alex standing in the doorway of the study. He leaned back in his chair and indulged himself by giving her a top-to-toe look. A red-and-white blousy shirt was tied at her still-slim waist and flirted with the band of the sexiest, most flattering pair of cutoff jeans he'd ever seen. Her feet were bare, as was her face, and she'd pulled her thick blond mane into a loose bundle on top of her head. She'd never looked more beautiful, and he desperately wanted to take her to bed.

Friends. They were trying to be friends.

Worst idea ever.

Daniel glanced at his watch and then grinned. It was past nine and that meant that she'd had a solid night's sleep. Good. She'd needed it. He was happy to see that the blue smudges were gone from beneath her eyes.

"Hey, sleepyhead. I'm not going to ask you if you slept well, because you obviously did."

Alex walked into the room and hopped up onto the corner of the desk, facing him. "I did. And for your information, I did wake up during the night and I did hear the sea. The tide must've been in."

Alex liked being right and he couldn't blame her because he liked it, too. He smelled the mint on her breath and forced himself not to lean forward and have a taste. Man, this week was going to be a drag if he couldn't touch or taste her.

Daniel leaned back and linked his hands across his stomach. If he kept them there, maybe he wouldn't give in to the urge to scoop her up, haul her outside and lower her to the sun bed on the porch. Excitement pooled in his groin at the thought of stripping her down until only the sun, his fingers and his mouth were touching her soft, fragrant skin...

Pull your head out of the bedroom, Clayton.

"How are you feeling?" he asked. He darted a look at the small strip of bare flesh he could see above the band of her jeans. Nobody would ever suspect that she was pregnant.

"Fine, actually. I haven't had any morning sickness or cravings for weird food." She smiled as she answered him, banging the heel of her foot against the leg of the desk. "And... Yay... I still fit into all my clothes, which is a definite plus."

Alex picked up a glass paperweight from the desk, turned it over and lifted her eyebrows. She carefully replaced it and when she looked at him again, her eyes were bright with astonishment. "That's Baccarat crystal and super expensive."

Daniel didn't care if it was a solid-gold nugget. He wanted to talk about her and the baby growing inside her. "Have you seen a doctor?"

Alex nodded. "I visited the clinic and had a blood test to confirm I was pregnant. I was prescribed some vitamins, given a handful of pamphlets to read through and was recommended a couple of books. I need to visit an ob-gyn when I get back and have an ultrasound scan. That way the doctor will get a better idea of my due date. It's also to check that the baby is growing as it should."

Daniel leaned forward, opened his online calendar and sent her an expectant look. "When is the appointment?"

"Do you want to come with me?"

She sounded surprised. "When are you going to realize that you're not alone, Lex? That we are in this together?"

Alex rattled off the date and time and Daniel tapped the it into his calendar. He was determined to be the exact opposite of his father—and his mother—who'd missed every milestone of his life, from his birth to football games to graduation.

Alex sent him a grateful look. "Thanks. Knowing you will be there will make me feel less—" she hesitated before completing her sentence "—alone. I've never missed my mom more than I have in the past few weeks and I dare not even think about Sarah. If I do, I won't stop crying."

Daniel placed his hand on her knee, his skin several shades darker than hers. He started to stroke back and forth, and then reminded himself that he was touching her in comfort, not for pleasure. "Your mom and dad died when you were pretty young. Do you remember them?"

Alex wrinkled her nose. "A little. But I'm not sure if my memories are my own or because I heard so many stories about them. I can't tell what's real or what's been planted."

"Does it matter, if they are good memories?" He didn't have any good memories of his mom, of his early life. He'd been so damn busy trying to survive, to get through the day, the week, until he could next visit The Silver C and his grandmother. On the ranch, under that big blue Texas sky, riding and exploring, he could let go, find a little peace.

Alex touched her stomach with her fingertips. "I just wish she was here."

Daniel squeezed her knee, choosing to express his sympathy through touch rather than words. Then he removed his hand because there was only so much temptation he could take.

"Have you eaten? There's a fruit salad in the fridge. Or I can make you pancakes. And bacon."

Alex's eyes widened in disbelief. "You cook?"

"Yes, smarty-pants, I can cook. In fact, I intend to catch and then cook our lunch."

Alex gestured to the ocean beyond the open windows. "I'm impressed. Maybe you should get to it, because the fish might not be in a cooperative mood. I haven't seen any fishing rods lying around."

"They are in the storage shed, along with fins, goggles and a Jet Ski. And a spear gun, which I'm going to use."

"Marvelous idea." Alex looked deeply skeptical at his abilities to provide her with food. She smirked. "If you come back empty-handed, I suppose we can always have peanut-butter-and-jelly sandwiches."

"Oh, you of little faith." Daniel heard the ping indicating that he had a new email and leaned forward to check the screen. He read the subject line and released an annoyed groan.

"Problem? Can I peek?" she asked. He nodded, her legs tangling with his bare ones as she leaned forward to look at the screen. He smiled at her squint.

"Do you need glasses to read, Lex?"

"Bite me." Lex cheerfully responded before frowning. "'Please date me.'" She read out the subject line for an email. There were more, some more direct than others. "'I'm your soul mate. I think I may be in love with you. I have really big…'" Alex's laughing eyes met his. "Did you register for a dating site or something? Or place an ad for a date on some skanky message board?"

Daniel glared at her. "No, that's the response from that article Grandmother made me do to promote the auction, and what it's like being one of the state's most eligible bachelors."

Alex giggled. "Oh my. This one says she's a bit of a nymphomaniac. How on earth did they get your email address?"

"They printed the ranch's website address. The public can email the ranch through the website. As they did." He gestured to the screen and grimaced. "Repeatedly."

Alex peered at the screen again. "Hey, this one is from a guy. The subject line mentions that the two of you have a mutual acquaintance."

"Not interested." Daniel leaned forward, highlighted all the offending emails and deleted them in one swift move. There was only one woman he wanted, and she was sitting next to him, driving him insane.

Daniel closed the lid of the laptop and stood up. Putting his hands on Alex's hips, he gently lifted her off the desk. But after placing her on her feet, he didn't— couldn't—let her go. How could he? She smelled like expensive soap and sunscreen, and her upturned mouth looked soft and inviting. Too much temptation—he had to kiss her, taste her. It had been so damn long.

Daniel threaded his fingers through her soft, up-swept hair and held the back of her head as he covered her lips with his, keeping his kiss gentle, exploratory. It would be so easy to fall into heat and passion, but he didn't want to scare her. He just wanted to kiss her in the sunlight, skim her body with his fingers, be with her in this moment with only the blue sea and the hot sun as witnesses.

She tasted like coffee and spearmint and sexy woman, a combination that made his head swim. Daniel skimmed her rib cage, brushed his knuckles over her waist and laid his palm possessively over her stomach, his hand almost covering her from hip to hip. Pulling his head back, he looked down and emotion tightened his throat.

He pushed the words out. "Somewhere in there is my baby."

Alex's big smile was a kick to his heart. She lifted her hand and pushed back that annoying curl that always fell down his forehead. "I hope our baby has your beautiful eyes."

"I hope he has yours," Daniel whispered back. "You are so lovely, Lex."

"You're not too bad yourself, cowboy," Alex murmured, her lips moving against his. Daniel sucked in his breath as her breasts pushed into his chest. Then Alex pulled away and Daniel felt her arms tightening around his neck as her nose burrowed into the side of his throat. He barely heard her words, but somehow they still lodged in his soul. "Having a baby is scary, Dan."

"I know, sweetheart. But I'm here with you, for you."

Alex pulled back and he noticed the brilliant sheen

in her eyes. He cradled her face and tipped his head to the side. "Why the tears, Lex?"

"If you are going to leave me, Dan, do it now. Before it hurts too much."

Leave her? His child? No chance. "I'm not going anywhere, Lex. I promise."

Alex forced a laugh before stepping back to wipe her eyes with the heels of her hands. She sent him a smile that was part embarrassment, part fear. "Ignore me. That's just hormones."

He nodded to give her an out, to allow her to walk away with her pride intact, but he knew that outburst had nothing to do with pregnancy hormones and everything to do with her fear of him disappointing her. Again.

Didn't she know that he would give her everything he was able to? His time, his support, his money, all his effort. Except his heart. He wouldn't give her that roughed-up organ. He liked it right where it was, thank you very much.

Daniel was either a very competent fisherman or the lady fish simply flung themselves onto his spear, thrilled to be caught by such a luscious merman. Alex was convinced the latter was true because they'd been eating from the ocean a lot lately, including tonight's dinner of a lobster salad. She could easily imagine the below-the-waves conversation:

Yes, Daniel, of course I will sacrifice myself for your eating pleasure.

No, take me.

He's mine to die for.

"What are you smiling about?" Daniel asked.

"I'm imagining a lady lobster's last words," Alex

confessed, sitting down in the chair he pulled out for her. She was a modern girl, living a modern life, but she never tired of being the recipient of his gentlemanly manners.

"You are very weird," Daniel commented as he took his seat to the right of her. He reached for the bottle of white wine in the middle of the table and twisted the bottle to show her the label. "I found this in the cellar. It's nonalcoholic. Would you like some?"

"Drinking nonalcoholic wine is like drinking coffee with no caffeine," Alex grumbled.

Ignoring her, Daniel merely lifted a brow. Alex pushed her crystal wine goblet toward him. "Oh okay, then."

His mouth twitched as he poured the wine. Or, more accurately, grape juice. Alex gestured to the food. "Thank you for preparing dinner again. You're spoiling me. It's going to be difficult going back to Houston and having to look after myself. I've been living in the lap of luxury at the Lone Wolf and now here, with you. Real life is going to be a bit of a shock."

Daniel handed her a glass of wine and lifted his beer bottle in a silent toast. Alex sipped her wine—not too shabby, as it tasted like a decent chardonnay—and watched him in the low light, courtesy of the single candle between them and the firepits dotted around the pool. She sighed. How could she *not* look at him? They were on a private island in the Caribbean, her surroundings were absolutely exquisite, but still they paled in comparison to Daniel.

Graceful but masculine, mysterious and sexy with a thick layer of smart. His body was a masterpiece, and she could literally gaze at that face forever. She craved to hear his laughter fill the air, his lips drawing patterns on her skin. She wanted him. She would for the rest of her life.

And that was why she'd mentioned Houston, spoke about life after Galloway Cove. Because she needed a reminder that having Daniel in her life on a full-time basis was impossible. Deep down she knew this, and she couldn't allow herself to be seduced by a hot man who cooked for her.

She wasn't that weak.

Okay, she *was*, but wasn't identifying the problem the first step to finding the solution?

Daniel, bless him, helped her pull herself together by changing the topic to one she expected. "Tell me about your job offer."

She could talk about work—it was a nice, neutral topic of conversation. "Mike and I joined the company I still work for shortly after we left college. He left about six months ago to start his own business. He's asked me to join him—"

"This is in PR?"

Alex wrinkled her nose. "We don't handle public relations in a traditional sense. I specialize in creating social media strategies that best display and promote a brand or a company's image in the digital space."

Daniel grimaced. "Sounds like hell."

She flashed him a quick smile. "It would to someone who has absolutely no social media presence."

Daniel smiled at her and her stomach flipped over. "You stalking me, Slade?"

She'd never admit that in a thousand years. "I cyberstalk lots of people. But you should be embarrassed that your grandmother is very active on social media and you are not."

"Yet I'm not embarrassed." Daniel reached for the

lobster salad and the serving utensil. He spooned food onto the plate in front of Alex before dishing up his own food.

"And this guy, Mike, wants to give you a partnership," Daniel asked, returning to the subject at hand. "Why would he do that?"

Alex forked up some lobster and groaned when the creamy sweetness hit her taste buds. Midchew, a thought hit her and she gripped Daniel's arm, her nails digging into the exposed muscle beneath his rolled up shirt sleeve.

"Problem?"

"I don't know if I should be eating shellfish," Alex said, pulling a face. "I think I read something about it not being safe for pregnant women."

Surely that was an old wives' tale. How could she be expected to walk away from all that bright, tasty, luscious salad? Resisting Daniel was hard enough, and now life was throwing another temptation in her way? Two words.

So unfair.

"I checked and it's safe to eat during pregnancy as long as its fresh and properly cooked. I caught and cooked it, and it's fine." Daniel waved his fork at her plate. "Eat."

Alex felt touched that he'd checked. It had been a long time since she felt protected, cosseted, fussed over. It was a nice feeling but dangerous. She couldn't allow herself to get used to being the center of any man's attention. Especially since that attention, along with love and respect and commitment, had the tendency to vaporize.

"You were telling me about Houston," Daniel prompted, leaning back and picking up his bottle of beer.

"Mike loves dealing with the clients—he's a born salesman but he's not so fond of overseeing the staff or paperwork. And the financial aspects of running a business. He's offered me a full partnership if I take over that side of the business."

Daniel looked out into the inky darkness. Alex followed his gaze and could just make out the boulders on the beach, the white bubbles of waves hitting the shoreline. "And you have to be in Houston to do that?"

Initially, Mike had suggested that she could spend the bulk of her time in Royal, commuting to Houston only a few days a month. Theirs was a web-based business and there was little that couldn't be managed over email and by video calling. It was Alex who'd pushed to move to Houston, who'd felt the need to get away from Royal and a certain sexy cowboy.

Yeah, that plan had worked out so well.

"I think I should be in Houston," Alex said, keeping her voice low.

Daniel took a few more bites of his dinner before pushing his food away. He used his thumb to trace the lines of the bamboo place mat. "What the hell happened to us, Lex?"

"We had sex and I got pregnant."

Daniel ignored the sarcastic retort. "I mean…back then."

To her, it was simple. He'd chosen The Silver C and Rose over her. What was there to discuss?

Daniel's eyes met hers and she almost whimpered at the pain she saw in his depths. "I asked for a long-distance relationship when you went off to college. You told me that it had to be all or nothing. Why? Why did you insist that my leaving was the only way I could prove that I loved you?"

"Because I needed you—I needed *someone*—to choose me, to make being with me the most important thing they could do."

Daniel sat up and linked his hands behind his head. "I needed to stay on The Silver C. I couldn't leave, Lex."

"No, you *wouldn't* leave. Rose said no, and you just did her bidding. You didn't fight for me, Daniel."

Alex pushed back her chair and stood up, taking her nonalcoholic wine over to the edge of the pool. She sat down and dipped her bare feet into the sun-warmed water and stared out to sea. The rising moon was the silver blue of a fish scale, the flash of an angel's wing. It was a night meant for passion, for making love in the sweet, fragrant air. It felt wrong to be opening old wounds under the light of a benevolent moon.

She heard Daniel crack open another bottle of beer and then he was sitting next to her, thigh to thigh, leg to leg, feet touching in the tepid water of the pool.

"I'm sorry I hurt you, Lex," Daniel said in a raspy voice, and Alex heard the sincerity in it.

"I just wanted you to come to college with me, Dan. To be somewhere else with me, away from our grandparents and their disapproval and their stupid feud. I wanted to see who we could be when we didn't have all of that hanging over us."

"I couldn't and wouldn't leave, Alex. And it wasn't because I didn't want to."

Alex pulled her thigh up onto the stone rim of the pool and pushed her hair off her forehead. Half facing him, she ran her hand down his arm until she found his fingers. His spread open in welcome and her hand was quickly enveloped by his. She took a breath, knowing that she shouldn't ask a question she wasn't completely sure she wanted the answer to. But she was going to anyway.

"Explain it to me, Dan, because I still can't work it out."

Daniel pulled her hand from his and leaned back, his hands behind him. He tipped his head up to look at the stars, and Alex knew that he was looking for his words. Instead of answering her question, he turned his head and swiped his lips across hers, his tongue sliding into her mouth. Alex instantly ignited, and she wound her arms around his neck, falling into his touch. How could he fire her up with just his mouth on hers, his big hand holding the back of her head, anchoring her to him?

God, he was a magnificent kisser...

He was also, she dimly realized, brilliant at avoiding the subject. Reluctantly, Alex pulled back and scooted a few inches from him. "Nope, I'm not going to be distracted, Clayton. Talk to me."

"I always envied you, you know," Daniel quietly stated. "I know that you lost your parents when you were really young but, God, you had this family that was pretty damn awesome."

"How would you know that? I mean, thanks to the feud, it's not like we saw much of each other growing up."

"Before I came to live with Grandmother full-time, I saw you when I was visiting. At church, at the town parade, the cookout at the community center." A small smile touched Daniel's face. "And maybe I saw more of you than I should've..."

"Meaning?" Alex demanded.

Daniel lifted one powerful shoulder. "I used to sneak onto Slade land, head for the tree house and watch you and your brother." He grimaced. "I'm sorry, that sounds creepy as hell, but I was young and, I suppose, lonely. After I moved to The Silver C, I started at school and life became busy and I stopped sneaking onto Slade land."

"Until the day you came across me in the high meadow. You were trespassing."

Daniel's mouth twitched. "I was on Clayton land."

"You wish you were," Alex retorted, her voice holding no heat, because how could it? Memories washed over her, as sweet as that summer's day. They'd started arguing about who was trespassing and before they knew it, they were inching closer and then Daniel grabbed her hips and she his biceps, and their lips touched.

"And then you kissed me."

"You kissed me," Alex replied because she was expected to. Soft laughter followed their familiar argument and Alex dropped her forehead to rest it on Daniel's muscled shoulder. "We loved each other so much, Dan, but it vaporized. I don't understand how that happened."

Daniel moved his head so that he could kiss her hair. "You asked me to do the one thing I could not do. You told me that leaving was the only way I could prove my love and that you would only carry on loving me if I did what you asked."

Alex frowned. "I don't remember saying that."

"Trust me, I heard it. And then you made me choose, Alex."

"And you chose The Silver C."

"I did."

His easy agreement hurt, but for the first time since she was eighteen, Alex felt the need to push aside the pain and understand. Daniel wasn't a guy who was careless with people's feelings, and she wanted to know and understand what drove him back then.

And now.

She was having a child with the man, so she had the right to try to understand him.

"I have no idea who my father is. He left before I was born, or so my mother said. She also said that he left after I was born, so who the hell knows what's true? I was raised in apartments, in trailers, in rented rooms and, for one memorable month, a women's shelter."

Dan ran his hand through his thick hair, then over his face. This wasn't easy for him and Alex respected him for opening up.

"Life with my mother was a matter of measuring the depth of the trouble and debt we were in—sometimes it was nose-deep and we were about to drown, and sometimes it was only ankle-deep. But it was always there… and she created most of it."

Alex kept her eyes on his face, scared to move in case he had second thoughts and stopped talking. She schooled her features because she knew that sympathy would make him clam up as quickly as inane platitudes would.

Stay still, don't breathe and just listen, Slade.

"When Stephanie tired of me or couldn't cope, she'd send me to Grandmother at The Silver C. Or my grandmother would ask to have me. Either way, she had to pay to have me at The Silver C. I once tried to work out how much she paid my mom and I stopped counting after fifty thousand dollars."

A low whistle escaped.

"Yeah, my mom was a piece of work," Daniel said, his voice steady and unemotional. But Alex could see the pain in his eyes and noticed the tiniest tremble in his bottom lip. His mother's lack of maternal instinct and his father's lack of interest still had the power to hurt him, Alex realized.

"So yeah, I watched you and seeing you with your family, with Sarah, I was envious of how much you were loved. How secure you felt." Daniel placed his hand on her thigh and skimmed the tips of his fingers across her knee. "That summer, I know that you argued with Gus, with Sarah—you were angry with them so often."

Of course she'd been angry with them, as well as with Daniel. She loved him, he loved her, they wanted to be together and they were being kept apart because of a stupid feud. At eighteen, it had been all about her and what she wanted, and to hell with anyone else.

Ashamed of herself, Alex lifted her hand and gently touched Daniel's jaw. "Why did you let me leave, Dan? Why did you let me go?"

"You needed to go and I needed to stay." Daniel lifted his hand to rub the back of his neck. "Grandmother wanted me to stay, to learn about The Silver C. It was going to be mine someday and I needed to learn the ropes. I assumed that leaving with you meant risking the land, my job, my inheritance."

Alex jerked back, angry. "She said that?"

"No, you're not listening. I said I *assumed* that. The truth was, I didn't want to leave Royal. I felt safe there—welcomed, protected."

"And I asked you to leave it, to risk it."

"In hindsight, I know that I used my assumption of my grandmother disinheriting me and her displeasure as an excuse, but I couldn't tell you that I—"

"That you loved The Silver C more than you loved me."

Daniel started to deny her words but then stopped

talking and shook his head. "I don't know, Lex. Maybe. All I know for sure was that I didn't want to leave. But neither did I want to let you go. I was so hurt, confused, unable to tell you what I was feeling."

"And I wanted you to make the grand gesture, to prove that you loved me," Alex admitted hoarsely.

"Stephanie did that, all the time. If I did x, I loved her. If I did y, I didn't. As a child I was constantly re-assuring her of how much I loved her, tying myself up in a knot trying to please her. After I went to live with Grandmother, I swore I'd never allow anyone to use love as a weapon against me again."

And by linking his love to his actions, she'd done precisely that. Ironically, the one thing she needed was the very thing her couldn't give her. What a mess.

Alex closed her eyes, trying to keep the tears away. "We were so young, Dan, dealing with feelings far beyond our comfort zone."

"And a raging attraction. It was like God gave the keys to a Formula 1 car to an eight-year-old. We were bound to crash and burn."

Alex touched her stomach and gave him a wry grin. "And it's happening again."

Daniel pushed his hand under hers so that his palm lay across her stomach. He placed his lips against her temple before drawing back. "The one thing I know we can handle is our attraction to each other. We can be friends and lovers, Lex. Trust me on this."

He sounded so sure, but Alex was still convinced that that toxic combination had the potential to blow up and rip them apart. Alex made the mistake of looking into those eyes—more umber than chocolate tonight—and saw need and desire swirling within those dark depths.

She felt herself yielding, relinquishing her grip on common sense.

I'm exposing myself—I know that I am—but Daniel needs me.

And God knew, Alex needed him. Because here, right now, Daniel was silently telling her that he chose her, that he wanted her in his arms, in his bed.

No, he more than wanted her—he craved her.

As she did him.

Alex leaned forward and stroked the pad of her thumb over his lower lip. "Take me to bed, Dan."

She heard his sigh of relief and then his body tensed again. "Are you sure? You said this wasn't a good idea."

She lifted her shoulders and let them drop. "It isn't. We haven't found a long-term solution, and we should do that, but not tonight, not right now."

Daniel followed her to her feet and loosely held her hips. "What do you want us to do tonight, Lex?"

"I want you to love me, Dan. As only you can."

Eight

Instead of entering the house, Daniel led Alex down the deck and into the master bedroom, through the open sliding doors.

At the foot of the bed, he stopped and cupped her face in his hands, his thumbs tenderly stroking her cheekbones. In this dark room containing shadows and secrets, Daniel realized that right here, right now, for as long as it may last, they were about to reignite their love affair.

There had never been anyone else like her, no one who captured his imagination as thoroughly as Alexis Slade did. Whether she was lying in a meadow, hair in two plaits, or standing on a stage, raising money for a worthwhile cause, or lying on his bed, she entranced him.

He wished he could say otherwise but that was what Alex did. Entranced and ensnared. How was he ever going to let her go?

But that was the problem for Royal. Here, he wasn't a Clayton with commitment issues and she wasn't a scared Slade. They were Dan and Lex, lovers.

"God, you are so beautiful, Alexis."

Alex smiled at the use of her full name; she knew he only used it when he was overcome by strong emotion. Unable to wait another moment to taste her, Dan dropped his head and, not trusting himself to go caveman on her, gently touched his lips to the corner of her mouth. *Such sexy lips*, he thought. He wanted them on his, moving over his skin, wrapped around his—

No, if he went there now, before he'd even started, he'd lose it. No, tonight was about Alex and how best he could show her how much he lov—*adored* her.

Alex released a long sigh. "Daniel. The way you make me feel…"

Daniel dropped his hands to caress her neck and sighed when her tongue traced the seam of his lips, asking for entrance. His small release of air allowed her to slip inside to touch his tongue, and he was lost—control was vanquished. Daniel released a deep groan and he placed his hands on her hips and boosted her up, grateful when her legs locked around his hips, bringing her hot core against his harder, desperate dick. Wrenching his mouth off hers, he sucked in a breath, telling himself to calm down, that they had all night, that this wasn't a onetime deal. He had time tonight, tomorrow and the day after next.

Would it be enough?

Would forever be enough?

And why was he thinking of forever if this was just flash-in-the-pan lust?

"Lean back, Lex," Daniel growled. Frustrated with himself, he pulled her shirt up her body.

"Let me help." Alex whipped her shirt off and unsnapped the front clasp of her bra, allowing the lacy garment to drop to the floor and his mouth to close around one watermelon-pink nipple. Laving it with his tongue, he pulled back to blow on the puckered bud, smiling as he noticed her tan line, the darker and white flesh. Alex groaned and pushed his head toward her other breast, and he was happy to lavish attention on that bud, as well. It gave him time to lecture his dick, to remind it to go slow, to take it easy.

This was about Lex; it would only ever be about Lex.

Daniel lowered Alex to the bed and bent over her to tug her jeans apart, to pull the battered fabric down her hips and over her pretty toes. Running a hand down her long thigh and shapely calf, he blew on her aqua-lace-covered mound, pleased at her aroused scent—sex and sea and sun. Two cords held the triangle in place and Daniel's impatience had his thumbs and fingers gripping the cord and twisting, easily snapping the thin fabric. He pulled the fabric away from her and stared down at her.

"You're pretty and perfect. And mine, Lexi. Right now, tonight, you're mine."

He saw her gasp of surprise, caught the flash of pleasure in her eyes.

Standing up, Daniel whipped his shirt off, pushed down his board shorts and looked down at his lover, the mother of his child, the woman who'd slid under his skin at eighteen and whom he'd never been able to dislodge.

Mine. Only mine.

Daniel looked at her face, expecting her attention to be on him, and he frowned when he noticed that she was looking past him. If she'd changed her mind, he'd punch a hole through that expensive wooden screen that separated the bedroom from the bathroom. Replacing it would cost him an arm and leg, but it would be worth it.

Daniel pressed his forehead against hers. "Lex? Do you want to stop?"

Instead of replying to his question, Lexi placed her hand on her heart and sat up. When she finally looked at him, Daniel realized that he could see the moon in her eyes.

Literally. The moon was in her eyes.

He turned slowly and his mouth dropped in astonishment. The moon was as wide as the sky and he thought that if he leaned off the deck, he could run his hand across its silvery surface.

It was blue and aqua and silver and white…and absolutely magnificent.

"Daniel, it's so lovely."

He looked back at Lexi and slowly shook his head. The moon couldn't hold a candle to her. She was more radiant, more entrancing than any Caribbean moon hanging outside their bedroom window.

He ran his hand over her shoulder, his finger burning when it met her sun-touched skin. "I need you, Lex."

Lexi smiled and his heart spun in his chest like a damn prima ballerina. "Can I have you and the moon?" she asked, her eyes darting from him to the view outside.

He touched her nipple and rolled it between his fingers, his erection swelling when her eyes clouded with desire. Then Lexi's hand encircled him and the world stopped turning. He felt a tremor shoot him and told himself that he couldn't plunge… He had to hold still.

Lexi's voice was soft but sure. "I want you and the moon, Dan."

Since his brain didn't operate without blood, which

was plunging south, Daniel shook his head to indicate his confusion.

Lexi kneeled and sent him a sultry smile. "Come behind me, Daniel. I want you to hold me, cover me, envelop me, make me scream. And I want to watch the moon while we do that. It's going to be a memory I'll always treasure."

Daniel moved to kneel behind her, his hands stroking the length of her back before placing his hand on her stomach to pull her back, to tilt her hips up. Wrapping his arms around her, he slowly entered her, his eyes burning at the sheer perfection of this moment. His completing her completed him.

He moved, slow, sexy movements that raised them up and up, closer to that silver orb hanging in the sky. His every sense was amplified: he heard the wind in the trees and the waves hitting the sand. Lexi's smallest whimper, her sighs of pleasure, were loud in his ears. Her scent filled his nose and when she turned her neck to find his mouth, he caught her eyes and they were an intense shade of touched-with-moonlight blue.

Lodged deep inside her, Daniel felt the rush of warmth, felt her contract and allowed himself to caress the moon and grab the stars.

In the Royal Diner, Gus looked up from his biscuits and gravy and into Amanda Battle's lovely face. The owner of the diner was one of his favorite people and he stood up to drop a kiss onto her cheek. "Good morning, beautiful."

Amanda laughed. "Should you be flirting with me now that you are married, Gus Slade?"

"Just stating a fact, ma'am." Gus took his seat again and sent a grinning Rose a wink. How wonderful it was to see his wife relaxed and smiling, happy in her skin. He'd done that, Gus thought, feeling proud. He'd made her glow from the inside out.

Amanda turned to Rose and bussed his wife's cheek with her own. "It's so nice to see you, Miss Rose. Congratulations on your wedding. I'm so happy for you."

Rose thanked Amanda for her kind words and for refilling her coffee cup. Amanda passed the carafe of coffee on to a passing waitress and tipped her head to the side. "So, the latest gossip is that you two sent your grandkids off on a honeymoon in your place? Are you crazy? Do you know how beautiful Galloway Cove is?"

Rose poured some cream into her coffee. "Those two are like two mules fighting over a turnip."

Amanda laughed at Rose's pithy saying. "Have you heard from them?"

"They managed to find a computer and have been in contact." Gus finished his breakfast and wiped his lips with his napkin. "They both sent us polite, gentle thank-you notes—"

Amanda swatted his shoulder. "They did not!"

"No, they didn't," Gus admitted. "But neither have they, after three days, called to be picked up or, as far as we know, killed each other."

"They might kill us when they get back, though," Rose said, wrinkling her nose.

"They'll work it out," Amanda assured her. "Or at the very least, they might be mad for a while, but they'll come around. You're family and they love you."

Amanda turned at the sound of her chime and Gus followed her gaze to the front door. Amanda frowned at the tall, well-built man entering the diner, his sharp business suit at odds with the rest of the customers' more casual attire. Amanda turned her back on him and looked at Rose. "Miss Rose? That man—do you know him?"

Rose leaned to the side to look at the Latino man and Gus saw the flare of appreciation in her eyes. Yeah, yeah, he was good-looking, but she wore his ring now.

"Rosie…" he warned.

Rose flashed him an impudent grin and turned her attention back to Amanda. "He looks a bit familiar, but no, I don't know him. Why?"

"He was in here the other day, looking for you. I think someone gave him directions to The Silver C."

"Since the wedding, I've been staying with Gus at the Lone Wolf," Rose said, blushing.

They really had to work out where they were going to live on a permanent basis, Gus thought. Strangely, Rose seemed more at home in his house than she did in hers. He'd been on tenterhooks, waiting for Rose to suggest that he move into Ed's house and still didn't know how to respond—he didn't think an "over my cold dead body" would go down well—but Rose had yet to make the request. That being said, they needed a house that was theirs, one neither of them had to share with the ghosts of the past.

"I should go to The Silver C, check up on the work."

"Daniel's foreman is a good man and no doubt Daniel is issuing his orders from Galloway Cove." Gus stroked the inside of her wrist to reassure her. He tipped his head back in a subtle gesture to the stranger. "Do you want to see what he wants?"

Rose shrugged and then nodded. "I'm here. He's here. Might as well." Rose looked at Amanda and smiled. "Would you mind sending him our way, Amanda, honey?"

Amanda nodded and glided, graceful as ever, away.

Gus turned in his seat as dark, flashing eyes snapped to them. Gus looked at him, instantly recognized those eyes—funny that Rose didn't—and sighed. Oh hell, this could be either very good or very bad. The man slid off his chair at the counter and walked over to him.

The man stopped by their table and Gus could feel the tension rolling off him. He primed himself, ready to jump up and defend his woman. He might be old, but his reflexes were still sharp. Nobody would ever be allowed to hurt his Rosie again.

"Ms. Clayton—"

"That's Mrs. Slade to you, son," Gus growled.

"My apologies." The man held out his hand to Rose, and Gus felt his temperature rise, when instead of shaking it like a good Texan would do, he lifted Rose's knuckles to his lips. "My name is Hector Lamb and I believe I am—"

"Daniel's father." Rose snatched her hand out of his grip, leaned back and sliced and diced him with her laser-sharp eyes.

"Where the hell have you been and why are you only showing up now?"

At the top of the trail, Daniel stopped, turned and looked at her as if he were surprised to see her on his heels. "Are you sure you're pregnant?" he demanded, hands on his hips, his eyes shaded by the brim of a well-worn ball cap.

"What makes you say that?" Alex removed her own cap and wiped her forearm across her forehead before resetting the cap on her head. They were deep into the mini jungle that covered most of the island, and it was humid as hell on a rainy day. She couldn't wait to get to the swimming hole that was reputed to be at the end of this long trail.

"You aren't experiencing morning sickness, you haven't had any weird cravings, you haven't been moody," Daniel replied. "And you're still as slim as you always were…"

Admittedly, it was taking some time for her to show, but there were signs. "The band of these shorts is tight and my boobs are definitely bigger."

Daniel sent her a steady look but she caught the devilry in his eyes. He lifted his hands and placed them on her bikini-top-covered breasts. "I don't believe you. I have to check."

His thumbs immediately found her nipples and Alex tipped her head up to receive his kiss. Oh, she liked this Daniel, this relaxed, funny, thoughtful man. For the first time since she'd moved back to Royal, they were connected on both a mental and physical level, and yeah, they gelled.

Whenever they weren't making love—which seemed to happen morning, noon and night—they talked and laughed. They had their differences, but their value systems were the same, their priorities were in sync. Respect and independence of action and thought were important to them and family always came first.

Family came first. But by moving to Houston, striking out on her own, she was deliberately putting time and space between not only the baby and Daniel, but the baby and its grandparents, uncle and her friends. Was she making life harder for herself in her effort to protect herself?

Daniel broke the kiss, took her hand and they continued walking alongside each other until the path narrowed and she was forced to fall into step behind him.

She didn't *have* to move to Houston; it wasn't a condition of the partnership.

Alex bit her lip and stared at the back of Daniel's head, her eyes tracing his broad shoulders, muscles rippling under the red T-shirt he wore. She'd traced those muscles with her tongue...

Wrenching her eyes off Daniel, she pulled her thoughts back. The point was, she had options. Or, deep breath now, she could also move in with Daniel and give this—whatever *this* was—a shot. They could be a couple, raise their child together, day in and day out. Alex sucked in her breath and placed her hand on her sternum as she waited for the wave of unease to pass through her. When it didn't, she tipped her head, surprised. Huh. So moving in with Daniel didn't scare her as much as it did a week ago.

Her heart skipped a beat. They didn't need to get married but they could make this work. They had fantastic sex, enjoyed each other's company, had the same priorities...

Of course she knew the risks involved. Back in Royal, they would have to deal with real life, two careers, a baby on the way, their grandparents and...stuff. The mundane and the boring and the tedious. And there was always the chance that Daniel would one day decide that this wasn't the life for him and, well, leave.

Could she cope with that? Would she be able to watch him walk away without her world falling apart? Yeah, it would hurt when—if—he left, but he might not.

Could she do this? Dare she take a chance on Daniel, on the life he was offering?

Alex could feel her heart racing, and a fine sheen of perspiration covered her forehead. Feeling her courage well up inside her, she started to speak, but no words came out.

How was she supposed to tell him she'd come to a decision without saying the words?

"Here we are."

Alex pulled her attention from her thoughts and looked around, her mouth falling open at the tall waterfall plunging into a pool below their feet. Flat boulders dotted the natural swimming hole, providing a perfectly flat surface to stretch out on, to soak up the sun's rays after a chilly dip in the pool.

"Awesome." Daniel walked down the path to the first boulder, dropped his backpack to the rock and kicked off his trainers. Whipping off his shirt, he dropped it at his feet and then shimmied out of his shorts. What was it with this man and his need to swim naked? Not that she was complaining but...

Daniel sent her a wicked smile. "Secluded. No one else here. No one to see me and you've—"

"Seen it all before," Alex said, completing his sentence.

"Strip and join me," Daniel suggested, waggling his eyebrows. Yeah, she could live with Daniel looking at her like he'd been waiting his whole life to make love to her in a pool at the bottom of a pretty waterfall. Heat and warmth rushed to that special place between her legs and her nipples pebbled with expectation.

Alex felt beautiful, desired and wanton. Daniel stood in front of her, utterly unselfconscious, the sun touching his tanned skin. The wind ruffled his jet-black curls, and as her eyes traveled over his impressive physique, his erection jerked as he hardened before her eyes.

Having such a masculine, focused man want her

made Alex feel intensely feminine, immensely powerful. She was life, she carried life, a goddess of the glen.

Alex quickly stripped down and stood in front of her
man, sighing when the sun's warm rays caressed her
bare back and buttocks. She pushed her breasts into his
chest before dragging her nipples across his skin, her
hand lifting to encircle him, her thumb brushing the tip
of his cock. Daniel groaned and pushed into her hand.

"Make love to me, Dan. Here, in the sun, on this
rock. On our secluded island."

Daniel nodded and she had a moment's warning
when his eyes glinted and his mouth twitched. Strong
arms wrapped around her and then she was flying off
the rock, hitting the freezing cold water with a heavy
splash.

Alex spluttered, shivered and kicked her way to the
surface to see Dan's wicked smile and laughing eyes.

"You are such a child," Alex told him, launching a
wave of water into his face.

Daniel ducked, grabbed her and she instinctively
wound her legs around his waist only to find out that
cold water had absolutely no effect on his erection at all.

Well then. It seemed like a shame to waste it.

Nine

After making love, they swam some more until they realized it was past lunchtime and they were hungry. They dressed, Alex in her fuchsia bikini and Dan in his board shorts, and then they ate the sandwiches Alex had prepared earlier and polished off the apples they had also brought along.

Feeling relaxed, Daniel replaced the cap on his water bottle and, after rolling up his towel, lay on his back and tucked the towel beneath his head. Enjoying the sun, he opened one eye to look at Alex. "Come lie down with me."

Alex curled into his side, her head tucked under his chin. The gentle breeze blew a strand of hair across his mouth. He picked up her hair and tucked it behind her ear.

"Best forced holiday ever," Alex murmured, her fingers idly drawing patterns above his heart.

"Best holiday ever," Daniel corrected her. "I love spending time with you, honey. I always did."

Alex opened her mouth to speak but closed it again. She had something on her mind—he knew that she was toying with a decision. Did he dare to dream that she'd reconsidered her living arrangements, that their forced week away—yeah, yeah, thanks old-timers—had worked?

"What's going on in that beautiful head of yours, Lex?"

Alex took a while to answer. "That job I was offered... I could actually stay in Royal and still take the partnership."

Daniel forced himself to stay still, but inside he was leaping to his feet, punching his fist in the air. "Are you thinking of doing that?" he asked carefully.

"Maybe. I sort of allowed you to believe that I had to move to Houston to take the partnership. I could stay in Royal and work remotely, traveling a couple of times a month."

He wanted to sit up, to whoop with delight, but he knew he had to tread softly because Alex was like a skittish colt that needed careful handling. Which was okay—he could tiptoe with the best of them. As long as he got what he wanted in the end, he didn't care how he got there. And he wanted Alex. In his arms, his bed.

And in his life.

"I'm scared of starting something, because I'm terrified I could lose it."

Daniel turned her words over in his head, trying to make sense of her out-of-the-blue statement. Pulling his head back, he looked at her but her eyes remained closed. He ran his hand up her spine, keeping his touch light and comforting.

"Care to explain that, Lex?"

Alex sat up, crossed her legs and he pulled himself up, bending his knees and allowing his hand to dangle between them.

"I don't like being left, Daniel. It's happened too often, and I don't think I can do it again."

He thought he knew where she was going with this but asked her to explain anyway.

"As we discussed earlier, losing my parents when I was young was a sad time, but Gus and Sarah stepped in and I was okay. However, when I was twelve, I lost my best friend Gemma, too. I don't know if you remember her—she was a redhead?"

He had a vague memory of seeing the two girls together, but he remembered the town's grief at Gemma's death more than he remembered the child herself.

"I was devastated. I thought my world ended." Alex pushed her hair back over her shoulder. "I had friends at school but nobody I was close to. I didn't want another friend who could die on me. So I kept my thoughts and feelings to myself and Sarah became my best friend. Then, in a meadow, I met and kissed you and I felt my heart opening up, expanding, and it became so full of you. That summer, you were my everything and I thought I was your world."

Alex touched the tip of her tongue to her top lip and when she looked at him, Daniel noticed the tears in her eyes. "I know it sounds dramatic but losing you felt like losing Gemma again. But somehow it was worse because you weren't only my best friend but my lover. All I wanted you to do was to choose me, to stick with me."

He suddenly understood. "You were angry that your parents and Gemma and, later, Sarah left you. You felt abandoned."

He got it.

"But I'm not allowed to be angry with them because they didn't have a choice to stay or to go."

"But I had a choice and I didn't choose you."

Alex nodded and scratched her head above her ear. "Being all grown-up, I thought I could handle having a fling with you. I thought I would sleep with you and keep it light and fluffy. And I was okay when I called it quits. I mean, I missed you but I knew that I could live without you. I think it helped that we didn't make an emotional connection, that it was all about sex."

They didn't make that connection because they'd both been too damn scared to go there. They still were. "Anyway, as for our current predicament… It makes sense for us to be together, to live together, to raise our child together," Alex quietly stated.

Thank the baby Jesus…

"But it also doesn't."

Crap.

Daniel looked at her and waited for her to continue, conscious of his heart thudding in his chest. Where was she going with this? "Carry on, Lex. Tell me what you are thinking."

"I'm scared of moving in with you, falling for you and then having to deal with you leaving, whether that's by death or a woman or whatever life might throw my way."

She was worried that he might leave her for someone else? Yeah, that wasn't going to happen. Not now, not ever. Alex pulled her bottom lip between her teeth. "I'm scared, Dan. I'm scared to try this, terrified that it won't work. I'm scared that you will become the center of my world again and when the day comes for you to make a choice, it won't be me."

She was a lot stronger than she gave herself credit for. They were both strong people; they'd both, in their different ways, survived so much. They could handle this.

He had to touch her, so he used the tip of his index finger to stroke the inside of her wrist. "I know you're scared, sweetheart. But there's something more frightening than fear and that's regret."

Alex released a heavy sigh and lifted her shoulders in a tired shrug. He could see that she was feeling overwhelmed and out of her depth. So was he but his childhood of rolling with the punches had taught him to not make decisions when he was emotional, that it was always beneficial to step back and look at a situation with some distance.

As much as he wanted to install Alex in his house as soon as he got back to Royal, he needed to give her time to find her way back to him. It was going to be hard, when his instinct was to take control, but if he wanted a family—this family—he had to take it slow.

"Can you see yourself staying in Royal? Is that something you can do?"

Alex stared at the pool below them and it took all of Dan's patience to remain silent. Eventually she nodded her head. "Yeah, I think that's a decision I am comfortable making."

Thank God. Do not punch the air, Clayton. You are not a child. Daniel held himself still. *You still have work to do but, God, that was a massive hurdle overcome.* "Okay then. Good."

He put his hands on her knees and waited for her troubled eyes to meet his. "Lex, you don't need to make any more decisions today. Take some time, think it through."

Alex bit her bottom lip. "What if I'd decided to move to Houston?"

He pushed his hand through his hair and met her eyes. "I don't know, Alex. It would've been more complicated, financially and logistically. But I like to think that we would've made it work."

Daniel prayed that she wouldn't pursue this line of questioning, that she wouldn't ask whether he would've moved to Houston and left The Silver C. Maybe. Possibly. Yes. But admitting that was a step too far. He was opening the door to his heart a bit too wide. Alex needed time and so did he.

"Rose and Grandpa are going to pressure us to get married," Alex said, directing her words to the pond and refusing to meet his eyes.

The last time he asked, she almost drew blood, her reply had been so cutting. "Do you want to get married?"

Alex shook her head. "I'm still coming to terms with my decision to stay in Royal. I can't think much beyond that. But, Lord, the gossip!"

"You speak as if the Claytons and the Slades haven't been gossiped about before," Daniel said, his tone wry. "Let them talk, Alex. We're working on our timeline, no one else's. We only have to answer to each other, nobody else."

Alex lifted her eyebrows. "Have you met our grandparents?"

He smiled at her quip but shook his head. "We don't have to be in a rush to figure this out. Let's take it step by step, day by day. Today you decided to stay in Royal—let that be enough for now."

Alex looked down at her hands before her deep blue eyes met his. "Okay. But I have one request."

Didn't she realize that he'd give her anything he could. "What, sweetheart?"

"I don't do well when there's no communication, when I think I am drifting on the wind. I need to be able to talk to you and you to talk to me. I feel better when we talk, when we have these conversations. I might not have the answers, but I don't feel so alone."

Touched beyond measure, Daniel clasped her neck with his hand and leaned forward to kiss her forehead. He'd watched her as a child, kissed her as a girl but this woman next to him? She was phenomenal.

"Do you know how many boys named Daniel were born in the greater Dallas area in '91?"

Rose looked from her kitchen at The Silver C to the informal dining table in the open-plan entertainment area and caught Gus's eye. How handsome he looked, she thought. How lucky she was to be married to him.

"How many?" Gus asked Hector Lamb, pushing the bottle of red wine in his direction. The red wine came from Ed's cellar. He'd collected the expensive wines because he thought it a classy thing to do but never drank the stuff. He'd never allowed anyone else to drink his collection, either. In the years since his death, Rose had sold the more collectible bottles and given away other bottles as gifts. She intended to drink the rest.

Rose pulled the cheesecake out of the fridge and looked around her immaculate kitchen. It was large and spacious and far too big for her and Gus. On the fridge was a magnet Ed had brought back from New York City, inside that drawer were his steak knives. She kept the flour in the same canister his mother did, the sugar in another. The windows were too small, the storage space badly designed.

Rose yanked open the second drawer and cursed when it became stuck before it was fully out. She was sick of sticky drawers and old furniture and poky rooms. She hated this house and was finally in a place where she could admit to it.

"Five thousand six hundred and sixty-two little boys were born during September and October of that year," Hector replied. "I knew the dates when Stephanie and I slept together—it happened over a week, so I gave Stephanie a little leeway in case the baby decided to be late."

Daniel was, in fact, early. "Hold on, boys, I want to hear how you tracked Daniel down," Rose told them, expertly slicing even portions of cheesecake. She scowled down at the half-cut dessert. When had she become so pedantic, so perfectionistic, so boring?

Rose defiantly cut the cake up into oddly shaped, differently sized pieces and wrinkled her nose. That didn't make her feel any better. She knew exactly what would…

After picking up the cake and three side plates, she walked over to the table and banged the cake down in the center of the table. She darted a quick glance at Hector before dropping an openmouthed kiss on Gus's lips.

Gus looked at her, shocked. No wonder. Regal Rose never ever engaged in public displays of affection.

"Are you okay, darlin'?" Gus drawled, surprise quickly turning to concern.

Rose nodded. "I hate this house."

Gus leaned back in his chair, rested his hands across his still-flat stomach and lifted his heavy gray eyebrows. "Do you now?"

"I don't want to live here anymore."

Hector cleared his throat and pushed his chair back. "Excuse me, please. I need to visit your bathroom."

Rose smiled, grateful to be able to speak to Gus alone. "Hurry back, Hector. This won't take long."

Hector nodded and walked away from them to the powder room just off the hall. Rose sat down next to him and placed her chin in the palm of her hand.

Gus smiled at her, a sweet, slow smile that was part devil, all charm. "Now, where are you wanting to live, Rosie? With me? My wife might have something to say about that."

She knew he was teasing but she was too nervous to smile. He'd adored Sarah. How was he going to react to her suggestion?

"You can tell me anything, Rose."

"I want to move into Sarah's house. I feel at home there, like she would be happy I was there, happy that I made you happy."

Gus's hands covered hers. "She missed you so much, Rose."

"I know. I missed her, too." Gus's wife, Sarah, had been her closest friend and Rose didn't know if she'd ever forgive herself for walking away from Gus and her best friend, the two people who knew and loved her best. How stupid young people could be! And that was why she felt no compunction in meddling in Daniel's and Alex's lives. If they couldn't see the wood for the trees, she'd damn well provide them with glasses and a chainsaw.

She had more to say and she might as well get it all out there. "I'd like Alex and her brother to choose what pieces of Sarah's furniture they'd like, and if there's anything special of hers you'd like to keep, I'd understand but—"

"But?" Gus asked gently.

"But I'd like a house of my own. I inherited most of everything that's in this home from my parents and great-grandparents and Ed didn't see the point of buying new when old worked as well as new." She was being silly but maybe Gus would understand. "I want my own stuff, Gus, new stuff. *Our* stuff."

Gus nodded once. "Then that's what we shall do, darlin'. And maybe Daniel and Alex can move in here. Alex will want to renovate and redecorate, do all that stuff new wives want to do but old wives don't let happen."

Rose grinned. Hearing Hector approaching her, she turned her attention back to him and smiled. "I am so sorry. We've been so rude. Tell us how you tracked down Daniel. And why did it take you so long?"

Alex looked out of the window of the private jet and saw the familiar landscape of Texas thousands of feet below her. In a half hour they'd be on the ground, and she and Daniel would be hurtled back into real life.

Dammit.

Real life meant deadlines and doctor's appointments, conversations with Gus and Rose, meetings with Mike. Real life wasn't lazy mornings, waking up tangled in Daniel's arms, listening to the sound of gently lapping waves and a gentle, fragrant breeze blowing across her skin. Real life wasn't fresh fish caught straight from the ocean, skinny-dipping in the cove or in the pool, making love in the outdoor shower.

Real life was grown-up life and she wasn't ready for it. On the island it seemed a lot easier to imagine staying in Royal, commuting to Houston for work, creating a life with Daniel. Now, a half hour out from that life, Alex once again questioned whether staying in Royal was the right option for her and her child. Was she taking too big a risk believing that she and Daniel could make this work?

Had she been seduced by spectacular sex on a sun-kissed island?

Alex drummed her fingers on the leather-covered armrest of her seat and gnawed her bottom lip, wishing that Daniel would look up, see her nervousness and say something, anything, to reassure her. But ten minutes after leaving Galloway Cove, he'd connected his cell phone to the in-flight Wi-Fi and hadn't stopped working since.

"Dammit to hell and back," Daniel muttered.

At least he was talking to her. Sort of. "Problem?"

Daniel lifted his head and grimaced. "More responses to that interview I did on being one of the state's most eligible bachelors. I have a thousand emails asking for a date."

"A thousand, really?" Alex asked, skeptical. He was a hot, sexy guy and there were a lot of desperate, lonely women out there, but that had to be an exaggeration.

Daniel turned the phone toward her and she saw the stream of emails on his screen. Okay, there were a *lot* of emails. "I thought you were picking up emails on the island, so why didn't you see these then?"

Daniel looked down at the screen again. It took him a while to answer as his finger flew over the small keyboard. "After deleting that first batch, I only checked my private email account on the island. This one is more of a general and PR account." He flashed her a quick grin. "I've opened a few emails and a couple of women did make a contribution to your charity to bribe me to date them."

Sex sold and, dammit, Daniel was sex on a stick.

Alex tipped her head to the side and looked at him, dressed in his white button-down shirt and khaki pants, designer sunglasses hanging off his shirt pocket. If he ever became sick of being a cowboy/businessman, he could find another career as a male model. She could easily see him diving off a cliff, into a blue sea, swimming up to a boat and crawling all over a sexy, skinny model…

Modeling… Hmm…maybe next year she could do a skin calendar featuring Daniel and all the sexy, sexy men of the Texas Cattleman's Club. God knew there were a bunch of them.

Daniel narrowed his eyes at her. "No. Whatever you are thinking, just no."

Alex just smiled and didn't bother to argue. When the time came, she'd have him posing naked, maybe against a tractor or one of his fantastic quarterback horses, his Stetson covering his essential bits.

"Forget it, Slade," Daniel muttered, now looking nervous.

Alex handed him a coy smile and glanced at her watch. "So, what are your plans for today?"

Daniel tapped his index finger against his thigh. "I need to catch up with my foreman, get my PA to reschedule some meetings I missed, return calls. You?"

"Pretty much the same. Except that I am scheduling some time to kill my grandpa."

Daniel laughed. "Come on, honey, I thought we'd partially forgiven them. After all, we are back together."

What did that mean? Was she now his girlfriend, his partner, his lover? Alex looked out of the window as the plane started to descend. They'd only spoken in general terms about her staying in Royal… Did he still want her to move in? Was she supposed to look for a house to rent in Royal itself? What did they tell Gus and Rose?

Where, exactly, did they stand?

All she knew for sure was that she'd agreed to stay in Royal. Was she sure that was the right thing to do? For her and the baby…?

The baby. Alex frowned. "What's the date today?"

Daniel tossed out the date and she slapped her hand against her forehead. "Dammit, I nearly forgot that I have an appointment with the ob-gyn this afternoon."

"This afternoon?" Daniel demanded. "Didn't I put that into my calendar?" he glanced at his cell phone and nodded. "Yeah, here it is, five thirty."

Alex nodded. "She's fitting me in as her last patient of the day."

He sighed, ran a hand across his face and glanced down at his phone. He quietly cursed. "Can you reschedule? I've got a crazy day."

"I don't think I should. I should've seen her already and I won't be able to get an appointment for another two weeks if I miss this one," Alex told him. She lifted her hands and lied. "I can go on my own—it's not that big a deal."

"It's a very big deal and I told you I want to be there," Daniel retorted. "Today is just not a good day."

"I can't help that," Alex pushed back, becoming annoyed herself. "When I made this appointment, I didn't know we were going to be kidnapped and out of touch for a week."

Daniel scrubbed his hand over his face before speaking again. "Okay, let's calm down. You said the appointment is at five thirty? Where?"

Alex gave him the doctor's address before adding,

"I'll understand if you can't make it, Daniel." Well, she'd try to understand.

Daniel leaned forward and covered her hand with his. "I said that I'd make you and the baby a priority, Lex, and I mean it. It would help if I could meet you there."

Alex linked her fingers in his and squeezed. She felt the warmth his words created and instantly relaxed. This was going to be okay; *they* were going to be okay. "Sure, we can do that."

Daniel leaned forward, brushed his mouth against hers and smiled. "Ready to go home?"

Alex smiled against his mouth. "No."

"Me neither. And please don't kill Gus. Prison orange is not your color."

Ten

Much later that day, Daniel gripped the bridge of his nose and closed his eyes. A headache pounded at the back of his skull and his shoulders were flirting with his ears.

It felt like he'd been back in Royal eight months instead of eight hours and he didn't know if he could fight another fire. He had cattle missing, he'd had to call the vet for a sick mare and one of his best men—who also happened to be one of his most experienced hands— had suddenly decided to retire.

On top of all of that, his PA had a stack of messages he needed to return, he had a pile of checks to sign and his accountant needed to speak with him urgently. Damn. He needed another vacation. But more than that, he needed Alex. Needed to see her smile, hear her voice.

Daniel looked at his watch. It was four twenty, which mean he'd need to leave the ranch by five to be on time for Alex's doctor's appointment. An image of Lex, rounded and beautiful, carrying his baby, flashed through his mind. He smiled. His woman was staying in Royal and in a few months' time, he'd meet the first of what he hoped would be a few children they'd make together.

Daniel heard the knock on his office door, jarring him from his thoughts, and looked up to see his grandmother's face between the frame and the door itself. He forced himself to keep his face blank, refusing to allow her the satisfaction of knowing her plan had worked out. Sort of.

"Can I come in?"

Daniel folded his arms as Rose stepped into the room. She looked good, he thought, and content. He liked seeing her happy but dammit, he wasn't going to smile at her...yet. "I'm not happy with you."

Rose didn't look even a little intimidated. "I don't care. I did what I needed to do."

Daniel spread his arms open. "Do I look like a little boy who needed your help?"

"You looked like a man who was going to allow the best thing in your life walk away from you." Rose walked over to his desk and placed her hands on the back of a visitor's chair. "I was not going to let her and that baby walk out of your life. And ours."

He couldn't help the smile that lifted the corners of his lips. "Be honest, you just want to dote on the baby."

Rose's smile made her look fifteen years younger. "I *so* do." She bit her lip and looked up at him, her eyes luminous. "So how did it go?"

Daniel smiled. "Do you use that look on Gus? Does he just fall at your feet and agree to anything you ask?"

"Of course he does," Rose replied. Daniel laughed

and Rose surprised him by walking around the desk and winding her arms around his waist. He knew Rose loved him, but she wasn't given to spontaneous bursts of affection. Closing his eyes, Daniel gathered his grandmother close, resting his chin in her hair. This woman had been his rock and his safety net, his moral compass and his true north. He might not have had a father or much of a mother, but she'd filled the gaps with her no-nonsense attitude and her integrity. And her love. She wasn't a hugger but he'd always known that he was loved.

But yeah, he was going to hug the hell out of his kid.

Daniel dropped a kiss on Rose's head and started to step away. He frowned when his grandmother's arms tightened to keep him in place. "Gran? Everything okay?"

Rose stepped back and he was shocked to see tears on her face. Bending so that he could see into her eyes, he gently held her biceps. "Are you okay? Is Gus okay? Did something happen? Crap, something has happened! Alex, is she okay?"

"Alex is fine, darling." Rose smiled and waved her hands in front of her face. "Do you have a handkerchief?"

Who used those anymore? Daniel cast an eye over his desk, saw a marginally clean bandanna and scooped it up. He found the cleanest corner and gently wiped away Rose's tears. "What's going on, Gran?"

Rose held his hand and led him to the leather couch that stood against the far wall. Daniel waited for her to sit before taking the seat next to her. Rose immediately took his hand in both of hers.

A million butterflies in his stomach started to beat their wings. What the hell was going on? "Okay, you are starting to scare me."

Rose stared down at his hands before releasing a sigh. "Have you checked your emails lately?"

Weird question. "I've been keeping up-to-date, mostly on my private email account. I glanced at the emails on the general account and now know that there are a lot of desperate women in Texas. Who sends an email asking a perfect stranger out on a date just because they read an article about him in a magazine?"

"Lonely girls who want to marry a good-looking, rich cowboy. You're a real-life fantasy."

Daniel snorted his disagreement. The only person he wanted to fantasize about him was Alex. The thought of Alex reminded him that he had to get this conversation moving or he'd be late. "What's your point, Gran?"

"You might have missed it but there have been a couple of messages to you from a Hector Lamb."

Hector Lamb? He recognized that name. "Did he send me a message on the ranch account, saying he wanted to meet me to discuss a mutual acquaintance?" The butterflies started to take flight. "I presume he is talking about Stephanie."

Rose nodded.

Daniel ran a hand across the back of his neck. "What does he want? Does he know that we haven't had any contact with her since I was a kid?"

This wasn't the first time one of Stephanie's marks showed up at their door, demanding restitution. When he was younger, it had been a common enough occurrence—money frequently changed hands to keep Stephanie out of jail—but even after she broke off communications, there had been a few men who tried their luck trying to extort money from them.

"He doesn't want anything," Rose replied. "No, that's not true. He wants to meet you."

"Me? Why?"

Rose's eyes brimmed with tears again. "Hector was in Austin for business. He met your mom. They had a weeklong affair. He left and when he returned five months later, it was obvious that she was pregnant. Your mom told him that the baby was a boy, that it was his and that she was going to name him Daniel."

Daniel felt the room tilt, his vision go blurry. He forced himself to concentrate on Rose's words, to make some sort of sense of what she was saying.

"Stephanie was still married to her loser ex and she was using his name. Hector offered to look after her and his baby, and he returned to Houston to rent her a flat, to buy furniture and a car. She was supposed to arrive in Houston two weeks later but—"

"She never arrived."

"Because, you know, Stephanie could never make life easy for herself. She went back to using the name Clayton and Hector couldn't find her. More important, he couldn't find you."

Daniel forced the words out from between clenched teeth and dry lips. "He looked for me?"

"He never stopped." Rose's smile was gentle. "He saw that picture of you in that magazine article and just recognized you. He knew you were his."

"How?" Daniel croaked the word.

"You look just like him, darling. You couldn't be anyone else's child." Rose placed her hand on his shoulder. "Honey, you're trembling. I know it's a shock, but he wants to meet you, wants to know you."

Daniel scrubbed his hands over his face, his heart banging inside his chest. He took a couple of deep breaths before he remembered that parental attention and love always came with a price. Why was his father here? What did he want? What was in it for him?

And, crucially, how much was he prepared to pay to have his father in his life?

Rose's hand drew big circles on his back. "Do you want to meet him?"

He'd have to meet him to discover why he was here, what he wanted. "Yeah, I guess."

Rose's smile was pure delight. "Excellent!" She jumped to her feet and clapped her hands. "Because he's waiting at the main house with Gus. He wants to meet you, too."

Today? Now? Jesus...

Alex left the doctor's room, clutching a black-and-white picture of her baby, who looked—admittedly—more like a peanut than a baby. But the heart was beating strong, and everything, as the doctor had informed her, was progressing normally. She was as healthy as a horse and the baby was thriving. Could she come back in two months, and would the baby's father be joining her at future appointments?

Well, no. Because she was going to Houston, to start a new life there.

Alex looked up and down the street and glanced at her watch. Daniel had missed the appointment and was nearly two hours late. Obviously, she and the baby were not the priority he'd promised her they would be.

It was better, Alex told herself as she slid behind the wheel of her car, that she found out now and not later. She could still leave, she could wrench herself away from Daniel and Royal, and start afresh in Houston.

He didn't love her, and he would never put her first. They'd landed ten hours ago, and Daniel had already forgotten about her, forgotten that he'd promised to accompany her to this appointment. He'd looked her in the eye and told her that she and the baby were his top priority, that he'd put them first. It only took him ten hours to forget that promise, to put his work and The Silver C in front of her.

Alex felt the tears slipping down her face as she stared at the picture of their baby. Her heart cramped and she felt the familiar wave of uncertainty. Since breaking up with Daniel a decade ago, and reinforced by Sarah's death, she'd avoided emotional entanglements and this was why. Because she couldn't handle the disappointment, the fear and the uncertainty. Relationships made her needy, vulnerable and so very insecure. She'd spent so many years running away from those weak emotions, and by sleeping with Daniel, she'd opened herself up to them again. What a fool she'd been to think that they could raise this child together and that, maybe one day, she could trust him enough to build a future with him.

She couldn't even trust him to keep a damned appointment, so how could she trust him with her love, her feelings, her very scarred heart? No, it was better that she return to Houston, and in a few months, she'd contact him and make arrangements for him to be part of the baby's life. Hopefully by then, she'd be stronger and mentally together.

Her passenger door opened and a gust of cool, wet wind accompanied Daniel into the car. He slammed the door shut and fiddled under his seat for the lever to push the seat back. Leaning back, he stretched out his long legs as far as they would go before turning to face her, looking weary. "Hi. Sorry I'm so late."

Daniel rubbed his hands over his face as if to wake

himself up before looking at her again. "How did it go? Are you okay? Is the baby okay?"

He was asking the right questions, but he sounded distracted, like he had more pressing problems on his mind. "God, it's cold out there."

Wow. He was talking about the weather. Could he not see that she was upset, that his missing the appointment had rocked her world? While Alex tried to make sense of his preoccupation—was he so oblivious that he couldn't see that she'd been crying?—Daniel reached for the sonograph. "Is this him? Her? Did they know what sex the baby is?" Okay, she now heard a little more interest in his voice. He cared about his child, that was obvious, but he hadn't cared to keep his commitment to her. She hadn't meant for it to be, but today turned out to be a test.

And he'd failed.

Daniel looked at her and frowned. "Are you okay?"

Well, no. "Do I look okay?" Alex asked, her voice soaked with emotion.

Daniel lifted his hand to touch her face and his expression hardened as she pulled back. "Look, I'm sorry I was late."

"You're not late, Daniel. You missed the entire appointment!"

"I know but—"

Alex banged her hand on the steering wheel. "No, no *buts*, Clayton! I asked you to be there, and you said you would."

"Something happened, Lex. If you'd just let me explain—"

She doubted that he could say anything that would make a difference. The fact of the matter was, once again, his precious ranch was more important to him than she was. "You believe that actions speak louder than words, Daniel. You told me this morning that I was your number one priority, that you would be here. Your actions disprove that."

Alex heard the frost in her voice, a direct contrast to the heat of Daniel's curse. She had to walk away—she couldn't do this for the rest of her life. She couldn't love him and not have him love her back. Great sex wasn't a good enough reason to stick around.

"Alex, for God's sake, let me explain."

She couldn't risk being persuaded to trust him, this would just happen again and again. Their time on the island had been a holiday romance, something that couldn't be replicated in real life. Real life wasn't sun and good sex and sparkling water; it was a chilly overcast day in Texas and two people who couldn't give each other what they needed. No, she had to end this today. *Now.* "I'm going back to Houston. That was my first instinct and I think it's the correct one."

"You're leaving Royal? Again? What the hell?"

Alex stared at the still-busy street, her eyes clear of tears. She was too hurt to cry, too empty to fight. She was in survival mode, simply doing what she could to emotionally survive.

"You're leaving because I missed one damn appointment?" Daniel's loud words reverberated through the interior of her car. "Are you completely insane?"

"No, I'm leaving because you can't keep your word! I'm leaving because I'm not a priority in your life and I can't trust you to be there for me!"

Daniel scrubbed his hand over his face. Looking up, he frowned at her, his dark eyes as cold as wind-battered boulders on an Arctic beach. "Jesus, Slade."

Alex gritted her teeth, leaned across him and opened his door. "Get out!"

Daniel pulled the door shut, leaned against the door and looked at her, his face now expressionless. She hated that blank look, the shutters in his eyes. Alex wanted to squirm under his penetrating gaze and forced herself to stay still, to lock stares with him. Daniel broke the heavy anger-charged silence. "You were just looking for a reason to run, weren't you?"

That wasn't fair. He was the one who'd let her down, who hadn't stuck to his word. Alex tapped the picture of the peanut. "Funny, I didn't see you there when I listened to our child's heartbeat. I didn't hear you asking questions."

"If I made it today, then something else, soon, would've made you run," Daniel gritted out.

"That's not fair."

"Oh, it so is. When you get scared, you run as fast and as hard as you can."

His words were as sharp and as bitter as the tip of a poison dart.

"I'm not scared," Alex protested.

"You acted out of fear when, ten years ago, you ran instead of trying to find a way to still go to school and see me. We started sleeping together last year and as soon as we started laughing together, talking, you broke it off."

"Our grandparents—"

Daniel leaned forward, his face harsh. "Don't! Don't you dare blame this on them! This is about you and me and the fact that whenever you find yourself in deep water, emotionally speaking, you swim back to shore!"

That was because she didn't want to drown. She knew what it felt like to lose air, to feel like you were dying without the people you loved in your life.

Daniel shoved both hands into his hair and tugged his curls in frustration. "We could have such an amazing life, Lex, but you value protecting yourself above loving me, loving us." Daniel dropped his hands and, in his eyes, Alex saw the devastation she'd put there.

"I can't keep trying to prove my worth to you, Alexis. I did that constantly as a child and I refuse to do it as an adult. You either want us—me—or you don't. I'm not going to continuously try to prove myself to you." Daniel picked up the photograph of their baby and looked at it for a long time. "I'm tired of fighting for us on my own, Lex. I want you. I want my family, but I need you to want it, too. And I'm not going to sit here and beg you for that chance. Go back to Houston, live in your safe cave."

She heard the words, thought that was what she wanted, so why did it feel like he was ripping her soul in two? Daniel opened the door, swung his long legs out of her small car and looked at her over his shoulder. "I'll contact you in a few weeks to check up on my kid."

Daniel left those parting words behind as he exited her vehicle. To check up on his child, not her. She'd pushed him, and she'd got what she wanted. A Daniel-free life. Alex ran the tips of her fingers over her forehead, utterly confused. She felt like she'd placed the last piece into a giant puzzle only to find that the focal piece of the picture was missing. What had she missed?

Acting on instinct, she flew out of the car and saw him walking away, his shoulders hunched and his head bent. "Daniel!"

He stopped at her shout, hesitated and finally turned to face her, lifting a dark eyebrow. "What?"

Hold me. Take me in your arms and soothe my fears.

Tell me that you'll never let me down. Never leave me. Love me, please.

"Why were you late?" she asked.

A small smile touched his mouth but didn't reach his eyes. "Oh, that little thing?" He hesitated, drawing the moment out. "A half hour before I was supposed to meet you, my father walked back into my life."

Eleven

The next morning, Daniel rested his forearms on the whitewashed pole fence and watched as one of his stable hands led Rufus, his prize stallion, from the barn to spend the day in the paddock behind his house.

Rufus had it made, Daniel thought. He and Rose and every other hand petted and pampered him and treated him like the king he was. Rufus got fed and brushed and stroked, and he could frolic and mate with a variety of mares.

Lucky Rufus. His life had certain parallels with his favorite horse. He thought he could go through life running his ranch, socializing with his friends and falling into the arms and bed of any available woman who caught his fancy. He thought that was living, but as it turned out, he hadn't had a clue.

Truth was, he wanted what he couldn't have. He wanted Alex, he wanted his child, he wanted a life together. Early-morning coffee in bed, long trail rides over the Clayton and Slade ranches, alone or with their child safe between his arms and knees. He wanted to walk into his house and see her there, watch her grow rounder and bigger, kiss her mouth when she brought their child into the world. He wanted to make dinner with her, listen to her read stories to their children, snuggle with her at night.

He wanted to love her body and nurture her soul.

He simply wanted the opportunity to love her.

Daniel scratched his forehead, his head pounding from sadness, stress and the half bottle of whiskey he'd consumed when he got home last night. He'd missed one appointment—and had a damn good reason for doing so—and she'd written him off as being untrustworthy, inconsiderate. She should've allowed him to explain and then decided, not jumped the gun. If he spoke to another woman, would she think he was having an affair? If he was a minute late, would he be in for a night of receiving the cold shoulder? He wasn't perfect; no man was, and Alex didn't seem to allow any room for him to maneuver.

He couldn't love someone who only loved you back when you proved your worth, who was only happy when you did what she wanted you to do. He loved Alex but he wanted a wife and a partner, not a shadow. He wanted a friend and a lover, not a prosecutor, cross-examining him on his every move.

Sighing, Daniel stared at the empty paddock. Maybe she was right, maybe they were better off apart. Maybe they'd been living in a fool's paradise while they were on vacation at Galloway Cove, allowing the fresh tropical breezes and the island's sultry allure to sway them into believing that they could have the impossible.

How many times were they supposed to try? Shouldn't he just accept that he and Alex were not meant to be?

"Morning."

Daniel turned to see Hector approaching him, dressed in an Italian suit. He looked down at his jeans and worn denim jacket over a flannel shirt and thought that while he and his father looked so alike, he didn't have Hector's taste in clothes.

"Hey."

Daniel hadn't had the chance to have a private moment with Hector, to take him aside and find out what he really wanted. The meeting at Rose and Gus's had carried on and on, and his grandmother had been less than pleased when he insisted that he had to go because he had a prior commitment that couldn't wait. Hoping to catch the tail end of Alex's appointment, he'd floored it to Royal, but he'd been too late.

And because he was late, his world had fallen apart.

"We didn't have time to have a one-on-one conversation last night," Hector said, coming to stand next to Daniel. "Your grandparents are extremely hospitable, and they love you very much."

"Rose is my grandmother. Gus is a new addition to the family," Daniel replied. Tired, upset and not wanting to indulge in small talk, he looked Hector in the eye. "What do you want?"

Shock passed over Hector's face before he schooled his features. "What do you mean?"

"Money? An introduction? A new sports car? A loan?"

Hector cocked his head to the side and instead of anger or annoyance or shame, Daniel saw sympathy in his eyes. "None of those."

"Well, what?" Daniel demanded, his voice ragged.

Because there had to be a reason he was here, back in his life.

"I have more than enough money, and I don't need your connections. I own six sports cars and I am excessively liquid." Humor touched Hector's mouth. "But thank you for offering."

Daniel pushed a hand through his hair. "Then why are you here?"

Hector placed his hand on his shoulder and squeezed. "I am here because you are my son. I have three daughters with a lovely woman who has been my life for more than twenty-five years, but you are my firstborn, my son. I am here because I need to know that you are happy, healthy, okay. I also wanted you to know that I never stopped thinking about you, that I was always looking for you. There's no price to pay, Daniel."

Daniel stared at him, shocked. "What did you say?"

Hector sent him a soft smile. "I didn't spend much time with Stephanie, but it didn't take me long to work out that life was a series of exchanges with that one. Do this for me and I'll do this for you. Pay me this and I'll do that. Pay me more and I'll pretend to love you.

"Why do you think I was so determined to find you? Apart from the fact that you were mine, I didn't want your life being a series of transactions."

Oh God, that was exactly what life with Stephanie had been like.

Daniel felt like he needed to say something, anything. "I've always thought that was what love was. Up to now, it's all I've known. My grandmother married Ed to make sure her mother was cared for… Stephanie only allowed Gran to have me if she paid for the privilege." A muscle ticked in his jaw. "And then, of course, there's Alex. She dumped me ten years ago when I refused to leave The Silver C with her."

"She was a teenager and, as such, stupid," Hector said, his voice mild. "I'm sure you hurt her, as well."

He had. By refusing to leave The Silver C, choosing the ranch over her, he made her feel abandoned. To a girl who'd been left by so many people, she felt any loss more keenly than most people did. She'd been scared and was still scared…

So was he. When there was so much to lose, love was goddamn terrifying.

Earlier, instead of explaining, instead of reassuring her, he'd turned the tables on her, accusing her of wanting to run. Guilt coursed through him. Rather than trying to see things from her perspective, he'd cast blame, got angry. He'd been confused and upset about Hector dropping back into his life, worried that the man he instinctively liked would disappoint him by putting a price on fatherhood.

Driving to Royal, he remembered thinking that his life had been so much less complicated last year: he'd had affairs that had the emotional depth of a puddle, his grandmother wasn't in love with her oldest enemy and Alexis Slade was a girl he saw around town, whom he was determined to keep at arm's length.

His life had been safe. But, God, so boring.

He didn't want that. He wanted to watch his grandmother fuss over her new husband, and he wanted to get to know this man who'd looked for him for the better part of three decades. He wanted his woman, his child, the two most important things in his life.

Because while he loved this land, loved The Silver C, the *love of his life* was probably packing up her car and heading south.

Daniel looked at Hector and lifted his shoulders and his hands. "I'm running out on you again but it's not because I want to, but…"

Hector smiled. "But there's a girl leaving, and you want to stop her."

Rose and her big mouth. Daniel smiled. "I intend to make that girl your daughter-in-law."

Hector grinned. "Sounds good to me." He pulled a card out of the top pocket of his suit and handed it to Daniel. "When you are ready, come to Houston, bring Alexis, meet my family. Or come alone, whatever…"

Daniel took the card and nodded once before scuffing his boot over the short dry grass. He cleared his throat, pushing down the emotion that threatened to strangle his words. "Thanks for looking for me."

Hector squeezed his shoulder again. "It's what fathers do. Go get your girl, son."

Son. Daniel heard the word and closed his eyes. He was finally someone's son. It felt good, wonderful. But it would be freakin' fantastic to be Alex's husband and the peanut's dad.

Alex recognized the sound of Gus's ancient ATV and wondered how much longer he'd continue to nurse that ancient beast. It sputtered and belched smoke and was in the shop for repairs more often than it was on the road. Gus had access to three brand-new ATVs a couple of steps from his front door but his loyalty to that old, paint-deprived quad bike remained constant.

Her grandfather was the most loyal of creatures. He'd loved Sarah—of that she had no doubt—and he'd treated her like a queen, but when he was with Rose, he glowed. Her hard, tough, frank-as-hell grandfather was putty in Miss Rose's hands. He loved her to the depths of his soul, beyond time, for eternity.

Rose, she was surprised to find, seemed to love him just as much. Rose was now Gus's world and Alex was happy for him. Happy that he'd spend the rest of his life loving and being loved.

She couldn't help feeling a little envious, but she shrugged it away, thinking that love like that perhaps now only existed for people of a certain age, a particular generation. She and Daniel were modern people, living in a modern world, and they'd been conditioned to be selfish, to be self-obsessed. How could true love flourish in a society that was so materialistic, self-loving and narcissistic? It was all about them, only about them. She was a classic example because she'd been so caught up in her own drama, in thinking how badly Daniel had treated her in failing to make the doctor's appointment, that she'd brushed aside his explanations. *Her* feelings, *her* heartache had been all she'd been worried about.

Daniel meeting his dad had been a damn good excuse to miss her doctor's appointment, and if she hadn't reacted so selfishly, she might not be sitting in the chair on Sarah's deck, her car fueled and packed, ready to make the journey to Houston and a new life.

She was thoroughly ashamed of herself. And now, more than anything, she wanted to know how he was dealing with his father's reappearance. What did Daniel think of his dad? Was the reality of meeting him as an adult as good as the dream he'd had of him as a boy? But no, because she'd acted like a selfish brat, he was dealing with this all alone.

Alex sighed as she heard Gus's footsteps on the wooden stairs that led to the tree house. Her grandfather's shadow fell over her and she lifted her head and greeted him. Gus nodded, dropped into the Adirondack chair next to her and propped his old boots on the railing. His pushed his ancient but favorite Stetson back with one finger like she'd seen him do a million times before. Old ATV, old boots, old Stetson, Rose.

The man never gave up on the things he loved. Alex bit her lip as the thought struck home. Gus didn't give up; few Slades ever did. So why was she?

Gus cleared his throat and Alex turned her head to look at his profile. "Do you remember when Gemma died?"

Alex jerked her head back, surprised at his question. That was the very last thing she expected him to say. "Sure. I remember getting the news. I thought my world had stopped."

"Do you remember the funeral?"

Alex shook her head. "Not so much, actually. I remember the coffin, the flowers, Sarah holding my hand."

Gus stared at the barren winter landscape beyond the river. "We woke early that morning, the day of the funeral. Sarah looked into your room but you weren't there, and we couldn't find you. We looked everywhere. You never took your hound with you that day. You two were never apart and that scared me."

Olly had died in her arms only a few months later after being kicked by a horse. It had been another loss in a string of losses. "I eventually saddled a horse and told your dog to find you. We went for miles and I eventually found you in the top paddock, the one that borders the Clayton land."

The one where she first kissed Daniel. Yeah, she knew it well. "It was the farthest point you could go without crossing onto Clayton land, and you were standing right on the boundary line."

Alex tried to remember but nothing came back. "I don't remember any of this."

Gus rubbed the back of his neck. "You told me that you were running away, that you couldn't go back. That going back would make it too real."

That sounded like her.

Gus slid down the seat, rested his head on the back of the chair and closed his eyes. Alex waited for him to continue but he just sat there, soaking up the winter sun. She flicked his thigh and he cranked open one eye. "What?"

"Aren't you going to tell me that I run away from stuff I don't want to have to deal with? That I did it ten years ago when I left Daniel—"

"In fairness, I did encourage you to do that," Gus said, his eyes still closed.

"So why aren't you pointing out that running away is what I do, that it's the way I deal with life when things get hard? That I push people away when I think they can hurt me? Why aren't you telling me that?"

"You seem to be doing a right fine job working this out on your own, sweetheart. Seems to me that you don't need my input."

Alex glared at him before dropping her gaze to her hands, which were dangling between her thighs. Running, hiding, staying away—emotionally, as well as physically—was what she did. She dipped her toe in and yanked it out when the water got deeper, the current stronger. As Daniel suggested, she played in the shallows, too scared to take a chance.

"I'm so scared, Grandpa," Alex whispered, her voice so low, she wasn't sure he had heard her small admission.

"So?" Alex looked at him and he shrugged. "Be scared. Be whatever you need to be, but instead of running, be scared while you stand in one place, while you try something new." Gus stood up and pinned her to her chair with his don't-BS-me blue eyes. "I loved your grandmother, Alex. I really did. But a part of me always regretted walking away from Rose, for missing out on fifty years with her. Regret is a cold hard companion I don't want you to live with. Daniel is a good boy—"

Alex couldn't help putting her hand on her heart and feigning shock at his praise of a Clayton.

Gus blushed and waved her mockery away. "Yeah, yeah. But he is a good man—he's loyal and hardworking, and God knows you two burn hot enough to start a wildfire."

Alex grimaced. That wasn't something she wanted Gus noticing. Gus bent down to kiss her cheek. "Don't run this time, Lexi. Stay still and see what happens. Gotta go. Need to check on the calves in the stable paddock."

He had hands and Jason to do that for him, but Gus would ride back on the wheels-on-death because he wanted to. No, because he *needed* to. Alex watched the best man she knew walk away, his back still strong, his gait still steady. He was hard and tough and frank, but her grandfather had an enormous capacity for love. For his family, both present and past, for his land and for his beloved Rose. He'd lived and loved and cried on this land. He tended it and it repaid him by providing a good livelihood for his kids and grandkids. His beloved wife and children and pets were buried in the family graveyard, and every inch held a memory. The land was an intrinsic part of him, just as Clayton land was a part of Daniel.

And they belonged here. Both of them, on this land. Together.

It was time, Alex thought as she stood up, to put this latest, most stupid Clayton-Slade feud to bed.

Her car was filled to the brim and Alex knew that if anyone saw her driving it, they would immediately assume she was leaving Royal and the gossip would fly around town. She and Daniel had created enough gossip lately, so she decided to quickly unpack her vehicle before tracking down Daniel.

She wouldn't take all her worldly possessions back up to her room, as that would take far too long, so Alex decided to dump them in Gus's spacious hall until she returned. She parked her car as close as she could get to the front door of her childhood home, exited her car and walked around to the other side. She had a heavy box of books in her arms when she heard the low rumble of a powerful pickup. Turning, she squinted into the sun and saw the dusty white truck with The Silver C's logo on the side panel.

Alex held the box, conscious that her mouth was as dry, as Gus would say, as the heart of a haystack. Watching as the truck stopped next to hers, Alex stared wide-eyed as Daniel flew out of the car, his face radiating determination and a healthy dose of kick-ass. He was at her side in two seconds and then the heavy box was yanked out of her hands and tossed, with very little effort at all, into the back of his truck. The corner of the box hit a fence post and the box split open, spilling books over the bed of the truck.

Before she could protest, Daniel grabbed her biceps and slammed his mouth against hers in a hard kiss, but as Alex started to sink into the kiss, he whipped his mouth away. Holding her arms, he easily lifted her away from her spot by the door and grabbed a suitcase and a toiletry bag, tossing both into the bed of his pickup.

Since that was exactly where she wanted her stuff, Alex watched him, her shoulder pressed into the side of the car as he emptied her car in a matter of minutes. She wished he'd taken a little more care in moving her potted plants, but she was sure they'd be okay.

When her car was completely empty—Daniel had even chucked her bag and phone onto his passenger seat—he stormed back to her and placed his hands on his hips, his chest heaving.

"You are not going to Houston," he stated, his voice gruff.

She'd gathered that already. Alex just resisted throwing herself into his arms and it took everything she had to lift an insouciant eyebrow. "You kidnapping my stuff, Clayton?"

"I couldn't give a damn about your stuff," Daniel muttered. He jerked his head toward the pickup. "Get in."

There was something wonderful in seeing her man slightly unhinged, Alex thought. She was quite curious to see what he'd do if she dissented. "And if I don't?"

Alex expected him to toss her over his shoulder, to bundle her into his car, and she was turned on thinking about Daniel going caveman on her. But instead of utilizing his physical strength, he lifted his hand to gently touch her face. "I need you, Lex. Right now, I need you to get into my truck because I have things to say…"

"Like?"

Daniel rested his forehead on hers. "I want to tell you that I need you, period. In my bed, my house, my damned life. Nothing makes sense without you."

Alex turned her cheek into his hand, refusing to

drop her eyes from his. This was Daniel, naked and exposed in a way she'd never seen him before. "We make sense, Alexis. We made sense ten years ago, but we were too young and dumb to know it. We made sense three months ago, but we were too scared to acknowledge it. You and I, we're two puzzle pieces that interlock. You're…"

Alex felt the moisture on her face, saw the sheen of emotion in his eyes. "What am I, Dan?"

Daniel held her face within both of his hands as her heart slowly slid from her chest to his. "You're everything, Lex. You're both my future and my past, my baby's mother and the beat of my heart. Please don't go to Houston. Stay here with me."

"Okay."

Daniel yanked his head back, a smile hitting his eyes with all the force of a meteor strike. "Are you being serious?"

Alex nodded. "When you roared up, driving like a crazy man, I was actually unpacking, not packing. I was coming to look for you."

Daniel's thumb skated over her cheek. "Why?"

Alex gripped his shirt, bunching the fabric in her hands. Preparing to jump, she gathered her courage. "I want to stay. I want to be here with you. Raising our children together."

More shock. Daniel looked down at her stomach and jerked his head up. "We're having twins?"

Alex laughed. "Not this time. I was talking about the future, the future I see with you."

"Damn. Twins would've been fun." He brushed her hair off her forehead, his expression tender. "How do you see our future, Lex?"

"Pretty much as you said earlier. I know that I have

some issues, Dan, but I don't want to live my life fearing something that may not happen. I'd rather have any time I can have with you than no time at all. I'm not saying that I'm not going to be insecure, to worry. I probably will but I'll try not to be ridiculous about it."

"And instead of getting frustrated, I'll just hold you tighter and tell you that I'm never going to let you go."

He was gruff and bossy and powerful and sometimes annoying, but he was also perfect. She tipped her head back. "I love you, Daniel. I'm crazy in love with you."

Daniel's smile was pure tenderness. "I love you, too, sweetheart."

Alex's mouth lifted to meet his and she tasted love on his lips, relief in his touch, happiness dancing across his skin. She was feeling pretty damn amazing herself. The kiss deepened, became heated and Daniel pulled her into his hard body, chest to chest, groin to groin. Tongues tangled as love and belonging and desire merged into a sweet, messy ball. This was the start of a new chapter and Alex couldn't wait for the rest of the book.

Daniel's hand came up to cover her breast and it took all her willpower to pull away from his touch. She gestured to the busy stables to the left of the house, blushing when she saw Gus and Jason leaning against the wall, unabashedly watching them.

"Jerks," she muttered.

"On the plus side, I didn't get my head blown off," Daniel murmured, laughter coating his words.

"Actually, Grandpa quite likes you," Alex told him. "He'd like you more if you married me."

Daniel jerked back, frowned and then released a strangled laugh. "I'm not sure what to say to that." He rubbed his jaw. "How do you feel about that?"

"Getting married?" Alex cocked her head to the side, pretending to think. "I think that sounds like a fine idea." She grinned at his astonishment and held up her hand to keep him from grabbing her again. "Slow down, cowboy, I'm not getting engaged with tear tracks on my cheeks and blue rings around my eyes and with my male relatives watching us like hawks. But do feel free to propose in the high meadow, preferably with a lovely ring and a bottle of champagne."

Daniel pretended to consider her statement. "Hmm, the ring I can do. But it'll have to be nonalcoholic champagne, and whose land will it be on?" He smiled and Alex's heart flipped over.

"Ours," Alex said, the words catching in her throat. "Yours, mine, ours."

Daniel nodded, raw, unbridled emotion in his eyes and on his face and in his touch. Alex watched his eyes as he bent to kiss her, silently saying a heartfelt thank-you to whatever force had brought them to this point. They were going to have a hell of a life and she couldn't wait for it to start.

"Hey, you two, what's the status?" Alex jumped, startled, and she turned to see her Gus a few feet from them, waving his phone in the air. Since when did he carry a phone? Alex wondered. "Rosie wants to know."

Daniel gently banged his forehead on her collarbone. "God."

"Everything is sorted," Alex told Gus, making a shooing movement with her hand.

"Rosie, let's hallelujah the county! Call everyone— we're going to paint the house. And the porch." Gus flipped his phone closed—so old she was surprised it still worked—caught Daniel's eye and gestured to the truck. "Well, come on, then. This stuff isn't going to move itself. Take it into the house and we can have a chat about what comes next."

The last thing she wanted to do was to talk to Gus, or anyone. What she really wanted to do was to divest Daniel of his clothes and make love to him as his future wife.

Daniel looked from her to his truck, adjusted his ball cap and shook his head. "As much as I appreciate the offer, sir, I'm going to stick to my original plan."

"And that was?" Alex asked as his hand enveloped hers.

"To kidnap you and your stuff." He flashed a grin at Gus as he wrapped an arm around her waist and easily carried her to his truck. He bundled her into the passenger seat and saluted Gus. "I try to learn from my elders, sir."

Epilogue

At six months pregnant, Alex required a wedding dress with an empire waistline but, catching a glance at her reflection in the gleaming glass door as she stepped out of the TCC function room, she saw that she still looked pretty amazing. The dress's bodice gathered into a knot behind her breasts and the chiffon overskirt, which was dotted with embroidered roses, flowed to the floor. She was, as everyone kept telling her, glowing. Alex knew that had as much to do with her husband of two hours as it did her pregnancy.

She was married. Alex looked down at the band of diamonds Dan had put on her ring finger earlier, a companion piece to her sapphire-and-diamond engagement ring, and took a moment to count her many blessings. Her partnership with Mike was smooth sailing, and while commuting was a pain, so far it was working. She was living in Dan's house and they were deciding how to completely renovate Rose's old house together. In Rose she found both a mentor, a friend and an ally. And in getting to know Sarah's oldest friend, she felt like she had a piece of her grandmother back.

Best of all, she woke up with Dan and fell asleep with him, secure that her heart was safe in his hands.

"Have I told you how stunning you look?"

Alex turned at her husband's voice and smiled. He didn't look too shabby himself, looking almost as hot in a tuxedo as he did in worn jeans and a T-shirt. But Daniel naked? Couldn't get sexier...

Daniel approached her, held the back of her head and tipped her chin up to brush her lips. "We haven't had a moment to ourselves since we walked into that church."

Their friends and family—including Daniel's father, his wife and his three half sisters and their spouses and many children—all wanted some time with the new bridal couple. While Alex appreciated their well wishes, her cheeks were sore from smiling, her feet ached and she just wanted to step into Daniel's arms for a cuddle.

"You doing okay?" Daniel asked, placing his hand on her round stomach.

"A little tired." Alex looped one arm around his neck and rested her cheek on his chest. "I'm so thrilled that we are going back to Galloway Cove for our honeymoon, Dan. I just want you and the sun and the sea."

"I just want you. Naked," Daniel muttered. He gathered her to him and she felt his erection against her stomach, and felt his hand cupping her butt.

"I missed you last night," Alex told him before pushing up onto her toes and placing her lips against his. Daniel immediately responded, his tongue sliding into her mouth and sending heat to her core.

Alex, as she always did, melted and wondered if anyone would notice if they sneaked away.

"My beautiful, sexy wife. How I love—"

The door behind them banged open and Daniel cursed at the interruption. Stifling her groan, she turned to see Rachel in the hallway, Matt Galloway a step behind her. Still leaning against Daniel, she lifted her hand at her matron of honor.

Rachel rubbed her arm. "Are you okay, Alex? You're looking a bit flushed."

That was because her husband still had his hand on her butt.

"Just taking a breather," Alex told her, turning to look at Matt. "I was just telling Dan that I'm so excited to be going back to Galloway Cove for our honeymoon."

Matt nodded. "I was surprised when Dan asked me. I thought that since you were basically kidnapped and tossed off the plane onto my island, it wouldn't be your first choice for a honeymoon."

Alex shook her head. "No, I loved it!" She loved making love to Daniel at the waterfall and by the pool and on the bench, in the outdoor shower…

Rachel lifted her eyebrows at her, Alex lifted hers back and they both burst out laughing. Yep, she was pretty sure that Rachel liked the island, too. And not only because it was a place of immense natural beauty.

The door opened again, and Tessa glided through, followed by Ryan. "Alex and Rachel, there you are! I've been looking for both of you."

Alex put her back to Daniel's chest, linking her hand with the one that now rested on her stomach. Her bridesmaid looked radiant and about to burst with news. Alex held up her hand as Caleb and Shelby joined their party, followed by James and Lydia. They were just missing

Brooke and Austin, but Alex had barely finished that thought when they walked into the hallway from the main entrance, Austin carrying a frame covered in brown paper.

"The gang's all here," Ryan commented.

"Alex, I want to run something by you—" James started to speak, only to be interrupted by Tessa.

"Wait, hold on, I need to—"

"Austin, honey, we need Rose and Gus," Brooke said a second later.

Alex laughed and tipped her head up to look at Daniel. He grinned down at her before lifting his fingers to his mouth to let out a shrill whistle. Their friends immediately quieted down. "We need to get back to our guests, so make it snappy." Daniel pointed to Tessa. "Tess, you're up."

"Alex, would you and Rachel both be my matrons of honor?"

Alex jumped up and down and Rachel squealed with excitement. Alex wanted to hug Tessa but Daniel held her tight. "Fantastic," he said. "Not meaning to be rude, but we need to hurry this along. I want to cut the cake, have a first dance with my bride and get to the fun part of the night."

Daniel pointed his finger at Caleb. "Go."

Shelby rested her temple on Caleb's arm. "We're having twins."

Alex let out a whoop, tore away from Daniel's hold to hug Shelby. As everyone else congratulated the happy pair, Alex took the chance to hug Tessa and then, because she was overflowing with happiness, to hug Rachel, as well.

Daniel gently hooked his finger into the back of her dress and tugged her back into her previous position. "We really do need to get back inside."

Alex nodded. "I know. Rose is going to have a fit if she finds us hanging out in the hallway with our friends."

Daniel grinned and jerked his head at James. "What's up?"

"Nothing that can't wait. I was just thinking that maybe Alex could do another fund-raising function next year."

Alex nodded enthusiastically, her mischievous side surfacing. "Absolutely. I was thinking about a skin calendar, tentatively called 'The Rogues of Royal.' I'd need you all to model. I hope you are comfortable stripping down in front of a camera."

The five male faces in front of her paled in unison. Alex looked up at her husband, who was laughing. "You know that I have no problem stripping down," he murmured before looking back at the group. "To be discussed later. Much, much later. Brooke, what have you got there, honey?"

Yet again the door opened, and Alex winced when she saw Rose's unamused face. "Ladies and gentlemen, the party is inside, not out here." This time, twelve grown men and women shuffled their feet at the displeasure in Regal Rose's voice.

Alex opened her mouth to apologize, but then her grandfather slipped past Rose, his eyes on the package in Brooke's hand. "Rosie! It's here!"

Rose clasped her hands in delight and joined Gus at Brooke's side. Alex stepped away from Daniel and wondered what was going on. "What is it?" she asked.

Rose beckoned her to come closer. The group made a circle behind them and Daniel dropped to his haunches, his hand on the frame. Alex heard movement behind Ryan and glanced over to see Hector joining the group, his eyes not moving from Daniel's face.

Gus nodded, and Daniel ripped the paper away. Alex took a moment to absorb the significance of Brooke's painting. A wolf rested in the first of three circles—one each for her, Daniel and Jason—and beneath it, Brooke had carefully painted the words *The Silver Wolf Ranch*.

Daniel turned to look at her and she saw love and adoration in his eyes. He stood up and took her hand and raised her knuckles to his lips. "Equal partners, Slade?"

"Equal partners, Clayton," she murmured.

Daniel kept her hand in his as he led her back to their wedding reception and their guests. "One dance, the cake cutting and then I'm hauling you out of here, Lex."

Alex grinned at him. "As you already know, I'm always up for a good kidnapping, my darling."

* * * * *

UNDER HIS TOUCH

CATHRYN FOX

This one is for you, Amanda W.
You are a gem! So glad to call you my friend.

CHAPTER ONE

Megan

"HE WANTS YOU to do what?"

Heavy spring rain pummels the Manhattan streets, along with the café's windows as I sip my mocha latte and take in Amanda's wide-eyed stare. Thick, black lashes blink rapidly as she works to absorb this crazy turn of events; and for God's sake if she doesn't pick her jaw up from the table, she's going to catch the fly buzzing around her jelly-filled doughnut.

"I know. Insane, right?" I say to my best friend, and give a slow shake of my head, still unable to believe what billionaire James Carson has asked me to do. Although, I have to admit, I'm more shocked that I actually agreed to do it. I mull it over for a second and a burst of unease moves through me as I think about putting his plan into motion. Am I making a big mistake? Maybe I shouldn't have agreed to it at all.

Amanda lifts her mug to her mouth and looks at me over the rim before asking, "Is the man losing his mind?"

"He's ninety." I flip my hand over. "So, I get why you'd think that, but after talking to him it's clear he's as sharp now as he was when I met him back in high school. Hard to believe he's playing with a full deck, though, considering what he wants me to do."

Every time the bell over the door chimes as it opens, my stomach does a little somersault. I'm far more nervous about this afternoon's meeting than I thought I would be. It's been eight years since I've set eyes on Alec Carson. Eight long years and I've never stopped thinking about him. Never stopped wanting to stab him in the eye with a fork.

"Okay, so let me get this straight," Amanda says. "James Carson wants you to find his grandson a wife?" She rubs her finger between her eyebrows, one of her cute quirks when she's trying to wrap her brain around something. Her nose crinkles. "But you're an event planner, not a matchmaker."

"I know, and I don't know the first thing about matchmaking. Cripes, the last time I used a dating site, I ended up with a narcissistic lawyer who probably feasted upon the dreams of innocent children." I give a low, slow whistle. "Not going there again."

Amanda laughs, and my stomach comes alive when the bell jingles again. By the time Alec arrives, I'm going to be a jittery mess. I need to keep it together, but facing the boy I once loved, the boy

I gave my virginity to, is messing with my mind and body in the worst kind of way. Then again, he's not a boy anymore and I'm not some innocent, naive love-struck teen. Truthfully, I never expected the grandson of billionaire magnate James Carson—a sweet, generous old man who always put family first—to walk away from me after a beautiful prom night in St. Moritz, without so much as a backward glance. We spent nearly all of senior year together, and I thought he was different. I thought we had something special. Thought he didn't care that I was from the wrong side of the tracks.

I thought wrong.

He always teased that I was the girl-next-door type, and I thought he liked that about me. In the end, however, it was just another thing I was mistaken about. I guess bigger and better, more glamorous, was waiting for him at Harvard. He didn't want the poor, parentless girl from Philly holding him back. Now he's a financier at Blackstone Venture Partners, working his way through the ranks at the multimillion-dollar holding company, one harsh corporate takeover at a time.

Ah, what was that you just said about feasting upon the dreams of innocent children?

"And Alec actually agreed to this?" Amanda asks, her damp blond hair brushing over her shoulder as she shakes her head, incredulous.

I run my hand over my own curls, a frizzy mess from the weather, and work to make myself presentable. Jesus, am I seriously preening for the jerk? Suppressed anger surfaces as I reach for my latte, take another fast sip, irritated with myself.

"His granddad set this up, and Alec is meeting me here, so he must have agreed," I say.

"I get why you're doing it. You find him a wife and throw him the royal wedding of the century, no expenses spared. That will take you from obscurity in the event planning world to the most sought-after consultant in Manhattan, but why would *he* agree? What's in it for him? From what I've read about 'Manhattan's most eligible bachelor' in the tabloids, he doesn't seem like the settling-down type."

Not only does Amanda know him from the tabloids, as my best friend since college, she knows how close Alec and I once were, and how he ditched me after prom. I look past Amanda's shoulder, and my heart jumps into my throat when Alec walks in. The air of authority about him draws the attention of every single woman in the room, and some not-so-single ones. Then there's the impeccable suit he's sporting, one that was undoubtedly tailor-made for his tall frame and athletic body. The men in the room begin to posture in his presence, but there's no point. Alec is breathtaking, the most impressive guy here, and for a moment I can't think, let alone breathe as he smooths his hands over his tie in much the same way his grandfather did during our meeting. With a laser focus, he casts a quick glance around the café. Intense blue eyes find mine, and the muscles in his square jaw ripple as he clenches down, giving me the impression that he had no idea it was me he was meeting.

Wouldn't James have told him?

As our eyes hold and lock, my insides burn like I've just been hit with a high-voltage Taser. Damn, he hasn't changed a bit. No, that's not true. He's grown from a boy to a man, his body wider, thicker, filling out his clothes in a way the young Alec never could. I swallow. Hard.

"I guess I'm about to find out what's in it for him," I squeak out.

Amanda's eyes pop open again. "I take it he just arrived." Her head angles, and I touch her hand and stop her before she can turn and gawk.

"Yes, he's here. Right on time, as I suspected." He always was conscious of the time, a stickler for the rules. Except now, something in my gut tells me he no longer plays by them. "Please don't look."

Amanda picks up her mug and half-eaten jelly doughnut. "Then I'm gone. Text me later," she says. "I can't wait to hear all about this."

I stand with her, and run my damp hands over my skirt. No need to greet him with a wet palm and let him know what the sight of him is doing to me— even after all this time. It's best I give a professional vibe, and the appearance that I'm completely unaffected by him.

If only that were true.

He nods to Amanda as she walks past him to put

her mug in the tray, and his overwhelming presence weakens my traitorous knees as he crosses the room to stand over me. All six feet of pure power and testosterone takes my mind back to the night we made love. Scratch that. To the night we had sex. Yeah, lovemaking involves emotions. If there were emotions involved, he wouldn't have walked away the next day, letting me know in no uncertain terms that there was nothing more between us. If only I'd gotten the memo back then, before I went to his hotel room and seduced him.

I lift my gaze to meet his, and even though he's offering me a smile, I catch a hint of uncertainty in his gorgeous blue eyes as they roam my face. Obviously, this is as awkward for him as it is for me. His arms lift, like he's about to embrace me, but professional event planner that I am, I keep it together and hold my hand out.

He stares at it for a moment, his smile dissolving, morphing into confusion, and then he gives me a tight, fast nod as he closes his big hand over mine.

Yeah, that's right. That's the way it's going to be. I'm in charge here.

"Megan," he says, his voice deeper than I remember it. "Nice to see you."

"Alec," I say. "Nice to see you, too. It's been a long time. You're well?" I say, always the master at small talk. A wedding planner has to be a good communicator, and I thank the Lord for my training.

Another tight nod. "Yes, you?"

"Never better," I say and give him my best smile despite the storm raging inside me.

He gestures with a nod to Amanda as she disappears out the door. "Am I interrupting? Granddad told me to be here for two."

"Two is correct and you're not interrupting at all. I was just meeting with Amanda to go over some details for the upcoming Bar Mitzvah I'm planning. She's a caterer. Perhaps you've heard of her business. Kitchen Door Catering, in Hell's Kitchen. I actually rent office space from her."

He gives a slow shake of his head. "Sorry, never heard of it."

I'm not surprised, really; making a name in Manhattan and competing with already established businesses that own the core market share is hard. I can throw money at the marketing budget all day, but the rich and famous prefer the status quo, and rarely give newbies like Amanda and me a chance. Any company used by James Carson, however, will become a household name and that's what I'm banking on.

Alec's gaze moves from my face to my near-empty coffee mug with pink lipstick staining the rim. "I'm going to grab a coffee. Can I get you anything?"

"That's my second cup. I'm already jittery," I say, a little breathless as he gazes at me with those mesmerizing blue eyes.

One brow raises. "Lemon-filled doughnut?"

Okay, now I really can't breathe. Why would he ask that, or even remember that? I open my mouth, but my damn voice is stuck in my tight throat, so I just shake my head no. He hesitates for a moment, and I take that opportunity to lower myself into my seat and dig my planner out from my bag. He smooths his hand over his tie again and turns, giving me a reprieve from his hot stare, and even hotter body. I take a fast breath and fuel my lungs. Honest to God, a man who had sex with me, and then walked away, shouldn't remember my favorite kind of doughnut, or my favorite kind of anything. Damn him for giving me a moment of hesitation, a seed of hope that he might have actually cared about me the night I gave myself to him.

I open my planner with a little too much force, grab my pen and scribble "Alec Carson" on the first blank page. I don't need to look up to know he's back at the table with his coffee. His presence, and the warm enticing scent of fresh soap and something uniquely Alec—a crisp new day after a hard summer rain—reaches my nostrils. My stomach squeezes slightly. I pinch my eyes shut for a second, to darken all the images that are clamoring to resurface. Alec is a world-class jerk, and I'm not going to waste a second remembering the way he touched me that night, with such deft, gentle hands. Or the way he talked to me, using sweet soothing words, as he *fucked* me. Over.

He sits, and my gaze goes to his big hands as he drinks his coffee. Still black, no sugar. Some things never change. Then again, some things do, and maybe that's for the best. I'm not sure I could work with him if I was still harboring a stupid schoolgirl crush.

Oh, but it was so much more than that, Megan.

"Okay," I say, shutting down that inner voice and working not to sound as breathless as I feel. "I want to be honest with you. I'm an event planner, not a matchmaker, but I'll do my very best to set up an appealing online profile for you and help find your soul mate." He goes perfectly still for a moment, and then he laughs, and the dark, jaded sound raises the hair on my neck. "What?" I ask.

"I'm not looking for a soul mate, Megan." He leans toward me. "I don't even believe in marriage."

I sit up a little straighter, and let my gaze roam his handsome face. Every visible muscle is strained, like an overtightened wire about to snap. "If you don't believe in marriage, what are we doing here?"

He goes quiet, thoughtful for a moment and takes a drink from his mug. He sets it on the table, leans back and folds thick arms over his chest.

"I'm here today because my aging grandfather won't stop breathing down my neck. He doesn't like my lifestyle, or my business practices. He says it's bringing a bad name to the Carson family. He wants me to clean up my act and marry a nice girl."

Appreciating his honesty, I tap my pen on my notepad and nod in understanding. The tabloids have been having a field day with Manhattan's most eligible bachelor. He's been photographed with different affluent women—far outside my social circle—on his arm every week. It can't be easy having no privacy.

Don't feel bad for him, Megan.

"I can understand that," I say.

He angles his head, a thick lock of hair falling forward, and I note that he's wearing it longer than usual. He rakes it back and asks, "Can you?"

"Sure," I say and glance at my planner. "But what I don't understand—"

His big warm hand closes over mine. The weight is heavy, and it takes my mind back to the way he once caressed me. Unnerved and aroused by his touch, my gaze flies to his. "It's like this, Megan. I'll get married, but it will be in name only. I'm not interested in anything more. A nice girl will get my granddad off my back, and the stability of marriage will look good to the board of directors who are handpicking Blackstone's next chief financial officer." My jaw drops open as he lays the cold, ugly truth out for me. So, this is what's in it for him? He would actually marry to better his position in the company. What kind of a man would do that? Perhaps the better question is, how did I not see this side of him all those years ago? I pull my hand back fast and wipe my palm on my skirt.

His eyes darken, the black bleeding into the blue as he zeros in on me. "If you have a problem with that…"

CHAPTER TWO

Alec

KEEP YOUR SHIT TOGETHER. *Play it cool. You've got this, Carson.*

Yeah, right!

I can lecture myself all I want, but I don't "got this." Not even a little bit.

I draw in a deep breath. "Do you?" I ask again, working to maintain a rigid, professional-like composure, despite the fact I'm telling the one woman I've always wanted but can never have what I want in a future wife.

How the hell did we end up here, negotiating a wife for me? Granddad, that's how. Now that my cousins Tate and Brianna are married, it was only a matter of time before he came after me. I'm not even sure the man's as weak and frail as he lets on. It could very well be a trick to get what he wants. But can I really take a chance and say no to him? He was there for me my whole life, stepping in to take the place of my dad—his son—when he up and left our family.

I want to make my grandfather happy, and if it means getting married… I clench down on my jaw with an audible click and grind my back teeth together.

I focus back on Megan. She's clearly shocked at what I'm telling her, struggling to digest my words. It takes every ounce of strength, and I mean every ounce I possess, not to press my lips to hers, lose myself in her sweet honeyed taste like I did on prom night.

You can't go there with her.

I stiffen my spine, present cold indifference like I do at every negotiation and study her tense body language. I might not have seen her in eight long years, but I know her well enough to know she's trying to wrap her mind around my need for a loveless marriage. Only problem is, I can't tell her the real truth.

"I… I suppose not." She blinks a few times, picks up her empty cup and sets it down again. "I mean, it's your life." She shrugs. "But I'm not so sure you're going to find a woman who would want a marriage in name only."

I let loose a low, deep humorless laugh. It gives me great pleasure to see that after all these years, little Megan Williams is still as sweet and innocent as the day I met her. I don't ever want her to change, which is one of the reasons I need to keep my hands and mouth to myself. I'm the last guy she needs in her life.

Where the hell was that resolve on prom night?

"You're wrong about that," I say.

Quizzical eyes that once looked at me with adoration narrow, and her thick lashes fall slowly, only to open again. "What makes you say that?"

"Women like power and are influenced by wealth. I'm willing to give whoever we pick exactly that. They can have it all, the money, jets and lifestyle, with the exception of my heart. That's not on the negotiation table."

"What…what about intimacy," she blurts out, then slams her mouth shut and glances around to see if anyone overheard her.

I lean toward her, note the pink flush crawling up her slender neck, pooling on the exact spot I'd like to place my mouth. I take a moment to look her over. At eighteen she was sweet and adorable, but she's grown more beautiful in the passing years. Prominent cheekbones, beautiful full lips, a body any man would kill for. Perfect then, and even more so now.

"Intimacy? Are you asking if I plan to have sex with my wife?"

She takes a deep breath, and as her chest heaves, my gaze slides downward, to her silky white blouse. From my height, and with the top two buttons undone, I'm gifted with a view of her creamy cleavage. I don't deserve to look. Don't deserve anything from her. Despite that knowledge, heat prowls through my blood, and my dress pants become increasingly uncomfortable.

"People…well, people have needs," she whispers.

I lower my voice to match hers. "True, and I'm not ruling sex out, but right now I have other concerns."

"Such as?"

"I'm used to living alone. I need a woman who won't be underfoot in my home. She must be intelligent, likable and a good conversationalist since she'll be attending dinners with board members." She stares at me for a moment, disbelief and a measure of repulsion evident in her big doe eyes. Good, that's the only way I can have her look at me, otherwise… "Perhaps you should be writing this down."

"Oh, right." Her pen flies over the blank pages as she fills it with my criteria. She taps the tip on her chin when done, and stares at her notepad. "Do you care if she works?"

"I'd like for her to have her own life. She won't need to work, but if she chooses to stay home, I'd like to see her involve herself in charitable work." Her eyes lift. "It will look better to the board," I say. Yeah, I get it. I'm coming off like a grade A prick, but that's what I want. That's what I need. If this woman gives me so much as a seed of encouragement, a hint that she might still want me, I could very well lose my shit. I can't—won't—let that happen. She deserves better than that. She deserves better than me.

Last week, when Granddad took me to his study

and plied me with brandy, I knew he was up to something. I agreed to his terms, saw the truth in his words. Sure, I come from wealth, but I want to make my own mark in the financial world, want to become Blackstone's youngest CFO. A wife will help with that and help with my reputation, which will hopefully get the damn paparazzi off my back—Christ knows they destroyed my brother, Will, who is fulfilling the Carson prophecy. But until I walked into this café, I had no idea I'd be facing Megan Williams. The old man never prepared me for her, and I can't help but think he left the event planner's name out on purpose. Smart man, because had I known I'd be coming face-to-face with the sweet girl I screwed over in high school, I never would have agreed to any of this.

I'll never forget the day I met her. It was the summer before our senior year. I was friends with her cousin Sara Duncan, and after Megan's parents died in a car accident, she moved from Philadelphia to Manhattan to live with her aunt and uncle, who are friends of Granddad's. Sara introduced us, and just like that I was lost in her and trying hard to keep it platonic. We were pretty inseparable for the rest of the year, then prom night. Jesus, prom night in St. Moritz. She knocked on my door, and when I opened it…

"Alec?"

Shit.

"Sorry, what?"

"If I'm going to fill out your online profile, I have to know what kind of woman you're attracted to."

Ah. I need to be careful here. My gaze rakes over Megan, and the frizzy state of her auburn hair, my absolute favorite color. It brings a smile to my face. She always hated it when it rained, but I think her wild locks are adorable. With light brown eyes—the color of a root beer Popsicle—fair skin clear of makeup, save for her pink lipstick, she still has that same girl-next-door look going on.

And that, my friends.

Right there.

Is the kind of woman I'm attracted to.

"I prefer blonde," I say, and as she nods her head, her drying auburn locks bouncing, she jots it down.

She plants her elbow on the table and rests her chin in her palm. She goes thoughtful for a long time, then blinks her eyes back into focus. "Can I ask something?"

"Yes, but it doesn't mean I'm going to answer," I say, wanting to be as honest with her as possible, but there are some things I just can't divulge.

"You date all the time. Thanks to the tabloids, I see the gorgeous women on your arm. Why not one of them? If it's to be a loveless marriage, and you think women want you for power and money, and they're probably on your arm because of that, why not just ask one of them to marry you?"

It's a legit question that deserves an honest answer. I might be a tough negotiator, but deep down

I do have morals and I respect integrity as much as the next guy. With Megan, though, I have to be less than forthright with this answer, for her own good.

"The women from my circle aren't suitable for what I need."

"How so?"

"They're glamorous, over-the-top, high mainte-nance."

"So, you're looking for a sweet girl next door?"

"Yeah."

"The kind of girl you're not really attracted to," she says, her voice so low I have to strain to hear it. But before I can answer—and I have no idea how to respond—she blinks up at me. "Does eye color matter?"

I finish my coffee and check the time. If I'm going to have a nice girl in my home, her appearance at least must be the antithesis of Megan's. Otherwise the daily reminder of what I want and can never have would drive me over the edge. "No, but I do prefer blue."

I watch her throat work as she swallows, and my insides twist. Jesus, that sad look she's trying to hide is ripping me wide-open. Hurting her is the last thing I want to do. But it's also killing me that she looks at me with distaste. Maybe I should put a stop to this. End it now before we go any further.

"Megan," I say.

"Yes."

"Look at me," I command in a soft whisper. Her

eyes slowly lift, lock on mine, and as she stares, a bolt of need grips my chest. I fight it down and ask, "Do you really want to do this? We have a history."

She takes one deep breath, lets it out slowly and lowers her pen. "And that's exactly what it is, a history." The chirpiness is her voice contrasts the visible pain in her eyes. "It's all in the past, where it needs to stay. We're both adults and both professionals and it comes down to this—you're not the only one getting something out of this. You see, Alec, once I find you a wife and throw you the best damn wedding Manhattan has ever seen, I'll be the talk of the town. It will get my business off the ground in a crowded market and skyrocket me into prominence."

"I guess we're both doing this to get ahead, then?" I say.

Her brows knit together. "When you put it that way." She casts her eyes downward for a second. "Looks like we're not so different after all. I'm scratching your back and you're scratching mine, so to speak."

"Tit for tat." As soon as the words leave my mouth, my gaze once again goes down to take in the curve of her breasts. I catch a hint of white lace, and my dick thickens. I want her. I've always wanted her. But am I going to do anything about it? No fucking way. Being around her might just kill me, and I'm going to need a drink, or an entire bottle, by the time we're done here. Because now that I know what's in it for her, I can't walk away and find another event planner. I clear my throat. "Is there anything else you want to know?"

She instantly switches back into professional mode and pulls a laptop from her bag. She sets it between us and boots it up. "Are there any particular dating sites you prefer?"

"Never been on one."

She clicks a few buttons. "I've not had much luck myself—"

"You use dating sites?" Why the hell would a woman like Megan need to use a dating site? She must have men falling at her feet.

"I have in the past," she admits.

I pinch the bridge of my nose, and glance at the barista, anything to keep my mind off Megan in bed with another man. I have no hold on her. She can date any guy she likes, but goddammit, the thought of any man's hands but mine on her still bothers me. Eight years later.

"I see the ads for that Match Made in Heaven site all the time," I say. "Should we try that?"

"It's a good jumping-off point. If we don't get any matches, we can set you up elsewhere. Although I'm sure you'll have a million matches in the first hour."

"What makes you think that?"

"Look at you," she blurts out. Her gaze moves from my chest to my face. "Ah, I mean, you're not bad to look at, and you're successful. All we need is a catchy bio. Let's have a look at it, see what other criteria I might need before I set you up." She points to the seat beside her. "Why don't you sit here, so we can look at the screen together."

"Coffee first. We might be here for a while. Do you want something?"

Her gaze slides to her empty cup. "I guess I'll have another mocha latte."

She reaches for her purse, but I hold my hand up to stop her. "I got it," I say and walk away, needing a moment to pull myself together before I sit close to her.

I order our drinks, and as the barista makes them, I grab a lemon-filled doughnut and a piece of cheesecake. I press my Apple Watch to the payment terminal and hold until it vibrates. After the charge goes through, I carry the sweets to our table.

She shakes her head. "I didn't want—"

"They're for me. I came here straight from the gym and I'm starving. The barista will bring our coffee over."

I lower myself into the seat next to her, and her sweet scent reaches my nose. I devour her with my eyes and throw up a silent prayer. Sweet mother of God, give me strength. Her gaze goes from the pastries, to my fork. Her eyes narrow in on the silverware, and her fingers curls into fists.

"You got something against my fork?" I ask.

"No." She shakes her head as if to clear it. "I was just remembering my mom's Philly cheesecake," she adds, and I get the sense she's redirecting the conversation. "Best in the world, and that's not a very healthy choice for after the gym," she says.

I grin at her. "Yeah, I know, Mom."

"Not funny," she says, and crinkles her nose, those cute freckles bunching together.

"I know but remember when we used to go to my place after school and raid the fridge before dinner. Mom used to—"

"Chase us into your bedroom with her broom, warning we were going to ruin our appetites," she pipes in, finishing my sentence, much like we used to do years ago. "But we were always hungry back then."

We both laugh, but it sizzles out fast, the space between us going perfectly quiet.

"Yeah," I say after a moment, breaking the silence.

"Yeah," she repeats, and then angles her head to glance at my clothes as the barista delivers the coffee. "You put a suit on after the gym?"

"Mmm-hmm." I pick up the doughnut and take a big bite. "Damn, that's good."

"Do you always wear a suit? Everywhere?"

"Yes, always. Except in the gym, the shower or in bed." I wink at her. "I like casual sex, and wearing a suit to bed just makes it formal," I say and wonder what the fuck I'm doing. I shouldn't be teasing her, flirting with her.

Her cheeks darken. "Well, some dates will be more casual than others. What if you go skydiving, or to the movies, or even a romantic hansom cab ride around Central Park?"

"When was the last time you took a horse ride around Central Park?" I ask.

"Ah, well. Never. It's something I've always wanted to do, but I'm not dating right now, and we're talking about you, not me."

A thrill I don't want to feel races through me. "Are you trying to say you want to dress me, Megan?"

"If that's what it takes to find you a wife, then yes. I want complete control."

Megan in bed, completely in control. Yeah, that visual is helping my cock. I take another bite of the doughnut and moan as I hold it out to her. "Try it."

She stares at it for a moment, and her mouth goes slack. "It does look good."

"It is good."

I hold it closer and she bites into it. Her lids close and lemon oozes from the doughnut as powdered sugar gets all over her face and nose.

I chuckle. "You always were a messy eater." I reach out, brush my thumb over her cheek.

She draws in a fast breath, and my hand freezes. Jesus, how can I do this? How can I spend the next month, possibly the next two, with this woman, without giving in to the things I feel?

I'll be fucked if I know, but somehow I have to find a way.

CHAPTER THREE

Megan

"He sounds like quite the asshole. I think you dodged a bullet after prom. I know it didn't feel like it then, but he did you a solid by walking away," Amanda says, as we toss our damp towels over our shoulders and walk through the gym to the locker rooms.

I nod in agreement and take in the near-empty establishment. I guess it being a Friday night and all, people have better things to do than sweat it out. Although I can think of other, more fun ways to get in a workout. *Good Lord, Megan. Get your thoughts out of the gutter.* It's just that it's been so long since I've been physically touched by a man. I'm sure that's the only reason my body is all amped up. Yeah, it has nothing to do with coming face-to-face with Alec last week.

Liar.

I wonder what he's doing on this Friday night, which glamorous, high-maintenance woman he has on his arm, and whose bed they'll be falling into later. The sooner I get him married, the better it is for my business—and for my sanity. But the questions on the Match Made in Heaven questionnaire that goes with his profile are very personal, and we'll need to fill it out together when he's back from his business trip. I don't know *this* rigid, detached Alec. He's far different from the boy back in high school. Heck, if answering the questions were left to me, he'd probably be matched to a hungry hyena with a toothache.

I snort at that and step into the change room with Amanda.

"Pajamas, romantic comedy and popcorn tonight?" she asks.

"There is no other way I'd want to spend tonight, and no one I'd rather spend it with," I say, and she rolls her eyes.

"I love you, too, but I'm sorry, Megan. I'd take a nice fat dick on a Friday night over a rom-com and popcorn at home, anytime."

I burst out laughing and glance around, but the few women getting changed still have their earbuds in and are paying us zero attention. "Okay, me, too," I admit and instantly hate myself when my thoughts stray to Alec again. Inside my bag, my phone pings, and I dig it out. My heart does a stupid little tumble when the display informs me that it's none other than the man plaguing my thoughts.

Alec: I'm free tonight to plug the holes in the questionnaire. My place, eight?

Swallowing, I tense up and Amanda leans over to see who the message is from. "Hmm," she begins, "Friday night, his place. Sounds like it's not just the holes in the questionnaire he's interested in plugging."

My gaze flies to hers, and I catch her smirk. "Not funny and not going to happen. Not in a million years."

Amanda hikes her bag over her shoulder and blows a wet strand of hair from her forehead. "Whatever you say."

"He doesn't like me that way." I laugh but it comes out sounding like a wounded animal on crack. "I'm actually the complete opposite of the women he's attracted to. Which is fine, because I have zero interest in him either."

"Good, because he hurt you once, and I don't want you to set yourself up for that kind of disaster now that you know what kind of man he is." We push through the locker room door.

"I won't. Fool me once, fool me twice. I get it." We walk through the gym, and step out into the warm spring night. Flowers growing in pots outside the storefronts reach my nostrils and we walk down the sidewalk, passing numerous up-and-coming restaurants on the way to our apartment building.

"If he hurts you in any way…" She stops and

makes scissor motions with her hands. "I will give him an up close view of his farm parts."

"Farm parts?" I laugh and shake my head. Not hard to tell she grew up in Texas's cattle country.

"That's right. Otherwise known as gonads around these parts," she says in her best Texas accent.

I laugh and shake my head. "He can't hurt me if I feel nothing for him. I guess his farm parts are safe."

"Good." She gestures with a nod to the phone in my hand. My God, I'm gripping it so hard my knuckles are turning white. "Now, are you going to answer him, or what?" she asks.

I lift the phone and text back.

Megan: Just finished working out. I'll hit the shower and come over.

Alec: What's your address? I'll send a car.

Am I really doing this? Am I giving the man my address, so he can send a car to drive me to his place, where we'll be all alone? My stomach jumps like I've just eaten a handful of Mexican jumping beans. I give him my address and shove my phone into my bag as we make our way inside. We take the stairs to the second floor, and I give Amanda a hug.

"Movie and popcorn tomorrow night?" I ask.

"You bet, and I want all the details from tonight." She exits the stairwell and I climb to the next floor and enter the apartment right above hers. Amanda moved into this building in Hell's Kitchen a couple years ago, and now is walking distance to her work. When the apartment above hers became available, I jumped on it, and moved my business to one of the spare offices in her warehouse. It's nice to have my best friend close. We're there for each other at a moment's notice, plus she cooks for me all the time. A good thing, considering I'm pretty lousy at it, and she's an amazing chef who is always experimenting and in need of a guinea pig.

I step into my apartment, lean against the door. I probably shouldn't be going to Alec's place, and should have insisted we meet on neutral ground, but I don't want him to think he affects me in any way at all. This is a business relationship, and I plan to keep it that way. My bag rolls off my shoulder when I lean forward, bracing myself.

You got this, girl. All you're doing is finding a wife for the man you once loved. Easy peasy.

On that note, I pull myself up to my full height, and head to the bathroom for a hot shower, even though I should probably take a cold one. Since I have no idea how long his car will take, I soap up quickly and wash my hair. Once done, I give it a fast blow-dry, and pin it to the top of my head in an unflattering mess. I'm not out to impress the man. I'm out to get him married, so I can get my business off the ground.

As I make my way through my small apartment to my bedroom, I can't help but wonder why James

Carson insisted I was the *only* girl for the job. His words not mine. I hadn't seen the elderly gentleman in years, and really, how did he even know I was an event planner? He sold me on the job based on the fact that it would get my name out in the right circles, and while this is a once-in-a-lifetime opportunity, there is a part of this whole thing that just doesn't sit right with me.

I plan numerous weddings, and honest to God, I can tell within five minutes if the couple will make it past the first year. It kind of guts me when I know they won't. Yeah, it's true, I'm a romantic at heart. I want people to find love and live happily ever after. I honestly think there's someone for everyone.

I might not like Alec, but I hate that he doesn't believe in happily-ever-after and has no problem with a loveless marriage. What the hell happened to him over the years? Back in the day he was the sweetest guy, captain of the football team, and always the big brother to all the guys on the team and everyone in our social circle. I never once thought of him as a brother, though. Not even for a second. Which is why during prom in St. Moritz, compliments of a very generous James Carson, I showed up at Alec's hotel room door with nothing but a sexy silk nightie on under my coat. We were friends, close as two people could get, and not once had he tried anything sexual with me. I'd decided to make the first move. Heck, maybe he slept with me out of pity, or had too much to drink. All I know is in the morning, he barely spoke to me, and that summer he made himself invisible before he left for Harvard. Maybe all the blame isn't on him, though. I'm the one who read the situation all wrong. Clearly an intimate relationship wasn't what he wanted, and my stupid actions ended up ruining a good friendship.

But my God, the way he touched me that night, the heated kisses, hungry caresses and a soft touch to soothe the pain that turned to pleasure as he took my virginity. For a brief second I think about running to my room to use my vibrator, but my doorbell chimes.

Dammit.

I tug on a pair of yoga pants and a comfy Taylor Swift T-shirt, then swipe a streak of pink across my lips. I give myself a once-over in the mirror, grab my purse and laptop bag, and head for my door. I retrace my steps down the stairwell and find a tall man dressed in a suit at the security door, both hands clasped behind his back as he rocks back and forth.

"Megan Williams?" he asks when I step outside.

"Yes, that's me," I say, and he holds his hand out and gestures to the sleek, black limousine with its back door open.

"Right this way, Miss Williams," he says with a smile that instantly puts me at ease. The man has a warm, fatherly presence about him, which suddenly has me missing my own. I was fortunate that my aunt Jeannie—my mom's sister—and Uncle Dave took me in after my folks died in the car accident. And while I grew close to my cousin Sara, we're like sisters today, it was never the same as having my own family. I miss that. I want that. Unfortunately, I've been working harder, and dating less. I'm not sure there are any decent guys left in Manhattan.

"Call me Megan." I make my way down the stairs and take in the shiny vehicle that costs more than I make in a year. Yeah, Alec and I really do come from different worlds. But he isn't so different from my adopted family. Uncle Dave is a very successful stockbroker and his family lived a completely different lifestyle than mine. I slide into the backseat. Alec was so kind and caring back then, and there were nights when I was incredibly sad, and Alec and I would text for hours. There was even that one time when he snuck in through my window, held me in my bed while I cried for the loss of my folks.

I swallow down the memories and stare at traffic as the driver takes me to Alec's home. Close to thirty minutes later, we're in New York's Upper East Side. The car slows in front of a luxury Manhattan apartment. Staring out the window, I crane my neck but can't see the top of the building.

The driver takes me to the front entrance, and before I can reach for the handle to let myself out, he's right there, opening the door for me. It feels a little odd to a girl who's used to taking care of herself.

"Thank you," I say. Wait, do I tip him? Cripes, I'm a little out of my element here. I reach for my purse, but he gives me a nod and waves his hand toward the doorman, who seems to be waiting for me.

"The concierge will take you from here," he says.

"Thank you. I didn't get your name?"

His head rears back, just slightly, like my interest in him has taken him by a surprise. Perhaps the women Alec normally has chauffeured to his apartment don't bother chitchatting with the help.

"Phillip Andrews," he says.

"It was nice to meet you, Phillip," I say.

He takes my hand in his and closes both of his palms over it. "The pleasure was all mine, Megan."

He lets me go, and I walk up the marble stairs leading to the massive front entrance. "Hi, I'm Megan Williams," I say when I reach the middle-aged man, with a big toothy smile. I hold my hand out, and he shakes it. "I'm here to see Alec Carson, and Phillip said you'd be taking me from here."

"That's right, Miss Williams, please come in."

"Call me Megan, and you are?"

"I'm Derek," he says, and pulls open the big glass door.

"Nice to meet you, Derek."

"You, too," he says with a nod. "Alec has been expecting you. I trust your drive was pleasant."

"Very," I say, and follow him into the spacious lobby tastefully decorated with glass and chrome that gives the place a welcoming, airy feel. We step onto the waiting elevator, and he puts a key in, and presses the top floor.

"Beautiful night," I say to Derek.

"Spring is here," he says, tugging at the lapels on his black jacket. "My favorite time of year."

"I'm a fall girl," I say. "Sweaters, lattes, falling leaves."

"Tourists," he laments, and we both laugh as the elevator opens on the top floor. "Here we are." He waves his hand and I glance out to find Alec outside his suite waiting for me.

Leaning against the doorjamb, feet crossed at the ankle, he's dressed in a pair of jeans and a comfy-looking blue T-shirt that brings out the color of his eyes. A dressed-up Alec is one thing, but this comfortable, laid-back version has my stupid ovaries doing the *macarena*. He has the sex appeal of a hot fudge brownie delight with a cherry on top, and here I am wishing I had a big spoon.

"Megan," he says, his deep octave throbbing through me and settling at the needy juncture between my legs. "No problems getting here?"

"None whatsoever. Phillip was very nice, and so was Derek."

I turn to see Derek off and give him a little finger wave. He nods before the doors ping shut, locking the world out, and Alec and me in.

"Phillip and Derek," he says. "You know their names?"

I face Alec, and once again I'm blasted with a bolt of lust I wish I didn't feel. "Yes," I mumble.

He swipes his tongue over his bottom lip, his gaze

leaving my face, to take in my T-shirt and yoga pants. In turn, I examine him. "You're not in a suit."

He arches one dark brow, and that's when I notice his hair has been cut. Long or short, he's as handsome as ever. "And you're very observant."

"Did I catch you showering, sleeping or having sex?" I ask.

His grin is so goddamn sexy I reach out and place my hand on the wall to maintain a vertical position. "Well, we might as well be comfortable while going through the forms. I dressed for comfort," I say, and wave my hand over my clothes.

He glances the length of me again and makes a sound. For a brief second I think it might be a moan, but I have to be mistaken. Right? I stash that thought to examine it later as he pushes off the frame and waves his hand to the open door behind him. "Are we doing this in the hall, or do you want to come in?"

Doing this in the hall.

Get it together, Megan. He is not talking about sex.

He turns to his side, and I slide past him, trying to ignore his enticing scent and the heat of his body as I step into his beautiful penthouse suite. I resist the urge to give a low, slow whistle. The door closes and as the lock clicks into place behind me, a warm shudder moves through my body.

"Cold?" Alec asks, mistaking my reaction. "I can turn on the fire."

My gaze goes to the propane fireplace that separates the living room from the kitchen, glass on both sides. "I'm okay, thanks." I scan his place, and take in the amazing view of the Hudson River, the mosaic of stars suspended over the New Jersey skyline. His place looks like it's been professionally decorated in cool grays, and the only homey touches are a picture frame on one of his side tables with a plant beside it. His mother had a lot of plants in the house when he was growing up, but Alec doesn't strike me as the type of guy who could keep one alive. Maybe the designer insisted on it, and his housekeeper waters it or something.

I step up to the table, pick up the frame and smile as I take in a young Alec in his Harvard graduation robe, his arm thrown over his younger brother, Will. Alec has a smile on his face, but it doesn't quite reach his eyes, and for some reason that just doesn't sit right with me. Does he ever laugh anymore, like we used to do when we were teens? God, the times we laughed until we cried. My heart pinches, missing those times.

"How is Will?" I ask, a stupid hitch in my voice as I turn to face Alec. Last I remember was seeing a picture of him in the tabloids in bed with a woman who wasn't his fiancée.

He stares at me a long time before answering. "He's well."

"And your mom? How is she?" I miss his mom. She was always so kind to me, welcoming me into their home, treating me like the daughter she always wanted and never had.

He scrubs his chin. "Mom is well. She stays busy with her charity work. How is Sara, and your aunt and uncle?" he asks.

"Good," I say. "When was the last time you saw Sara?" I ask. They both went to Harvard and maintained their friendship there. I was sure Sara had a thing for him, and there was a time I thought they'd become a couple. Who knows, maybe they did hook up on campus. Then again, Sara is an oversharer about such things and would likely have told me. I never did tell her about what happened on prom night. I was too mortified.

"A few months back. Is she still with Edward and Smith Law Firm?"

"She is. Working hard to make partner," I say, and I'm about to switch the conversation back to him and ask about his dad, but I'm not sure if I should. He left when Alec and Will were young. The guys maintained a relationship with him, but it was strained. How could it not be? He left for a much younger woman. I take in the tension in Alec's body, and sense he wants to get down to business. Ending my trip down memory lane, I turn and place the picture back down.

"Where should we set up?" I ask, and spin back around to find Alec standing right there, so close all I'd have to do is go up on my toes if I wanted to kiss him. Which I don't. At all.

"Why not right here," he says, his voice hoarse, an octave lower as he points to the sofa facing the hearth.

"Okay." I step around him, and plop down on the comfy gray sofa. I set my purse on the floor and tug my laptop from the bag. "These questions are going to take forever, so you might as well make yourself comfortable. We could be here all night." I tuck my legs underneath myself and glance up at Alec. The intensity in his eyes as they roam over my body sends a spark of need rocketing through me. What the hell is going on here? If I didn't know better, I'd think he likes what he sees. But I do know better.

He clears his throat. "I'm going to need a drink." He disappears into the other room, comes back with two glasses. One with white wine, and one with brandy. He swirls the amber liquid in the crystal, and I chuckle softly.

"Something funny?"

"You're so much like your grandfather. You have a lot of the same mannerisms. He swirls his brandy like that and you both have a habit of smoothing down your tie. I noticed you doing that at the café last week."

"Tate does it, too. So does Will. Granddad's clearly rubbed off on all of us." He smiles. "But you always were a people person. Not much gets by you. I'm sure that's what makes you an amazing event planner."

I beam at the compliment. "I am an amazing event planner. It helps when you love what you do."

He hands me the glass of wine. "I like that you own your successes and don't apologize. No point in being modest."

"You own your successes, too," I say, as I recall an article in *Forbes*. He's a financier who restructures businesses and makes no apologies. "Do you like what you do?" I ask.

He eyes me for a moment. "Do you think I'm the big bad wolf, Megan?"

"I never said that."

"You didn't have to, and if you do, you'd be right. I'm not a nice guy."

He might make deals that destroy businesses and people's lives, but I'm not here to insult the man. I'm here to get him married. Changing topics, I sip the wine and the tart flavor bursts on my tongue. "This is delicious."

"Dry, the way you like."

My pulse leaps in my throat. "You remember that?"

"I remember everything," he says, and as he lowers himself beside me, I can't help but think his thoughts have gone to the same place mine have. To the night I seduced him.

I take another sip of wine, stalling before I have to speak, since I'm sure my voice is about to fail me again. "Mmm," I say. I turn on my computer and pull up the profile I began last week. "If we want to match you with the right woman, you have to answer honestly."

"I always try to be honest, and I'm not looking for the right woman," he says, those blue eyes roaming my face, and for the briefest of seconds I wish I were her. Wish I were the right woman for Alec Carson. I practically snort as that stupid thought goes through my head. "I'm looking for a *suitable* woman, remember?"

"You won't at least try?" I say as I shift to face him, legs tucked securely underneath me. "I think everyone has a match, and true love really does exist. You just have to be open to it."

The muscles in his neck bunch as he rolls his shoulders, like the strain of the week is sitting heavily on top of them.

"I'm not open to it," he says, his voice so firm and adamant, it instantly shuts down my rebuttal. "Let's get at this."

Disappointment courses through me but I shove it down. This is Alec's life not mine and if he's against love and marriage, who am I to try to change things. "Okay."

Beside me, he shifts and his leg rubs against my knee as he stretches out and crosses his ankles. He swirls the brandy and takes another drink. The liquid settles on his bottom lip and all I can think about is licking it off. Except he does it for me, and I want to tangle our tongues, taste the brandy from his mouth. A bolt of heat moves through me and I tear my gaze away, try to read the words before me as my stupid libido kicks into high gear.

"Okay, the first set of questions is to generally describe your personality."

"Go on."

"You have three choices for your answers—*not at all*, *somewhat* or *very*." He nods, and I continue with "Bossy?"

He grins, and I click *Very*.

"I'm pretty sure I could have gotten that one right," I say, and rest my head against the sofa pillow. "Remember that time we went to King's Palace amusement park?"

He nods, and looks at the big window, like his thoughts are a million miles away. "It was right after you moved in with Sara."

"You gathered up a few of your football friends, and we all went for the day." He turns back to me and the smile that comes over his face is so genuine and happy, my pulse leaps. As I look at Alec now, I see the boy from my youth. I relax on the sofa and take another sip of my wine. I place it on the table and laugh. "You were so bossy. The guys all wanted to hit the race cars, but you said no, and we did every other ride in the park until it closed and it was too late for any of us to ride."

"Megan," he says, the smile falling fast from his face, a look of horror moving in to take its place. "You'd just lost your parents in a car accident. I couldn't let…what if it reminded…"

"Oh, my God," I say under my breath as the room spins around me. "I… I didn't realize." My heart crashes so hard against my chest, breathing becomes difficult. He did that…for me. "That was so…" Tears prick my eyes and I fight them off. "So considerate of you."

He shrugs like it was nothing.

"The guys were so pissed off," I say, my voice breaking a little. "I thought for sure Dillon Fraser was going to rip you a new one."

"I'd rather that over you…"

"I had no idea." I swallow down the lump in my throat. "Thank you."

He finishes off his brandy and pushes to his feet. "Wine refill?" he asks, and averts his eyes.

"Yeah, sure," I say, certain I'm going to need more alcohol to get through this. "But I'm a lightweight."

"I know." He picks my glass up and leaves, and I press my palms to my eyes hard enough to make me see stars, before I cry over the loss of a young, thoughtful boy who used to watch out for me. He comes back and hands me the wine. I take a huge gulp and find him studying me carefully as I set it on the coffee table.

"You've been asking all the questions, but I have one of my own," he says.

"What?" I ask, unease moving through me.

"Why are you still single?"

Way to get right to the point.

"Well, you see, Alec. There are two kinds of people in this world, those who like Neil Diamond and those who don't." I bite back a grin, and wait for him to get it. When a wide smile splits his lips, we both burst out laughing and the sound is music to my ears.

"How many times did we watch that movie," he says.

"What About Bob?" I shake my head. "It definitely was our go-to movie."

Our laughter dies down, and he turns serious again. "You still want it all don't you. The family, kids, white picket fence."

"You say it like it's a bad thing."

"It's just that it's not for me."

He reaches behind his head and squeezes the back of his neck, and I want to ask why it's not for him, but I don't. When we were young, we shared our hopes and dreams, but having a family of his own was never something he talked about. That didn't mean I didn't think he wanted one, though. I just assumed it wasn't something guys talked about. But I guess in the end it just solidifies that we want different things and would never work out.

"You deserve that, Megan," he says in a voice so soft it wraps around my heart and hugs tight. While we might be different now, he was the one guy who got me, the one guy who understood I needed a family of my own. I can't replace the one I'd lost, but I needed something that was just mine.

"I'm not seeing it happening anytime soon," I say,

and give an exaggerated sigh. "I work long hours and I've pretty much given up dating."

"You haven't been with anyone in a long time?" he asks, quietly.

"No," I say, and look away.

"It's nothing to be embarrassed about. Guys are assholes, I get it."

That makes me laugh. "Takes one to know one," I reply, teasing him with something we used to say when we were young.

"Hey, I resemble that comment."

This time we both laugh, hard, and if I close my eyes really tight, I can almost pretend we're back at his childhood home, hanging out in his bedroom.

But we're not, and I'd be wise to remember this isn't the Alec I once loved.

My heart thuds as I blink up at him. A second passes, then another, and then my laptop fan kicks in, pulling me back. I take a calming breath. "We better keep going," I say, getting the night back on track. I quickly go over the rest of the traits, and avoid reminiscing, even though many of his answers bring back warm memories.

Alec shifts, moving a little farther down on the sofa. "Okay, now we're on to how skilled you are at things."

"Then we're done, right?"

I snort. "No, we have a million more things to answer."

He sighs. "You're right. We are going to be here

all night. In that case, how about a pizza, extra pineapple even though pineapple belongs nowhere near a pie?"

I laugh. He used to tease me about that so much when we were teens. "We don't have to get pineapple. You don't like it."

"Yeah, but it could quite possibly be the only nutritious thing I've put in my mouth today."

At the mention of putting things in his mouth, my nipples tingle, and another wave of heat rushes up my neck. Alec's gaze drops to my pinkening flesh, no doubt aware that my thoughts might not be so pure. I bite back a groan, and work for casual when I say, "You used to be so health conscious back when you were playing football." My gaze travels the length of him. "Not that your current diet isn't working for you."

"I work out, try to stay fit, but there isn't much time for eating healthy."

"My best friend Amanda is a chef, remember. We can set you up with healthy meals delivered right to your door."

He gives me a look I can't quite decipher and for a minute I wonder if I'm overstepping boundaries as an event planner/matchmaker. "Not a bad idea," he finally says, and pulls out his phone. He punches a bunch of buttons, and gestures with a nod to my computer. "Pizza will be here in thirty minutes. Next question."

Okay, clearly he wants to get this over with. For

the next half hour we run through the questions, and when a knock comes on his door, I pinch my strained eyes shut for a brief second to give them a break. Alec pushes off the sofa, and his hard body holds my gaze as he pulls his wallet from his back pocket and crosses the wide expanse of polished wood floor. I stand and stretch out my limbs.

A moment later he comes back with the pizza and drops the box onto the coffee table. The smell reaches my nose and I give a low moan. When I look up, I find him standing perfectly still, lips pinched tight, his Adam's apple bobbing as he swallows.

I open my mouth to ask if he's okay, when he bends and flips the box open. "Mario's does great pizza."

"I've never had it," I say, letting my question go as I look at the huge pineapple-filled pizza.

"It's my go-to place. Dig in." He waits until I pull a cheesy slice free, and then he grabs one for himself. We both plop back down on the sofa, a little closer this time, and I bite into my slice. I chew and swallow.

"This is so good."

"Told you."

I make a few more moaning sounds and note the way Alec is shifting uncomfortably beside me. Maybe he has that disorder I recently heard about. What was it called? Misophonia. Yeah, that's it. A hatred of sounds that causes negative emotions, even violence. I stop moaning, and chew as quietly as I can. Heck, I don't want to be the one getting a fork in the eye. I wash my slice down with my wine, and the next thing I know my glass is half full again. A yawn pulls at me, but I stifle it. I want to finish this form here and now. Another hour in his apartment just might do me in.

"Another?" he asks.

"Pizza after the gym, now that's conducive to staying fit."

"You're perfect, Megan."

Perfect? Alec thinks I'm perfect?

Okay, maybe the alcohol is getting to him, and to me. Last time I had too much, I took my clothes off for this man.

I finish off a second slice and wipe my mouth with the napkins. "Should we get started again?" He nods. "Okay, now we're on to, 'How well do each of the following describe you?'"

"Can't wait," he says, and I laugh.

"You answer with *not at all*, *somewhat* or *very*."

"Got it."

"First one—you tell your partner everything. How well does that describe you?"

He goes quiet for a moment and my mind goes back to all the secrets we shared, all the hopes and dreams we only told one another.

"Very," he says, and I like his answer. A person should be open and honest with their partner.

"You are good at keeping secrets."

His hand goes to his jaw and he scrubs it roughly. "Very," he says.

"Me, too," I say under my breath.

"What?" he asks, and my gaze lifts to his.

He leans forward, finishes off his brandy. "Next question," he asks.

All righty, then.

"Monogamous," I say. "Answer with *not at all, somewhat* or *very*."

He jumps to his feet, and paces to the window. "Is this all really necessary?" he asks, his empty glass dangling by his side. He angles his head to see me.

I stand and go over to him to take in the skyline. "I… Yes, it's necessary," I say, his blue eyes burning through me. As my body turns traitorous, and I'm no longer able to hold his gaze, I turn my attention back to the sky and work to pull myself together. His glass hits the table, and the noise cuts through the deafening quiet.

"Megan."

I turn to face him, take in the stiffness of his posture. "Yes."

"It's late and you're tired." He leans toward me, and I wobble slightly, partly from the wine and partly from his close proximity. "Phillip has probably clocked out, and I don't want you in an Uber alone this time of night."

"I appreciate your concern, but I'm a big girl."

"I know that but why don't I just drive you home myself."

He's a big guy and the alcohol wouldn't have hit him like it's hit me, but I lost Mom and Dad in a drunk driving accident, and I'm sensitive about touching a single drop and getting behind the wheel. "We've been drinking," I say.

He pauses, and nods in understanding. "You're right. I'm sorry. I wasn't thinking. I never should have suggested that. I know how you feel about it, and I feel the same way." He rakes his teeth over his bottom lip as he takes a measured step closer to me. "I guess the only logical answer here is for you to sleep over."

CHAPTER FOUR

Alec

Sleep over?

Logical?

What the ever-loving fuck was I thinking? I wasn't—can't when she's around—and therein lies the problem. But how the hell can I be expected to have clear thoughts, or reason with any sort intelligence, after all our reminiscing. Not to mention the fact that I no longer have any blood left in my brain. Christ, hanging out with Megan like this, talking and laughing about old times and listening to her make those sweet moaning sounds that have been imprinted in my brain for eight long years, is preventing my synapses from firing.

"I…" she begins, looking about as flustered as I feel.

"I have lots of spare rooms," I say quickly. I don't want her to get the wrong idea here, or the right idea, or… As my blood rushes south, I have no idea what's right and wrong anymore, and so help me, if she gives me one sign, some tiny indication that she might want me to touch her, I'm not sure I have it in me to fight it. "I can call Phillip in the morning, or take you back myself," I say in a firm voice reserved for the boardroom, a reminder to us both that what's going on here is a business meeting and nothing more. "Whatever you prefer. Right now, I don't want you in an Uber alone, and why wake Phillip when we have other options."

She gives a wave toward her computer and stifles a yawn. "We didn't finish answering all the questions. I guess if I stayed over we could do it first thing in the morning. That will save travel time and help get the ball rolling sooner rather than later." She nods, like she's fully convinced and continues with, "I want to get you married as fast as we can this coming summer. A lot of women get engaged in the fall or at Christmas. I want my name to be the one on the tips of their tongues."

"Thinking like a true businesswoman. Then it's settled," I say, a knot in my stomach as the reality of what we're really doing—finding me a damn wife—comes crashing over me. I take a distancing step back before I do something I can only regret later. Something like pulling her into my arms, kissing her sweet mouth and making love to her until morning. "I have some clothes you can wear."

Her back goes straight and she frowns. "Alec, I

don't want to wear clothes that were left here by some woman you dated."

"And I wouldn't want you to either. I have some sweats that tie at the waist, and a T-shirt. It will be big on you, but should be okay to sleep in."

Relaxing slightly, the alarm leaving her pretty face as her doe eyes soften, she says, "Oh, okay, that will work. Thanks."

"For the record, I don't have women's clothes in my place. I've never brought a woman here before..." My home is my sanctuary, the one place where I can lock the world out and just be me, away from the watchful eyes of the paparazzi.

Manhattan's most eligible bachelor. What a load of shit.

She gives me a quizzical look, the freckles around her nose bunching. "I'm a woman."

"I know," I answer. Boy, do I ever know, but no need to go there with her. "Special circumstances and all, plus maybe it's a good idea for me to have a woman here, trying it out for size since our goal is to find me a wife."

The corners of her mouth turn up. "Looks like I'll be popping your cherry." Her brown eyes go wide. "Wait, I mean..."

"I know what you mean," I say, coming to her rescue.

Flustered, her chest rises and falls, and a few curls fall from the clip at the top of her head. Damned if she doesn't make that look sexy. My fingers itch to release that fastener, watch all those silky locks fall—over my pillow.

"My God, I don't know why everything is coming out wrong tonight," she says. "Must be the wine."

"Must be," I say, but I'm a negotiator, a man who reads others for a living, and right now, being alone in my place is fucking with her as much as it is with me, and I need to shut this shit down right now.

"I think I need sleep," she says, and the slight blush that forms on her cheeks has my dick thickening in my pants.

Uh, hello, pal. Didn't you just lecture yourself on shutting this shit down?

I take another measured step back to put distance between us. It's a start, but knowing she's in the next room, sleeping in my clothes, might call for a hot shower, and a little extracurricular activity under the spray. Otherwise I'll never get a wink of sleep, and I have some reports I need to go over in the morning, after we finish the ridiculous questionnaire. What's the point of it, anyway? No way am I going to find the perfect match, not when she's standing right before me and I can't have her. For as long as I've known Megan, she's had white picket fence all over her. She might still be single, and evaded my question on why that is, but she wants—needs—a family of her own. No one deserves it more than her, especially after everything she's been through.

A guy like me, well, I can't give that to her. The men in my family are unable to remain in a monogamous relationship. My father is still in my life since he left, as well as my younger brother, Will's—when he's not off honeymooning with a girl he'll eventually leave. Christ, that man goes through women faster than a drunk goes through one-dollar bills at a strip joint. The mess he made of my mother when he left still haunts me, and no way would I ever want to rip a woman apart like that.

Honestly, I can't even count how many times my father warned me I was just like him—that I didn't have monogamy in me. None of the Carson men do. The sad thing is, my mother said the same, and warned me to walk away from sweet Megan Williams before I hurt her because in the end it was inevitable.

I'm truly holding out hopes for my cousin Tate. He and his wife, Summer, do seem happy together, but the Carson track record is an ugly one. Megan herself said I remind her of Granddad. That man is still going strong in his nineties. I'm pretty sure he hooked up with his old friend Delilah when they reconnected at Tate and Summer's wedding in St. Moritz last summer. Although I really don't want to think too hard on that. At the end of the day, I'm a chip off the old block, unable to be faithful, and I'd never, ever put Megan through that. She's had enough to deal with in life already. It's better for her to think I'm a prick, a hard-assed businessman who isn't interested in love.

"Come on," I say, and she follows me down the

hall to my bedroom. She stays at the door, shifting from one foot to the other as I dig through my closet and come back with clothes for her.

"Thanks," she says. "You wouldn't happen to have a spare toothbrush."

"Yeah, in the bathroom off your bedroom. I keep it stocked for Will. Sometimes he crashes here. You should find everything you need." I walk her to the room beside mine and open the door for her.

She steps in and goes to the window with the view. "This is beautiful."

"Yeah," I say, but when she turns back, it's her I'm looking at. "Do you need anything else?"

She wraps her arms around her slim body and shakes her head. "I don't think so."

"Okay, you know where the kitchen is if you get hungry, and if you need anything through the night, you know where to find me."

I leave her alone to change and make my way to my own room, where I head straight for the shower. I strip off, run the water and climb into the hot spray. As it rains over me, and I envision Megan stripping down in the next room, I take my thick cock into my hand and stroke from base to crown. Hell, it might feel good, but the only thing that could make it better was if I was sliding into Megan with her moaning my name. I take a breath, brace one hand on the wall by the nozzle, and pump a couple more times until I shoot my cum into the stream. Feeling a measure of relief, I rinse off, dry my body and flop down into my bed.

I toss and turn, but sleep continues to elude me. A noise in the other room reaches my ears and I sit up and listen. I kick off my sheets, and tug on a pair of boxers. Is Megan trying to sneak out under the cover of darkness or does she need something? I push open my door, and pad quietly down the hall. When I round the corner, and find her curvy ass aimed my way as she bends over the coffee table, and tucks the tab into the cardboard pizza box, my cock instantly thickens.

"Megan," I say quietly.

She jumps and faces me, and my gaze drops to her breasts, her nipples precisely, and the sexy way they press against the worn material of my white T-shirt.

"Alec, you scared me."

"What are you doing?"

She picks her computer bag up from the floor. "I couldn't sleep, and I came out to get my laptop," she says quickly, her voice breathless, like she's been in my bed, and I've been doing dirty, delicious things to her body.

Get those thoughts out of your head, dude.

"I saw the pizza was still out, and thought I'd put the rest of it in the fridge. Nothing like cold, firm pizza for breakfast," she says, her edgy laugh stroking my balls.

I step up to her and pick up the cardboard box, my

hand brushes hers and she sucks in air. "You always had a thing for leftover pizza with cold cheese, and a firm crust. Must be a weird Philly thing," I tease. She whacks my stomach, and I capture her hand, bring it to my chest.

"It's…it's not weird, and it's not a Philly thing. A lot of people love leftover pizza," she says, her voice hitching as her body vibrates. I step closer, crowd her, brush my thumb over her wrist as I keep her hand pressed to my chest.

"I'm not one of those people. I don't get the appeal." I dip my head and focus in on her wet lips. I drop the box and put my thumb under her chin. Her lips part slightly, and that's exactly the kind of encouragement I want, or rather don't want.

"What's…what's not to get?" she asks, her chest rising and falling faster now, her sweet minty breath washing over my face.

I shrug. "I don't know. I guess I like warm things in my mouth."

Don't do this, Carson. Go the fuck back to your room.

Unable to stop myself, I let go of her hand to grip her small rib cage, and my thumb lightly brushes one hard nipple. "Oops, sorry."

I wait for a kick to the nuts, but instead, she lets loose a sexy moan that fuels the hunger in me. Goddammit, she's as responsive to my touch today as she was all those years ago.

"You asked a lot of questions tonight," I say,

"questions about myself and what I find important in a relationship."

"Yes," she says, and swipes her tongue over her bottom lip.

Want zings through me. "You never asked how I liked to have sex."

"I'm… I'm not sure it's on the form," she says, her eyes dimming with desire.

"What if it is? Some of those questions are pretty damn personal."

"True."

"What if I'm called to a business meeting tomorrow morning and I'm not able to help you finish the questions. The sooner we get this done, the better it is for both our careers, right?"

My gaze roams her face, takes in the need in her eyes. It wraps around my dick and squeezes. I've never needed a woman in quite the same way as I need her. But I should put a stop to this. I have to put a stop to this. I briefly pinch my eyes shut and pray for the strength to walk away.

"What are you suggesting, Alec?" she says in a soft, seductive whisper that nearly makes me come in my boxers.

Fuck me.

"That maybe I should show you." In this moment, as need zaps my balls, every reason I have for staying away from her vanishes into thin air. The only thing I know is if I don't get this woman into my bed this very second, I might just spontaneously combust. "You'll want to find someone who's compatible sexually, and this way you'll know what you're working with when vetting dates. It might speed up the process in matching me correctly."

"It's the logical thing to do," she murmurs, and I swipe her nipple a little harder, and widen her legs with my knee. The laptop bag in her hand falls with a thud and she moans as I shimmy closer, rub her sex with my thigh.

"When you moan like that… Jesus."

"You don't like it?"

I laugh and shake my head. "Oh, I like it. I like it a lot."

A sexy chuckle bubbles in her throat. "I thought you might have had misophonia."

I place my palms over her breasts, give them a little squeeze. This time she emphasizes the moan, and I like the way she's teasing me. "Mis-a-what?"

"Never mind," she whispers, her head rolling back as she moves on my leg, a slight rocking of her hips, enough to rub the swollen little cleft I can't wait to put in my mouth.

"I'm hungry, Megan," I growl into her ear.

"Pizza," she murmurs.

"Haven't we already established that I like to put warm things in my mouth," I say, my voice deeper, thicker, dripping with lust. "Any suggestions?"

Her body stiffens, and her eyes fly open. She pushes away from me, and in that moment, I get it. I hurt her in the past and my question just pulled her from her lust-induced state and snapped her back to her senses. Now she's having second thoughts and I don't blame her one bit. I was a stupid, needy prick for starting this in the first place.

She inches back, her eyes locked on mine, and I swallow as the gap of air between us cools. We stand there for a long time, our eyes locked like we're in a Mexican standoff. I want to speak, say something, do something, anything, but the next move has to come from her.

Her gaze drops to my caged erection, and a visible quiver moves through her body. After a few speechless moments of checking me out, her eyes slowly travel back to mine.

She grips the hem of her too big T-shirt. In one sexy movement she peels it over her head, gifting me with a view of her gorgeous, full breasts and hard pink nipples.

Sweet mother of God and all that is holy.

"Will these do?" she asks.

On that note, I take a labored breath, then another, and in two fast steps close the distance between us. I cup both breasts, revel in the softness of her skin and meet her heated gaze. "Yeah, these will definitely do," I say, and bend forward to take one turgid nub into my mouth. Our moans mingle, and she arches her back as her hands go around my almost naked body. She drags her nails down my arms, palms my muscles, and my dick jumps in my boxers.

The honeyed scent of her skin fills my senses as

her breast fills my ravenous mouth. Greedy man that I am, I suck hard, and widen my lips to take more, until she's writhing and crying out my name. I back off a bit, clench down on one nipple, and her cries of joy burst around me.

I lick and suck and eat at her like she's going to bolt at a moment's notice—leave me starved for another eight long years—but she doesn't. Instead she puts her hand on my cock and gives it a little squeeze.

I release her nipple and give it a soft lick to soothe the sting. Then I scoop her up, ready to make up for lost time, over and over again. I carry her to my bedroom and set her on my bed; she falls backward, and her auburn hair tumbles.

"Look at you," I murmur, taking pleasure in the sight of her. She's so goddamn sexy and I'm the luckiest guy on the planet.

The heat between us, the chemistry that has only grown stronger, flared brighter in our years apart, scorches the air we breathe. I drop to my knees in front of her, lean over her body and press my nose to her stomach, breathing her in. I missed the smell of her.

I go back on my heels, and she sits up, her breathing rough and ragged as she reaches for me, runs her fingers over my flesh. Raw hunger claws at my insides, and I take a breath, work to slow myself down. We both understand there can't be a tomorrow or a next week, we have opposite goals, but we have tonight, and I plan to take things slow, make it last well into the morning.

I untie the oversize sweats and grip the band. She goes back on her elbows and lifts her hips for me. I tug them down slowly, and leave her lacy thong in place. Fucking sexy. I toss her pants away, and slide my finger into the top of her lacy underwear. I swipe it back and forth, coming close, but not quite touching the spot swollen with need, clamoring for my touch.

"Alec," she cries out, and I love hearing my name on her tongue, the sexually frustrated sound as she lifts her hips, trying to force me closer. I tug on her panties and pull them upward until her beautiful lips are hugging the thin band. I wiggle the material back and forth, massaging her clit with the lace.

Her gasp curls around me, her body a quivering mess of need and pleasure. "Oh, yes," she cries out, and as her head goes from side to side, I can't take teasing her anymore. I need my mouth on her body, everywhere, anywhere, all at once—all night long. Delirious with need, I grip the scrap of material in my hand and in one quick thrust tear the flimsy thong from her body.

She gulps and sits up a little straighter. "Alec," she cries out, her brown eyes wide, full of lust and desire.

"Good thing you removed your T-shirt or I might have ripped it from your body, too." Her chest heaves and I bite back a smile. "Now spread your legs," I command in a soft voice and she immediately obliges, offering herself up to me so nicely a groan catches in my throat. I cup her ankles and place her feet on the edge of the mattress. With her knees pointed at the ceiling, I grip her thighs, squeeze slightly and widen her legs even more to accommodate my wide body. Her warm aroused scent turns me on even more, and my heart nearly gives when I glimpse her pink wetness, wide-open and ready for my mouth. I gaze at her for a second, then blink, wanting to capture this moment in a still frame.

"Megan," I murmur, and settle myself on the floor between her thighs, stroking her quivering sex from top to bottom. "So fucking pretty." Her body practically levitates off the bed as I pet her, and my cock throbs, grows another inch until it's bursting through the elastic band of my boxers. Reaching up, I cup one breast and give a squeeze as I slide a finger into her. Christ, she's soaking wet.

A moan rolls out of her throat and a growl catches in mine as her wet heat squeezes around my finger. Her pussy is so hot, tight and beautiful, this could very well be over before it even begins. But I need to hold it together. We're not teenagers back in my room at St. Moritz, where we fumbled and clumsily learned each other's bodies. Yeah, we were young and inexperienced, but up until this moment, it was the best night of my life.

Her sexy sounds of pleasure massage my balls, and my dick throbs even harder, leaving me a little off-kilter. But I can't think about what being intimate with her again is doing to me, how screwed up I'll become tomorrow. No, tonight I just want to feel, and bring her all the pleasure she deserves.

I slide another finger inside her for a snug fit, and small spasms begin at her core. She's already so close, it's insane. Then again, who am I to talk. Precum is pooling from my slit, and my cock is begging me to take her already. But I won't. Not until she comes for me first. I might be called a lot of things, but at the heart of it all, I'm a gentleman and I'm not between the legs of some random woman here. This is Megan Williams, and the fact that she's actually giving herself to me again, when I don't deserve anything from her, well, I don't take that lightly. With her pleasure paramount, I take her swollen clit into my mouth and suck hard as I move my finger in and out. Her pussy grows slicker beneath my ministrations, and I clamp down slightly on her cleft.

Air leaves her lungs in a whoosh, and her whimpering sounds reach my ears as I soften my tongue, lave her aching clit as her body writhes beneath me. I lift my mouth, glance up at her to find her on her elbows, watching me. Our eyes meet, lock, and my heart misses a few beats as I struggle to refill my lungs. My God, she's breathtaking.

"You taste so good," I murmur when I can finally breathe again, and she reaches for me, rakes her hand through my hair and guides my mouth back to her hot core. Loving that she knows what she wants, and isn't afraid to take it, I chuckle against her clit, and fuck her with my fingers, changing the pace, rhythm and depth until she's shaking and crying out my name. I love seeing her like this. Damned if I don't want to make her feel this good every day of my life.

I circle her clit with my tongue, then press against it as I deliver hot, openmouthed kisses to her sweet pussy. She rocks against me, a shameless display of need, as she takes what she wants. Attagirl. She rides my fingers, moving faster and faster and soon enough she's a beautiful hot mess tumbling over the edge.

"Alec," she cries out, the clench of her muscles drawing my fingers in deeper and deeper and making me crazier and crazier. My dick throbs, aching to feel those clenches. "I'm…oh, God, Alec." Her sweetness explodes on my tongue and I drink her in, not daring to miss a drop. I want her flavor in my mouth, want to taste her on my tongue a week from now. She spasms around me, and I stay between her legs and let her ride out the waves until her body goes slack and she's panting for her next breath.

I climb over her body, brush my tongue over both nipples on my way to her mouth. Her legs wrap around me, and through my boxers my cock presses against her hot core. My lips find hers. I kiss her deeply, thoroughly explore her mouth with my tongue, and she kisses me back, the same sweet way she kissed me all those years ago.

I'm about to push off her, grab a condom when

she gives me a hard shove. I roll to my back, and catching me by surprise she climbs over me, straddles my legs. "What are you doing?" I ask, my voice rough and labored.

She tugs my boxers down and my cock springs free. She takes me into her hands, weighs me in her palms as she examines the long length of my dick. Her eyes are heavy lidded when her gaze lifts to mine. "Did you miss the part where I said I like firm, too?" she asks.

"Oh, Jesus," I say as she bends forward to lick my cum, like it's her goddamn job. With a slow slide of her tongue, she cleans my crown, before taking me to the back of her throat. "Megan," I croak out, and grip her tumble of hair. I wrap it around my hand and move it to the side to watch my dick slide in and out of her mouth. It's the sexiest thing I've ever seen. "That is so good," I manage to say.

She moans, and the vibrations of her mouth zap my balls. She takes them into her palm and massages gently as her hand works the long length of me and her tongue swirls around my swollen head. The perfect trifecta. Her moans grow louder, more heated, and the way she's worshipping my cock—loving every second of it—fucks me over in so many ways. Blood fills my veins and as much as I like what she's doing, if she keeps it up, I'm going to shoot my load down her throat. But I'm not ready for this to be over. I want, need, other things from her tonight.

"Megan," I growl, and give a little tug of her hair

to pull her off me. Her mouth is wet as I bring her to me for a kiss. "I need to be inside you," I say.

"Yes," she murmurs. I roll until she's underneath me, and then I go up on my knees to reach into my nightstand to pull out a box of condoms. I rip into it, pull out a foil package and quickly sheathe myself. I fall over Megan, who hasn't taken her eyes off me. "You ready for me to fuck you?" I ask.

Eyes heated, she widens her legs and wraps them around my waist, answering my question without words. I position my crown at her entrance and it throbs as I give her an inch. She moans, thrusts upward for more.

"Alec, please," she cries out.

"You need it, Megan? You need my cock?"

"I need you to fuck me," she whimpers, and in one quick thrust I power my hips forward and fill her completely. "Holy God," she cries out, her nails digging into my back. I go perfectly still for a moment, and concentrate on how good she feels as I give her a second to catch her breath. "I feel you, Alec. Feel you throbbing inside me."

"You are so hot and tight, it's all I can do to hang on. I'm already more than halfway there," I groan.

She begins to rock, and I move with her, pulling almost all the way out, only to slide back home again. We move together, each giving and taking, and every time I power into her sweet core, it pulls a cry from her throat. Her hands go to her breasts and she rubs her nipples. Jesus, that's hot. My lips find hers again as my balls tighten, scream for release. I grind into her, stimulate her clit with each downward slide, and soon enough she's chanting my name again, her muscles clenching in an explosion of passion.

"I'm there," she murmurs, her skin warm and slick as she shatters around me. Her hot cum singes my cock, drips all over me, and I've never felt anything more satisfying in my entire life. Perfection.

I change the rhythm and pace, driving deeper, harder, but unable to get enough. "Yes, yes, yes," she chants, and when her eyes roll back in her head, her body explodes for the third time tonight. There is nothing in the world better than this. Megan in my bed, coming all over my cock. Her pussy squeezes my dick hard, and I can no longer hold on. I throw my head back and growl as I come high inside her. My muscles spasm and shudder with my final pulse, and once depleted, I collapse on top of Megan, press her into the mattress. Her heart pounds hard against my chest, and I bury my mouth into her neck, where I press feather-soft, openmouthed kisses to her delicate flesh. I stay there for a long time, revel in her scent and enjoy the light caress of her fingers stroking my back. I breathe in contentment as I bask in my postorgasmic bliss.

Soon enough my cock grows flaccid and with much reluctance, I pull out of her and discard the condom. Sprawled out on my bed, her eyes heavy lidded and struggling to remain open, her hair is a tangled mess beneath her. I've never seen her look more beautiful. Her breathing changes, grows softer, and I fix the blankets around us, pulling her into my arms so we can get a few hours of sleep.

She moans, and my pulse beats a bit faster as she snuggles into me, a well-sated woman. I let my gaze fall over her again, and my chest swells, loving that I was the one who did this to her.

I drop a soft kiss onto her forehead, and as reality begins to trickle back in, I struggle to calm my racing heart. Just like eight years ago, Megan rocked my world in a way no other woman ever has or ever will. But it shouldn't have happened then, and it shouldn't have happened now. What the hell is wrong with me? Why can't I be stronger around her? Why would I go and seduce the one girl in the world I need to keep my distance from?

CHAPTER FIVE

Megan

I SLEPT WITH ALEC.

Omigod, I slept with Alec. Last night, after a couple glasses of wine, it seemed like a good idea. I'm a grown woman who's in charge of her sexuality, so why not, right? Why not take what I want from a man who was willing to give it. We're both single, consenting adults and I haven't been touched in a long time. Not that any man has ever touched me the way Alec has, or ever brought me such intense pleasure.

But now, under the stark light of morning, a headache brewing in the back of my head, I'm second-guessing my decision-making abilities. Truthfully, as much as I want to blame it on the alcohol, I can't. I wanted him. I wanted my hands on his body, his on mine. I wanted to feel his hard cock inside me, taking me to places no man has ever been able to take me. But why did he want me in his bed, if I'm clearly not his type?

I guess his cock didn't get the memo.

I lay perfectly still between the warm sheets, sorting things through as I listen to his soft breathing. I told him I hadn't been with a guy in a long time, and Alec and I have a history. Perhaps I reeked of desperation, and he was just doing me a favor. Still, desperation or not, he wanted it, too.

Nevertheless, I should go, get out of here before we have our second—eight years later—awkward morning after. But what are the chances that I can get out of here without waking him, and move to Canada before he figures out I'm even gone?

"You okay?" he asks quietly.

I flinch at the sound of Alec's voice. So much for sneaking out. The mattress moves as he rolls my way, and the warmth of his fingers on my chin as he angles my head until we're eye to eye awakens my body all over again. In his sleep-rumpled state, his hair an unkempt mess, he's even more beautiful than ever.

And I slept with him.

But the real problem is, I want to do it again.

Then keep doing it.

A groan catches in my throat as his gaze moves over my face, assessing me. "Hey," he whispers, the softness in his voice, the genuine concern in his eyes, warming me all over. "What is it?"

"Nothing," I squeak out, but he frowns at the lie.

"Are you overthinking this?" he asks. I can't hide anything from this man. He knows me far too well. And he's right. I'm overthinking this. Like I always do. Heck, for the last eight years I've been overthinking the night I seduced him.

"Actually, I was just thinking about moving to Canada," I say, a successful attempt to lighten the mood, judging by the smile spreading across his face. When that smile reaches his eyes, my heart leaps because in this instant, I realize I'm looking at the boy from my youth, not the anti-love guy who says he's not a nice man. What I'd do to have the old Alec back full-time. I swallow against a tight throat, and it's all I can do not to weep for the loss of our closeness.

He lightly brushes my hair back, those intense blue eyes roaming my face. "Did you enjoy yourself, Megs?"

Megs, oh, God, the nickname.

"Immensely," I say, my sated body aching in all the right places.

"Good. Me, too."

"But we need to make one thing clear. It was just sex. I'm not looking for or asking anything else of you. I don't want you to get the wrong idea about me," I add.

"I won't."

"Good."

"It was just sex," he says. "I get it. Not a problem."

"I shouldn't have seduced you," I blurt out, and avoid adding *again* to the end of the sentence.

A crooked grin curls one corner of his luscious mouth and all I can think about is how his lips felt on my body, between my legs. "You think…" he begins but stops when I pull the blankets up to cover the red blush crawling up my neck. "Hey, wait, no need to be embarrassed," he says. "We're adults, doing what adults do."

"I've been hired to find you a wife and plan your wedding, Alec," I point out. "We shouldn't have done this."

His entire body stiffens at the blunt reminder, and a second later he gives a curt, almost dismissive nod. "You're right, and we have work to do this morning." He tears his gaze away and gone is the softness in his voice, his face…his posture. My God, the man is such a contradiction, soft and sweet one minute, all business the next. If I'm not careful I'm going to end up with whiplash. "Let's chalk it up to a night of fun, and put it behind us."

"That's exactly what we need to do," I say, but my heart is already warning me that it won't be as easy for me as it will be for him. I can't—won't—fall for this man again. I want a loving marriage and family, and his goals are in complete contrast to that. We both know that. Any more time in his bed, fun or not, might just draw me back into a place I simply refuse to go.

From the other room my phone buzzes, the special ringtone letting me know it's Amanda. Great, just great. She's going to want a play-by-play rundown, and no way will I be able to hide this from her. One look at me and she'll know I had sex with

Alec. He'd better hide his farm parts. But oh, what amazing parts he has.

Stop thinking about his equipment, already.

"You going to get that?" he asks, his voice lacking warmth, as he kicks his blankets off, exposing his nakedness to me. He stands and stretches and my goddamn mouth waters.

"Ah, what are you doing?" I ask.

"Going to grab a shower." He glances down at his bare body. "Oh, I didn't think… I mean, you've seen me naked."

"It doesn't mean I want to again."

That's a lie.

I do.

"You better grab your phone. Whoever's calling doesn't seem like they're about to give up." With that he walks to the bathroom, his cute ass dragging my focus the whole way. It's only when he shuts the door that I'm able to think again. "Jesus," I murmur under my breath, and search the floor for the sweatpants he gave me to wear last night. I scoop up my ripped underwear and ignore the quiver careening through my blood. I've never had a man rip my panties from my hips before. Okay, stop thinking about how hot that was.

I scan the floor for my T-shirt and that's when I remember I took it off in the living room. Oh, hell. I open the bedroom door, and dash through the apartment. I grab the shirt and quickly tug it on. Feeling a whole lot less exposed, I dig my phone from my purse and swipe my finger over the screen.

"Where are you?" Amanda asks.

"What…uh…what are you talking about?" I feign innocence, but I'm guessing she won't have any of that.

"I'm standing outside your apartment with two lattes. We have yoga this morning, or did you forget?"

"I forgot."

Silence for a moment, and then, "Oh, my God, you slept with him."

I glance over my shoulder. "Amanda…" I begin quietly.

"Jesus, Megan, what were you thinking?" she huffs out.

"Last night I was thinking, why the hell not," I say.

"And today, what are you thinking today?"

How is it everyone can read me so well? Am I that much of an open book? "I'm thinking I had a great time, and now we're back to business. It won't be happening again. Maybe it was just something we needed to get out of our system." *Okay, girl, get it together. Overthinking and rambling. My two specialties.*

Amanda goes quiet again and I can visualize her rubbing that spot on her forehead. "Are you okay?"

I walk to the window and look out at the Hudson River below. I take a deep yoga breath and let it out slowly, instantly calming myself down. "I'm perfectly fine."

"Don't shit me," she warns.

"I'm fine. We had sex, talked about it, and now we're getting back to the business of finding him a wife."

A pause and then, "One more question?"

"What?"

"Did he make your eyes roll back in your head?"

"Three times," I say, and cover my mouth to stifle a chuckle.

"That's good, then. I'm drinking your latte and going back to bed. When you get back, wake me and I want all the details."

"Everything okay?" Alec asks, coming into the room dressed in nothing but track pants. My gaze falls, takes in his bare chest, the oblique muscles that are guiding my eyes down.

"Yes, it was my friend. I forgot that we had yoga this morning."

He points upward. "I'm doing laps in a few. You can join me if you want to get in some exercise." I look up at his ceiling and he explains. "Rooftop pool."

"It's a bit chilly for that, isn't it?"

"The pool is heated and glassed in. Coffee?"

"Yes, please," I say, and follow him into the kitchen. I glance around the massive space and take in the state-of-the-art appliances as he goes to his coffeemaker, but it's not just any coffeemaker. With all the spouts, buttons and gadgets, it's the fancy kind you'd find at a high-end coffee boutique.

"Mocha latte?" he asks.

"You're kidding, right?"

"I never kid about my coffee," he says, and I laugh. Even when we were teens he loved his coffee. He glances at me over his shoulder. "I need to get my laps in this morning. I have some paperwork that needs my attention this afternoon. To speed things up, would you mind asking questions while I exercise?"

"Uh, I guess not."

He pours milk into a metal cup, sticks it under a spout and steams it. "You're welcome to swim if you want."

"I don't have a suit."

The muscles on his back ripple, the same way they did when I ran my fingers over his body. He finishes making my coffee and hands it to me. I take a seat at the gigantic island and breathe in the welcoming scent.

"If you'll excuse me for a minute," he says. He disappears into the other room and comes back doing something on his tablet. He hits a few buttons, and I assume it must be some work emergency, then he goes back to making his coffee.

"Do you still like Pop-Tarts for breakfast?" he asks.

"No, I kind of gave that up when I became an adult. I usually have yogurt, toast or sometimes just a protein bar." My stomach takes that moment to grumble. "I seem to be hungrier than usual this morning."

Way to bring up all the sex we had, Megan.

"It was a late night," he simply says. "I'm not that well stocked, but I do have bread in the freezer. That will get us by, and after our swim I'll order us in a proper breakfast. We'll have it at the pool."

"You don't have to do that. Toast will do, and I should head out right after we finish the question-naire. I have some work to do on a Bar Mitzvah today."

He makes his coffee, takes a sip and eyes me over the rim. "If you think I'm letting you leave here with-out properly feeding you—"

"Bossy much," I say. "Glad they asked that on the form. We wouldn't want any woman to think you were easy to get along with."

"It's settled, then," he says, not bothering to dis-agree. He opens the freezer, pulls out the frozen bread and places four slices in the toaster. "I have butter, jam and peanut butter."

"Strawberry jam?"

"Is there really any other kind worth having?" he asks, and pulls it from the fridge.

"This coffee is so good," I say, and take a big sip. "I'm going to have to invest in one of those machines. I'll need an engineering degree to figure out how to use it, though."

He chuckles softly. "It's not so hard." He takes

another sip of coffee and goes serious. "How is this all going to work? Once you set up the profile for me, then what?"

"Well, I'm going to pretend to be you online. Vet the women to see if I think they'd be a good match. I'll set up the date, tell you where to be, at what time and what to wear. I probably should check your wardrobe."

"You'll find mostly suits and gym clothes."

"Then we might need to go shopping."

"Do you think that's necessary?"

"Absolutely."

"I don't think—"

I hold my hand up to stop him when the toast pops. "I'm in charge here. That's the only way this is going to work. If you want me to find you a 'suitable' wife…" I pause to do air quotes around that one word "…then you have to put yourself in my hands."

His muscles tighten, and I'm almost one hundred percent sure his cock just twitched at my poor choice of words. He mumbles something under his breath, pulls two plates from his cupboard and slides me two slices. I twist the lid off the jam as he grabs a spoon from his drawer and comes around the island to sit next to me.

"Here's the thing, though. You're kind of well-known, so I was thinking maybe we should use your middle name and we can take a sideways picture or something distant. Give them enough to work with but maybe not identifiable as you."

He hands me the spoon, and my fingers brush his as I accept it. The heat from his flesh trickles through my traitorous body and I work to ignore the frisson of need as I dip the spoon into the jar and come out with a big scoop of strawberry jam. I coat my toast and hand the spoon back, this time taking care not to touch him.

"Are you afraid my real identity will scare them off?"

"I'd just rather a woman walk in without any pre-conceived notions."

"Makes sense, but I'm not going to hide the fact that I'm looking for a wife in name only."

I open my mouth to ask if he'd at least try, but quickly stop myself. The man is stubborn, and bossy, and when he has his mind hell-bent on something, there is no way I'm going to change it. I'd just be fighting a losing battle.

"Do you have any out-of-town trips that I should know about?" I ask instead.

"Not unless something unexpected comes up."

"I'm going to need a copy of your work agenda and meeting times if I'm going to be scheduling dates for you."

"I'll have my assistant get that to you." He angles his head. "Anything else, boss?"

I roll my eyes at him. "Not that I can think of right now."

"Will you need a key to my place?"

"And risk the chance of walking in on you in the

middle of…" I let my words fall off as I envision Alec in his bed with another woman, doing all the things to her that he's recently done to me. *Get it together, Megan.* "Actually it might be a good idea," I say. It's best if he doesn't think I care if he's here with another woman, considering that's the whole reason for me being here in the first place. And really, I don't care. Not one little bit. "If you bring a woman back here, I'd like to have your kitchen stocked a bit better, and a few homey touches would be nice. I can arrange that. I want things perfect. We need this to work for both our sakes."

"I'll get you a key," he says, like he's not happy about the whole thing.

I bite into my toast, chew and wash it down with a mouthful of delicious coffee. Alec does the same and then turns to me. With a piece of toast halfway to his mouth he asks, "You're really going to pretend to be me online?"

"Yes, except more charming."

He goes perfectly still for a second before he lets loose a laugh. "You don't think I'm charming, Megs," he asks, and nudges my chin with his fist.

"I don't really know you anymore, Alec," I say, and it instantly changes the mood. He pulls his hand back, more aloof than usual as he finishes his toast. He stands to put his plate in the dishwasher when the doorbell rings.

"Expecting company?" I ask.

"Yes," he says, and I check the time as he disappears around the corner. Who could he be expecting on a Saturday morning at ten? I glance at my clothes and jump from the stool, panicked. I'm hardly dressed to greet his guests, and what if it's a woman—one of his many. But then I remember he doesn't bring women into his home, and I'm only here because he's trying it on for size. Maybe that's why my seduction worked. Maybe he was trying a woman out in his bed for size, too.

Okay, Megan, stop overthinking everything.

I'm about to hurry down the hall when the door closes, and Alec calls me into the living room. I peek in to make sure he's alone. "What's going on?" I ask, when I see a dozen boxes sitting on his coffee table. He had a delivery, this time of day?

I slowly walk into the room, and can't believe it when I see the boxes are from Bianca's Boutique, Manhattan's very expensive, very elite lingerie shop.

"These are for you," he says. "Size six, right?"

"I…uh…yes, how do you know that?" He arches a brow at my foolish question. Of course he knows that. His hands were all over my body, and since he's reached out and touched more women than Hallmark, he's probably an expert at guessing sizes. "What have you done?"

"I kept you from your yoga this morning. Now you can swim instead." He settles himself on the sofa, and gestures for me to sit in the cushiony chair across from him. "You don't like Bianca's?"

I step around the coffee table. "I… I've never shopped there?"

"I know Bianca quite well. She's very particular, and her swimsuits are high quality. She personally put this order together for me this morning."

I throw my hands up. "You just called her up and put an order in? This morning? That's what you were doing on your tablet?"

He taps a finger to his lip, like he's amused with all my questions. "Yes."

"I can't believe you did this."

"What's the big deal?"

Okay, this man obviously operates in a different world than I do. "How many did you order?"

He shrugs. "A few. I wasn't sure what fit or style you liked."

"You know you're insane, right?"

He scrubs his chin, and nods. "One of the nicer things I've been called."

"I bet," I say, and he just smirks at me. I lift the lid off one box and pull out a gorgeous designer bikini with a floral print top that ties in the front, and high-waisted bottoms. I've been lusting after a suit like this for a while now, but it wasn't in my budget. "I can't keep all these."

"There's no return on swimwear. They're yours. You're welcome to use my pool anytime. Perhaps your friend Amanda would like to join you sometime."

Flabbergasted I drop the bikini into the box. "That's a nice offer, but this is too much."

"You don't like that one. Try this," he says, and hands me another box. The man is generous, and I have no doubt he'll give his wife all the material things she wants, but is that really enough to keep the marriage alive? Won't she eventually want his heart, too?

I open it, but this time I find a lacey white thong. I pull it from the box, run the expensive material through my fingers.

His grin is sheepish when I glance at him. "Replacement. For the pair I ripped," he explains.

"This is way nicer than what I was wearing."

"I liked what you were wearing," he says almost under his breath, and my gaze shoots to his. He jumps from the sofa. "Did you want to shower before you swim?"

I nod. "Yes," I say. The sooner I get the scent of his skin off mine the better.

He nods. "I'll head up and get some laps in. There's a private elevator in the hall. It takes you up to the roof. No one has access but me."

"The rooftop is just for your use?"

"Yes." He disappears for a second and comes back with a key. He presses it into my palm and closes my fingers around it. "This will get you into my apartment, and to the roof. I'll meet you there."

He heads to his room to get changed, and I open a few more boxes, until I find a pretty black-and-white suit that covers a bit more than the others. Not that it matters. We've seen each other naked. I hurry to the spare bedroom, shower and tug on the suit. Key in hand, laptop bag over my shoulder I make my way to the rooftop, and hurry to the glassed-in pool. Dressed in tight swim trunks, Alec's long, lean body glides through the crystal clear water and he surfaces right in front of me.

"You made…" he begins but his voice falls off as his gaze moves over me, a long leisurely inspection from my dry mouth to the tips of my toes, and all the way back up again, stopping to linger on my breasts—and nipples that are no doubt poking hard against the thin fabric. A moan catches in his throat and my entire body lights, like a match to dry tinder.

Honestly, if he's about to marry someone else, why the hell is he looking at me like he wants to eat me alive?

CHAPTER SIX

Alec

I PICK MY cell phone up from my desk, glance at it and set it down with a little more force than necessary. Fuck. Here it is late Friday morning and I haven't heard from Megan since last Saturday—when she joined me at the pool and I damn near devoured her with my gaze.

Well done, Alec, well done.

I worked to hide my arousal and keep things casual as we did laps, had breakfast and finished the questionnaire. I'm not sure I pulled it off, though. After the round of sex we had, you'd think I'd be sated, gotten her out of my system, but it only made me want her more. How I'm going to get through this and keep my hands to myself is beyond me. She made it clear what we did can't happen again, and I have to agree with her.

I glance at my phone again and check the time. I have a late afternoon meeting, but I need a breath of fresh air before sitting down with the board and hashing out the details on the next deal. My job looks harsh in the eyes of most, I can understand that. We finance investors who buy undervalued assets in companies. Once they secure controlling shares they restructure, changing leadership and management. People frown at what I do, some call me a monster, but I'm good at it—and it's a sure way for me to carve my own way in this world, which is important to me. What they don't know is I always make sure to help those who lose their jobs. Granddad owns half of Manhattan, and with the charity I run, we're always in need of new blood and top management expertise.

I push from my chair and take the elevator down to the main floor. I make my way to my Tesla, press the fob and climb in. Before I realize what I'm doing or where I'm even going, I find myself driving along Ninth Avenue through Hell's Kitchen looking for Kitchen Door Catering.

I slow my vehicle to glance at the storefronts, and a chorus of cars honk from behind. I simply flip them all the finger and pull over to check my GPS. I punch in the name and a second later I'm given directions to the business. I pull back into traffic and follow the route until I'm outside the industrial-looking brick building. I kill the ignition and step out into the warm sunshine and make my way down the busy sidewalk. Delicious scents of ginger and spices reach my nostrils as I enter the shop, and a little bell

over the door jingles to announce my presence. Behind the counter, Megan's friend Amanda glances
up, and behind her glasses, her brown eyes go wide
when she sees me.

"Alec," she says, and wipes her hands on her
apron.

"Nice to see you again, Amanda. I never got a
chance to say hello at the coffee shop but Megan told
me about your catering business."

I quickly catalog the space. The front of the shop
has fridges and freezers with take-out food, and behind Amanda there is a wide-open space with three
big butcher-block tables, where numerous chefs are
working away.

She takes her glasses off and sets them on the
counter. "Do you have an event you need catered?"
she asks, her eyes wide and hopeful.

"No, but when I do I'll be sure to keep you in
mind. Megan also mentioned you do personalized
meal delivery. That's something I'm definitely interested in." That brings a big smile to her face. "Speaking of Megan, is she around?" I ask.

She jerks her thumb over her shoulder. "She's in
her office. I'll get her for you. In the meantime, why
don't you look this over." She hands me a colorful
brochure, picks up her phone and presses a button.
She turns her back to me, preventing me from hearing her conversation, and I walk over to the fridge
to check out today's specials.

I've never really seen an innovative business quite

like this. Not only do they cater events, they make extras and sell it fresh daily. Behind me the door jingles and in walks a woman with four small children, three boys and one girl. They run straight for the cupcake display as Amanda greets the woman, then glances at me quickly. "She'll be right out."

As the kids pick out what cupcake they want, I grin, and think back to my own childhood. How many times did Granddad take me and Will, and our cousins Tate and Brianna, out for treats. The man was a saint and had so much patience with us. Is it any wonder each of us would do anything for him—even get married? Although I still can't quite believe I agreed to it. Must have been all the brandy he used to loosen me up. I must remember to ask him why he hired Megan, or how he even knew she ran an event business. Then again, even at ninety he keeps his ear to the ground.

"Hey," Megan says as she comes around the counter, her hair a tumbled mess, like she's been running her fingers through it. "What brings you here?"

"I thought I'd check out Amanda's kitchen." I wave my hand around the place. "The idea of fresh, healthy home-delivered meals sure would make my life easier." Not a lie. I rub my gut. "Eating out is beginning to take its toll."

"You probably could lay off the doughnuts," she says with a grin. "And stop fishing for compliments." I laugh at that, and she adds, "I'm glad you're here. I was going to text you. It's been a crazy week, and

I should have reached out earlier, but I had a last-minute emergency with the Bar Mitzvah venue. A pipe broke in the yacht club, and I had to scramble to find a new location."

I dip my head and try not to stare at her mouth. "If you ever run into that again, just give me a shout."

"Really?"

"Granddad owns numerous properties that I oversee, and we'd be happy to help you out. Pick up the phone and call me before you take it out on your hair." Her eyes go wide for a second, and then she laughs and finger combs her curls. "I see you never lost the habit of running your fingers through your hair when you're stressed. Remember after exams—"

"Oh, my God, don't remind me. I always came away looking like a sheepdog who went through the dryer without a static sheet."

I laugh out loud. "You were adorable." I glance over her shoulder to see Amanda watching us. "Anyway," I say, and clear my throat, returning to professional mode and getting back down to business. Why does being around her make me forget to keep my guard up? "You were going to text me?"

She pokes my chest and I wish she hadn't. That innocent touch makes me want to pull her into my arms, and kiss the smudged lipstick from her lush mouth. "You have a date tonight, Alec."

While one part of me is happy to get the ball rolling and get this over with, the other part is dreading the idea of picking out a wife. Even if I wanted to back out now—run as far away as possible despite what it could do for my image and career, not to mention pleasing Granddad—I can't. Megan has a lot riding on this, and I can only assume her friend does, too, since she'll be catering my wedding, and getting her food in the hands of some very prominent members of society.

"You found me someone who fits the criteria?"

"Yes. Her name is Danielle. She's an elementary school teacher and she sounds perfect. I made a reservation for seven at Il Mercato. Italian is her favorite. I want to go over some things we talked about so you're up to speed when you meet her."

I gesture with a nod to the door. "Sounds like a good plan. Should we do it over lunch or have you eaten?"

"Lunch is perfect. We can eat in my office where we'll have privacy. How about ginger squash soup, and roasted chicken sandwiches?" She breathes in deep and when she does her chest expands, and behind her silky white blouse, her nipples reach out and taunt me. "It's been cooking all morning and I'm dying to have some."

"We can eat here?"

"Sure. Come on." She glances at her friend. "Amanda, I'm going to grab two bowls of soup and two sandwiches. Put it on my tab," she says. Amanda rolls her eyes at us. I step around the counter, and my gaze travels the length of Megan as I follow her into the kitchen. She's dressed in a curve-hugging skirt that shows off her long, shapely legs and high heels I want her to keep on in bed the next time I put my face between her thighs. Shit, what am I saying? There isn't going to be a next time.

I pull myself together as Megan introduces me to the staff. After an exchange of pleasantries, she goes up on her toes, stretching her hands over her head to pull two bowls from the shelf.

"I could have gotten those for you," I say, as I hover at least a foot over her head.

She shrugs. "It's okay. I'm an independent woman used to doing things myself."

I nod but for some reason that ticks me off. I love that she's independent, but it would be nice if she had someone to rely on, someone to call when, oh, I don't know, when she's stuck and needs to find a new venue. She's so different from the women in my circle, and it makes me want to help her all the more.

She fills the bowls with thick, creamy soup, and hands them to me. "Take them in there," she says, and nods to the office at the end of the hall. "I'll grab us some sandwiches."

I balance the soup and carefully make my way down the hall. I glance in, find a desk scattered with papers, and know I've come to the right place. I set the soup down. One in front of her big comfy chair and one across from her.

"I see you're still messy," I say when she comes in.

"Excuse me," she says, pretending she's offended

by the remark, but the grin lingering on her lips tells another story. "It's called organized chaos."

"Oh, is that what we're calling it now? I'll be sure to remember that." She sits across from me, and smiles. My God, she is so beautiful. "Amanda has a nice setup."

"She's really hoping to grow. If we pull off the wedding of the century, her business is going to sky-rocket. I really want that for her."

I dip my spoon into the soup and taste it. "If everything she makes tastes this great, I'd be happy to hand her name around."

"You'd do that?" she asks, beaming, and for some reason being able to make her this happy thrills me and fucks me over at the same time.

"Yeah, sure," I say, like it's nothing, but it's obviously not nothing to Megan.

"Thank you," she says, and I love how much she cares about her friend's well-being. She always was kind and thoughtful, a giver. My mind rewinds to the way she gave me her body, and my cock thickens. Shit.

"Okay, so fill me in on what I need to know," I say, getting us both back on track.

As we eat, Megan opens her laptop and turns it my way. I read through the conversation and get myself up to speed. "I must say. I'm impressed. You're pretty good at pretending to be me."

"After going over all those forms I think I know you better than I know myself."

We both nod at that, and I lean back in my chair and bite into my sandwich when her phone rings. "Excuse me for a second." She swipes her finger across her phone. "Hey, Sara, what's up?" she asks. I busy myself with the brochure Amanda gave me and listen to the one-sided conversation. It doesn't take long to figure out Sara is putting together a last-minute anniversary party for her folks, and Megan is organizing it.

"You're never going to believe who is sitting across from me this very minute," Megan says, glancing at me. "Nope…nope…nope," she says, and winks. "You give up? Okay, I'll give you a hint. He helped me get you home from that party when you thought it would be a good idea to drink too much and dance on the table." She laughs and nods her head. "That's right, none other than Alec Carson." A moment and then she responds, "He's good. Yeah, sure we can all get together soon, talk about old times." She goes quiet for a minute. "Well, I can ask him, but I'm not sure he'd be interested. He's a busy guy." Megan grabs a pen, takes a couple notes as Sara talks, then she responds with, "I'm, ah… working on an event for him. I'll explain the details later, over drinks tonight at Onyx when we hash out the details for the anniversary party."

After she ends the call, she crinkles her nose. "Sorry about that."

"She wants you to invite me to the anniversary party?"

"Ah, yeah. You don't have to go, of course."

"I'll go."

Her brow furrows.

"Sure, why not," I say. "I always liked your aunt and uncle. It would be nice to see them again."

"Oh, okay. Sara was out of town on business, and I'm scrambling to pull this off in two weeks. Thank God, Amanda could fit us in and cater the event."

"About this schoolteacher," I say.

"Right." She shows me the woman's picture, and with blond hair cut short, she's cute enough in that girl-next-door way, but she's no Megan.

Megan frowns and glances at me. "I'm not sure you should wear a Gucci suit. I'd like for you to dress just a bit more casual for your first meeting."

I arch a brow. "Is this where you take me shopping?"

"Do you have the time?"

I check my watch. "I have a couple hours."

She grabs her purse from beneath her desk. "Then we should get at it."

"What did you have in mind?"

She tosses her purse over her shoulder and gives me a once-over. "Casual pants, shoes, sweater. A little more of a relaxed look, I think. Why don't we hit Fifth Avenue?"

"Shopping is not my favorite thing, especially on Fifth Avenue."

She plants her hand on her hip and arches a brow. "Alec—"

"Fine, fine," I say, and hold my hands up in surrender. "You're the boss," I say, following her out of her office.

"We're off to do some shopping," she says to Amanda, and I tuck the brochure into my pocket.

"You'll be hearing from me soon," I say, and open the door for Megan. She squeezes past me, and her warm scent reaches my nostrils. I breathe her in, and work to marshal my desire as I step outside and guide her to my vehicle.

Two hours later, shopping bags in hand, she points to one more store. "Let's go in there," she says.

I hold the bags up; I'm so over this. "You don't think I've bought enough?"

She pouts, and her pink painted lips pucker as she blinks up at me. "Just one more," she says, her voice a pleading whisper, and I shake my head, unable to say no when she begs like that. Fuck, what I'd do to hear her beg like that in bed, let me know all the dirty things she'd like for me to do to her. We head inside some new trendy store and she gasps when she sees a blue sweater on sale. To her it's clearly something special; to me, it's a blue sweater.

"Try this on for me." She grabs a casual dress shirt from the shelf. "This, too."

"That's it," I say, giving her a warning glare. "No more after this."

"Go," she says, and waves me toward the changing room as she browses a few more items. I reluctantly walk to the back of the store and the sales clerk opens the room for me. I slip out of my suit jacket, unbutton my shirt and pull on the sweater.

"Can I see?" Megan asks.

I open the door, and her gaze falls over me. She makes a little noise, and I'm almost positive I see desire in her eyes. "That's it. That's the sweater you're going to wear tonight. Along with the new boots and chino pants. It's perfect." Her eyes move to mine, and hold for a second too long. "There's no way school-teacher Danielle won't fall for you," she says, almost regretfully.

"That's not really the goal."

She rolls her eyes at me. "You know what I mean." She steps into the change room with me. "Hang on," she says, then puts her arms around my neck to adjust the sweater on my shoulders and tuck the tag in. Her hair tickles my face, and when I catch her honeyed scent again, my traitorous hands slide around her waist, pull her against me. She gives a small gasp, and when she lifts her face to mine, confusion mixed with need brimming in her dark eyes, I can no longer fight the battle. I dip my head, press my lips to hers.

At first her mouth is pinched tight, and I'm about to pull back, curse myself for my weakness, but then she softens against me, and I slide my hands down, run my palms over the curve of her gorgeous ass. She moans into my mouth, and I slide my tongue to hers, taste her warm sweetness. My cock grows in my unforgiving dress pants, and she moves against me, massaging my dick with her stomach. I back her up, push her against the mirror and practically dry hump her right there in the changing room with the damn door open.

Someone clears their throat and we break apart, fast. I spin and tuck her behind me as I come face-to-face with the sales clerk. "Perhaps you two should get a room," he says, and I nod.

"Sorry about that." I grin at him. "She liked my sweater. A lot."

"You'll be taking it, then?" he asks, and folds his arms, his foot tapping a steady rhythm on the carpeted floor.

"I'll take ten. Mix up the colors," I say. "Toss in a couple of the dress shirts, as well." My way of apologizing for our inappropriate behavior.

A smile lights up his face. "You got it," he says, and steps away. I turn back to Megan. Her hands are covering her face and she's peaking at me through her spread fingers.

"Oh, my God, how mortifying."

"It's fine, and don't worry. He's getting a big commission because of our PDA."

Her hands fall, and her eyes narrow. "Why did you do that?" she asks, her brow crinkled. "Why… why did you just kiss me?"

"Because I have a date with a 'girl-next-door' schoolteacher," I say, doing air quotes around the words.

She smooths her sexy mess of hair down. "That still doesn't explain—"

"I don't usually date nice girls, remember? It's been a week since you were in my bed, and I needed a reminder on how nice girls kiss, so I don't screw tonight up."

Lame, Carson. So lame.

She's not buying it any more than I'm selling it, but she nods her head. "You're up to speed now?"

"Yeah," I say, even though I want to kiss her some more—everywhere, all afternoon.

"Then we probably shouldn't do it again."

"You're right." She's about to move past me when I block the door. "Can I ask you something?"

"Yes, but it doesn't mean I'm going to answer," she says, throwing my words back at me.

I grin. "You're going to Onyx for drinks with Sara. It's across the street from Il Mercato. Did you choose that lounge so you could keep tabs on me?"

"That's exactly why I chose it."

"Are you worried I'm going to screw things up?"

"I'm worried about a lot of things, Alec."

CHAPTER SEVEN

Megan

YEAH, I'M DEFINITELY worried about a lot of things, especially this afternoon's heated kiss in the men's change room. My God, what was he thinking, and then to play it off as practice? I don't know what was going through his head, I only know what was going through mine, and that was to shut the damn door and finish what he started.

I toy with my wineglass and stare out the window as I wait for Sara to arrive. I came to Onyx a bit earlier, wanting to catch a glimpse of Danielle, and possibly to see Alec dressed in the clothes we picked out for him today. I have no doubt he's going to charm the pants right off the sweet schoolteacher, or rather the pretty blue dress, as that's what she was wearing when she got out of the cab. She came here alone, but I have a feeling she won't be leaving solo.

Shoes tapping on the floor catch my attention and I turn to see Sara rushing toward me, dressed in a pencil skirt similar to mine, and a blue blouse similar to my white one.

"Sorry, I'm late," she says, and leans down to give me a hug. "I got caught up at work, and you know how that is." She sits across from me, and the hostess lets us know our server will be with us shortly. "Are you eating or are we just having drinks?" Sara asks as she flicks her auburn hair from her shoulders. We might be cousins, but we look so much alike we could easily pass as sisters.

My stomach grumbles, a reminder that I haven't eaten since lunch with Alec. "I could use some food," I say, and flip open my menu. The server comes, and Sara orders a glass of white wine, while I get a refill on mine. Maybe alcohol will help me forget I just sent the man I used to love, and recently had sex with, on a date in his quest for marriage.

"Tell me, what is this event you're setting up for Alec?" Sara asks, and I angle my head, glance across the street again when the front doors of Il Mercato open. Alec arrived before Danielle, dropped off by his driver, and they've been in there for a half hour now. I shouldn't expect them to be finished so soon but I can't help myself from checking every five seconds. "Something interesting over there?" Sara asks, and scans the street.

I take a sip of wine. "Very," I say.

She leans toward me, almost conspiratorial. "Do tell."

"New York's most eligible bachelor is in that restaurant, with a woman who might be his future wife."

Sara's jaw drops open, and she blinks several times. "Alec is getting married?"

"Something like that."

"Wow, I never thought I'd see the day." We both go quiet when the waiter returns with the wine. She takes a sip, waits until he leaves and then asks, "Who's the lucky girl?"

"Don't know yet."

She toys with the stem of her glass and gives me a look that suggests I might be losing my mind.

"Wait, I'm confused—"

"That's because it's confusing," I say, and lower my voice. "Alec hired me to find him a wife. Technically his grandfather hired me."

"That's insane," she says. "Alec has no trouble finding women on his own. I read the tabloids."

"Yeah, but he wants a nice girl, a girl-next-door type. Tonight he's on a date with an elementary schoolteacher. I set it up."

"Since when did you become a matchmaker?"

"If I find him a woman I get to plan his wedding. Imagine what that will do for my career."

"That's amazing," she says, "but a nice girl doesn't seem like his normal type. Not anymore, anyway."

"What do you mean?"

"When you came to live with us, you had girl next door written all over you, and I assumed he liked that since you two were inseparable."

"We were just friends," I say.

"Yeah, tell that to the million girls who wanted to go out with him senior year, but he only had eyes for you. We all had a crush on him."

"He never once hit on me. We were friends." I learned that the hard way. "I kind of thought you had a crush on him."

"Who didn't. I wasn't going to do anything about it, though. You're my cousin and I'd never do anything to hurt you. I thought you liked him."

I loved him.

"I didn't know," I say.

"So why is he looking for a nice girl now? I don't get it."

"He needs a 'suitable' wife if he wants to step into the CFO position at Blackstone. He doesn't believe in love or happily-ever-after. He wants a wife in name only."

"I never knew he was so romantic," she mocks.

"Right?" I give a sad shake of my head.

She snorts out a laugh. "Oh, well, at least whomever he marries will get good sex out of it. I'm sure that man fucks like a god," she says, and I nearly spill the wine in my glass as I bring it to my lips.

Don't blush, Megan. Don't think about the way he fucks and give yourself away.

Too late.

Fortunately, before Sara notices the color on my face, the waiter comes and takes our order. He jots it down and I close my menu and hand it over. When he disappears, I turn my attention to Sara. "How are things with Doug?"

She groans. "We're done. Doug turned out to be a dud." She gives a humorless laugh. "Maybe Alec is on to something, because I'm beginning to believe there is no such thing as love or happily ever after either." She glances out the window. "What about you? How's your love life going?"

"Let's just say I'm about to buy shares in Duracell." She laughs at that, and I pull a notepad from my purse. "How's work going?" I ask.

"Busting my ass 24/7, but the senior partners keep overlooking me. I have more experience than Laura Sweeny, but her husband golfs with them, so she got the last promotion." She scoffs. "I need a husband who golfs. Maybe that will help me get ahead, but there are just no decent guys out there and I've given up on trying to find a needle in a haystack."

"I hear you. Okay, so two weeks to plan a party. You're not giving me much time."

She crinkles her nose. "Sorry, I was out of town for work, and time just got away from me. Will you be able to pull it off?"

"I'll get the invitations out the second we secure a venue, which might be hard this late in the game."

"Don't kill me, but I was actually hoping to have it at the Skylark."

"Sara—" I'm about to tell her there's no way in hell I could get that last minute when she blinks at me and cuts me off.

"I told Mom, and now she has her heart set on it."

I groan and sit back in my chair. "I'll see what I can do, but Amanda won't be able to cater. They don't allow that."

"You'll make it up to her with Alec's wedding."

"True," I say. "I'm not making any promises. But I'll make some calls first thing tomorrow."

I open my notepad and we spend the next fifteen minutes going over the guest list, the menu and decorations. Our meals arrive and after every bite, both Sara and I glance out the window, looking for lover boy and his date.

I tap my pen on the table. "Oh, I forgot to tell you. Alec said he'd come to the anniversary party."

"Maybe he'll bring his fiancée," she says, and wipes the corner of her mouth with her napkin. But as I think about Alec showing up with his fiancée, the chicken I just swallowed sits like lead in my stomach. "What?" Sara asks me when she notices I've gone quiet.

I blink. "Nothing."

"Mcgan, please don't tell me you're still hung up on him."

"I was never hung up on him," I say. I glance out the window again and sit up a little straighter in my chair when the door opens, and the handsomest guy I've ever set eyes on steps outside.

"It's them," I say, and hope Alec can't see us staring. Or can he? His head lifts and his gaze zeroes in on me. Surely he can't see me watching from the dim light in the restaurant. He lifts his hands and gestures for a cab. It arrives, and he pulls money from his pocket and hands it over as Danielle gets in the backseat, no kiss goodbye.

The cab drives off, and he immediately starts our way. "What's he doing?" I ask.

"I think he sees us," Sara says. "He's on his way over here. I don't think the date went well."

"Great," I say, hating the relief I feel. I don't want Alec. I don't even really like the man he's become. I don't think.

I grab my napkin, twist it in my hands and scan the restaurant to find Alec stalking toward us. He doesn't look angry, and I'm glad for that. Maybe the date went better than I thought.

"Megan," he says, and steps up to the table. He bends, drops a kiss onto Sara's cheek and flashes her a smile. "Nice to see you again, Sara. I'd like to get caught up, but right now I need to talk to Megan. Would you mind?"

Sara drops her napkin onto the table. "Actually, we're finished here." She checks her watch. "I need to get going. Work never stops. Megan, I'll grab the bill on the way out."

Sara snatches up her purse and leaves, and I sit there staring at Alec. What the heck is going on? He's scrubbing his chin, his gaze latched on to mine.

"Have a seat," I say.

"Can you come with me?"

"I… Sure." I stop twisting my napkin and reach

for my bag. Alec slides his hand around my body and places his big palm at the small of my back as he leads me out. "Where are we going?"

"I need air," he says.

He guides me to the limousine that picked me up that first night and opens the door for me. I slide into the back.

"Hi, Phillip, it's nice to see you again."

"You as well, Megan." He gives me a big smile, like he's actually delighted to see it's me getting into the backseat.

"What's going on?" I say to Alec as he climbs in beside me. I scan his face, still unable to read him. He clearly has his guard up. "Did the date go well or not?"

"Not," he says. "Phillip, how about a drive through the city."

"Very well, Alec." With that Phillip presses a button on the dashboard, and the privacy divider goes up.

"What happened with Danielle?"

"She was a good choice. I can see why you picked her. She fit my needs, but when I came right out and told her I wasn't looking for love, things fizzled from there." He shakes his head. "Here I thought it would be easy."

"Maybe girl-next-door types aren't impressed by your wealth." Is it weird and awful that I'm happy he didn't go home with her tonight? *Yes, yes it is, Megan. You need to get him married. Not just for your business but for Amanda's, too.*

He moves closer, and his thigh touches mine. The air around us instantly charges. I suck in a fast breath, sexual tension arcing between us. "Yeah, maybe," he says, his voice dropping an octave.

"We'll keep trying." Dammit, I hate how raspy my voice sounds. "There has to be a nice girl out there who will be happy with the lifestyle you're willing to offer."

"Maybe I need to switch tactics, figure out how to impress a nice girl."

"That's probably a good idea."

"Are you willing to give me a hand?" he asks, his voice low and husky, and so goddamn sexy my nipples harden, and I grow damp between my legs. How can this man turn me on with a simple question? That in itself is a huge problem, and if I knew what was good for me, I'd knock on the glass and ask Phillip to pull over so I can run far away from this man, and this spell he seems to have over me.

I open my mouth, about to end this, but instead find myself asking, "What do you have in mind?"

Good Lord, girl.

He reaches into a cabinet and pulls out a bottle of my favorite white wine. He opens it and hands me a glass. I take a sip and moan. "Mmm, delicious."

"Impressed?"

"I'm impressed that you knew my favorite kind of wine. I've always liked dry white, but my favorite brand has changed over the years, so how did you know?"

"I asked Amanda when I called her shop to put an order in."

"Ah, I'll have to talk to her about telling my secrets. What else did she divulge?"

"Nothing, and I'd rather find out your secrets myself. A nice girl would like that, right?"

"She probably would, and thank you for supporting Amanda's business. I really appreciate it."

"You're a good friend. We should all be so lucky."

I'm about to ask him about his friends when another thought hits. "Wait, why do you have my favorite wine in the car. Were you planning this?"

Instead of answering, he presses a button and the moonroof opens. A cool night breeze brushes over us, but my body is so hot, it's refreshing. I glance out to take in the mosaic of stars shining in the velvet sky.

"Wow, so pretty."

"Want to be really impressed?" he asks, and takes my wine from me.

"Sure."

"Stand up," he says, and shifts to the seat across from me. I stand, and poke my head through the opening in the roof as his hands go to my waist to balance me. Wind rushes through my hair, but fortunately we're going slow enough that it doesn't steal my breath. I glance around, take in the traffic and all the bright lights of the bustling city. I'm about to duck back inside when Alec's hand dips beneath my skirt, and slides upward, dragging the fabric with it.

Oh, my God.

As he exposes the lower half of my body, I flatten my hands on the roof of the vehicle and can't believe that I'm shifting my stance, giving him access to the spot that has been craving his touch since we parted last Saturday. Okay, that's a lie. I've been craving his touch since our night in St. Moritz. Still, this is wrong. He had a date with another woman tonight. A date *I* set up.

His hand slides a little higher and a moan catches in my throat. Okay, maybe I'll just let him touch me for a second, give me one glorious orgasm, because goddammit, I'm fighting a losing battle here. He rubs my clit through my lacy underwear, the panties he bought me last week. If I didn't know better—and I'm not entirely sure I do—I'd think I wore the thin lace on purpose, in case something exactly like this might happen tonight.

He tugs the panties to the side, and cool air washes over my pussy, but the second his mouth closes over me, my temperature skyrockets. "Oh, yes," I cry out, as he licks me from top to bottom, circling my clit in that little way that makes me insane.

He dips one thick finger inside me, and rubs the bundle of nerves that takes me higher and higher. He pulls his finger out and slides two back in, filling me so nicely. "Please," I murmur, even though I'm sure he can't hear me, but then he changes the pace and depth, touching me places so deep, I can barely fill my lungs.

From the sidewalk, a group of teens raise their fists and pump air as they cheer me on, like they're privy to what's going on down below, and for some reason, I'm not even embarrassed. This man, the lust he arouses in me is melting all my reserve, not to mention my brain cells. Seriously, though, I can't for one minute believe I'm in a limo, driving through New York, as Alec finger fucks me from the backseat. Does it get any better—any dirtier—than this? Jeez, maybe deep down, this girl next door is a little more adventurous and a whole lot more naughty than she ever knew.

In a fast move, he rips the material from my hips, and I can't believe how much I like his impatience. The soft blade of his tongue swipes over my clit, a hot stimulation that curls my toes and my fingers.

"Yes," I moan, and lift my gaze to the sky, not able to focus on anything but the pleasure coursing through me. He takes his fingers from my pussy, and I groan, but when he pushes his tongue in and slides his hands around my backside, massaging my cheeks and spreading them, a new kind of need takes hold.

Is he going to…

He touches my back opening, rolling his finger around the rim, and dipping in slightly, and the sensations are so foreign and so delicious, my entire body pulses. What the hell? With his tongue inside me, his finger gently probing my backside, I buck forward and grind my clit on his face. His growl of approval reaches my ears, thrills me, and a second later a gasp crawls out of my throat, and I grip the hood of the vehicle as a powerful orgasm tears through me, stealing my ability to breathe as well as to stand. As my hot release drips down my thighs, my legs weaken, and Alec pulls me in.

His eyes are dark, intense, but there is a small smile playing on his gorgeous face. He likes playing with me, likes trying new dirty things to gauge my reactions. Well, if that orgasm didn't tell him I liked it a little filthy, nothing would. And who knew? Surely not me. My sex has always been vanilla. How could I ever go back to boring missionary after this?

I'm about to fall back onto my seat when he pops the button on his chinos, and pulls out his cock. My mouth waters as I take in his huge thickness, and before I can even think about what I'm doing, I straddle his lap, and sink down until every inch of him is buried deep in my body.

"Alec," I cry out, and press my mouth to his, taste myself on his tongue.

"You feel so fucking good," he murmurs into my mouth. He cups my breasts through my blouse, and brushes his thumbs over my aching nipples. I arch into him, and his big fingers fumble with the buttons. "I want to rip this off you," he growls. While I want that, too, I don't want to be caught exiting the vehicle with my clothes torn apart. He finally gets the buttons opened, and unhooks my bra from the back. I shrug out of it and as I move up and down, slide his cock in and out of me, he clamps down on one nipple and I go perfectly still.

"So good," I moan, and as he sucks on me, his other hand massages my breast. He growls and my sex muscles ripple around his pulsing cock. I want to feel him. That's when some small working brain cell reminds me I jumped on his cock without a condom.

"Alec," I say, a hint of panic in my voice. There is more than pregnancy to consider here. "Protection."

My nipple pops from his mouth, and he curses. Before I can think better of it, even though there is a part of my lust-induced brain warning this is a bad idea, I cup his face, and say, "I'm clean and I'm on the Pill."

He exhales, almost painfully. "I'm clean, too, Megs. I always use a condom. I promise."

"I trust you," I say, shocking myself with that admission. He might be a lot of things but the Alec I knew and loved would never do anything to hurt me.

"I don't want to stop," he says, his cock still buried deep inside me. "I want to fill you with my cum."

"I want that, too," I say, even though I'm not sure why. Maybe it's because I want to do something special with him, something I've never done with another man. Or maybe it's because I want a part of him in me, a reminder of this night when I watch him walk down the aisle with another woman.

"Good," he growls.

"Then we can do this?"

He grips my hips, lifts me up and then pulls me

back down again. Heat and need roll through me. "Yeah, we can fucking do this."

I gasp and press my forehead to his. We breathe together as he repeats the movement, and lifts his hips to power into me. My hands go to his shoulders, palm his muscles through his sweater.

"You are so overdressed," I say, almost giddily as he takes me higher and higher.

"I'll get naked for you later," he says, and shifts me to take my other nipple into his mouth.

Later, yes. Later I can spend time with my mouth on his body, his beautiful cock. Wait, no, there can't be a later. Later I'll be stronger. Later I'll somehow find the willpower to stop this from happening. I lift my arms, brace them on the roof, as he licks, nibbles and sucks on my turgid nipples, each slide of his tongue so beautiful and artful, I feel the pull deep between my legs.

"I'm so close, Megs," he says, and pulls me to him, his arms wrapped tight around my body, his mouth buried in my neck.

"I feel you. You're throbbing." I moan, lift high and when I sink back down, I come all over his cock.

"Jesus, you're so hot."

His teeth scrape the tender flesh of my shoulder as he powers into me and goes completely still as he finds his release. I hold my breath, concentrate on each pulse, as well as the sensations he rouses deep inside me.

When he finishes, I suck in a gasping breath and

he cups my face. "Breathe, Megs. Breathe with me." I gulp and he inhales, and I follow his lead for a few minutes until I'm no longer panting.

Catching me by surprise, he brings my mouth to his for the softest, sweetest kiss. The tenderness in his lips wraps around my heart and squeezes. Damn, that is not good.

"I see you have a thing for ripping panties," I say, trying to make light of this.

He chuckles. "Just yours."

I lift myself from his cock. He groans, and opens some compartment and pulls out a tissue. He wipes me between the legs and my heart wobbles at the gesture. I fix my skirt as he cleans himself and disposes of the tissue, and that's when a bit of reality creeps in.

"Do you think he heard?" I ask, staring at the privacy panel.

"No, it's soundproof." He zips up and leans toward me, a dirty, wicked grin on his face. "I would never put you in a situation where someone could hear or see you, Megan. Not unless you wanted that."

"Oh," I say for lack of anything else as I put my bra and blouse back on. This guy really is kinky, and I kind of like that.

He presses a button, and says, "We can head to Central Park now."

The vehicle turns, and I sway into Alec as he comes to sit beside me. He glances out the window, and from the heavy way he's breathing, to the way he's gone quiet and pensive, I get that he has something on his mind. Maybe he, too, is trying to figure out why we keep doing this. As though moving of its own accord, his hand closes over mine and squeezes. I swallow against the tightness in my throat.

"Central Park?" I ask. "Why there?"

"Something I want to show you," he says quietly without taking his gaze from the road. We sit in silence and a few minutes later, the car stops. Alec opens the privacy barrier. "Thanks, Phillip, we shouldn't be too long."

"Take as long as you like, Alec."

Alec nods, climbs from the car and holds his hand out to me. I accept it and slide out. "Come on," he says, and I follow him blindly through the park, toward the crowd gathering at the pond.

"Oh, my God, we're here to see the Mandarin duck, aren't we?"

He grins. "You ruined the surprise."

I plant one hand on my hip and eye him. "I've really been wanting to see it. Did Amanda tell you about this, too?"

"No, I figured this one out all on my own. You always used to love coming here to feed the ducks." A chill goes through me, and he tugs me to him. One arm circles my body and he runs his hand up and down my arms to warm me.

"You remembered," I say quietly, touched that he took me here—then and now.

"I remember."

My heart pinches. On my saddest days missing

my parents, Alec used to take me to the pond. It was a distraction, and it always helped me clear my head, get it on straight and figure out my future.

We make our way to the edge of the pond to see the beautiful, multicolored duck. "How do you suppose an Asian duck made it to Central Park?" I ask.

"Don't know. He's kind of mean, though," Alec says as the duck nips at a local mallard.

"He's probably just unsure and feeling lost and territorial," I say, understanding those emotions exactly after seeing Alec with Danielle tonight.

I glance up at Alec, and his eyes are serious and intense when they meet mine. If I'm not careful, this man is going to ruin me. I turn back to the pond and once again, as I stand here, I realize what's real, what's not and what my future holds.

"Let me just say, I don't really think you have a problem impressing nice girls. I've been chatting with another woman online. I'll set you up a date for next week." Forcing a smile, I add, "She's a librarian. Maybe she's one of those women who are all quiet during the day and real wild at night." It's cliché, but I thought that would pull a smile from him, but no, he's still staring at me like he wants to eat me alive again.

Okay, I get it. There is tension between us, enormous tension, enough to light up Central Park in a blackout, for a week. Maybe Sara was right. Maybe he did like me back in the day, but decided not to start anything because he wasn't the marrying type, and I wanted the family and kids. Fine, I can live with that rejection now, especially knowing he doesn't believe in marriage, or love. But at the end of the day, why can't we continue to have some fun together until I find him a wife. We're both single, and we clearly fit in the bedroom—or the back of a limo. The man drove straight for my sex when I poked my head through the roof, and I'll be damned if I didn't want that. Why deny myself earth-shattering orgasms? If I keep my heart out of it, I can't see why I should.

"I was thinking," I say.

"About?"

"You might need more help than I first thought. Maybe it's a good idea if I continue to be of assistance. You know, to give you practice impressing the girl next door."

His nostrils flare and even in the dim light I can see the black of his eyes bleed into the blue. "Do you think that's a good idea?" he asks, and I get it, he wants me physically but he's as unsure about this idea as I am.

"No, not even a little bit."

CHAPTER EIGHT

Alec

WITH THE MORNING board meeting finished, I tug on my jacket and I'm about to push from my chair and leave the boardroom when Malcolm Blake, CEO and chairman of the board, holds his finger up to me.

"Can you hang back a moment, Alec," he says, and I give a curt nod as everyone exits the room.

"What can I do for you, Malcolm?" I ask when we're alone.

He crosses the room, leans against the massive table and puts his hand on my shoulder. "I had a drink with your grandfather on Sunday."

"I'm sure he enjoyed the visit. Was he his usual pleasant self?" I ask, thinking about how he grumped about the stock market after my last visit. He might be in his nineties, but he keeps up with the news, and watches his investments closely. I'm pretty sure he's on the ball way more than he lets on. He might fool the other grandkids, but he's not fooling me.

He laughs, like he's privy to some inside joke, and says, "He told me you're getting serious with a woman. That we should be hearing wedding bells in the near future."

"He did, did he?" What. The. Fuck.

"You know, James never was much good at keeping secrets."

Or keeping his nose out of his grandkids' business. But it's best I don't say that.

"We'd love to meet this girl," he says. "Stability goes a long way with the board of directors, and that will definitely come into play when we choose the next CFO. Karl will be retiring in the fall, and of course we have a few other candidates, but marriage will definitely give you a leg up. You'd be the youngest CFO in Blackstone's history."

I grin. "It would be my honor."

He slaps my shoulder. "Summer is just around the corner and you know what that means."

"Blackstone's annual golf tournament." Every year the event is held at Malcolm's own personal golf course, and the members and their families all convene, eat and drink. I usually play a round of golf and hightail it out of there before every grandmother tries to set me up with their granddaughter.

"That's right, and we expect you to bring your young lady."

"We'll be there," I say.

"That's what I wanted to hear," he says. He pushes off the table and I stand. He walks me to the door and I can't help but want to strangle Granddad for telling him I was getting serious. Well, not really, but shit, did he have to tell Malcolm?

I nod to my assistant, step into my office and close the door. Circling my colossal desk, I sit, and stare out the window to take in all that is New York. The sun is warm today and getting warmer as summer approaches. I tug my phone from my pocket and it buzzes in my hand. My heart leaps, hoping it's Megan. When I see her name, I want to kick my ass. I shouldn't be this happy to hear from her, and agreeing to sleep together the other night, yeah, not my brightest moment. But I can't seem to keep my hands off her. Maybe this is for the best. Keep having sex with her and get it out of my system once and for all. Like I actually believe that's going to happen. But what choice do I have? Keeping my hands to myself clearly isn't working.

Megan: I hate to ask, but can you help me with something?

Alec: Does it involve getting you naked?

Megan: Is that all you ever think about?

Alec: No sometimes I think about other things too. Want to hear?

Megan: I bet and no, I don't want to hear.

Alec: Hey, what is it you need help with and why do you hate to ask?

Megan: I am trying to secure Skylark as the venue for my aunt and uncle's anniversary party, but I keep getting the answering machine. Time is short. I was wondering…

Alec: Yes, I know the owner, but it's going to cost you, and if you think I'm talking about the venue being expensive, you'd be wrong.

Megan: That's blackmail.

Alec: That's right.

Megan: You didn't forget about your date tonight did you?

Alec: How could I when you keep reminding me. What should I wear?

Megan: I'm going to swing by your place around 4. I have a client I need to meet near your place. I'll lay out your clothes. Karla the librarian loves sushi, so pretty casual.

Alec: Give me the details on Skylark. I'll make some calls, and don't ever worry about asking me for a favor.

Megan: Thank you Alec.

I stare at my phone as she sends me the details, my heart pounding a little faster. When we finish texting, I pinch the bridge of my nose, and open my laptop. I have a ton of work to get through this afternoon, but now my thoughts are filled with Megan, and doing things for her, making her life a bit easier. I make a few calls, talk to the right people and in no time at all I secure her venue. I could call her and tell her, of course. But I'd rather do it in person so I can see her smile, her reaction.

Head down, I bury myself in my work, ordering in a sandwich for lunch, and eating at my desk. When late afternoon rolls around, I power down my computer, shove it into my bag and head outside. I find my Tesla in my designated spot and jump in. Maneuvering through the busy afternoon traffic, I make my way home, my pulse jumping in anticipation as I get closer.

I hit the button to open the garage door and drive into the well-lit underground parking area. The smell of gas and fumes lingers in the air as I wait for the elevator to arrive. When it does Derek greets me and waves his hand for me to enter.

"You're home a bit early today, Alec," he says, making small talk like we always do.

"I have some things to take care of at home," I tell him, and he grins at me like he knows exactly what I'm up to.

"Miss Williams has already arrived," he informs me.

I scrub my face to hide my smile. "Yes, we have some business to take care of." Derek puts his hands behind his back and whistles softly as we make our way to the penthouse. "How's Peggy?" I ask. Last time we talked about his wife, she was in the hospital with complications from pneumonia. At the time, it was easy to tell Derek was distressed, and worried about the hospital bills.

He gives me a toothy smile. "She's doing well. She's back to work, and feeling herself again."

"Glad to hear that."

"We sure would like to thank whoever took care of our medical expenses."

I nod. "I'm sure if they wanted a thank-you, they would have given you their name."

"You're probably right about that. Best I let it go."

"For the best, I think."

When the elevator stops at my penthouse, I practically leap off.

Derek chuckles slightly. "I don't remember ever seeing you this happy," he says, and that's when it occurs to me that I am happy, and haven't been this happy since…high school. "You have a wonderful day," he adds before the doors ping shut.

"You, too," I say, and pull my key from my pocket. I open the door quietly, not wanting to startle Megan but wanting to surprise her just the same.

I drop my laptop bag and kick off my shoes. From my bedroom, she's humming something and I pad quietly down the hall, following the sound as it wraps around my dick and strokes hard. I stop at the doorway and damn near swallow my tongue when I find Megan bent over my bed, arranging clothes for me to wear. From my viewpoint, I take in the soft swell of her ass in her sexy black-and-white-striped dress, which rides up her creamy thighs as she moves my clothes around.

I clear my throat and she spins around, her hand going to her chest. Eyes wide, she stares at me. "Alec, you scared me half to death."

"Sorry," I say, as my gaze races over her, my dick thickening even more.

"What…what are you doing here?"

"I live here, remember."

She plants a hand on her hip, and glares at me. Damned if that doesn't turn me on even more. "I told you I was going to take care of your clothes."

"There's something else that needs taking care of," I say, and she gives me a quizzical look.

"Oh, what might that be?" she asks, but the blush crawling up her neck lets me know she gets it.

"You, Megs. You need to be taken care of." Christ, all I can think about is laying her on that bed and giving her a dozen orgasms.

"Me? What do I need taken care of?" she asks, her chest rising and falling a bit faster.

"I secured your venue. Skylark is booked for the party," I say, and my heart crashes against my chest when her eyes go wide and a huge smile splits her lips. Catching me by surprise, she rushes across the room and throws her arms around me. I pick her up and her legs go around my back. Fuck, yeah.

"Alec, this means the world to me. My aunt and uncle will be so happy." She hugs me tight and her breath is warm on my neck. "I have no idea how to thank you."

"I do," I say, my voice a little deeper. Her head slowly inches back. Our eyes meet and her expression is filled with equal amounts of curiosity and desire.

"Do you now?" she asks, her lips quirked, and I love that she's playing along. "Care to explain?"

"It involves hot water, and soap." I shift my hands under her ass to hold her, walk to my bathroom and set her on the counter. Her arms fall to her sides as I step back, and let my gaze race over her beautiful face and body. God, she's so perfect.

I shrug out of my suit jacket and loosen my tie. "I need to wash up and get ready for my date. I haven't showered with a good girl yet, and I believe I'm going to need your assistance."

"Oh, well." Her legs widen on the counter, and her dress rides farther up her thighs. Fuck, she is so sexy. "Yes, we did agree that I would help you practice impressing nice girls." She gives a sigh. "The things I do for you, Alec."

I remove my tie and unbutton my shirt. Her eyes drop, take in my near nakedness. Christ, I love the way she looks at me. "I think it might be beneficial to us both." I remove my shirt and tug open my pants. Her fingers go to the small buttons lining her dress, and man, do I ever want to rip it off her. She toys with the top button, but doesn't open it, and I can't help but think her thoughts mirror mine.

"Yes, that's right. You get to become CFO, and I get all the perks that come with planning your wedding."

I kick off my pants and socks then remove my boxers. Her breathing changes when I take my hard dick into my hand and start stroking. "Well, yes, there's that," I say, and step up to her. I slide my hand up her thighs, and push her panties to the side. "But maybe a few other perks, too."

"Such as," she asks breathlessly, her hips moving, squirming, as her hot core beckons my touch.

I slide a finger into her. "An orgasm or two."

"Alec," she gasps, her hands going to my shoulders as I fuck her soaking wet sex with my finger. I love finding her like this, love how aroused she gets for me. Her eyes slip shut and her lips part as she tosses her head from side to side, her hair a tumbling mess over her shoulders. With my finger moving in and out of her, I slide my tongue over her bottom lip, then lean in for a taste. She kisses me back, her soft sexy moans of excitement curling around my cock.

She reaches down, takes my thickness in her hands and I let loose a loud growl. "This is very impressive," she says, and as she strokes me, her pussy grows wetter. I chuckle and slide another finger in, wanting to bring her to orgasm so I can taste her. I press my palm against her clit, and stimulate it as I finger fuck her and her hands grip my dick tighter. Her pussy starts rippling and I pull out of her. Her hands fall from my cock, and she braces them behind her and lifts herself slightly as I slide her panties down. I toss them away, grip her legs and widen them even more. Desperate to taste her, make her come all over my tongue, I bury my face between her legs. I lick her, put my tongue inside her and circle her clit with my thumb.

"Alec," she cries out, and a second later her hot juice spills from her beautiful pussy. I growl and lap at her, drink her in, not wanting to miss a damn drop.

"You taste so good, Megs," I say as she continues to ripple and ride out the pleasure. Her hips move, buck against my face, and when her body stops spasming, I stand and wipe my wet mouth with the back of my hand. Her eyes are glazed, and her chest rises and falls.

Fucking sexy.

As she sits there, struggling to catch her breath, I turn on the shower, and come back to lift her from the counter. Her body slides down mine, the tiny buttons on her dress scraping my flesh.

"Are you fond of this dress?" I ask.

"I have another just like it," she says, her eyes dimming with desire.

"Good." In one quick tug, I rip it open and the buttons fall to the floor and scatter. She gasps and

I tear it from her body and let it fall to her feet in a rumpled heap. "But I'll still replace it."

"You don't have to do that."

"Want to," I say.

I reach behind her and unhook her bra, freeing her beautiful breasts. "I haven't spent enough time here." I brush my thumb over her hard nipple, and bend to take it into my mouth. I lick softly, and squeeze her breasts together so I can taste both at the same time. "I'm going to fuck you here," I say, and she whimpers in response. "I'm going to fuck you everywhere."

"I don't see as we have a choice," she says playfully. "We have to cover everything so you're ready for your dates."

"Exactly," I say and back up, stepping into the stream and bringing her in with me. The warm, needlelike spray falls over us and I grab the bar of soap. I lather my hands and run them all over her body, and she moans as I touch her. I remove the nozzle, rinse her off and spend a few extra minutes with the spray between her legs. She's a quivering mess when I replace the nozzle and she reaches for the soap, washing me in turn. My dick is a steel rod by the time she takes it into her hands. Bubbles form as she soaps me, and I move my hips, power into her hand, but I don't want to come, not yet. There are so many things I need to do to her first. I grab the nozzle again and rinse my body, but before I can turn the spray off, she drops to her knees and takes my dick into her mouth.

"Fuck, Megs," I say as she takes me to the back of her throat and chokes a little. I push her wet hair from her shoulder, revel at the way she sucks me deep. One hand goes to my balls, and she gently massages. She works her mouth over me, taking me closer and closer to the edge. I need her to stop as much as I need her to continue. I fuck her mouth a few more times, and then pull back. She moans at the loss.

"I want you to come in my mouth," she says.

"Me, too. Come on."

I grab a towel and wipe her down, then quickly dry myself. Reaching for her hand, I take her back into the bedroom.

She sits on the edge of the mattress, and widens her legs to show me all her pretty pink wetness. I remove the clothes she laid out, and nearly bite off my tongue as she showcases her body.

I step up to her, push my thumb into her mouth and she sucks me so hard, I nearly shoot off. "You want my cum?" I ask, and she nods. "You want me to fuck this pretty mouth and shoot my cum down your throat?" She nods and squirms on the bed. "Is that what nice girls want?" I ask pulling my thumb out so she can answer.

"It's exactly what nice girls want," she says.

"Get on the bed, and squeeze those gorgeous tits together. I want to fuck them," I say, and she visibly quivers. She goes down on her hands and knees, pointing her sweet ass my way as she crawls to the middle of the mattress. I growl. "Megs," I say.

She looks at me over her shoulder. "Yes," she asks innocently.

I take my dick in my hand and stroke. "You shake your ass at me like that and it makes me think you want it fucked."

She drags her teeth across her bottom lip. "Maybe I do. Maybe I don't," she says, and I shake my head. This woman is going to be the death of me.

Pre-cum pools on my crown and I rub it around to lubricate my cock as she sprawls out, offering herself up to me completely. I climb over her and she squeezes her beautiful breasts together just like I asked. I place another pillow under her head and angle it, so her mouth can take my dick.

"Perfect," I say, and straddle her body. I slide my cock between her tits, and she opens her mouth when my crown presses against her lips with each forward thrust. I rock into her, and she swirls her tongue over me. "Yeah, just like that, baby," I say. "Show me how much you want my cum."

She quivers at my words, and I love the dirty side of this sweet girl. In fact, I love everything about her. But I can't think about that, not when her tits are squeezing me so tight, and her mouth is doing crazy things to my dick. I thrust into her harder, faster, chasing an orgasm as she moans around my crown, the vibrations going right through me.

"Yes," she cries out between each thrust.

"You've got me right there, baby," I growl, every muscle in my body tightening, as my orgasm mounts.

"You ready to taste me?" She nods and I reach down, slide my hand around the back of her neck and fill her mouth with my hot cum. She swallows and drinks me in, but I come so much she can't take it all. It spills from her lips and when I finally drain myself and pull out, she licks her mouth, cleaning every last drop.

I can barely catch my breath as I watch her. When she licks the last of my release, I turn her around and put a pillow beneath her hips, to lift her ass. "I plan to fuck you here," I say, and slide my finger between her sweet cheeks. I circle her tight opening, probe slightly. "It won't be tonight. It will take time to prepare you properly." She moves against my finger, and writhes on the bed and even though I just came, my cock grows hard again. I can't get enough of this woman. I slide a finger into her hot core, and she cries out my name. "Do you need my fat cock in here?" I ask.

"Yes, please," she says, and I chuckle.

"My dick is hard for you again," I say. "And this is exactly where it wants to be."

She wiggles her ass and I push my finger in as I position my cock at her dripping opening. In one hard thrust I drive home and she lets loose a cry.

"Alec, yes," she says, and reaches up to grip the headboard to hang on for the ride. I pull out and drive back in again. I slide my hand between the pillow and her body to stroke her clit.

"You like that, baby? You like my cock in here?"

"I do," she cries out, and I work my finger in her ass, stretching her, letting her get used to the new sensations.

"And my finger. You like my finger in this sweet virgin ass of yours?" Her reply is muffled as she buries her face in her pillow and comes all over my cock. Her muscles ripple around me, and I can't even believe I'm coming again. I spurt into her, and after filling her beautiful body, I fall over her back.

I push her hair to the side, and press kisses to her shoulder. She goes still beneath me, sated and spent, judging by the soft sounds of contentment crawling out of her throat. Not wanting to crush her, I roll over and pull her with me. She snuggles into me, and her hair tickles my face. I take deep breaths and let them out slowly as my heart rate settles to normal.

She lifts her face to mine, her gaze roaming over me, her smile, soft and seductive. "You keep looking at me like that, and we'll never get out of this bed," I say.

She chuckles slightly. "How exactly am I looking at you?"

I coil a strand of hair around my finger and give it a tug. "You know exactly how you're looking at me."

"Sex has never been this good," she admits.

"Impressed?" I ask, to stop myself from telling her it's the best sex I've ever had, too.

She laughs. "Very." But then all humor disappears from her face. "It's getting late, and I need to get you up to speed on Karla before your date."

I nod, but what I really want to do is crawl under the covers and spend the night with her. Except I can't do that. I'm not the guy for her and we both know it. Right? Wait, am I seriously thinking I am the guy for her? That I might have staying power?

Just then my cell rings…and rings and rings.

"You should probably get that," she says.

I go in search of my phone, and find it in my pants on the bathroom floor. I slide my finger across the screen. "Hey, Mom."

"Is it true?" she asks.

I pinch the bridge of my nose. "Is what true?"

"You hired Megan Williams to find you a wife?"

"Technically Granddad hired her."

A beat of silence then, "Alec…"

I can hear the worry in her voice, the fear… maybe even a hint of disappointment. She always liked Megan and was the one who warned me to distance myself from her all those years ago. Honestly for as long as I can remember, my mother criticized the Carson men, and constantly reminded me that I'd grow up to be no better, and would only end up breaking a woman's heart. It wasn't easy to hear I was cursed when I was just a boy, when I didn't really understand the history of my family. The older I got, the more I struggled with it, and I swallowed it down until I met Megan. I was so goddamn scared of hurting her, I had no choice but to walk away, even though it was, by far, the hardest thing I ever had to do.

"Mom…"

"Alec, do you still have feelings for Megan?"

"I need to get married and she's helping me."

"You didn't answer the question."

"She's a nice girl and—"

"And you'll just end up breaking her heart." I swallow. Hard. "Have you talked to your father lately?"

"No, why?"

She snorts. "He's got a new young thing on his arm."

"I didn't know."

"How could you at the rate he goes through them. The Carson men just can't commit, Alec. I'm sure you don't need me to bring up Will and the splash done on him in *Starlight*."

"No. I remember it well."

"Thank God, Naomie found out and left him before she became other casualty." She makes a tsking sound. "How embarrassing for him, and the entire Carson family." She goes quiet for a second. "Alec, honey," she says, softening her voice. "You know I love you. I'm just trying to save you from falling into your father's footsteps. I want you to be better than that, and I don't want to see your private *affairs* made public."

I cringe. She has about as much faith in my ability to remain monogamous as the rest of the Carson family. "I'm looking for a wife in name only," I tell her.

"I see."

"I know what I'm doing," I tell her, even though I'm pretty sure I don't. "I have to go. I'll talk to you later." We say our goodbyes and I end the call. I make my way back to Megan, who is looking at me with concern.

"Everything okay?"

"Yeah, you were going to tell me about Karla. Karla the librarian, who wants to go out for sushi on a Tuesday night. Although I shouldn't complain. The sooner I find someone, the better, right?"

"Right," she says, and pulls the blankets up to cover herself. Now, why did that feel more like a kick to the nuts? Oh, maybe because someplace deep inside me I want her to tell me not to go out, that she's the girl for me and we can make forever work. But there is no forever in my world, as I was just reminded, and I'd be wise to remember that.

Yeah, I'm totally fucked.

CHAPTER NINE

Megan

IT'S BEEN FOUR WEEKS. Four glorious, yet horrible weeks and not one of the dozen women I've set Alec up with have been "suitable." While one part of me is far too thrilled about that—seeing as I end up in his bed every night—the other part of me is distraught. The clock is ticking, and Blackstone's annual golf tournament where Alec is to introduce his fiancée is coming up fast. He needs to have a woman on his arm, and a ring on her finger, if he wants to impress the aging board of directors, with their old-fashioned values.

I rush around my apartment and get ready to meet Alec. At least I've convinced him to stop scaring the women off by blurting out that he wants a marriage in name only, and he promised he'd at least try to find common ground and give the relationship a chance. Yet none of the women have measured up to what he needs. Or so he says. I have the feeling he's not trying hard enough, and the women are the ones back-ing away, which is why I am now stepping in to go on a date with him. I want to see firsthand what he's like, how he acts and treats his dates. If he's com-ing off as some hard-assed, guarded businessman, no wonder he can't get a second date.

We're going to my favorite Mexican restaurant, and with the weather warmer and the nights grow-ing longer, I slip into one of my favorite dresses, a little black number that can be dressed up or dressed down. As it slides down my sides, the soft material scraping my skin, the sudden visual of Alec tearing it from my body sends heat to my core.

"Oh, my," I say under my breath as I fasten the button at the back and contort my arms to zip it up. I put on a bit of mascara, a light dusting of blush and swipe my favorite pink lipstick across my lips, which are still kiss-swollen from last night, and all the nights before.

The buzzer sounds, and I rush to my front door and press it, giving Alec access to the building. A moment later a knock comes on my door, and I take a deep breath. Why the hell am I so nervous? This is Alec, and I've been in bed with him numerous times.

You've never gone on a date, though.

But it's not even like it's a real date. We both know that. I'm only doing this to critique him. Right?

Okay, stop overanalyzing things, Megan.

I slip on my shoes and smooth my dress down, and pull myself together as I walk to the door. I swing it open, and when I find Alec standing there, looking casual and yummy in his chinos and button-down shirt, I nearly falter in my heels.

With one hand behind his back, he reaches out, touches the tumble of hair flirting with my shoulders. "You're beautiful," he says, his gaze slowly sliding down the length of me.

"You are, too," I say for lack of anything else.

He grins at me, a grin so sexy and so full of mischief and promise, I almost forget how to breathe. Surprising me, he produces a bouquet of flowers from behind his back.

"Nice touch," I say. Jeez, I can't remember the last time a guy gave me flowers, a real date or not.

"I thought so."

"Modest, too. For the life of me I don't understand why you can't get a second date," I tease.

"I'm not sure I'd use the word *can't*."

"Your ego won't allow that?" I tease.

"I told you, those women weren't right. You're doing a good job picking them. They fit all my criteria on paper, but there's something missing when we meet face-to-face."

"You have to stop being so picky," I say as I take the flowers into the kitchen. I fill a vase with water and drop them in. I turn back around and reach for my purse. "Ready?" I ask.

"Yeah," he grumbles, and follows me to the door. We step into the hall and I lock up. A few minutes later we're in his Tesla heading to Lindo's. Alec finds a parking spot and comes around my side of the car to let me out.

"So far, so good," I say to him. "That would impress any woman, I'm sure."

He grins. "I'm not an ogre. I do have manners. Plus, you're grading me, so I'm pulling out all the stops." He slides his arm around my body, placing his hand on the small of my back, and a fine shiver moves through me. "Cold?" he asks, his brow furrowed with genuine concern, and I hate how much I like that.

"Not really." No sense in lying. The man is well aware of what his touch does to me.

"Ah," he says, his grin widening. "We could skip dinner and head straight to my place."

"Alec," I warn, even though I'm in love with the idea. "We need to focus."

"Fine, fine," he says, and opens the restaurant door. I step inside and breathe in the delicious scents as I glance around the dimly lit, cozy and somewhat romantic restaurant. Alec stands close as the hostess comes our way, so close I can smell his freshly soaped skin as well as the aroma that is uniquely Alec.

Alec gives his name and reservation time, and the hostess checks her tablet before leading us to a small table in the back corner. Light from the candle dances across his handsome face as we take our seats.

"Nicest table in the place," I say to him, and look

around, noting the way some woman keeps casting glances our way. A former lover? My stomach knots at the thought and I push it down. Not my business, nor my issues.

Alec opens the wine list and hands it to me. "What would you like?" he asks.

"I'd love a glass of chardonnay," I say, and hand it back. The waiter comes to take our drink orders, and Alec orders wine for me and a soda for himself.

"You're not having anything?" I ask.

"I'm driving," he says and my heart wobbles in my chest.

"I wish you would have met my parents, Alec. You would have liked them."

"I'm sure I would," he says. "I feel like I know them anyway, from all your stories."

I swallow down the lump in my throat. "You were always such a good listener, so patient with me when I was sad. You barely knew me, and yet you took such good care of me. I don't think I would have made it without you." I pause for a moment as my mind trips back to high school. "In thinking back, I don't think it was fair of me to put that burden on you. I wasn't your problem."

His hand slides across the table and captures mine. "Megs, come on. You were going through a hard time, and I wanted to be there for you."

"Why?" I ask, and hold back the question I really want to ask.

Why did you leave me after prom?

"Sara and I were friends, and you were her cousin. You were like a lost puppy and I kind of have a thing for puppies," he says with a grin.

"You just lost points."

He sits up straighter, his shoulders square, and I can't help but grin at his cute yet confused expression. "What did I do?"

"Somehow in there, I think you called me an ankle biter."

He bursts out laughing, and I laugh with him, the mood around us softening, mellowing. The waiter comes with our drinks, and we place our food orders, and fall into easy conversation. The woman two tables over, however, keeps an eye on Alec and I do my best to ignore her.

Our meal arrives, a dinner for two, and in the center of the table the waiter sets out an enchilada, a burrito, a taco and a chimichanga for us to split.

"Looks amazing," I say as Alec slices the enchiladas in half and divvies them up on our plates.

"I haven't had Mexican in years," he says.

"Remember when we used to eat it every weekend?" I ask him. "It was always between pizza and Mexican."

"And nine times out of ten you always won the thumb war and got your way," he says.

I glance at his big hands. "Wait, did you let me win on purpose?" I bite into my food and moan at the delicious flavors.

"Me, let you win?" He arches a brow. "Are you forgetting how competitive I am?"

"Nope, you were competitive."

"Still am."

I take a sip of wine. "Win or die trying, right?"

He laughs. "Something like that?" He forks the enchilada into his mouth, and nods. "This is good," he says.

"Try this one." I cut the chicken burrito into two and put half on his plate. He takes a generous bite, and moans. "I think this beats pizza every day."

"Pizza has its place," I say, remembering the first night we shared a pie at his apartment and the way we played afterward. *Okay, get your mind off sex before your nipples poke through your dress. It's all fun and games until someone puts an eye out.* Changing topics, I ask, "You're still coming to the anniversary party tomorrow night?"

"Still planning on it, unless you're sending me out on another date."

"I'm not. I figured you needed a night off."

"I'm looking forward to catching up with Sara." A little sound escapes me when he brings up my cousin. "What?" he asks, and takes a drink of water.

"Did you know back in high school all the girls had a crush on you."

"Nope. Didn't know."

"Apparently they wanted a piece of Alec Carson." I lean toward him. "But they all thought we were an item."

He doesn't laugh at that, like I thought he would. Instead he says, "I can see that. We were pretty inseparable."

I dig deep, gather courage, and I'm about to ask him what happened to us, when the woman who's been staring takes out her phone and aims it our way.

"I think that woman just took a picture of us," I say to Alec.

"Shit," he says under his breath.

The woman pushes her chair back and steps up to our table. "Alec," she says. "Alec Carson."

He angles his head. "What can I do for you?" he asks, and from the way he's looking at her I get the sense they don't know each other.

"Rumor has it New York's most eligible bachelor is soon to get married." Her gaze slides to me, and she has a weird smirk on her face. "Are you the lucky lady who's finally pinned him down?"

"If you'll excuse us, we're in the middle of dinner," he says, his voice hard and agitated but holding a measure of politeness, even though the woman doesn't deserve it.

"But it's breaking news, Alec." She bats well-painted eyelashes at him, and does a flirty toss of her red hair. "I'm sure *Starlight* would love to do a spread."

Starlight is a tabloid magazine that emphasizes sensationalized crime stories and gossip about celebrities. It wasn't long ago that Will was on the cover...in bed with a woman who wasn't his fiancée. He must have gone into hiding, keeping his head down and nose clean, because he hasn't been in the news for a long time. Could this be the reporter who outed him?

The brazen woman turns to me. "And what is your name?"

"Her name is none of your concern," Alec answers through clenched teeth. His jaw is so tight, I'm sure he's going to crack his back teeth.

My pulse beats a little faster, and my heart goes out to Alec as I take in the tension in his body. I've seen the pictures of him in the papers, of course. But never knew how aggressive and downright rude the paparazzi could be—to his face—until this very second.

"Don't worry, I'll find out who she is." She laughs as her gaze moves over me. "Although you don't really seem like his type." She taps her finger to her chin, and puckers her lips. "Tired of playing with models, going for the plain Jane instead?" she asks, her gaze zeroing in on Alec.

Alec stands so fast, his chair shoves backward, but it doesn't faze the woman at all. "Don't you dare talk about her like that."

"Oh, my, I've never seen this protective side of you before, Alec. She must be pretty special," she says, giving me another glace before walking away.

Alec slowly sits back in his chair and smooths his hand over his chest.

"I'm sorry. It's awful what you have to put up with. Do you want to leave?"

He takes a deep breath, lets it out slowly. "Let's finish our meal and not give her that kind of power over us."

"Do you think she'll print the picture?"

"I don't know. We're having dinner. Nothing to really sensationalize over that."

"Does this happen a lot?" I catch a glimpse of the woman as she breezes out the door, looking quite smug with herself. "When you were on other dates, were you harassed?"

"Sometimes."

Perhaps that's why things never worked out. No one wants to be accosted, photographed or belittled during dinner.

"She's wrong, you know," he says.

"Wrong?"

"You're not a plain Jane. You're beautiful."

I set my fork down, my pulse jumping in my neck. "Thank you," I say quietly as he divides the taco, and puts half on my plate, but I no longer have an appetite. "How do you think she found out? Who would have said you were soon to get married?"

"Granddad is spreading it all around town. I'm going to have a talk with him."

"Don't be too hard on him. He's just excited for you. I think…" I let my words fall off. I don't want to say anything to upset him.

"You think what?" he asks, pushing the matter.

"I don't think he's very well, Alec. He was doing a lot of fading in and out when he hired me, like he was forgetting his words, and I think he just wants to see his grandkids happy and settled down before…" I can't bring myself to finish the sentence. I've always loved Alec's granddad. He was so good to me when we were younger, and the thought of losing someone else I care about cuts me deeply.

"Yeah, I guess." Alec pinches the bridge of his nose. "I'm not so sure his mind is going, though."

"Really, why?"

"He had enough wits about him to convince me to get married, and drag you into it all."

"He didn't drag me. I went into this willingly."

"Even though you knew it was me."

"Yes."

"Even after…" He looks down, like his thoughts are now a million miles away. Or more like eight hours away by plane. The amount of time it takes to go from New York to St. Moritz.

The waiter comes, interrupting the moment, and asks if I'd like a refill on wine. I decline, and set my fork down, finished with dinner and wanting to leave, just to go somewhere we can be alone.

"Ready to go?" Alec asks.

"Yes. You?"

He gestures to the waiter to bring the bill, and after he pays, we make our way out into the dark night. I breathe in the fresh spring scents before climbing into the Tesla. Alec circles the car, his strong, confident movements drawing my attention, and a few minutes later, he pulls into traffic, but instead of taking me back to my place he goes in the opposite direction.

"Where are we going?" I ask.

"It's a surprise."

"I don't like surprises," I say.

He laughs. "Like hell you don't. You screamed your head off when I got you those Rolling Stones concert tickets for your birthday."

"Well, okay maybe I do," I say. "As long as it's a good surprise."

His hand slides across the car and sits heavy on my thigh as he gives it a squeeze. His warmth seeps through me, and my insides quiver with all the crazy things I feel for this man. All the emotions that have resurfaced in his presence. Suddenly I'm not so sure any of this was worth it. Not if it means I spend another eight years mending a broken heart.

I stare out the window, take in the pedestrians and shops as he drives, and soon enough we're at Central Park. "Are we here to feed the duck again?" I ask.

"Nope." He parks and comes around to my side of the car. I climb out, and he hits the fob to lock the doors. "Let's go," he says, taking my hands in his. A breeze blows over us as I follow him through the lit park and he stops at the hansom cab.

"A carriage ride? Are you serious?" I ask.

"You said you've never been in one but would like to." He grins. "How many points does this get me?"

"A lot," I say, a little touched and surprised that

he remembered. He boosts me up until I'm situated on the seat. He talks to the driver for a second, and then climbs in beside me. I snuggle close, and he wraps his arm around me.

The buggy starts, and I glance around to admire the sights and the people. "This is so nice," I say.

"Yeah, it is."

His mood is mellow, but there is heat in his eyes as he gazes at me. His hand brushes my hair from my face. "I want to be inside you," he whispers.

My heart stalls. "I want that, too."

"My place or yours?" he asks.

I grin at his cheesiness. "How about winner chooses," I say, and take his hands in mine for a thumb war. He laughs out loud and the sound takes me back, reminding me of the Alec I once knew. Only problem is, I'm beginning to like this version of him a little too much.

CHAPTER TEN

Alec

PHILLIP PULLS THE limo up to the curb, and I thank him as I exit the vehicle.

I step inside the building where the anniversary party is well underway and take the elevator to the top floor. I'm a bit late but I had some last-minute things to take care of that kept me tied to my desk. When I enter the Skylark, I look around and finally spot Megan talking to Sara. My heart kicks into gear the second I see her, but then worry seeps into my bones. I can't tell what they're discussing but from Megan's body language, I'd hazard a guess that it's something very important. I take a step toward her when I'm stopped by Megan's aunt and uncle.

Jeannie opens her arms wide, her smile sincere and genuine. I always loved that about her. She was down-to-earth, and very motherly, which was something Megan needed after losing her folks.

"Alec," she cries out, ecstatic to see me, and I

bring her in for a big hug. "I understand you're to thank for all this," she says, widening her arms and glancing out the floor-to-ceiling window, with the view of the Hudson River, Empire State Building and Midtown Manhattan.

"Just made a call. This is all Megan," I say, giving her the credit.

"How are you, son?" Dave asks, and gives my hand a shake.

"Doing well. How about you?"

"Counting down the days to retirement," he says, and we both laugh. "Come on, what are you drinking?" He puts his hand on my shoulder to lead me to the bar. I excuse myself from Jeannie, who is already greeting other arriving guests, and take in the cozy atmosphere as we head to the bar at the back. We both take a seat and I order a brandy.

"What's this about you getting married?" Dave says, and I laugh. He always was one to get right to the point, much like Granddad, which is why they've always hit it off.

"I guess you've been talking to Granddad."

"Ran into James on the golf course the other day."

"Granddad was playing golf?" I say. Yeah, he's far more agile and sly than he's letting on.

"Winning, too," he says with a chuckle. "He told anyone who would listen that his grandson would soon be making a big announcement."

"I bet he did."

"Who's the lucky girl?" he asks, and my gaze in-

stantly goes to Megan. Dressed in a sexy black cock-
tail dress, with her hair pinned up, showcasing her
neck, she's the most stunning woman in the room.
Jesus, I've never seen her more beautiful. Maybe
that's not entirely true. A well-sated Megs in my
bed, all sleepy, and warm. Yeah, that's one hell of a
look on her. But those days must come to an end. My
own brother couldn't keep his dick in his pants—the
spread in *Starlight* proved that—and he was engaged
to a woman he loved. We just don't have it in us and
I can't—won't—hurt Megs like that.

I turn back to Dave, who is watching me carefully, and try to get my shit together. "We'll be making an announcement soon," I say. "Right now, it's
hush-hush."

Dave laughs at that. "Well, it's nice to see you and
Megan together again. Here I used to think you'd one
day put a ring on her finger."

I give a humorless laugh. "We're just friends," I
say, the lie catching in my throat.

"That's what she says, too." He takes a long drink
from his glass, draining the amber liquid. "James
also told me about the great things you're doing at
the university."

Fuck, are none of my secrets safe with that man?
And honestly if he's so disgusted with my lifestyle
and what I do for a living, why is he talking about
my charity work. I keep that private.

"There you are," Megan says, coming up to us.

Her gaze goes back and forth between the two of us. "Wait, what was that about the university?"

"Nothing," I say quickly.

"Oh, okay," she says, my words taking her back a bit, judging by the way she's blinking rapidly. "I was beginning to think you changed your mind about coming."

"Just had some last-minute things to take care of," I tell her.

She gives me an odd, almost edgy look, and I frown, hoping everything is okay between her and Sara.

Dave stands. "Well, I must go mingle," he says. He gives Megan a kiss on the cheek. "Thanks again for all this, sweetie. Your aunt is over-the-moon happy."

"My pleasure," Megs says and hugs him.

When he's gone, she turns to me. "What's going on?" I ask, my gaze raking over her face and taking in the tension in her body.

She shakes her head. "Am I that easy to read?"

"Yes."

I finish the brandy in my glass and gesture the bartender for another. "What are you having?" I ask.

"White wine."

I get her a glass, and say, "Want to step outside, get a breath of fresh air."

"Yes," she says quickly, her voice almost breathless.

We maneuver through the guests, and we end up

stopping at least a dozen times to make small talk. When we're finally outside alone, Megan takes a deep breath, and looks at the view.

"Gorgeous," she says, and I shift closer, pressing the side of my body to hers.

"Yeah," I agree, my gaze focused solely on her. She glances up at me, that odd worried look back in her eyes.

"I was talking to Sara."

"I saw that when I came in."

"She's smart, a lawyer as you know. A great conversationalist, too. She hasn't had much luck with men, and is pretty much done with the dating scene."

I eye her. Where the hell is she going with this?

She takes a drink of her wine, and I toss back my brandy.

"She's pretty, too. She doesn't have blond hair and blue eyes, but she does have those girl-next-door looks you mentioned."

I nod as understanding dawns. "What are you saying, Megan?" I ask, just to make sure.

"She's game, Alec."

"Game?" Why is it she can't quite bring herself to just say Sara wants to be my wife in name only?

"She's up for a sex-only marriage."

I rock back on my heels, toss the idea around in my brain. "I see. What are your thoughts?"

"I think it's an excellent idea. I mean, it's Sara. You two go way back so a fast engagement and marriage will be more believable, right?"

"True."

"Plus you've gone on numerous dates and can't find anyone suitable. Time is also of the essence."

"Yeah" is all I say.

"You were right, you know," she says so low I have to strain to hear her.

"About what?"

"She likes the idea of your wealth and power. It surprised me. But I guess there really are girls out there enticed by such things." She gives a humorless laugh. "You won't have to worry about her falling for you and asking for your heart."

"I guess I won't."

"Anyway, I changed the seating arrangement, and put you next to her. You guys can treat it like a date, get reacquainted and see if she's right for you."

She sips her wine, and it takes every ounce of strength I have not to bend forward and lick the moisture from her lips. Instead, I harden myself, and take a measured step back.

"We should get inside." She checks her watch. "Dinner will be ready in a minute."

She makes a move to go, and I cup her elbow. She spins back to face me. "Megs," I say.

"Yes?" As she looks up at me, with those big inquisitive brown eyes, I want to tell her the truth. I want to tell her she's the one for me, but I can't bring myself to do it. I love her and don't want to hurt her.

"Thanks."

"You're...you're welcome," she says, stammering a bit, and I hate myself even more.

"I'll leave you two to catch up."

I swallow down the bile punching into my throat as she pulls her elbow away and disappears inside. I follow her in, and make my way to the tables set up for dinner. I find Sara and she waves me over. She pulls the chair out for me and I sit next to her.

"Sara," I say.

"Alec." She shifts a bit closer to me. "It's so good to see you again."

"You, too."

"So," she begins. "Have you talked to Megan?"

I give a nod. "Is this something you want to do, Sara?"

She gives a laugh, and tosses her hair over her shoulder in a flirty manner. "I am so done with relationships, and I've been working my ass off at the firm, trying to make partner. Like your old-school board of directors, marriage and stability go a long way with my senior partners. It's the only way a partnership is going to happen for me, and I like the perks that come with being on your arm." I nod, not at all certain about this. Megan was right about everything. Sara is smart, and a great conversationalist, but looking at her reminds me of the woman I can't have. "But we don't have to rush into anything just yet," she says, as if she can read my hesitation. "Let's go on a few dates, see how compatible we are." She gives me a come-hither smile and I instantly understand she's talking about bed-room compatibility.

Megan takes a seat at the other side of the table, a few chairs down, and some guy who looks about her age, pounces into the seat next to her. He instantly engages her in conversation, and I wonder how well they know each other. Did she put him next to her on purpose? Is she interested in him?

Fuck me.

I tamp down the raging jealousy taking up resi-dency in my gut. I want her happy, and if that guy can do that for her, give her the family and happily-ever-after she wants, then I need to stop being a self-ish prick and get on board.

Soon enough our meals are served, and we all make small talk and dig in. Once dessert arrives, Dave stands, taps his spoon on his stemware to gain everyone's attention and smiles at those around the table.

"I would like to thank everyone for being here tonight to celebrate this special occasion," he be-gins. "Or maybe you're all here to give pity to Jean-nie for putting up with me for the last twenty-five years." Laughter erupts and when it dies down, he says, "She wasn't an easy one to catch, I tell you. But she was worth the chase." He bends down and gives his wife a kiss. "Jeannie," he says, "you are the best thing that has ever happened to me. You're kind, thoughtful, generous, have given me a beauti-ful family." I glance at Megan who has tears in her eyes. "Every day my love for you grows stronger, and every day my belly grows bigger, thanks to all the amazing meals you put on my plate." We laugh as his gaze moves around the table, and I swear he's talking to me and me alone when he holds my gaze and says, "If you're lucky enough to find someone who gives your life purpose, someone you can't wait to fall into bed with every night, and more importantly wake up to every morning, then hang on to her with everything in you, and if she doesn't see it your way, and she's worth the fight, then for God's sake fight." As we chuckle, he lifts his glass and we all follow suit. "Here's to the best twenty-five years of my life, and here's to many more."

After his speech, guests are socializing while dessert is being cleared, when Sara's phone rings. She reaches into her bag and checks the display.

"Shoot, I have to get this." She rolls her eyes. "Work."

"No problem," I say.

She excuses herself from the table and finds a quiet place to take her call. My gaze slides to Megan's and I find her talking to the guy beside her, but his gaze keeps drifting to her breasts. Son of a bitch. I push from my chair, and I'm about to grab him by the scruff and tell him to get some goddamn manners, when Sara touches my arm.

"I have to go." She goes up on her toes and puts her mouth to my ear. "This is so not how I wanted tonight to end."

"Yeah," I say as Megan excuses herself. She gives her aunt and uncle a hug, and heads toward the balcony. I relax slightly when douchebag doesn't follow. I turn back to Sara and try to focus on what she's saying to me.

"I'll call you tomorrow, and we'll make plans," she says. "I'm really looking forward to getting re-acquainted." She gives me a slow, simmering smile, one that tells me exactly how she wants our next date to go.

"I'll see you soon, Sara," I say, and bend to kiss her cheek. She's an attractive woman, but I feel no spark. I guess that's a good thing since I want a marriage in name only. We get a few raised eyebrows from those around the table and I suppose if we do go through with it, the display will go a long way.

After she disappears, others rise from the table, and I head to the balcony in search of Megan, but she's not there. If she's gone, there's no sense in me staying any longer. I say my goodbyes, head to the elevator and shoot Phillip a text. I step out into the chilly night and find Megan standing on the curb, hailing a cab and shivering in her tight dress.

"Hey," I say, and she turns to face me, a fake smile on her face.

"Oh, hey," she says as I step up to her, my body so close tension arcs between us.

"Did you like that guy?"

She frowns. "You mean the guy talking to my breasts?"

"Yeah, him."

A sound crawls out of her throat. "He's the son of my aunt's friend."

I nod and glance past her shoulder. "Where are you going?"

"I'm exhausted. I thought I'd call it a night, get to bed early. Wait, where's Sara?"

I dip my head, touch a strand of her hair and consider tugging on it until her mouth is open, mine for the taking. "She had some business to attend to."

"What do you think? Is she suitable?" Megan asks.

"Too early to tell."

"Oh."

Just then Phillip pulls up to the curb. "Come on," I say to her.

"No, it's okay. I can get my own lift."

"Get in the car, Megan."

"Alec—"

"In the car."

"You—"

"I'm still a single guy, Megan, and you're a single woman. Let me put my cock in you. One last time."

She blinks several times, and her body vibrates when I put my hand on her waist. "I… I…"

Even though she's stumbling over her words, she doesn't pull away, she steps closer to me. Taking that as a yes, I guide her to the car and open the door.

She aims her sweet ass my way as she climbs in and shimmies to the other side to make room for me.

"Hi, Phillip," she says, her voice as shaky as her body.

"Megan, always a pleasure."

"My place, please," I say and put my hand on Megan's leg, holding her in place. Tonight I want—no need—to be with her. Need to own and claim every inch of her body before I set her free again.

We sit in heavy silence as Phillip drives us home, and what feels like a lifetime later, he finally pulls up in front of my building. I open the door and Megan follows me out, the tension so thick between us, it's almost suffocating. I loosen my tie, and capture her hand to lead her up the front steps to the main door where Derek is standing guard.

"Good evening, Alec, Megan." He gives us a big toothy smile, and presses the button to the elevator. I clench down on my teeth when it takes too long to get here. We finally get on, and Derek inserts his key and takes us to the top floor. He doesn't make small talk like usual. I can only guess he feels the tension in the air.

We reach our destination, and we both hurry off, thanking Derek as I insert my key and drag her in with me. Finally alone, I push her against the door, and trap her body with mine.

"I've wanted my mouth here all night," I say, then press my lips to her, desperate to taste her. Her soft lips open, and she moans for me as I feed my starvation. Her hands slide around my body, and grip my ass. I chuckle slightly and push against her, rubbing my hard cock on her stomach. Our tongues tangle and her moans grow needy.

"You want my cock."

She nods, and I push my leg between hers to widen them and rub her hot pussy on my thigh. I slide my hand around her neck, undo the small button and unzip her dress. Not wanting to break contact, but wanting her naked, I step back. "Take it off," I say.

She wiggles her hips, a vicious little tease, and the dress slides down her body. I drink her in, devour her with my eyes as she stands before me in a matching bra and panties. "Turn around," I say. "Hand on the door."

She turns from me, and I close the distance, putting my hand on her ass to squeeze. I touch the tiny lace thong, and slide my hands around the front to dip into the lace. Her sex is sopping wet and a growl I have no control over comes out of me.

"I love that you're always ready for my cock," I say, and she breathes rapidly as she wiggles against my finger.

"Please, Alec," she begs. She pushes backward, and rubs that sweet ass of hers against me.

"I'm going to fuck you, Megan. I'm going to fuck you everywhere tonight," I say, and her body vibrates in anticipation. I slide my other hand around her body and up her breasts. "Tell me you want that."

"I want that," she says, as I tug her bra down and brush my thumb over her hard nipple.

"First I want you on my face. I want to eat you, while you rub that sweet pussy all over my mouth." She cries out my name, and I go to my knees to tug her panties down her legs. "The shoes stay on," I say. She lifts one leg and then the other and I tuck her panties into my pocket. I stand back up, and unhook her bra. "Face me."

I step back and she turns slowly. The heat in her eyes, glazed with lust, as her beautiful creamy flesh beckons my touch nearly has me coming in my pants. Her shaky hands reach for my suit jacket and she pushes it from my shoulders. It falls off and her fingers work the buttons on my shirt. I hiss when her fingers touch my flesh, burn through me. I unbutton my pants and kick them off. Her hand goes to my cock, and she rubs me through my boxers. "Fuck, yeah," I say, digging my fingers into the soft warm flesh of her ass. I pick her up, and her legs go around me as I carry her to the bedroom.

I set her on the bed. "Up on your knees." Her beautiful tits bounce as she positions herself, and I tug off my boxers and take my throbbing cock into my hand. Her gaze drops, and she wets her mouth. So sexy. "Touch yourself," I say.

She quivers and her small hand slides between her open thighs. When she runs her fingers over her hot pussy, her head rolls back, her little gasps and moans making me insane. I climb onto the bed with her, and flatten myself out. "Come here," I say. "Come ride my mouth."

She straddles me, and I grab her hips, position her right where I want to, right where I can worship her. I pull her down onto my face, and her sweet scent and flavor fill my senses and push me closer to the edge. She shamelessly grinds her sex on my face and I eat her, run my tongue over her clit and shove it inside her tightness.

"Oh, God, Alec," she says, and puts her hand on the headboard as she grinds harder, taking what she needs. That's a girl. She rolls her hips, a sexy move as she whimpers and chases her orgasm.

I pull her ass cheeks open, and slip a finger into her back passage. Over the last couple of weeks I've been preparing her, and tonight—the last time I'll ever have her in my bed—is the night I'm going to take her, everywhere.

She bounces on my mouth, her clit so hard and inflamed I take it between my teeth, roll my tongue over it, and she cries out as a hot gush of liquid heat dribbles into my mouth and over my chin, announcing her orgasm.

I growl and lap at her sweetness, tasting the depths of her as she rides out the waves. Panting and quivering, she needs time to come back down, but we're far from done here. I grip her hips and lift her from my mouth.

"Slide down," I say.

She shimmies down, and I position her so she's

on her knees, straddling my hips, her hot sex wide-open for me. So pretty. I slowly lower her onto my hard dick, and her hot tight walls hug me. Perfect. So damn perfect. I stretch her hot slick flesh with my girth and she wiggles, trying to force more of me inside, but I hold her hips and control the depth, even though I'm near delirious with need.

"Alec," she murmurs.

"You want it all?"

"Yes," she cries out.

"Don't worry, baby, I'm going to give you everything."

Her eyes flash to mine, and my heart thuds when I see the need reflected there. I pull her down a little more, sinking in a few more inches, and as she opens wider for me, I wish to God I could give her everything. But I can't. I just fucking can't.

Her body shakes all over and she gets hotter and wetter as I fill her. My balls ache and I power up, giving her every last inch of me, and she moans as I stretch her walls. She lifts up, sinks back down again, and as her pretty pussy devours my cock, the world around me melts away.

"Ride me, Megs. Work your sweet pussy over my cock. I want you to come again. I want you to drip all over me." Her movements become fast, more frenzied, and I inch up to take her bouncing breasts in my hands. She lifts up, sinks down and rubs her clit on my pelvis, and her entire body tightens around my cock. Jesus, it's the hottest thing I've ever seen.

I close my eyes, struggle to hang on as her release coats me and drips to my balls.

"Yeah, baby," I say.

The second she stops spasming, I sit up and lift her from my cock. Her face is flushed as I reposition her on the bed, until that sweet ass is in the air. Her body tightens, and I run my hand along her back to reassure her.

"Hey, Megs. Do you want this?" I ask.

"Yes," she cries out.

"I won't hurt you. I promise."

"I know. I just… I've never done this before."

I run my fingers over her spine, then gently slide them between her creamy ass cheeks. "I know." Christ, the fact that she trusts me with her body like this. It's an honor. "I can make it good for you," I assure her.

"I like the sensations when you put your finger in me," she says, and I love how open and honest we're being with each other.

"If at any time you don't like it, I'll stop."

"I want this, Alec," she says quickly, a new sort of desperation in her voice. "I want you to do this."

My pulse leaps. I get the sense that she needs to have me everywhere as much as I need to be everywhere. I lean over her, drop a soft, tender kiss on her cheek and slip a pillow under her hips. "So pretty," I say, and sweep my fingers over her flesh until goose bumps form.

I grab a bottle of lube from my nightstand, having bought it specifically for this occasion. I squirt a generous amount into my palm and rub it until it's warm. I touch her cheeks, widen them and put my finger inside her. She begins to writhe and I move it in and out, desperate to mark this beautiful woman everywhere. "Feel good?" I ask.

"It feels different, but nice. I like it." Her body relaxes, opens.

"Look at you," I say. "All warm and ready for me." I add another finger, and her breath rushes. I'm so goddamn hard just from touching her my balls are ready to explode. I spend a long time preparing her, then pour lubricant on my throbbing dick. I fall over her body, position my cock at her tight entrance and put my mouth near her ear. "Baby, you ready for me?" I ask.

She pushes back, and my cock breaches her opening. "Yes," she cries out. I glance down, revel in the way her beautiful body is taking me.

I go painstakingly slow, giving her time to adjust to each inch, until I'm finally balls deep inside her, my eyes practically roll back in my head. She sucks in a breath and my cock aches with the need to release, but I won't, not until I make her come for me one more time.

She moves against the pillow, rubbing her hot pussy over the cotton, but I slide a hand between her legs, and take control of her stiff clit. I press against her slick cleft, and apply pressure as I work my cock in and out of her ass. She rocks against me, and when she cries out and starts coming all over my hand, I nearly lose my mind. I pump deep, once, twice and on the third time, I spurt my cum high inside her, giving her everything I can give her.

"I feel you," she cries out.

I fall over her, press kisses to her back, and she softens beneath me, all warm and sated and sweet. We stay like that until I grow flaccid, and her breathing changes, slows.

"Don't move," I whisper, and dart to the bathroom. I come back with a warm cloth to clean her. "Roll over," I say quietly, and she's like a rag doll as she slowly goes to her back. I inch her legs open and wipe her with the warm cloth. She moans in contentment and I crawl back in beside her, pull her close. Her soft brown eyes close slowly, sleep pulling her under. I tuck her against me, and cover us up, as my mind goes back to what her uncle said about falling in bed together every night, and more importantly waking up together each morning. Yeah, I want that. I want it with Megan. Is there a chance I could be a better man for her? That I could find happiness, like my cousin Tate has.

Can I take that chance?

Can I not?

CHAPTER ELEVEN

Megan

IT'S NOT LIKE me to sneak out in the middle of the night—after the most intimate sex of my life—but that's exactly what I did after Alec fell asleep in his bed beside me. No way could I be there come morning, have him tell me to my face that our time together was over. I knew what I was getting into before I even went to his place.

Let me put my cock in you. One last time.

Before he committed to Sara, which we both knew he was going to, he wanted to have a little fun in the sack with me, a girl he wasn't worried about losing his heart to. Now that he's found a wife in name only—he made the decision Sunday morning, hours after I'd left his bed—I need to pull myself together. It's been two weeks since I fled, two weeks where he and Sara have been photographed together numerous times, even at the annual golf tournament, and I need to get my head back in the game and start thinking about their wedding plans, because any day now, they're going to announce them.

Amanda sticks her head into my office. "Lunch?"

Ignoring the storm stirring up my stomach, I give her my best smile, but she can see right through me, see the pain beneath the surface. Why oh why did I go and fall for him again?

Again?

Who am I kidding? I never stopped loving him.

"Actually, I had a late breakfast, so I'm going to pass," I say. I honestly haven't had much of an appetite lately.

She eyes me for a moment. "Hey, are you okay?" she asks, folding her arms as she leans against the door frame.

"Perfectly fine," I say, and lift my chin an inch, to prove I have it all together.

"Megan," she begins. "If you love him you need to tell him."

"I don't love him." I sigh and lean back in my chair. "Even if I did, I couldn't just tell him. It's a little more complicated than that," I say.

"What I don't understand is all the sex you two were having. He must have deeper feelings."

I think about that for a minute, remember the feel of his lips on mine, the way he took such good care of my body. Would a man not feeling something deeper be so gentle, so tender, so eager to mark every inch of me?

"It's just sex, Amanda. Two people having fun

while they're passing the time. Even if I did love him, we have different goals in life," I say to remind myself. "And I'd never tell a guy I loved him when he's made it perfectly clear he doesn't believe in love or happily-ever-after. After so much loss, having my own family isn't just something I want, it's something my heart needs."

She frowns. "Okay, I'm here if you need to talk."

Just then my phone rings, and I'm grateful for the distraction, until I see who's calling. "Thanks, Amanda," I say, and slide my finger across the phone. "Sara, hi."

"We finally set a date," she says. "And it's soon."

I grab my pen, and note the way my stupid hand is shaking. "Okay, give me the details."

"It's going to be a very formal wedding at the country club in two weeks. It's the perfect spot."

Funny, Sara and I have different opinions on the perfect spot. I want my wedding to be casual, my groom dressed comfortably, and I'd prefer it to be at a beach or a lake, not some snobbish country club. But it's not my wedding, so I have no say.

"Two weeks," I say, not at all surprised they're moving quickly.

"No sense in wasting time."

I begin to tell her all the things that need to be done ASAP, like the menu, cake, dress, invites, photographer, flowers, etc., but Sara goes silent on the other end.

"What's the problem?" I ask.

"The problem is that I have to be away for work."
Her voice sounds distant, like she's driving through
a tunnel. "Will you be able to just plan these things
without me? Oh, as far as bridal party goes, I'm
going to ask my best friend to be my maid of honor,
and that's it. No bridesmaids. I would have asked
you but with you planning everything, there would
be way too many complications."

"I totally understand," I say. No way could I stand
for her while she marries the man I'm in love with.
"So you asked Jessica?"

"Yes, and Alec is having Will as best man. All
of New York's most important people will be there.
This can only do good things for my career," she
says, a hint of excitement in her voice.

I still can't quite believe the two are marrying for
their careers. Doesn't anyone believe in love anymore? I pinch the bridge of my nose. "Are you telling me you don't care about the menu, or, or—?"

"Not really. This is your area of expertise, you
know what to do better than I do."

"What about the guest list?"

"I'll email you mine, and you can work with Alec
for his and all the other things you mentioned. The
two of you can pull it together, I'm sure of it."

Work with Alec?

That's the last thing I want to do.

With a headache brewing, I shake my head no,
even though she can't see me. "Sara, I don't know—"

"I'm going to be away for the next week. Maybe

more. I have a convention in Atlanta. The firm is sending me, and I have no choice."

"What about your dress?"

"Ah, can you just pick something for me? We're the same size."

My head begins to spin and I take a deep breath. "I can't pick out your wedding dress for you."

"Sure you can. We're the exact same size. If it looks good on you, it'll look good on me. I want to be a princess on my special day, so as long as it's a ball gown, I'll like it."

Years ago when I envisioned my wedding, I pictured myself in a ball gown. A real Cinderella. Now, however, I'd like something a little more streamlined.

"I… Is Alec okay with me planning everything?"

"I haven't had a chance to run it by him. Would you mind? I need to get packed and catch a flight."

"I don't think—"

"I just arrived home. I have to run."

My God, what kind of marriage are they going to have?

One in name only.

"Gotta go. Thanks, Megs, you're the best."

I sit there, dumbfounded as the line goes dead. She seriously wants me to pick a wedding dress for her. The menu and other things I can understand, but a dress? That's completely insane. I shake my head, and stare at my phone. How the heck is Alec going to feel about working closely with me. I haven't talked to him, or set eyes on him in weeks. I take a deep fortifying breath, and shoot him a text.

Megan: Sara has to be away for a convention, and she asked that I work on the wedding plans with you.

I stare at my phone, watch three dots appear and then disappear. He must be writing and deleting, unsure of what to say. His response finally comes in.

Alec: What do you suggest?

Megan: I'll need to meet with you to go over menu, guest list, etc. The sooner we get started the better. Do you want to come by my work, and we'll put together a menu to start things off?

Alec: Four o'clock okay?

Megan: See you then.

I must be out of my mind. With no time to waste, I pick the phone back up and start making calls, to set things in motion, and before I know it, the day is almost over.

I glance up when I hear footsteps in the hall— heavy steps that can only be Alec's. I smooth my hand over my hair after running stressed-out hands through it all day. I stand to greet him when he comes into view, his large frame eating up the doorway and completely overwhelming me. My mouth instantly goes dry. He does a quick sweep of my clothes, and in turn I look him over. Hair cut short, face clean-shaven, he looks handsome, composed…guarded.

Keep it together, Megan.

I give him a huge smile, and resist the urge to hurtle myself at him, and show him I'm the girl for him. But I won't. Because I'm not. It's over between us, and I need to remember that. "Have a seat," I say, and gesture to the chair across from me, thinking about the last time he was in this office with me, and the limo drive we took later that night.

Dressed in a suit that showcases his broad shoulders and fit body, he smooths his hand over his tie.

I sit, and I'm about to make small talk when he gives a curt nod. "You wanted to talk to me about a menu?" he says, getting right down to business.

All righty, then.

"As you know, Amanda will be catering, and thank you for that, by the way. She's thrilled."

"Her food is amazing. I've been getting deliveries to my door for the last week."

"She is amazing, and this is a once-in-a-lifetime opportunity for her."

"For you, too," he says, his blue eyes intense when they latch on to mine. "That's why you agreed to this, right? Because of what it could do for your career?"

"I… Yes," I say, but there is a part of me that's not one hundred percent sure of that. Maybe it was the thought of seeing Alec again, getting a glimpse of the young boy I once knew, and always loved, that had me agreeing. "Yes," I say again, not wanting him to think there were other reasons. He continues to stare at me, and I reach for the menu. What the hell is going on with him?

"Here is Amanda's menu. I'd suggest a beef, chicken and fish dish for the mains, and she does some lovely hors d'oeuvres to start the night." I glance up, but he's not looking at the menu, he's looking at me. The intensity in his eyes sucks the oxygen from my lungs, and nerves flutter in my belly. I wipe my suddenly wet palms on my skirt.

"I'm sure she does."

"Do you want to take a look?"

"No, I trust your judgment."

"Oh, okay," I say. "I won't let you down. This wedding will be talked about for years to come." He nods, and I wait for a response. When none comes, I say, "I hope your week isn't too busy. I've booked us for cake tasting, flower shopping—"

"Text me the times."

"What about tuxedos? I scheduled an appointment. Will you and your brother want my help with that? Oh, wait. Sara didn't tell me a color scheme. Her favorite color was always lavender, but I'll have to double-check that. You'll want your tie and cummerbund to match."

"You'll probably want to come to make sure we get the colors right. I know how you like to pick out my clothes."

Wait, was that a hint of humor? If it was, his face certainly isn't showing it.

"I have an appointment to look at dresses right afterward, so that shouldn't be a problem."

"Sounds like you have everything under control," he says.

"It's what I do." I stand and he stands with me. I walk around my desk to open the door, and his body brushes mine. Sparks arc between us, and I suck in a fast breath when he cups my elbow, a show of possession. I spin to face him. His head is dipped, eyes glossy, like he's a million miles away as his gaze fixates on my mouth.

"Alec," I say, my voice a breathless whisper.

"Yeah," he murmurs.

My entire body responds to the need in his voice. But we can't do this. He's engaged now. "I'll text you that schedule," I say in my best professional voice, and his head snaps up, like he's just been slapped.

"Right." He lets go of my arm and walks into the hall. I'm seconds from collapsing in a mess of hot tears and need when he turns back around.

"Megs," he says softly.

"Yes."

He opens his mouth, hesitates and scrubs his hand over his face. "I'll be waiting on that schedule."

CHAPTER TWELVE

Alec

FOR THE LAST WEEK, I've been everywhere with Megan, and so help me fucking God, it's been torture. Torturous not to kiss her at whim, not to pull her into my arms, carry her to my bed. I'll be glad when this wedding is done and over with and I won't have to spend every second with her. But will that stop me from spending every second thinking about her, fantasizing about her being in my arms, between my sheets.

Probably not.

Christ, I should have kept my mouth and hands to myself. Never should have given in to weakness. The last time she was in my bed, I was beginning to believe there could be more between us, but when I woke up and she was gone, it was the slap in the face I needed. I can't be the man she needs.

As I stand in the dressing room trying on my tux, my brother, Will, in the room beside me, and

Megan standing outside waiting, I think back over the week. Megan managed to get the invitation out in record time, considering the sizable crowd we're having. Since I cared little about the details, we picked peonies for the flowers, and vanilla for the cake, a popular crowd-pleaser and both Sara's favorites. I consider that a moment longer. I'm sure if it were Megs's wedding she'd pick daisies for the flowers and lemon for the cake.

I tug on my jacket, and glance at myself in the mirror. I'm not in love with the lavender color, but in the end does it really matter?

"Almost done?" Megan asks.

I open the door and her eyes go wide as she takes me in. "You look amazing," she says under her breath. Just then my cell pings, and I grab it from my pants on the chair.

"It's Sara," I say, and frown at the phone. "Shit."

"What?" she asks.

"She's stuck in Atlanta for the next couple days."

Will comes from his dressing room and smooths a hand over his lapels, breaking the moment.

"I'm not so sure about this color," he says scrunching up his face.

"Not your choice, bro," I say, with a slap to his back.

"Are you whipped already, Alec?" he teases. "Light purple. Couldn't we have at least picked something a little more manly?"

"Like soft blue," Megan says, and I take in the soft

blue dress she's wearing. I'm guessing that would be her color of choice.

"That would work," Will says, and gives himself a once-over in the mirror. "You owe me for this, bro."

I laugh. "When you get married, I'll wear pink."

Will's face drops, and he grumbles under his breath, something that sounds like "never going to happen," when the clerk steps up to us.

He pulls out a measuring tape and gets to work on sizing us up. Once we're both back in our regular suits, I step from the change room and find Megan on her phone. She glances up at me and smiles. "I guess you don't need me anymore."

Oh, how wrong she is.

She gestures with a nod. "I have to head next door to do a dress fitting."

"You're picking out Sara's dress?"

"Crazy as it sounds, I am. All designers want to be worn by your bride, so they're bending over backward for me."

Bending over backward.

Kill me now.

I check my watch. "I can come help, if you want."

"I'm sure you must have more important things to do on a Friday night."

"This is the highlight reel," I say, and she laughs.

"What about Will?" she asks, pointing a finger back and forth between the two of us as Will checks his phone. "You two must want to hang out."

She's giving me an out, and if I knew what was

good for me, I'd take it. I'm about to agree because any more time with her is going to do me in.

"Can't," Will pipes in. "I'm off to St. Thomas."

Megan frowns. "You have work in the US Virgin Islands?"

"A little work, but I plan to take some much-needed rest and relaxation before Alec's wedding," Will says.

"Why not go to St. Moritz?" Megan asks, and I note the way her gaze darts to mine at the mention of the ski resort. Have her thoughts gone back to the night she came to my room? "Your grandfather owns half the place."

"All the more reason for me to go to St. Thomas, where I have my own private villa," Will says.

"He likes his privacy," I say, and Megan nods.

"Okay, well, if you have nothing better to do, then come help me pick out a dress," she says to me. I shouldn't go. I should just go home and down a few brandies and forget all about Megan, but I'm clearly some kind of masochist, because I nod and follow her out of the store. We go to the bridal boutique one shop down and I open the door for her. Her body brushes mine and I bite back a moan of want as she slips inside.

We head to the back of the store where there's a dais and a series of mirrors. Megan introduces us to Maria, who will help her try on gowns, and I pick up a magazine and flip through it blindly when she's led into the change room. A few minutes later Megan comes out looking elegant in a big ball gown. While it's nice, and it fits her beautifully, it's not something I can see her wearing on her wedding day. Then again, it's not her who's going to be wearing it and walking toward me as I wait at the altar.

She steps up onto the podium and examines herself in front of the mirrors. I lean forward, brace my elbows on my knees. She's frowning when she turns to me.

"What do you think?"

"You look beautiful," I say. She smooths her hand over the big skirt, and the bling on her waist glitters. "Although the bling isn't you," I say.

"I know, but I think Sara would love it." I sit back and nod. "Wait, let's take a picture," I say, "and I'll send it to her." I pull my phone out, snap a picture and send it to Sara. As we wait to hear, Maria suggests we try on another.

Megan continues to try on different styles and send pictures to her cousin. But still no response from Sara. After the tenth dress, Megan comes from the change room and I nearly bite off my damn tongue.

"Holy shit," I say, as she walks to the podium in a strapless, body shaping gown that showcases her beautiful curves and creamy skin. I stand before I even realize what I'm doing and walk up to her.

"This one," I say. "This is the dress." I run my hand along the exposed skin on her back and when a shiver moves through her, Maria makes an excuse and rushes off.

Megan turns to me, a flush on her cheeks, her eyes wide as I touch her. "When we were kids you talked about a ball gown princess dress—"

"You remember that?" she asks, cutting me off.

"Yeah. But I have to tell you, Megs. This is the one. It's stunning. I've never… What made you try this on?"

"I just… It was a mistake." She lets her words fall off, turns from me fast, averting my gaze, but there is a hitch in her voice when she says, "I need to get out of this." She nearly falls as she steps down from the podium. I hurry to her, catch her in my arms, and when I do, everything I feel for her comes racing to the surface. I dip my head and at the same time she swipes her tongue over her lips like she's preparing her sweet mouth for me.

"Megs," I whisper, just as my damn phone pings.

Megan pushes away from my arms. "That's probably Sara," she says, her voice rough and breathless.

I glance at my phone. "She said to pick whichever one you like best. She has no preference."

"Oh, okay," she says, then disappears into the changing room. I sit back down and restlessly flip through the magazine, every nerve in my body agitated and on fire. When she finally comes out, her face is pale and she looks like she's just seen a ghost.

I jump from my chair, close the distance between us. "What is it?" I glance at the phone in her hand.

She's gripping the thing so hard her knuckles are turning white. "Are you okay?" She blinks once, then twice, then shoves her phone into her purse so I can't see what has her so rattled. "Megs?" I ask again.

"Everything is…fine," she says, but I know her well enough to know she's lying.

CHAPTER THIRTEEN

Megan

I'VE HAD A KNOT in my stomach since I received that text from Sara at the bridal boutique.

Sara: Met the hottest guy at the convention. He's a god in bed. Won't be home for a couple more days. Hope the planning is going well. You look amazing in all those dresses.

I didn't respond. Didn't know how. Jesus, she's engaged to Alec and having hot sex with a guy at her convention. Something tells me the convention was long over, and she was hanging back just to have a little bedroom fun. How the hell could she do this to Alec? Okay, yes, I get it. Alec and I have been having sex like bunnies, but the key words here are *have been*. We stopped the second he got engaged to Sara. Alec might be a lot of things. A LOT of things. But he's no cheater. He once told me he wasn't a nice guy. Fine. Maybe he does deals at work that destroy businesses and livelihoods, but when it comes right down to it, I know in my heart he's monogamous.

"What are you going to do?" Amanda asks from the chair facing my desk as she sips her latte. I reach for mine, grateful that I have a friend who knows when I need my favorite drink.

"I don't know what to do," I say. I'm an honest girl. At least I try to be. I only fib when I have to, when I know it's for my best and someone else's. When was the last time I fibbed? Oh, when I thought I could have sex with Alec and not feel anything more.

My lips tingle with the memory of him, and the intimate way he always claimed my mouth.

Stop thinking about him already.

I push from my chair. "I can't tell him."

"If it's a marriage in name only, will he even care?"

"I don't know. I mean eventually they'll have sex, right?" Unease worms its way through my veins. "I'm sure they're already having sex, actually."

"It's not too late, you know."

Pacing in my office, I spin to face my friend, who is staring at me with those astute brown eyes. "If you're suggesting I tell him how I feel, yes it's too late. He's getting married in less than a week, Amanda. Everything is set. I'm not about to jump in now and ruin this. Think about what this wedding will do for your business."

"If you're worried about me, don't. Some things are more important than fame and the bottom line."

I take a big breath and let it out slowly, wishing I'd gone to yoga this morning.

The bell over the front door jingles, and I plop back down into my chair as Amanda excuses herself and darts to the front. I put my head on my desk, but perk up when a familiar voice reaches my ears. Amanda pokes her head in, her eyes wide.

"Someone here to see you," she says.

I stand when James comes in, his cane banging on the floor.

"James, what are you doing here?"

"Now what kind of greeting is that, child?"

"Sorry. It's nice to see you. Please have a seat. Can I get you a coffee, tea?"

"Any brandy?" he asks and I grin.

"No sorry."

He waves a dismissive hand. "No matter."

"What can I do for you?"

"Just checking in to see how plans are going? Haven't seen Sara in some time now." His eyes narrow and I almost squirm under his scrutiny. It's like the man can see through me, see how I feel about his grandson.

I nibble my lip, and hate to lie to the man but say, "She got tied up at a conference in Atlanta."

"Tied up, huh?" he says, like he's privy to something I'm not.

"Can I ask you something?" I say, calling on all my bravado.

"Yes, but it doesn't mean I'm going to answer," he says, and I laugh.

"You sound like Alec."

"That boy means the world to me."

"I know he does and he'd do anything for you, James."

"He's one of the good ones."

That gives me pause. If he thinks he's one of the good ones, why did he tell Alec his image was hurting the family? Why is he pushing him to marry to clean up his act?

"How so?" I ask.

"Did he ever tell you about his grandmother?"

"When we were younger, he mentioned her. She was gone when I came into the picture."

"I'm not sure what it was, but out of all the grandchildren, they had a special bond. Oh, don't get me wrong, she treated all the grandkids the same, but she said there was a different light inside Alec." He pauses and smiles as if recalling and relishing an old memory. "They spent a lot of time in the garden. Did he ever tell you he has a green thumb?"

"No," I say, and smile at that. I couldn't keep a plant alive to save my soul. But then I remember the one plant at his place. I thought it seemed out of place, surrounded by his cool gray decor.

"Oh, yes, he spent a lot of time with his grandmother in the garden. He took it the hardest when she died."

"How…" I shut my mouth, not wanting to dredge up sad memories, but James's eyes flicker.

"Ovarian cancer," he says, frowning. "Damn cancer. That's why he set up a trust fund."

"Trust fund?"

"He didn't tell you."

"No."

"He finances a dozen deserving medical school students each year. Pays the entire shot. He's determined to find a cure. He's quite the philanthropist, that one."

If I wasn't seated, my knees would have given out on me. "He does?" My mind races, back to when he told me he wasn't a nice guy. Why would he do that? "Why wouldn't he tell me about this?"

"He's secretive. Very private. All my grandkids are. Not much wonder with the paparazzi in their faces all the time." James laughs, but it holds no humor. "The loss of his grandmother hit him hard, though and if the media found out about the charities, they'd dig deeper. His grandmother guarded her private life, and Alec goes to great length to ensure it remains protected, even after all these years."

"What do you mean?"

"Damn media will start asking questions on why he finances students, and he doesn't want any of his grandmother's business made public." A warm smile touches his mouth. "Deep down that boy is soft."

"He is?" I ask, even though I know it's true.

"Every time Blackstone puts someone out of work, he secretly makes sure he finds a position for them." He puts his finger to his lips. "That's a secret, too, though."

As my heart pounds behind my eyes, I try to make sense of this. Alec is a good guy, and his granddad knows it. Then why did Alec tell me otherwise, and why did James specifically ask me to find his grandson a wife and get him settled because his lifestyle looked bad on the family, dragged down the Carson name?

"James?"

"Yes, child?"

"Why me? Why did it have to be *me* to find Alec a wife and then plan his wedding?"

"How else was I going to get you two lovebirds together?"

CHAPTER FOURTEEN

Megan

I'VE BEEN WALKING around in a daze for the last few days, pulling together the last-minute details for tomorrow's wedding as I try to process what James told me. Lovebirds? Alec and *me*? He can't be right. If he is, then why is Alec marrying Sara?

Restless and on edge, I walk to my window, peer out at the street below, then go back to my sofa. Even though everything is set and I'm about to pull off a grand wedding that will make everyone stand up and take notice, I grab my journal and go through tomorrow's arrangements one more time, until a knock sounds on my door. My heart jumps into my throat, desperately wanting it to be Alec. For the last week I've wanted to talk to him, tell him what James said to me, but I couldn't bring myself to do it. The man rejected me once, all those years ago, and I'm pretty sure I can't go through that kind of humiliation again.

Stop being a chickenshit.

I shut down that inner voice, stand quickly and take a couple deep breaths. I don't want to appear too anxious or needy.

I pad softly to my door, pull it open and frown when I find Amanda standing there. "Oh, hi."

She huffs. "Nice to see you, too."

"I'm sorry." I widen the door to welcome her. "Come in. I am happy to see you."

"Are you expecting someone else?"

"No."

She lifts a bottle of wine. "Then maybe you'll want to drink this with me tonight."

I grin, even though I don't feel like smiling. "You know me too well."

I shut the door, set the lock and follow my best friend into the kitchen. She roots through my drawers, pulls out a corkscrew and opens my favorite wine, but when she does, my thoughts go back to Alec, and when he had my favorite brand of vino in the limo. God, that limo drive. Not only was the sex amazing, but when he took me to the duck pond, it touched my heart on a whole new level. The man knows me well, that's for sure.

But what I don't understand is why he told me he wasn't a good guy. Did he not want me to like him?

I reach for the stemware, and Amanda adds a splash of wine to each glass. We walk back to the living room and she moves wedding magazines and papers to sit in the comfy buttery-yellow chair across from me, then tucks her feet underneath her. I do the same. Once comfortable, Amanda takes a sip of wine and rubs the line on her forehead. I brace myself.

"What?" I ask.

"I spent the last week trying to wrap my brain around your relationship with Alec."

My stomach cramps, and I set my wine down, ready to straighten out my friend on where Alec and I stand. "Amanda—" I begin, but she cuts me off.

"No, really stop, Megan. Think about it. None of the women he dated were suitable. He couldn't commit. Maybe he was holding out for you. I mean he did ditch that one girl and take you on that dirty limo ride."

"Amanda—" I try again but she stops me.

"Maybe he's in love with you, but is afraid to commit for some reason. Something is holding him back, I feel that in my gut and my gut never lies. Maybe he settled because he was desperate with the golf tournament coming up. Maybe he had no choice. I've seen him and Sara together, Megs. There is zero chemistry, whereas you two damn nearly vibrate when you're near each other. The sparks. Insane." She puts her hands by her head and makes an explosion sound.

I pause for a moment, look past her shoulder and consider the heat between us. My entire body warms when I reminisce about the way he touched me, in and out of the bedroom. The stolen kisses, the way he couldn't seem to keep his hands or his eyes off me whenever we were together. His touch was so achingly tender and at times possessive. The last time we were in bed it was like he needed to mark every inch of me. I quiver just thinking about it.

Could Alec feel the same way about me as I do about him? Is something holding him back? If so, what? I let out a frustrated growl and I drop my head back on the sofa.

"Maybe I'm just clinging to something that isn't there. You of all people know I have a hard time letting go. Maybe I was good enough to have sex with, but not to marry. Maybe I don't fit the criteria of what he needs in a wife."

"Maybe you need to talk to him to find out." She sips her wine and swirls it in her glass. "Did you ever tell him you wanted more?"

"No, actually I told him I didn't want more from him."

"Maybe he's working with that information."

My heart beats a little faster in my chest. Is there really a chance that Alec and I can be together? Is something holding him back, some deeper fear?

"He's getting married to Sara tomorrow," I announce, my hope dwindling.

Amanda sets her glass down, and meets my gaze unflinchingly. "I want you to answer me seriously, Megan. Do you love him?"

Oh, God, I do. I love him so much. He's the best guy I know.

"Yes," I answer honestly, and Amanda stands.

"Get your purse," she says, pulling her phone from her back pocket.

"What?"

"Get your purse. I'm getting you an Uber. You and Alec need to talk."

"Amanda—"

"Stop overthinking this, girlfriend. Car's on its way. Move it."

I climb from the sofa and stand on shaky legs. The truth is I do love Alec, and before he goes through with this sham of a wedding tomorrow, I have to talk to him, tell him how I feel. Otherwise I'll spend the rest of my life regretting it and wondering what if…

"Okay," I say, my voice as shaky as my legs. I grab my purse, and feel equal measure of excitement and fear as Amanda walks me out the door, down the stairs and to the front of the building. As I stand there, I start to get cold feet. "Maybe this isn't a good—"

"Overthinking again," she says, and holds her hand up to stop me. "You have to know, Megan. You can't spend the rest of your life wondering what if."

"You're right. I can't."

An inky black car pulls up, and I slide into the backseat. "Text me," Amanda says. "I've got a good feeling about this."

I give the driver directions, and fold nervous hands on my lap. *Breathe, Megan, just breathe.*

I stare out the window and try to calm myself, a difficult task considering what I'm about to do. Will he be happy, mad? What about Sara? She's looking forward to being on Alec's arm. Can I do this to her? But Sara loves and cares about me. Surely if she knew how I felt, she'd want me to be with him. A short while later we pull up in front of his building, and I get out. My heart is in my throat as I walk up the stairs, forcing one foot in front of the other. Derek greets me at the door, but this time he doesn't offer me a toothy grin. No, this time he looks a bit confused.

"Megan, I wasn't expecting you tonight," he says, as he opens the glass door for me.

"Some last-minute wedding things I need to discuss with the groom," I say.

"Very well." He walks me to the elevator, inserts his key and I force myself to make small talk on the way up. I stammer a bit, and trip over my words. Is it any wonder? My damn brain is racing a million miles an hour.

"Thanks," I say when I step off. The elevator doors ping shut, and I stand in the hall and take a minute to pull myself together before I knock. I wait, but the door doesn't open. Has the groom gone to bed already so he'll be refreshed for the big day? I knock again, a bit louder this time, and slip my hand into my pocket to grab the key he gave me. Should I? I wait a few more minutes and when he doesn't answer, I decide to let myself in.

I open the door, and peer into the dark. "Alec," I call out quietly. If he's asleep, should I wake him? I tiptoe down the hall, and when I hear noises coming from his bedroom, I hurry my steps, but when I peer through the crack in his door, and find Sara in his arms, my vision goes fuzzy around the edges and I falter backward.

I lean against the wall, brace my hands on my knees and mentally berate myself. Why, oh why did I come here? Alec isn't in love with me. He currently has his arms wrapped around my cousin—his fiancée—like he's anxious to get an early start on their honeymoon.

Tears fall, and I swipe at them, hate them. Hate myself for believing there could be more between us. Amanda was wrong. James was wrong. Everyone was wrong, including me, and I never should have spent one minute thinking Alec could want me. I struggle to pull myself together, and when I finally get my legs working again, I retrace my steps, go out into the hall and lock up behind myself. I press the button for the elevator and pull my hair forward, not wanting Derek to see my red eyes. Grabbing my phone, I shoot Amanda a text.

Megan: Still have that bottle of wine.

Amanda: Oh no. Are you okay?

Megan: Not even a little.

Amanda: I'm so sorry Megs. I thought…

Megan: Not your fault.

I shove my phone back into my pocket when the elevator arrives, and I force myself to smile when the doors slide open.

"That didn't take too long," Derek says.

I clear my throat and hope to pull off casual. "Nope, all is good."

As if sensing my dark, shaky mood, Derek goes quiet and when we reach the lobby, I wave goodnight and rush outside to draw a breath. I call for an Uber and by the time I reach my apartment, I've pretty much cried myself out. I slide from the vehicle and find Amanda waiting for me.

"Hey," I say, and when she pulls me in for a hug, more tears fall.

"Come on. I have wine, and ice cream."

I let her guide me to my apartment, where we— and when I say "we," I mean *me*—finish the bottle of wine, and eat the ice cream. The next thing I know, I'm waking up with a killer headache, the sun shining in through my open curtains. Beside me, Amanda is asleep, and my heart misses a beat, thankful that she stayed to take care of me.

I glance at the clock and jolt upright. "Damn," I say, and give my head a minute to settle. With so many last-minute things to pull together before the ceremony this afternoon, I shake Amanda.

She groans, and I say, "We need to get moving."

Her lids flutter open. "Right," she says. "I'm moving."

"I need to shower," I say.

"Me, too." She sits up and rubs her eyes. "You okay?"

"Fine," I lie, wanting to busy my mind with the ceremony.

"You want to ride to the country club in the van with me? I'll make Jeremy sit in the back with the food and you can ride up front with me."

"No, I need to go earlier. I'll Uber and meet you there." I turn from her, unable to face the worry in her eyes as she looks at me.

I make my way to the shower to clean myself up, and once I'm washed and dried, I slide into a dress—presenting professional event planner—and glance at myself in the mirror. Ugh. With dark circles under my eyes, I look like a raccoon with a bad case of food poisoning. I stick my tongue out, groan some more and reach for my toothbrush. Feeling a little more human, I grab my purse, and make my way to the country club to ensure all the details are perfect for the wedding of the century.

I busy myself, checking on the photographer, flowers, table settings, minister and everything else. It's the only way I can get the image of Alec with his arms wrapped around Sara out of my mind. Soon enough the guests begin to arrive, and I hide in the back and help Amanda in the kitchen. Even though I'm probably more of a nuisance than an assistant.

She's got this catering thing down to a science and everything is warming in chafing dishes.

"Stop worrying about me," I say to Amanda, when I catch her watching me from the corner of her eye.

"Okay, okay," she says, and turns her attention to plating the hors d'oeuvres. I check my watch and leave the kitchen when I spot Sara, her maid of honor, Jessica, and Aunt Jeannie and Uncle Dave pull up in a limo. I swallow down the knot in my throat as she waves to me and I put on my best happy face.

Looking gorgeous and radiant in her ball gown, the one I picked for her, she comes toward me. "We need to get you inside," I say. "We can't let the groom see you." A groom I've been avoiding all day. I know he's here, I feel his presence, can almost smell his hypnotizing scent. I usher Sara and Jessica inside the country club, while her mom and dad head off to mingle before the ceremony begins in less than fifteen minutes.

"We need to talk," Sara says to me, the seriousness in her tone sending sparks of worry down my spine. "Jessica, do you mind. I need to talk to Megan alone."

"No problem," Jessica says, and steps away, her pretty lavender dress swishing as she turns.

Sara puts her hands on my shoulders. "I can't go through with this," she says. "In fact, I never ever planned to go through with it. I didn't even think things would go this far."

I shake my head, incredulous. "What are you talking about? You're here, you're dressed." I wave my hand toward the window. "Alec is outside waiting for you."

"You don't understand," she says, shaking her head, almost panicked. "I never wanted to marry him."

I pinch the bridge of my nose as the room spins around me. "What are you talking about?"

"I don't need to be married to make partner. I made that up."

"Sara, you're losing me."

"This you'll understand. He's in love with someone else. He always has been."

"Sara—"

"Why do you think I had you go dress shopping for me? Why do you think I went away for so long, or texted you to tell you I was sleeping with someone else? I wanted to wake you the hell up, so you'd see what that man means to you and vice versa. I thought spending time together would do it, but you're both so stubborn and dense."

I back up, stumble a bit and grab the nearest chair. "You set all that up on purpose."

"Of course. I wanted you two together. Heck, everyone knows you two belong together."

"Sara," I say. "I saw you two last night. I saw you in his arms. I went to Alec's apartment to talk to him and I saw you two together in his bedroom."

Her head jerks back, her eyes wide in surprise,

then she laughs. "I seduced him last night." My stomach knots, and I place my hand over it, fearing I'm going to be sick. "I did it to prove a point."

I shake my head, unable to wrap my brain around all the things she's saying to me. "He pushed me away, Megan. He rejected me because he's in love with you. I kissed him on purpose, to show him we have nothing together. I jumped in and said I'd be his wife, because I didn't want him marrying some schoolteacher or librarian or anyone but you. He loves you, Megan, and you need to be the one walking down that aisle." She reaches behind her head and begins to unbutton her dress.

"What are you doing?" I ask.

"Changing clothes with you."

"You can't be serious."

"Of course, I am. Now go out there, and show that man you love him. Isn't that how it's done in those romance movies you watch?"

"It's called the grand gesture, and for the record, I knew he loved her," Amanda says from behind me.

I spin to face her, catch her grin. God this is all happening too fast, I don't even have time to think it through. Amanda comes up and starts unbuttoning my dress, and the next thing I know, before I can even catch my breath, or get a word out, I'm being zipped up in Sara's wedding dress.

"This is insane," I say. "I can't do this. He's expecting you."

"And he'll be thrilled when he lifts this veil and finds you behind it," Sara says.

My heart beats like I've just had a triple shot of espresso. Could Sara be right? Does Alec love me? "He said he didn't believe in love or even want a family. Those are all the things I want."

"He wants it, he just doesn't know it," Sara explains. "You're going to show him he does. Now stop overthinking this."

I'm in a complete daze as my best friend and cousin practically drag me outside. I stand there looking at Alec through my veil as I try to catch my breath. Looking amazing in his tux, his brother, Will, beside him, he's rocking back and forth on his heels, the guests sitting in lavender colored chairs all stand when the wedding march begins. It's a beautiful wedding, a wedding of the century, and what's about to happen next will either make or break my business. But I can't think about that right now. I'm about to give Alec the shock of a lifetime.

Am I really going to do this?

Uncle Dave steps up to me. He grins, like he's in on all this, too. Has everyone been matchmaking? Sara shoves me from behind, to set me into motion, and I can barely make my legs move as I walk toward the man I love. From the corner of my eye I spot James, and he's grinning. He knows it's me!

Does Alec?

God, what will he do when my veil is lifted? I hesitate. I can't do this, it's insane. I'm about to bolt, but Uncle Dave holds my arm, to prevent me from fleeing. My heart pounds so hard, I can't think, can't hear, can't breathe.

When I finally reach Alec, I step up to him. His jaw is clenched tight, and the muscles are rippling. He reaches out, and I tense when he lifts my veil.

A gasp sounds in the crowd, and he goes perfectly still. Too still. His expression darkens, and deep blue eyes—angry eyes—narrow.

"Alec," I whisper.

"No," he says, and shakes his head as he backs away. "Not you, Megan. Never you."

CHAPTER FIFTEEN

Alec

"I'F YOU'RE GOING to get married, you should at least marry the woman you love," Granddad says as he swirls his brandy in his glass and relaxes into his recliner.

I pace around his den, so goddamn mad I can barely see straight. "I can't believe you set this all up. Just to get Megan and me together."

"You've been in love with her since high school and I'm not the only one who knows you two belong together," he says. "Look at what Sara did." He chuckles, but I find no humor in the situation.

I close my eyes, and my heart aches when the vision of Megan dressed in that wedding gown fills the darkness. The horrified look on her face, one I put there, rips a hole in my gut. It's been three days since she bolted from the country club, and I holed myself up in my penthouse until Granddad insisted on seeing me. Megan is the last person in the world I ever meant to hurt, which is why I can't marry her.

"You don't understand," I say through gritted teeth.

Granddad pushes from his chair, saunters across the room and refills his brandy. He pours a splash into another glass and hands it to me. "Then make me understand," he says.

I swirl the brandy, swallow it in one gulp and welcome the burn as it goes down my throat. I set the glass down, run my hand through my hair and walk to the window to glance out.

"I love her, Granddad," I finally admit out loud.

"I know."

"And that's exactly why I can't be with her," I say quietly.

"Now that makes no sense."

I spin, frustrated with this whole situation. "The Carson men have a hard time with commitment, you of all people know that. Even Mom warned me to stay away from her. If my own mother doesn't believe in me, how can I possibly believe in myself."

"Ah, I see," he says, and nods his head, like he just solved all the problems in the world.

I smooth my hand over my tie and pace back to the sofa across from Granddad. I drop into it, and brace my elbows on my knees. "What do you see?"

"You don't think you have it in you to be loyal."

A noise crawls out of my throat. "Name a man in our family who's been loyal," I say. "Christ, Will was in love and even he couldn't stay loyal. We just don't have it in us and I can't—won't—hurt Megan like that. She deserves someone better."

"You're wrong you know."

"What am I wrong about?" Restless and edgy, I shake my foot.

"I was loyal, son. I was very loyal to your grandmother. She was my everything."

I sit up a little straighter. "You've been with a lot of women, Granddad."

"I grieved for your grandmother for many years, Alec. But I knew she didn't want me to spend the rest of my life alone. It was many, many years after she was gone that I started dating again."

"Yeah, I guess I never really thought about that."

"You have a lot of me in you, whether you believe that or not. So does Tate. Look how happy he and Summer are. They're in it for the long haul. You'll see."

"They do seem happy." A sound catches in my throat. "And Megan did say I remind her a lot of you. She said we have the same mannerisms."

Granddad leans forward. "You don't think you can be loyal?"

"Not really."

"Let me ask you this. Have you slept with Sara?" I groan. In no way do I want to talk about my sex life with my ninety-year-old grandfather. "Answer me, son."

"No, I didn't sleep with Sara. She tried to get me into bed, but I pushed her away."

His brows arch. "Even though she was your fiancée, you pushed her away."

"Yeah."

Cloudy blue eyes lock on mine. "Why do you think that is?"

I shake my head. "I just...it didn't feel right."

"Why didn't it feel right?" he asks, and I wish he'd stop pushing.

"Granddad—"

"Answer the question, Alec."

I briefly shut my eyes and take a deep breath. "Because I'm in love with Megan, and being with someone else felt wrong."

"And there you have it," he says, and leans back in his chair, a smirk on his face.

I mull that over for a moment. I couldn't sleep with Sara, not after I'd had Megan in my bed. In fact, I made the decision to have a celibate marriage, because it felt wrong...disloyal to Megan.

Holy shit.

"Granddad...what have I done?"

"Nothing you can't fix."

I shake my head. "You're so wrong about that. Megan must hate me. Did you see the tabloids, see what they're saying about her and her business? Jesus, no one will ever hire her again. She has every right to hate me."

"Yeah, you were quite the dense ass," he says.

I scoff. "Why don't you tell me what you really think?"

"All right I will." He waves his hand toward the door. "Get up off the sofa, get out there and go fight for the woman you love."

"How?"

"You're a smart man, most times," he says with a grin. "I'm sure you'll figure it out."

I jump from the sofa, my heart and mind racing a million miles an hour. I need to make this right. I need to show Megan what she means to me. As an idea forms, I glance at Granddad. "I'm going to need your help."

"I thought you might say that."

CHAPTER SIXTEEN

Megan

"I CAN'T BELIEVE I let you talk me into this," I say to Amanda and give a slow shake of my head.

"When someone offers you a free vacation, you don't turn it down," she counters.

I glance out the window, take in the beautiful mountains, with their snow-peaked caps. The last time I was here, in St. Moritz, it was after prom, when I seduced Alec. I never, ever thought I'd find myself back in the place that holds so many glorious, yet painful memories. But James called me a few days after I ruined Alec and Sara's farce wedding, offering me use of his private jet and his villa here in the Alps. I flat out refused. But Amanda begged and pleaded with me, which is a little uncharacteristic of her. In the end I caved. Her business went down with mine last week. This is the least I could do to make it up to her.

The cab driver whistles from the front seat, and

I fold my hands on my lap, my heart still raked raw from Alec's rejection. But I don't want to think about him. This vacation is about getting him out of my mind and heart once and for all.

"I did a bit of research on this place," Amanda says. "Before we go to the villa can we go to Lej da Staz?" She blinks hopeful eyes at me.

I shrug. "Fine by me." I remember that lake. It has a long boardwalk out over the water, with the mountains as the backdrop. It's a beautiful spot. A perfect wedding venue, one I would have picked over a country club. But now, well, now I no longer believe in true love and happily-ever-after. I might as well start collecting cats.

Amanda leans forward and talks to the driver as I check my phone. No messages, no brides calling to book their future weddings. And why would they? They probably think I'm going to try to steal their grooms. I groan low in my throat and rest my head against the back of the seat.

A short while later the cab stops, and I'm grateful. After the long flight, I need to stretch my legs. I'm about to get out of the backseat, but out on the boardwalk there appears to be a wedding. My heart climbs into my throat and tears threaten as painful memories from last week bombard me.

"We should go," I say to Amanda. "Looks like a wedding and I don't want to disturb them."

"Let's just stretch our legs. We'll be quiet." She

opens her door and jumps from the cab. Unsure about this, I quietly open mine and slide out.

I shade the sun from my eyes and kick out my cramped legs. I glance around and see numerous tents set up. Under one, food is being laid out for the reception and it smells divine. In the distance I glance at the guests milling about, and note the soft blue colors and decorations.

"Come on, let's get a closer look."

"I think I've crashed enough weddings this week," I say, but Amanda, being a little pushy and persistent, grabs my arm and practically drags me along. As I get close, I slow my steps.

"Is that Uncle Dave?" I ask, my head rearing back in surprise. The sun is in my eyes, and I haven't slept for a week, so there is a good chance I'm hallucinating.

"You tell me," Amanda says, her voice a little amused.

I scan the crowd, and when I see my family and friends, my heart leaps. "What's going on?" I ask, but when I turn to Amanda, she's backing away. "What are you doing? Amanda, what the hell?"

"It's the grand gesture," she says. "The way it was meant to be."

I turn back to the wharf and when I see Alec coming toward me, dressed casually in a white shirt, beige pants and barefoot, tears sting my eyes. "Alec…" I choke out. "What's…going on?"

He steps up to me, takes my shaky hands into his.

"What's going on is that I was a complete idiot. But I plan to fix that."

"What…what are you doing?" I ask when he pulls a box from his pocket.

"Megan, I love you. I've always loved you."

Tears fall down my face. "You said never me, Alec. You looked me in the eye and said never me."

"Haven't we already established that I'm an idiot," he says. I nod, in agreement, and he laughs softly. "Megan, I've wanted you my whole life, but I never thought I could be loyal. The men in my family, well, you know all about them. I thought I was no different. Even my mother…" He swallows. "You're the woman I want."

"Alec," I say again, my brain trying to process.

"You were right when you said I was like my grandfather. He was loyal to Grandmother, and I am loyal to you. I know that because Sara seduced me and I couldn't touch her. Couldn't be disloyal to my love for you."

"You…love me?"

He laughs and goes down on his knees. "I love you, Megan. I want you to be my wife. Please say yes."

I look past his shoulders, take in all my family and friends, watching us. Amanda is nervously shifting from one foot to the other. I guess now I know why she was so adamant that we come here. "You did this? You set this up?" I choke out, returning my gaze to Alec.

"When we were teenagers, you described your perfect wedding to me. Do you remember that?"

"I do," I say. "I can't believe you remember, though."

"I remember everything, Megan. I remember every detail, right down to the casual way you wanted the groom to dress." He goes quiet for a moment, thoughtful, and I listen to his throat work as he swallows. "I remember the night you came to me in my room after prom. It was the best night of my life."

I nod. "Mine, too, until the morning."

"I'm sorry. I handled it badly."

"No, I understand now. You were trying to protect me." My heart swells as my throat tightens with all the things I feel for this man. All these years he was trying to protect me from himself, when all he wanted to do was love me.

He holds the ring out. "I will love you forever if you let me."

"I don't love you like you think," I say, and his face falls, sadness backlighting his gorgeous blue eyes.

"Megan—"

I press my fingers to his lips to quiet him. "You think women love you because of your power and wealth. I don't love you for that."

A relieved smile lights up his face. "So you do love me?"

"Of course I love you, you big dummy."

He laughs and tears fall down my face as he pulls the ring from the case, but I back up.

"Megan…what?" he asks.

"I wish I had my dream dress."

Once again relief moves into his eyes. "Sara," he calls out, and she comes forward with the strapless gown I tried on and fell in love with at the bridal boutique.

I give a big hiccupping sob. "Alec, I can't believe…"

"Marry me, Megan. Make me the happiest man on the planet."

"Yes," I say, and he slips the beautiful ring on my finger. A moment later he stands, and turns to the crowd.

"Whew," he says, wiping his brow. "It was touch and go there for a while but she said yes."

As everyone claps, he picks me up and spins me around. "I love you, Megs. I promise to be the best husband in the world."

"I love you, too," I say as he puts his mouth on mine for a deep, intimate kiss full of love and promises.

"Okay, let's get this show on the road," I say, as he laughs and pulls me to him, renewing my belief in true love and happily-ever-after.

* * * * *

FOR THE SAKE OF
THEIR SON

CATHERINE MANN

For my children.

One

Elliot Starc had faced danger his whole life. First at the hands of his heavy-fisted father. Later as a Formula One race car driver who used his world travels to feed information to Interpol.

But he'd never expected to be kidnapped. Especially not in the middle of his best friend's bachelor party.

Mad as hell, Elliot struggled back to consciousness, only to realize his wrists were cuffed. Numb. He struggled against the restraints while trying to get his bearings, but his brain was still disoriented. Last he remembered, he'd been in Atlanta, Georgia, at a bachelor party and now he was cuffed and blindfolded, for God's sake. What the hell? He only knew that he was in the back of a vehicle that smelled of leather and luxury. Noise offered him little to go on. Just the purr of a finely tuned engine. The pop of an opening soda can. A low hum of music so faint it must be on a headset.

"He's awake," a deep voice whispered softly, too softly to be identified.

"Damn it," another voice hissed.

"Hey," Elliot shouted, except it wasn't a shout. More of a hoarse croak. He cleared his throat and tried again. "Whatever the hell is going on here, we can talk ransom—"

A long buzz sounded. Unmistakable. The closing of a privacy window. Then silence. Solitude, no chance of shouting jack to anyone in this…

A limo, perhaps? Who kidnapped someone using a limousine?

Once they stopped, he would be ready, though. The second he could see, he wouldn't even need his hands. He was trained in seven different forms of self-defense. He could use his feet, his shoulders and his body weight.

He would be damned before he let himself ever be helpless in a fight.

They'd pulled off an interstate at least twenty minutes ago, driving into the country as best he could tell. He had no way of judging north, south or west. He could be anywhere from Florida to Mississippi to South Carolina, and God knows he had enemies in every part of the world from his work with Interpol and his triumphs over competitors in the racing world.

And he had plenty of pissed-off ex-girlfriends…. He winced at the thought of females and Carolina so close together. Home. Too many memories. Bad ones—with just a single bright spot in the form of Lucy Ann Joyner, but he'd wrecked even that.

Crap.

Back to the present. Sunlight was just beginning to filter through the blindfold, sparking behind his eyes like shards of glinting glass.

One thing was certain. This car had good shock absorbers. Otherwise the rutted road they were traveling would have rattled his teeth.

Although his teeth were clenched mighty damn tight right now.

Even now, he still couldn't figure out how he'd been blindsided near the end of Rowan Boothe's bachelor party in an Atlanta casino. Elliot had ducked into the back to find a vintage Scotch. Before he could wrap his hand around the neck of the bottle, someone had knocked him out.

If only he knew the motive for his kidnapping. Was someone after his money? Or had someone uncovered his secret dealings with Interpol? If so, did they plan to exploit that connection?

He'd lived his life to the fullest, determined to do better than his wrong-side-of-the-tracks upbringing. He only had one regret: how his lifelong friendship with Lucy Ann had crashed and burned more fiercely than when he'd been sideswiped at the Australian Grand Prix last year—

The car jerked to a halt. He braced his feet to keep from rolling off onto the floor. He forced himself to stay relaxed so his abductors would think he was still asleep.

His muscles tensed for action, eager for the opportunity to confront his adversaries. Ready to pay back. He was trained from his work with Interpol, with lightning-fast instincts honed in his racing career. He wouldn't go down without a fight.

Since he'd left his dirt-poor roots behind, he'd been beating the odds. He'd dodged juvie by landing in a military reform school where he'd connected with a lifelong group of friends. Misfits like himself who disdained rules while living by a strict code of justice. They'd grown up to take different life paths, but stayed connected through their friendship and freelance work for Interpol. Not that they'd been much help to him while someone was nabbing him a few feet away from the bachelor party they were all attending.

The car door opened and someone leaned over him. Something tugged at the back of his brain, a sense that he should know this person. He scrambled to untangle the mystery before it was too late.

His blindfold was tugged up and off, and he took in the inside of a black limo, just as he'd suspected. His abductors, however, were a total surprise.

"Hello, Elliot, my man," said his old high school pal Malcolm Douglas, who'd asked him to fetch that bottle of Scotch back at the bachelor party. "Waking up okay?"

Conrad Hughes—another traitorous bastard friend— patted his face. "You look plenty awake to me."

Elliot bit back a curse. He'd been kidnapped by his own comrades from the bachelor party. "Somebody want to tell me what's going on here?"

He eyed Conrad and Malcolm, both of whom had been living it up with him at the casino well past midnight. Morning sunshine streamed over them, oak trees sprawling behind them. The scent of Carolina jasmine carried on the breeze. Why were they taking him on this strange road trip?

"Well?" he pressed again when neither of them answered. "What the hell are you two up to?" he asked, his anger barely contained. He wanted to kick their asses. "I hope you have a good reason for taking me out to the middle of nowhere."

Conrad clapped him on the back. "You'll see soon enough."

Elliot angled out of the car, hard as hell with his hands

cuffed in front of him. His loafers hit the dirt road, rocks and dust shifting under his feet as he stood in the middle of nowhere in a dense forest of pines and oaks. "You'll tell me now or I'll beat the crap out of both of you."

Malcolm lounged against the side of the black stretch limo. "Good luck trying with your hands cuffed. Keep talking like that and we'll hang on to the key for a good long while."

"Ha—funny—not." Elliot ground his teeth in frustration. "Isn't it supposed to be the groom who gets pranked?"

Conrad grinned. "Oh, don't worry. Rowan should be waking up and finding his new tattoo right about now."

Extending his cuffed wrists, Elliot asked, "And the reason for this? I'm not the one getting married."

Ever.

Malcolm pushed away, jerking his head to the side, gesturing toward the path leading into the dense cluster of more pine trees with an occasional magnolia reaching for the sun. "Instead of telling you why, we'll just let you look. Walk with us."

As if he had any choice. His friends clearly had some kind of game planned and they intended to see it through regardless. Sure, he'd been in a bear of a mood since his breakup with Gianna. Hell, even before that. Since Lucy Ann had quit her job as his assistant and walked out of his life for good.

God, he really needed to pour out some frustration behind the wheel, full out, racing to…anywhere.

A few steps deeper into the woods, his blood hummed with recognition. The land was more mature than the last time he'd been here, but he knew the area well enough. Home. Or rather it used to be home, back when he was a poor kid with a drunken father. This small South Carolina farm town outside of Columbia had been called God's land.

Elliot considered it a corner of hell.

Although hell was brimming with sunshine today.

He stepped toward a clearing and onto a familiar dirt driveway, with a ranch-style cabin and a fat oak at least a hundred years old in the middle. A tree he'd played under as a kid, wishing he could stay here forever because this little haven in hell was a lot safer than his home.

He'd hidden with Lucy Ann Joyner here at her aunt's farmhouse. Both of them enjoying the sanctuary of this place, even if only for a few hours. Why were his buds taking him down this memory lane detour?

Branches rustled, a creaking sound carrying on the breeze, drawing his gaze. A swing dangled from a thick branch, moving back and forth as a woman swayed, her back to them. He stopped cold. Suddenly the meaning of this journey was crystal clear. His friends were forcing a confrontation eleven months in the making since he and Lucy Ann were both too stubborn to take the first step.

Did she know he was coming? He swallowed hard at the notion that maybe she wanted him here after all. That her decision to slice him out of her life had changed. But if she had, then why not just drive up to the house?

He wasn't sure the past year could be that easily forgotten, but his gut twisted tight over just the thought of talking to her again.

His eyes soaked in the sight of her, taking her in like parched earth with water. He stared at the slim feminine back, the light brown hair swishing just past her shoulders. Damn, but it had been a long eleven months without her. His lifelong pal had bolted after one reckless—incredible—night that had ruined their friendship forever.

He'd given her space and still hadn't heard from her.

In the span of a day, the one person he'd trusted above everyone else had cut him off. He'd never let anyone get that close to him—not even his friends from the military reform school. He and Lucy Ann had a history, a shared link that went beyond a regular friendship.

Or so he'd thought.

As if drawn by a magnet, he walked closer to the swing, to the woman. His hands still linked in front of him, he moved silently, watching her. The bared lines of her throat evoked memories of her jasmine scent. The way her dress slipped ever so slightly off one shoulder reminded him of years past when she'd worn hand-me-downs from neighbors.

The rope tugged at the branch as she toe-tapped, back and forth. A gust of wind turned the swing spinning to face him.

His feet stumbled to a halt.

Yes, it was Lucy Ann, but not just her. Lucy Ann stared back at him with wide eyes, shocked eyes. She'd clearly been kept every bit as much in the dark as he had. Before he could finish processing his disappointment that she hadn't helped arrange this, his eyes took in the biggest shocker of all.

Lucy Ann's arms were curved around an infant swaddled in a blue plaid blanket as she breast-fed him.

Lucy Ann clutched her baby boy to her chest and stared in shock at Elliot Starc, her childhood friend, her former boss. Her onetime lover.

The father of her child.

She'd scripted the moment she would tell him about their son a million times in her mind, but never had it played out like this, with him showing up out of the blue. Handcuffed? Clearly, he hadn't planned on coming to see her. She'd tempted fate in waiting so long to tell him, then he'd pulled one of his disappearing acts and she couldn't find him.

Now there was no avoiding him.

Part of her ached to run to Elliot and trust in the friendship they'd once shared, a friendship built here, in the wooded farmland outside Columbia, South Carolina. But another part of her—the part that saw his two friends lurking and the handcuffs on her old pal—told her all she needed to know. Elliot hadn't suddenly seen the light and come running to apologize for being a first-class jerk. He'd been dragged kicking and screaming.

Well, screw him. She had her pride, too.

Only the baby in her arms kept her from bolting altogether into her aunt's cabin up the hill. Lucy Ann eased Eli from her breast and adjusted her clothes in place. Shifting her son to her shoulder, she patted his back, her eyes staying locked on Elliot, trying to gauge his mood.

The way his eyes narrowed told her loud and clear that she couldn't delay her explanation any longer. She should have told him about Eli sooner. In the early days of her pregnancy, she'd tried and chickened out. Then she'd gotten angry over his speedy rebound engagement to the goddess Gianna, and that made it easier to keep her distance a while longer. She wouldn't be the cause of breaking up his engagement—rat bastard. She would tell him once he was married and wouldn't feel obligated to offer her anything. Even though the thought of him marrying that too-perfect bombshell heiress made her vaguely nauseous.

Now, Elliot was here, so damn tall and muscular, his sandy brown hair closely shorn. His shoulders filled out the black button-down shirt, his jeans slung low on his hips. His five o'clock shadow and narrowed green eyes gave him a bad-boy air he'd worked his whole life to live up to.

She knew every inch of him, down to a scar on his elbow he'd told everyone he got from falling off his bike but he'd really gotten from the buckle on his father's belt during a beating. They shared so much history, and now they shared a child.

Standing, she pulled her gaze from him and focused on his old boarding school friends behind him, brooding Conrad Hughes and charmer Malcolm Douglas. Of course they'd dragged him here. These days both of them had sunk so deep into a pool of marital bliss, they seemed to think everyone else wanted to plunge in headfirst. No doubt they'd brought Elliot here with just that in mind.

Not a freakin' chance.

She wasn't even interested in dipping her toes into those waters and certainly not with Elliot, the biggest playboy in the free world.

"Gentlemen, do you think you could uncuff him, then leave so he and I can talk civilly?"

Conrad—a casino owner—fished out a key from his pocket and held it up. "Can do." He looked at Elliot. "I trust you're not going to do anything stupid like try to start a fight over our little prank here."

Prank? This was her life and they were playing with it. Anger sparked in her veins.

Elliot pulled a tight smile. "Of course not. I'm outnumbered. Now just undo the handcuffs. My arms are too numb to hit either of you anyway."

Malcolm plucked the keys from Conrad and opened the cuffs. Elliot massaged his wrists for a moment, still silent, then stretched his arms over his head.

Did he have to keep getting hotter every year? Especially not fair when she hadn't even had time to shower since yesterday thanks to her son's erratic sleeping schedule.

Moistening her dry mouth, Lucy Ann searched for a way to dispel the awkward air. "Malcolm, Conrad, I realize you meant well with this, but perhaps it's time for you both to leave. Elliot and I clearly have some things to discuss."

Eli burped. Lucy Ann rolled her eyes and cradled her son in the crook of her arm, too aware of the weight of Elliot's stare.

Malcolm thumped Elliot on the back. "You can thank us later."

Conrad leveled a somber steady look her way. "Call if you need anything. I mean that."

Without another word, both men disappeared back into the wooded perimeter as quickly as they'd arrived. For the first time in eleven months, she was alone with Elliot.

Well, not totally alone. She clutched Eli closer until he squirmed.

Elliot stuffed his hands in his pockets, still keeping his distance. "How long have you been staying with your aunt?"

"Since I left Monte Carlo." She'd been here the whole time, if he'd only bothered to look. Where else would she go? She had money saved up, but staying here made the most sense economically.

"How are you supporting yourself?"

"That's not your business." She lifted her chin. He had the ability to find out anything he wanted to know about her if he'd just looked, thanks to his Interpol connections.

Apparently, he hadn't even bothered to try. And that's what hurt the most. All these months, she'd thought he would check up on her. He would have seen she was pregnant. He would have wondered.

He would have come.

"Not my business?" He stalked a step closer, only a hint of anger showing in his carefully guarded eyes. "Really? I think we both know why it is so very much my business."

"I have plenty saved up from my years working for you." He'd insisted on paying her an outlandish salary to be his personal assistant. "And I'm doing virtual work to subsidize my income. I build and maintain websites. I make enough to get by." Her patience ran out with this small talk, the avoidance of discussing the baby sleeping in her arms. "You've had months to ask these questions and chose to remain silent. If anyone has a right to be angry, it's me."

"You didn't call either, and you have a much more compelling reason to communicate." He nodded toward Eli. "He is mine."

"You sound sure."

"I know you. I see the truth in your eyes," he said simply.

She couldn't argue with that. She swallowed once, twice, to clear her throat and gather her nerve. "His name is Eli. And yes, he's your son, two months old."

Elliot pulled his hands from his pockets. "I want to hold him."

Her stomach leaped into her throat. She'd envisioned this moment so many times, but living in it? She never could have imagined how deeply the emotions would rattle her. She passed over Eli to his father, watching Elliot's face. For once, she couldn't read him at all. So strange, considering how they'd once been so in sync they could finish each other's sentences, read a thought from a glance across a room.

Now, he was like a stranger.

Face a blank slate, Elliot held their son in broad, capable hands, palmed the baby's bottom and head as he studied the tiny cherub features. Eli still wore his blue footed sleeper from bedtime, his blond hair glistening as the sun sent dappled rays through the branches. The moment looked like a fairy tale, but felt so far from that her heart broke over how this should have, could have been.

Finally, Elliot looked up at her, his blasé mask sliding away to reveal eyes filled with ragged pain. His throat moved in a slow gulp of emotion. "Why did you keep this—Eli—from me?"

Guilt and frustration gnawed at her. She'd tried to contact him but knew she hadn't tried hard enough. Her pride… Damn it all. Her excuses all sounded weak now, even to her own ears.

"You were engaged to someone else. I didn't want to interfere in that."

"You never intended to tell me at all?" His voice went hoarse with disbelief, his eyes shooting back down to his son sleeping against his chest so contentedly as if he'd been there all along.

"Of course I planned to explain—after you were married." She dried her damp palms on her sundress. "I refused to be responsible for breaking up your great love match."

Okay, she couldn't keep the cynicism out of that last part, but he deserved it for his rebound relationship.

"My engagement to Gianna ended months ago. Why didn't you contact me?"

He had a point there. She ached to run, but he had her son. And as much as she hated to admit it to herself, she'd missed Elliot. They'd been so much a part of each other's lives for so long. The past months apart had been like a kind of withdrawal.

"Half the time I couldn't find you and the other half, your new personal secretary couldn't figure out where you were." And hadn't that pissed her off something fierce? Then worried her, because she knew about his sporadic missions for Interpol, and she also knew his reckless spirit.

"You can't have tried very hard, Lucy Ann. All you had to do was speak with any of my friends." His eyes narrowed. "Or did you? Is that why they brought me here today, because you reached out to them?"

She'd considered doing just that many times, only to balk at the last second. She wouldn't be manipulative. She'd planned to tell him face-to-face. And soon.

"I wish I could say yes, but I'm afraid not. One of them must have been checking up on me even if you never saw the need."

Oops. Where had that bitter jab come from?

He cocked an eyebrow. "This is about Eli. Not about the two of us."

"There is no 'two of us' anymore." She touched her son's head lightly, aching to take him back in her arms. "You ended that when you ran away scared after we had a reckless night of sex."

"I do *not* run away."

"Excuse me if your almighty ego is bruised." She crossed her arms over her chest, feeling as though they were in fifth grade again, arguing over whether the basketball was in or out of bounds.

Elliot sighed, looking around at the empty clearing. The limo's engine roared to life, then faded as it drove away without him. He turned back to Lucy Ann. "This isn't accomplishing anything. We need to talk reasonably about our child's future."

"I agree." Of course they had to talk, but right now her

heart was in her throat. She could barely think straight. She scooped her baby from his arms. "We'll talk tomorrow when we're both less rattled."

"How do I know you won't just disappear with my son?" He let go of Eli with obvious reluctance.

His son.

Already his voice echoed with possessiveness.

She clasped her son closer, breathing in the powder-fresh familiarity of him, the soft skin of his cheek pressed against her neck reassuringly. She could and she would manage her feelings for Elliot. Nothing and no one could be allowed to interfere with her child's future.

"I've been here all this time, Elliot. You just never chose to look." A bitter pill to swallow. She gestured up the empty dirt road. "Even now, you didn't choose. Your friends dumped you here on my doorstep."

Elliot walked a slow circle around her, his hand snagging the rope holding the swing until he stopped beside her. He had a way of moving with such fluidity, every step controlled, a strange contradiction in a man who always lived on the edge. Always flirting with chaos.

Her skin tingled to life with the memory of his touch, the wind teasing her with a hint of aftershave and musk.

She cleared her throat. "Elliot, I really think you should—"

"Lucy Ann," he interrupted, "in case it's escaped your notice, my friends left me here. Alone. No car." He leaned in closer, his hand still holding the rope for balance, so close she could almost feel the rasp of his five o'clock shadow. "So regardless of whether or not we talk, for now, you're stuck with me."

Two

Elliot held himself completely still, a feat of supreme control given the frustration racing through his veins. That Lucy Ann had hidden her pregnancy—his son—from him all this time threatened to send him to his knees. Somehow during this past year he'd never let go of the notion that everything would simply return to the way things had been before with them. Their friendship had carried him through the worst times of his life.

Now he knew there was no going back. Things between them had changed irrevocably.

They had a child together, a boy just inches away. Elliot clenched his hand around the rope. He needed to bide his time and proceed with caution. His lifelong friend had a million great qualities—but she was also stubborn as hell. A wrong step during this surprise meeting could have her digging in her heels.

He had to control his frustration, tamp down the anger

over all that she'd hidden from him. Staying levelheaded saved his life on more than one occasion on the racetrack. But never had the stakes been more important than now. No matter how robbed he felt, he couldn't let that show.

Life had taught him well how to hide his darker emotions.

So he waited, watching her face for some sign. The breeze lifted a strand of her hair, whipping it over his cheek. His pulse thumped harder.

"Well, Lucy Ann? What now?"

Her pupils widened in her golden-brown eyes, betraying her answering awareness a second before she bolted up from the swing. Elliot lurched forward as the swing freed. He released the rope and found his footing.

Lucy Ann glanced over her shoulder as she made her way to the graveled path. "Let's go inside."

"Where's your aunt?" He followed her, rocks crunching under his feet.

"At work." Lucy Ann walked up the steps leading to the prefab log cabin's long front porch. Time had worn the redwood look down to a rusty hue. "She still waits tables at the Pizza Shack."

"You used to send her money." He'd stumbled across the bank transaction by accident. Or maybe his accountant had made a point of letting him discover the transfers since Lucy Ann left so little for herself.

"Well, come to find out, Aunt Carla never used it," Lucy Ann said wryly, pushing the door open into the living room. The decor hadn't changed, the same brown plaid sofa with the same saggy middle, the same dusty Hummel figurines packed in a corner cabinet. He'd forgotten how Carla scoured yard sales religiously for the things, unable to afford them new.

They'd hidden here more than once as kids, then as

teenagers, plotting a way to escape their home lives. He eyed the son he'd barely met but who already filled his every plan going forward. "Your aunt's prideful, just like you."

"I accepted a job from you." She settled Eli into a portable crib by the couch.

"You worked your butt off and got your degree in computer technology." He admired the way she never took the easy way out. How she'd found a career for herself.

So why had she avoided talking to him? Surely not from any fear of confrontation. Her hair swung forward as she leaned into the baby crib, her dress clinging to her hips. His gaze hitched on the new curves.

Lucy Ann spun away from the crib and faced him again. "Are we going to keep making small talk or are you going to call a cab? I could drive you back into town."

"I'm not going anywhere."

Her eyebrows pinched together. "I thought we agreed to talk tomorrow."

"You decided. I never agreed." He dropped to sit on the sofa arm. If he sat in the middle, no telling how deep that sag would sink.

"You led me to believe…" She looked around as if searching for answers, but the Hummels stayed silent. "Damn it. You just wanted to get in the house."

Guilty as charged. "This really is the best place to discuss the future. Anywhere else and I'll have to be on the lookout for fans. We're in NASCAR country, you know. Not Formula One, but kissing cousins." He held up his hands. "Besides, my jackass buddies stranded me without my wallet."

She gasped. "You're joking."

"I wish." They must have taken it from his pocket while he was knocked out. He tamped down another surge of anger over being manipulated. If he'd just had some warning…

"Why did they do this to you—to both of us?" She sat on the other arm of the sofa, the worn width between them.

"Probably because they know how stubborn we are." He watched her face, trying to read the truth in the delicate lines, but he saw only exhaustion and dark circles. "Would you have ever told me about the baby?"

"You've asked me that already and I've answered. Of course I would have told you—" she shrugged "—eventually."

Finally he asked the question that had been plaguing him most. "How can I be sure?"

Shaking her head, she shrugged again. "You can't. You'll just have to trust me."

A wry smile tugged the corner of his mouth. "Trust has never been easy for either of us." But now that he was here and saw the truth, his decision was simple. "I want you and Eli to come with me, just for a few weeks while we make plans for the future."

"No." She crossed her arms over her chest.

"Ah, come on, Lucy Ann. Think about my request before you react."

"Okay. Thinking…" She tapped her temple, tapping, tapping. Her hand fell to her lap. "Still no."

God, her humor and spunk had lifted him out of hell so many times. He'd missed her since she'd stormed out of his life.…

But he'd also missed out on a lot more in not knowing about his son.

"I can never regain those first two months of Eli's life." A bitter pill he wasn't sure how to swallow down. "I need a chance to make up for that."

She shook her head slowly. "You can't be serious about taking a baby on the road."

"I'm dead serious." He wasn't leaving here without them. He couldn't just toss money down and go.

"Let me spell it out for you then. Elliot, this is the middle of your racing season." She spoke slowly, as she'd done when they were kids and she'd tutored him in multiplication tables. "You'll be traveling, working, running with a party crowd. I've seen it year after year, enough to know that's no environment for a baby."

And damn it, she was every bit as astute now as she'd been then. He lined up an argument, a way to bypass her concerns. "You saw my life when there wasn't a baby around—no kids around, actually. It *can* be different. *I* can be different, like other guys who bring their families on the circuit with them." He shifted to sit beside her. "I have a damn compelling reason to make changes in my life. This is the chance to show you that."

Twisting the skirt of her dress in nervous fingers, she studied him with her golden-brown gaze for so long he thought he'd won.

Then resolve hardened her eyes again. "Expecting someone to change only sets us both up for disappointment."

"Then you'll get to say 'I told you so.' You told me often enough in the past." He rested a hand on top of hers to still the nervous fidgeting, squeezing lightly. "The best that happens is I'm right and this works. We find a plan to be good parents to Eli even when we're jet-setting around the world. Remember how much fun we used to have together? I miss you, Lucy Ann."

He thumbed the inside of her wrist, measuring the speed of her pulse, the softness of her skin. He'd done everything he could to put her out of his mind, but with no luck. He'd been unfair to Gianna, leading her to think he was free. So many regrets. He was tired of them. "Lucy Ann…"

She yanked her hand free. "Stop it, Elliot. I've watched you seduce a lot of women over the years. Your games don't work with me. So don't even try the slick moves."

"You wound me." He clamped a hand over his heart in an attempt at melodrama to cover his disappointment.

She snorted. "Hardly. You don't fool me with the pained look. It's eleven months too late to be genuine."

"You would be wrong about that."

"No games." She shot to her feet. "We both need time to regroup and think. We need to continue this conversation later."

"Fair enough then." He sat on the sofa, stretching both arms out along the back.

She stomped her foot. "What are you doing?"

He picked up the remote from the coffee table and leaned back again into the deepest, saggiest part. "Making myself comfortable."

"For what?"

He thumbed on the television. "If I'm going to stick around until you're ready to talk, I might as well scout the good stations. Any beer in the fridge? Although wait, it's too early for that. How about coffee?"

"No." She snatched the remote control from his hand. "And stop it. I don't know what game you're playing but you can quit and *go*. In case that wasn't clear enough, leave and come back later. You can take my car."

He took the remote right back and channel surfed without looking away from the flat screen. "Thanks for the generous offer of transportation, but you said we can't take Eli on the road and I only just met my son. I'm not leaving him now. How about the coffee?"

"Like hell."

"I don't need cream. Black will do just fine."

"Argh!" She slumped against the archway between the living room and kitchen. "Quit being ridiculous about the coffee. You know you're not staying here."

He set aside the remote, smiling as some morning talk show droned in the background. "So you'll come with me after all. Good."

"You're crazy. You know that, right?"

"No newsflash there, sweetheart. A few too many concussions." He stood. "Forget the suitcase."

"Run that by me again?"

"Don't bother with packing. I'll buy everything you need, everything new. Let's just grab a couple of diapers for the rug rat and go."

Her acceptance was becoming more and more important by the second. He needed her with him. He had to figure out a way to tie their lives together again so his son would know a father, a mother and a normal life.

"Stop! Stop trying to control my life." She stared at him sadly. "Elliot, I appreciate all you did for me in the past, but I don't need rescuing anymore."

"Last time I checked, I wasn't offering a rescue. Just a partnership."

If humor and pigheadedness didn't work, time to go back to other tactics. No great hardship really, since the attraction crackled between them every bit as tangibly now as it had the night they'd impulsively landed in bed together after a successful win. He sauntered closer. "As I recall, last time we were together, we shared control quite…nicely. And now that I think of it, we really don't need those clothes after all."

* * *

The rough upholstery of the sofa rasped against the backs of Lucy Ann's legs, her skin oversensitive, tingling to life after just a few words from Elliot. Damn it, she refused to be seduced by him again. The way her body betrayed her infuriated her down to her toes, which curled in her sandals.

Sure, he was beach-boy handsome, mesmerizingly sexy and blindingly charming. Women around the world could attest to his allure. However, in spite of her one unforgettable moment of weakness, she refused to be one of those fawning females throwing themselves at his feet.

No matter how deeply her body betrayed her every time he walked in the room.

She shot from the sofa, pacing restlessly since she couldn't bring herself to leave her son alone, even though he slept. Damn Elliot and the draw of attraction that had plagued her since the day they'd gone skinny-dipping at fourteen and she realized they weren't kids anymore.

Shutting off those thoughts, she pivoted on the coarse shag carpet to face him. "This is not the time or the place for sexual innuendo."

"Honey—" his arms stretched along the back of the sofa "—it's never a bad time for sensuality. For nuances. For seduction."

The humor in his eyes took the edge of arrogance off his words. "If you're aiming to persuade me to leave with you, you're going about it completely the wrong way."

"There's no denying we slept together."

"Clearly." She nodded toward the Pack 'n Play where their son slept contentedly, unaware that his little world had just been turned upside down.

"There's no denying that it was good between us. Very good."

Elliot's husky words snapped her attention back to his face. There wasn't a hint of humor in sight. Awareness tingled to the roots of her hair.

Swallowing hard, she sank into an old cane rocker. "It was impulsive. We were both tipsy and sentimental and reckless." The rush of that evening sang through her memory, the celebration of his win, reminiscing about his first dirt track race, a little wine, too much whimsy, then far too few clothes…. "I refuse to regret that night or call our…encounter…a mistake since I have Eli. But I do not intend to repeat the experience."

"Now that's just a damn shame. What a waste of good sexual chemistry."

"Will you please stop?" Her hands fisted on the arms of the wooden rocker. "We got along just fine as friends for thirty years."

"Are you saying we can be friends again?" He leaned forward, elbows on his knees. "No more hiding out and keeping big fat secrets from each other?"

His words carried too much truth for comfort. "You're twisting my words around."

"God's honest truth, Lucy Ann." He sighed. "I'm trying to call a truce so we can figure out how to plan our son's future."

"By telling me to ditch my clothes? You obviously missed class the day they taught the definition of truce."

"Okay, you're right. That wasn't fair of me." He thrust his hands through his hair. "I'm not thinking as clearly as I would like. Learning about Eli has been a shock to say the least."

"I can understand that." Her hands unfurled to grip the rocker. "And I am so very sorry for any pain this has caused you."

"Given that I've lost the first two months of my son's

life, the least you can do is give me four weeks together. Since you're working from home here, you'll be able to work on the road, as well. But if going on the race circuit is a deal breaker, I'll bow out this season."

She jolted in surprise that he would risk all he'd worked so hard to achieve, a career he so deeply loved. "What about your sponsors? Your reputation?"

"This is your call."

"That's not fair to make an ultimatum like that, to put it on me."

"I'm asking, and I'm offering you choices."

Choices? Hardly. She knew how important his racing career was to him. And she couldn't help but admit to feeling a bit of pride in having helped him along the way. There was no way she could let him back out now.

She tossed up her hands. "Fine. Eli and I will travel with you on the race circuit for the next four weeks so you can figure out whatever it is you want to know and make your plans. You win. You always do."

Winning didn't feel much like a victory tonight.

Elliot poured himself a drink from the wet bar at his hotel. He and Lucy Ann had struck a bargain that he would stay at a nearby historic home that had been converted into a hotel while she made arrangements to leave in the morning. He'd called for a car service to pick him up, making use of his credit card numbers, memorized, a fact he hadn't bothered mentioning to Lucy Ann earlier. Although she should have known. Had she selectively forgotten or had she been that rattled?

The half hour waiting for the car had been spent silently staring at his son while Eli slept and Lucy Ann hid in the other room under the guise of packing.

Elliot's head was still reeling. He had been knocked

unconscious and kidnapped, and found out he had an unknown son all in one day. He tipped back the glass of bourbon, emptying it and pouring another to savor, more slowly, while he sat out on the garden balcony where he would get better cell phone reception.

He dropped into a wrought-iron chair and let the Carolina moon pour over him. His home state brought such a mix of happy and sad memories. He was always better served just staying the hell away. He tugged his cell from his waistband, tucked his Bluetooth in his ear and thumbed autodial three for Malcolm Douglas.

The ringing stopped two buzzes in. "Brother, how's it going?"

"How do you think it's going, Douglas? My head hurts and I'm pissed off." Anger was stoked back to life just thinking about his friends' arrogant stunt, the way they'd played with his life. "You could have just told me about the baby."

Malcolm chuckled softly. "Wouldn't have been half as fun that way."

"Fun? You think this is some kind of game? You're a sick bastard." The thought of them plotting this out while he partied blissfully unaware had him working hard to keep his breath steady. He and his friends had played some harsh jokes on one another in the past, but nothing like this. "How long have you known?"

"For about a week," the chart-topping musician answered unrepentantly.

"A week." Seven days he could have had with his son. Seven days his best friends kept the largest of secrets from him. Anger flamed through him. Was there nobody left in this world he could trust? He clenched his hand around the glass tumbler until it threatened to shatter. "And you said nothing at all."

"I know it seems twisted, but we talked it through," he said, all humor gone, his smooth tones completely serious for once. "We thought this was the best way. You're too good at playing it cool with advance notice. You would have just made her mad."

"Like I didn't already do that?" He set aside the half-drunk glass of bourbon, the top-shelf brand wasted on him in his current mood.

"You confronted her with honesty," Malcolm answered reasonably. "If we'd given you time to think, you'd have gotten your pride up. You would have been angry and bullish. You can be rather pigheaded, you know."

"If I'm such a jackass, then why are we still friends?"

"Because I'm a jackass, too." Malcolm paused before continuing somberly. "You would have done the same for me. I know what it's like not to see your child, to have missed out on time you can never get back…"

Malcolm's voice choked off with emotion. He and his wife had been high school sweethearts who'd had to give up a baby girl for adoption since they were too young to provide a life for their daughter. Now they had twins—a boy and a girl—they loved dearly, but they still grieved for that first child, even knowing they'd made the right decision for her.

Although Malcolm and Celia had both known about *their* child from the start.

Elliot forked his hands through his buzzed hair, kept closely shorn since he'd let his thoughts of Lucy Ann distract him and he'd caught his car on fire just before Christmas—nearly caught himself on fire, as well.

He'd scorched his hair; the call had been that damn close.

"I just can't wrap my brain around the fact she's kept his existence from me for so long."

Malcolm snorted. "I can't believe the two of you slept together."

A growl rumbled low in his throat. "You're close to overstepping the bounds of our friendship with talk like that."

"Ahhh." He chuckled. "So you do care about her more than you've let on."

"We were…friends. Lifelong friends. That's no secret." He and Lucy Ann shared so much history it was impossible to unravel events from the past without thinking about each other. "The fact that there was briefly more…I can't deny that, either."

"You must not have been up to snuff for her to run so fast."

Anger hissed between Elliot's teeth, and he resisted the urge to pitch his Bluetooth over the balcony. "Now you have crossed the line. If we were sitting in the same place right now, my fist would be in your face."

"Fair enough." Douglas laughed softly again. "Like I said. You do care more than a little, more than any 'buddy.' And you can't refute it. Admit it, Elliot. I've just played you, my friend."

No use denying he'd been outmaneuvered by someone who knew him too well.

And as for what Malcolm had said? That he cared for Lucy Ann? Cared? Yes. He had. And like every other time in his life he'd cared, things had gone south.

If he wanted to sort through this mess and create any kind of future with Eli and Lucy Ann, he had to think more and care less.

Three

Lucy Ann shaded her eyes against the rising sun. For the third time in twenty-four hours a limousine pulled up her dusty road, oak trees creating a canopy for the long driveway. The first time had occurred yesterday when Elliot had arrived, then when he'd left, and now, he was returning.

Her simple semihermit life working from home with her son was drawing to a close in another few minutes.

Aunt Carla cradled Eli in her arms. Carla never seemed to age, her hair a perpetual shade halfway between gray and brown. She refused to waste money to have it colored. Her arms were ropy and strong from years of carting around trays of pizzas and sodas. Her skin was prematurely wrinkled from too much hard work, time in the Carolina sun—and a perpetual smile.

She was a tough, good woman who'd been there for Lucy Ann all her life. Too bad Carla couldn't have been her mother. Heaven knows she'd prayed for that often enough.

Carla smiled down at little Eli, his fist curled around her finger. "I'm sure I'm going to miss you both. It's been a treat having a baby around again."

She'd never had a child of her own, but was renowned for opening her home to family members in need. She wasn't a problem-solver so much as a temporary oasis. Very temporary, as the limo drew closer down the half-mile driveway.

"You're sweet to make it sound like we haven't taken over your house." Lucy Ann tugged her roller bag through the door, *kerthunking* it over a bump, casting one last glance back at the tiny haven of Hummels and the saggy sofa.

"Sugar, you know I only wish I could've done more for you this time and when you were young." Carla swayed from side to side, wearing her standard high-waisted jeans and a seasonal shirt—a pink Easter bunny on today's tee.

"You've always been there for me." Lucy Ann sat on top of her luggage, her eyes on the nearing limo. "I don't take that for granted."

"I haven't always been there for you and we both know it," Carla answered, her eyes shadowed with memories they both didn't like to revisit.

"You did the best you could. I know that." Since Lucy Ann's mother had legal guardianship and child services wouldn't believe any of the claims of neglect, much less allegations of abuse by stepfathers, there wasn't anything Lucy Ann could do other than escape to Carla— or to Elliot.

Her mother and her last stepfather had died in a boating accident, so there was nothing to be gained from dwelling on the past. Her mom had no more power over her than Lucy Ann allowed her. "Truly, Carla, the past is best left there."

"Glad to know you feel that way. I hope you learned that from me." Carla tugged on Lucy Ann's low ponytail. "If you can forgive me, why can't you forgive Elliot?"

Good question. She slouched back with a sigh. "If I could answer that, then I guess my heart wouldn't be breaking in two right now."

Her aunt hauled her in for a one-armed hug while she cradled the baby in the other. "I would fix this for you if I could."

"Come with us," Lucy Ann blurted. "I've asked you before and I know all your reasons for saying no. You love your home and your life and weekly bingo. But will you change your mind this time?" She angled back, hoping. "Will you come with us? We're family."

"Ah, sweet niece." Carla shook her head. "This is your life, your second chance, your adventure. Be careful. Be smart. And remember you're a damn amazing woman. He would be a lucky man to win you back."

Just the thought... No. "That's not why I'm going with him." She took Eli from her aunt. "My trip is only about planning a future for my son, for figuring out a way to blend Elliot's life with my new life."

"You used to be a major part of his world."

"I was his glorified secretary." A way for him to give her money while salving her conscience. At least she'd lived frugally and used the time to earn a degree so she could be self-sufficient. The stretch limo slowed along the last patch of gravel in front of the house.

"You were his best friend and confidant... And apparently something more at least once."

"I'm not sure what point you are trying to make, but

if you're going to make it, do so fast." She nodded to the opening limo door. "We're out of time."

"You two got along fabulously for decades and there's an obvious attraction. Why can't you have more?" Her aunt tipped her head, eyeing Elliot stepping from the vehicle. The car door slammed.

Sunshine sent dappled rays along his sandy-brown hair, over his honed body in casual jeans and a white polo that fit his muscled arms. She'd leaned on those broad shoulders for years without hesitation, but now all she could think about was the delicious feel of those arms around her. The flex of those muscles as he stretched over her.

Lucy Ann tore her eyes away and back to her aunt. "Have more?" That hadn't ended well for either of them. "Are you serious?"

"Why wouldn't I be?"

"He hasn't come looking for me for nearly a year. He let me go." Something that had hurt every day of the eleven months that passed. She waved toward him talking to his chauffeur. "He's only here now because his friends threw him on my doorstep."

"You're holding back because of your pride?" Her aunt tut-tutted. "You're throwing him and a possible future away because of pride?"

"Listen to me. *He* threw *me* away." She'd been an afterthought or nuisance to people her whole life. She wouldn't let her son live the same second-class existence. Panic began to set in. "Now that I think of it, I'm not sure why I even agreed to go with him—"

"Stop. Hold on." Carla grabbed her niece by the shoulders and steadied her. "Forget I said anything at all. Of course you have every reason to be upset. Go with him and figure out how to manage your son's future. And I'll always be here if you decide to return."

"If?" Lucy Ann rolled her eyes. "You mean when."

Carla pointed to the limo and the broad-shouldered man walking toward them. "Do you really think Elliot's going to want his son to grow up here?"

"Um, I mean, I hadn't thought…"

True panic set in as Lucy Ann realized she no longer had exclusive say over her baby's life. Of course Elliot would have different plans for his child. He'd spent his entire life planning how to get out of here, devising ways to build a fortune, and he'd succeeded.

Eli was a part of that now. And no matter how much she wanted to deny it, her life could never be simple again.

Elliot sprawled in the backseat of the limo while Lucy Ann adjusted the straps on Eli's infant seat, checking each buckle to ensure it fit with obvious seasoned practice. Her loose ponytail swung forward, the dome light bringing out the hints of honey in her light brown hair.

He dug his fingers into the butter-soft leather to keep from stroking the length of her hair, to see if it was as silky as he remembered. He needed to bide his time. He had her and the baby with him. That was a huge victory, especially after their stubborn year apart.

And now?

He had to figure out a way to make her stay. To go back to the way things were…except he knew things couldn't be exactly the same. Not after they'd slept together. Although he would have to tread warily there. He couldn't see her cheering over a "friends with benefits" arrangement. He'd have to take it a step at a time to gauge her mood. She needed to be reminded of all the history they shared, all the ways they got along so well.

She tucked a homemade quilt over Eli's tiny legs before shifting to sit beside him. Elliot knocked on the driver's window and the vehicle started forward on their journey to the airport.

"Lucy Ann, you didn't have to stay up late packing that suitcase." He looked at the discarded cashmere baby blanket she left folded to the side. "I told you I would take care of buying everything he needs."

His son would never ride a secondhand bike he'd unearthed at the junkyard. A sense of possessiveness stirred inside him. He'd ordered the best of the best for his child—from the car seat to a travel bed. Clothes. Toys. A stroller. He'd consulted his friends' wives for advice— easy enough since his buddies and their wives were all propagating like rabbits these days.

Apparently, so was he.

Lucy Ann rested a hand on the faded quilt with tiny blue sailboats. "Eli doesn't know if something is expensive or a bargain. He only knows if something feels or smells familiar. He's got enough change in his life right now."

"Is that a dig at me?" He studied her, trying to get a read on her mood. She seemed more reserved than yesterday, worried even.

"Not a dig at all. It's a fact." She eyed him with confusion.

"He has you as a constant."

"Damn straight he does," she said with a mama-bear ferocity that lit a fire inside him. Her strength, the light in her eyes, stirred him.

Then it hit him. She was in protective mode because she saw him as a threat. She actually thought he might try

to take her child away from her. Nothing could be further from the truth. He wanted to parent the child *with* her.

He angled his head to capture her gaze fully. "I'm not trying to take him away from you. I just want to be a part of his life."

"Of course. That was always my intention," she said, her eyes still guarded, wary. "I know trust is difficult right now, but I hope you will believe me that I want you to have regular visitation."

Ah, already she was trying to set boundaries rather than thinking about possibilities. But he knew better than to fight with her. Finesse always worked better than head-on confrontation. He pointed to the elementary school they'd attended together, the same redbrick building but with a new playground. "We share a lot of history and now we share a son. Even a year apart isn't going to erase everything else."

"I understand that."

"Do you?" He moved closer to her.

Her body went rigid as she held herself still, keeping a couple of inches of space between them. "Remember when we were children, in kindergarten?"

Following her train of thought was tougher than maneuvering through race traffic, but at least she was talking to him. "Which particular day in kindergarten?"

She looked down at her hands twisted in her lap, her nails short and painted with a pretty orange. "You were lying belly flat on a skateboard racing down a hill."

That day eased to the front of his mind. "I fell off, flat on my ass." He winced. "Broke my arm."

"All the girls wanted to sign your cast." She looked sideways at him, smiling. "Even then you were a chick magnet."

"They just wanted to use their markers," he said dismissively.

She looked up to meet his eyes fully for the first time since they'd climbed into the limousine. "I knew that your arm was already broken."

"You never said a word to me." He rubbed his forearm absently.

"You would have been embarrassed if I confronted you, and you would have lied to me. We didn't talk as openly then about our home lives." She tucked the blanket more securely around the baby's feet as Eli sucked a pacifier in his sleep. "We were new friends who shared a jelly sandwich at lunch."

"We were new friends and yet you were right about the arm." He looked at his son's tiny hands and wondered how any father could ever strike out at such innocence. Sweat beaded his forehead at even the thought.

"I told my mom though, after school," Lucy Ann's eyes fell to his wrist. "She wasn't as…distant in those days."

The weight of her gaze was like a stroke along his skin, her words salve to a past wound. "I didn't know you said anything to anyone."

"Her word didn't carry much sway, or maybe she didn't fight that hard." She shrugged, the strap of her sundress sliding. "Either way, nothing happened. So I went to the principal."

"My spunky advocate." God, he'd missed her. And yet he'd always thought he knew everything about her and here she had something new to share. "Guess that explains why they pulled me out of class to interview me about my arm."

"You didn't tell the principal the truth though, did you?

I kept waiting for something big to happen. My five-year-old imagination was running wild."

For one instant in that meeting he had considered talking, but the thoughts of afterward had frozen any words in his throat like a lodged wad of that shared jelly sandwich. "I was still too scared of what would happen to my mother if I talked. Of what he would do to her."

Sympathy flickered in her brown eyes. "We discussed so many things as kids, always avoiding anything to do with our home lives. Our friendship was a haven for me then."

He'd felt the same. But that meeting with the principal had made him bolder later, except he'd chosen the wrong person to tell. Someone loyal to his father, which only brought on another beating.

"You had your secrets, too. I could always sense when you were holding back."

"Then apparently we didn't have any secrets from each other after all." She winced, her hand going to her son's car seat. "Not until this year."

The limo jostled along a pothole on the country road. Their legs brushed and his arm shot out to rest along the back of her seat. She jolted for an instant, her breath hitching. He stared back, keeping his arm in place until her shoulders relaxed.

"Oh, Elliot." She sagged back. "We're a mess, you and I, with screwed-up pasts and not much to go on as an example for building a future."

The worry coating her words stabbed at him. He cupped her arm lightly, the feel of her so damn right tucked to him. "We need to figure out how to straighten ourselves out to be good parents. For Eli."

"It won't be all that difficult to outdo our parents."

"Eli deserves a lot better than just a step above our

folks." The feel of her hair along his wrist soothed old wounds, the way she'd always done for him. But more than that, the feel of her now, with the new memories, with that night between them…

His pulse pounded in his ears, his body stirring.… He wanted her. And right now, he didn't see a reason why they couldn't have everything. They shared a similar past and they shared a child.

He just had to convince Lucy Ann. "I agree with you there. That's why it's important for us to use this time together wisely. Figure out how to be the parents he deserves. Figure out how to be a team, the partners he needs."

"I'm here, in the car with you, committed to spending the next four weeks with you." She tipped her face up to his, the jasmine scent of her swirling all around him. "What more do you want from me?"

"I want us to be friends again, Lucy Ann," he answered honestly, his voice raw. "Friends. Not just parents passing a kid back and forth to each other. I want things the way they were before between us."

Her pupils widened with emotion. "Exactly the way we were before? Is that even possible?"

"Not exactly as before," he conceded, easy enough to do when he knew his plans for something better between them.

He angled closer, stroking her ponytail over her shoulder in a sweep he wanted to take farther down her back to her waist. He burned all the way to his gut, needing to pull her closer.

"We'll be friends and more. We can go back to that night together, pick up from there. Because heaven help me, if we're being totally honest, then yes. I want you back in my bed again."

Four

The caress of Elliot's hand along her hair sent tingles all the way to her toes. She wanted to believe the deep desire was simply a result of nearly a year without sex, but she knew her body longed for this particular man. For the pleasure of his caress over her bare skin.

Except then she wouldn't be able to think straight. Now more than ever, she needed to keep a level head for her child. She loved her son more than life, and she had some serious fences to mend with Elliot to secure a peaceful future for Eli.

Lucy Ann clasped Elliot's wrist and moved it aside. "You can't be serious."

"I'm completely serious." His fingers twisted in her ponytail.

"Let. Go. Now," she said succinctly, barely able to keep herself from grabbing his shirt and hauling him in for a kiss. "Sex will only complicate matters."

"Or it could simplify things." He released her hair slowly, his stroke tantalizing all the way down her arm.

Biting her lip, she squeezed her eyes shut, too enticed by the green glow of desire in his eyes.

"Lucy Ann?" His bourbon-smooth tones intoxicated the parched senses that had missed him every day of the past eleven months. "What are you thinking?"

Her head angled ever so slightly toward his touch. "My aunt said the same thing about the bonus of friends becoming…more."

He laughed softly, the heat of his breath warming her throat and broadcasting just how close he'd moved to her, so close he could kiss the exposed flesh. "Your aunt has always been a smart woman. Although I sure as hell didn't talk to her about you and I becoming lovers."

She opened her eyes slowly, steeling herself. "You need to quit saying things like that or I'm going to have the car stopped right now. I will walk home with my baby if I have to. You and I need boundaries for this to work."

His gaze fell to her mouth for an instant that felt stretched to eternity before he angled back, leather seat creaking. "We'll have to agree to disagree."

Her exhale was shakier than she would have liked, betraying her. "You can cut the innocent act. I've seen your playboy moves over the years. Your practiced charm isn't going to work with me." Not again, anyway. "And it wouldn't have worked before if I hadn't been so taken away by sentimentality and a particularly strong vintage liqueur."

Furrows dug deep trenches in his forehead. "Lucy Ann, I am deeply sorry if I took advantage of our friendship—"

"I told you that night. No apologies." His apologies had been mortifying then, especially when she'd been hoping for a repeat only to learn he was full of regrets. He'd stung her pride and her heart. Not that she ever intended to let him know as much. "There were two of us in bed that night, and I refuse to call it a mistake. But it won't happen again, remember? We decided that then."

Or rather *he* had decided and *she* had pretended to go along to save face over her weakness when it came to this man.

His eyes went smoky. "I remember a lot of other things about that night."

Already she could feel herself weakening, wanting to read more into his every word and slightest action. She had to stop this intimacy, this romanticism, now.

"Enough talking about the past. This is about our future. Eli's future." She put on her best logical, personal-assistant voice she'd used a million times to place distance between them. "Where are we going first? I have to confess I haven't kept track of the race dates this year."

"Races later," he said simply as the car reached the airport. "First, we have a wedding to attend."

Her gut tightened at his surprise announcement. "A wedding?"

Lucy Ann hated weddings. Even when the wedding was for a longtime friend. Elliot's high school alumni pal—Dr. Rowan Boothe—was marrying none other than an African princess, who also happened to be a Ph.D. research scientist.

She hated to feel ungrateful, though, since this was the international event of the year, with a lavish ceremony in East Africa, steeped in colorful garb and local delicacies. Invitations were coveted, and media cameras hovered at a respectable distance, monitored by an elite security team that made the packed day run smoothly well into the evening. Tuxedos, formal gowns and traditional tribal wraps provided a magnificent blend of beauty that reflected the couple's modern tastes while acknowledging time-honored customs.

Sitting at the moonlit reception on the palace lawns by the beach, her baby asleep in a stroller, Lucy Ann sipped her glass of spiced fruit juice. She kept a smile plastered on her face as if her showing up here with Elliot and their son was nothing out of the ordinary. Regional music with drums and flutes carried on the air along with laughter and celebration. She refused to let her bad mood ruin the day for the happy bride and groom. Apparently, Elliot had been "kidnapped" from Rowan's bachelor party.

Now he'd returned for the wedding—with her and the baby. No one had asked, but their eyes all made it clear they knew. The fact that he'd thrust their messed-up relationship right into the spotlight frustrated her. But he'd insisted it was better to do it sooner rather than later. Why delay the inevitable?

He'd even arranged for formal dresses for her to pick from. She'd had no choice but to oblige him since her only formals were basic black, far too somber for a wedding. She'd gravitated toward simple wear in the past, never wanting to stand out. Although in this colorful event, her pale lavender gown wasn't too glaring. Still, she felt a little conspicuous because it was strapless and floor-length with a beaded bodice. Breast-feeding had given her new cleavage.

A fact that hadn't gone unnoticed, given the heated looks Elliot kept sliding her way.

But her mood was too sour to dwell on those steamy glances. Especially when he looked so mouth-wateringly handsome in a tuxedo, freshly shaven and smiling. It was as if the past eleven months apart didn't exist, as if they'd just shared the same bed, the same glass of wine. They'd been close friends for so long, peeling him from her thoughts was easier said than done.

She just wanted the marriage festivities to be over, then hopefully she would feel less vulnerable, more in control.

Weddings were happy occasions for some, evoking dreams or bringing back happy memories. Not for her. When she saw the white lace, flowers and a towering cake, she could only remember each time her mama said "I do." All four times. Each man was worse than the one before, until child services stepped in and said drug addict stepdaddy number four had to go if Lucy Ann's mother wanted to keep her child.

Mama chose hubby.

Lucy Ann finally went to live with her aunt for good—no more dodging groping hands or awkward requests to sit on "daddy's" lap. Her aunt loved her, cared for her, but Carla had others to care for, as well—Grandma and an older bachelor uncle.

No one put Lucy Ann first or loved her most. Not until this baby. She would do anything for Eli. Anything. Even swallow her pride and let Elliot back in her life.

Still, keeping on a happy face throughout the wedding was hard. All wedding phobia aside, she worked to appreciate the wedding as an event. She had to learn the art of detaching her emotions from her brain if she expected to make it through the next four weeks with her heart intact.

"Lucy Ann?" A familiar female voice startled her, and she set her juice aside to find Hillary Donavan standing beside her.

Hillary was married to another of Elliot's school friends, Troy Donavan, more commonly known as the

Robin Hood Hacker. As a computer-savvy teen he'd wreaked all sorts of havoc. Now he was a billionaire software developer. He'd recently married Hillary, an events planner, who looked as elegant as ever in a green Grecian-style silk dress.

The red-haired beauty dropped into a chair beside the stroller. "Do you mind if I hide out here with you and the baby for a while? My part in orchestrating this nationally televised wedding is done, thank heavens."

"You did a lovely job blending local traditions with a modern flair. No doubt magazine covers will be packed with photos."

"They didn't give me much time to plan since they made their engagement announcement just after Christmas, but I'm pleased with the results. I hope they are, too."

"I'm sure they are, although they can only see each other." Lucy Ann's stomach tightened, remembering her mother's adoring looks for each new man.

"To think they were professional adversaries for so long...now the sparks between them are so tangible I'm thinking I didn't need to order the firework display for a finale."

Lucy Ann pulled a tight smile, doing her best to be polite. "Romance is in the air."

"I hope this isn't going too late for you and the little guy." She flicked her red hair over her shoulder. "You must be exhausted from your flight."

"He's asleep. We'll be fine." If she left, Elliot would feel obligated to leave, as well. And right now she was too emotionally raw to be alone with him. Surely Hillary had to have some idea of how difficult this was for her, since the alum buddies had been party to the kidnapping.

Her eyes slid to the clutch of pals, the five men who'd been sent to a military reform school together.

Their bond was tight. Unbreakable.

They stood together at the beachside under a cabana wearing matching tuxedos, all five of them too damn rich and handsome for their own good. Luckily for the susceptible female population, the other four were now firmly taken, married and completely in love with their brides. The personification of bad boys redeemed, but still edgy.

Exciting.

The Alpha Brotherhood rarely gathered in one place, but when they did, they were a sight to behold. They'd all landed in trouble with the law as teens, but they'd been sent to a military reform school rather than juvie. Computer whiz Troy Donavan had broken into the Department of Defense's computer system to expose corruption. Casino magnate Conrad Hughes had used insider trading tips to manipulate the stock market. He'd only barely redeemed himself by tanking corporations that used child-labor sweatshops in other countries. World famous soft rock/jazz musician Malcolm Douglas had been sent away on drug charges as a teenager, although she'd learned later that he'd been playing the piano in a bar underage and got nabbed in the bust.

The groom—Dr. Rowan Boothe—had a history a bit more troubled. He'd been convicted of driving while drunk. He'd been part of an accident he'd taken the blame for so his overage brother wouldn't go to jail—then his brother had died a year later driving drunk into a tree. Now Rowan used all his money to start clinics in third-world countries.

They all had their burdens to bear, and that guilt motivated them to make amends now. Through their freelance work with Interpol. Through charitable donations beyond anything anyone would believe unless they saw the accounting books.

Now, they'd all settled down and gotten married, starting families of their own. Was that a part of what compelled Elliot to push for more with her? A need to fit in with his Alpha Brothers as they moved on to the next phase of their lives?

Lucy Ann looked back at Hillary. "Did you know what Malcolm and Conrad were up to yesterday?"

"I didn't know exactly, not until Troy told me, and they were already on their way. I can't say I approve of their tactics, but it was too late for me to do anything. You appear to be okay." Hillary leaned on her elbows, angling closer, her eyes concerned. "Is that an act?"

"What do you think?"

She clasped Lucy Ann's hand. "I'm sorry. I should have realized this calm of yours is just a cover. We're kindred spirits, you and I, ever organized, even in how we show ourselves to the world." She squeezed once before letting go. "Do you want to talk? Need a shoulder? I'm here."

"There's nothing anyone can do now. It's up to Elliot and me to figure out how to move forward. If I'd let him know earlier…"

"Friend, you and I both know how difficult it can be to contact them when the colonel calls for one of their missions. They disappear. They're unreachable." She smiled sadly. "It takes something as earth-shattering as, well, a surprise baby to get them to break the code of silence."

"How do you live with that, as a part of a committed relationship?"

She couldn't bring herself to ask what it felt like to be married to a man who kept such a chunk of his life separate. She'd known as a friend and as a personal assistant that Elliot's old headmaster later recruited previous students as freelancers for Interpol. She'd kept thoughts about that segmented away, since it did not pertain to her job or their life on the race circuit.

But now, there was no denying that her life was tied to Elliot's in a much deeper way.

"I love Troy, the man he is. The man he's always been," Hillary said. "We grow, we mature, but our basic natures stay the same. And I love who that man is."

Lucy Ann could almost—almost—grasp the promise in that, except she knew Hillary helped her husband on some of those missions, doing a bit of freelance work of her own.

Lucy Ann stared down into the amber swirl of her juice glass. "Is it so wrong to want an ordinary life? I don't mean to sound ungrateful, but *normal,* boring, well, I've never had that. I crave it for myself and my child, but it feels so unattainable."

"That's a tough one, isn't it? These men are many things, but normal—delightfully boring—doesn't show up anywhere on that list."

Where did that leave her? In search of what she couldn't have? Or a hypocrite for not accepting Elliot the way he had accepted her all her life? She ran from him. As much as she swore that he pushed her away, she knew. She'd run just as fast and hard as he'd pushed.

"Thank you for the advice, Hillary."

Her friend sighed. "I'm not sure how much help I've been. But if you need to talk more, I'm here for you. I won't betray your confidences."

"I appreciate that," Lucy Ann said, and meant it, only just realizing how few female friends she'd ever had. Elliot had been her best friend and she'd allowed that to close her off to other avenues of support.

"Good, very good. We women need to stick together, make a sisterhood pact of our own." She winked before ducking toward the stroller. "Little Eli is adorable, and I'm glad you're here."

Lucy Ann appreciated the gesture, and she wanted to trust. She wanted to believe there could be a sisterhood of support in dealing with these men—even though she wouldn't be married to Elliot. Still, their lives were entwined because of their child.

A part of her still wondered, doubted. The wives of Elliot's friends had reached out initially after she left, but eventually they'd stopped. Could she really be a part of their sisterhood?

"Thank you, Hillary," she said simply, her eyes sliding back to Elliot standing with his friends.

Her hand moved protectively over to the handle of her son's stroller, her throat constricting as she took in the gleaming good looks of her baby's father. Even his laugh seemed to make the stars shimmer brighter.

And how frivolous a thought was that?

She definitely needed to keep her head on straight and her heart locked away. She refused to be anyone's obligation or burden ever again.

Elliot hoped Rowan and Mariama's marriage ceremony would soften Lucy Ann's mood. After all, weren't weddings supposed to make women sentimental? He'd watched her chatting with his friends' wives and tried to gauge her reaction. She knew them all from her time working as his assistant, and seeing this big extended family connected by friendship rather than blood should appeal to her. They'd talked about leaving their pasts behind countless times as kids.

They could fit right in here with their son. A practical decision. A fun life.

So why wasn't she smiling as the bride and groom drove away in a BMW convertible, the bride's veil trailing in the wind?

Shouldering free of the crowd, Elliot made his way toward Lucy Ann, who stood on the periphery, their son in a stroller beside her. Even though he'd arranged for a nanny who'd once worked for a British duke, Lucy Ann said she couldn't let her son stay with a total stranger. She would need to conduct her own interview tomorrow. If the woman met her standards, she could help during Eli's naps so Lucy Ann could keep up with the work obligations she hadn't been able to put on hold. The encounter still made Elliot grin when he thought of her refusing to be intimidated by the very determined Mary Poppins.

He stopped beside Lucy Ann, enjoying the way the moonlight caressed her bare shoulders. Her hair was loose and lifting in the night wind. Every breath he took drew in hints of her, of Carolina jasmine. His body throbbed to life with a reminder of what they could have together, something so damn amazing he'd spent eleven months running from the power of it.

Now, fate had landed him here with her. Running wasn't an option, and he found that for once he didn't mind fate kicking him in the ass.

Elliot rested his hand on the stroller beside hers, watching every nuance of her reaction. "Are you ready to call it a day and return to our suite, or would you like to take a walk?"

She licked her lips nervously. "Um, I think a walk, perhaps."

So she wasn't ready to be alone with him just yet? A promising sign, actually; she wanted him still, even if she wasn't ready to act on that desire. Fine, then. He could use the moon and stars to romance her, the music from a steel drum band serenading them.

"A walk it is, then, Lucy dear," he asserted.

"Where can we go with a baby?"

He glanced around at the party with guests still dancing along the cabana-filled beach. Tables of food were still laden with half shares of delicacies, fruits and meats. A fountain spewing wine echoed the rush of waves along the shore. Mansions dotted the rocky seashore, with a planked path leading to docks.

"This way." He gestured toward the shoreline boardwalk, all but deserted this late at night. "I'll push the stroller."

He stepped behind the baby carriage. Lucy Ann had no choice but to step aside or they would be stuck hip to hip, step for step.

Five minutes later, they'd left the remnants of the reception behind, the stroller wheels rumbling softly along the wooden walkway. To anyone looking from the looming mansions above, lights shining from the windows like eyes, he and Lucy Ann would appear a happy family walking with their son.

Tonight more than ever he was aware of his single status. Yet again, he'd stood to the side as another friend got married. Leaving only him as a bachelor. But he was a father now. There was no more running from fears of becoming his father. He had to be a man worthy of this child. His child with Lucy Ann.

She walked beside him, the sea breeze brushing her gauzy dress along his leg in phantom caresses. "You're quite good at managing that stroller. I'm surprised. It took me longer than I expected to get the knack of not knocking over everything in my path."

He smiled at her, stuffing down a spark of anger along with the urge to remind her that he would have helped in those early days if she'd only let him know. "It's just like maneuvering a race car."

"Of course. That makes sense."

"More sense than me being at ease with a child? I'm determined to get this right, Lucy Ann, don't doubt that for a second." Steely determination fueled his words.

"You used to say you never wanted kids of your own."

Could those words have made her wary of telling him? There had been a time when they shared everything with each other.

He reminded her, "You always insisted that you didn't want children, either."

"I didn't want to risk putting any child in my mother's path." She rubbed her hand along her collarbone, the one she'd cracked as a child. "I'm an adult now and my mother's passed away. But we're talking about *you* and your insistence that you didn't want kids."

"I didn't. Then." If things hadn't changed, he still might have said the same, but one look in Eli's wide brown eyes and his world had altered in an instant. "I don't run away from responsibilities."

"You ran away before—" She stopped short, cursing softly. "Forget I said that."

Halting, he pulled his hands from the stroller, the baby sleeping and the carriage tucked protectively between them and the railing.

Elliot took her by the shoulders. Her soft bare shoulders. So vulnerable. So...*her*. "Say it outright, Lucy Ann. I left *you* behind when I left Columbia behind, when I let myself get sloppy and caught, when I risked jail because anything seemed better than staying with my father. For a selfish instant, I forgot about what that would mean for you. And I've regretted that every day of my life."

The admission was ripped from his throat; deeper still, torn all the way from his gut. Except there was no one but Lucy Ann to hear him on the deserted walkway. Stone houses dotted the bluff, quarters for guests and staff, all structures up on the bluff with a few lights winking in the night. Most people still partied on at the reception.

"I understand that you feel guilty. Like you have to make up for things. But you need to stop thinking that way. I'm responsible for my own life." She cupped his face, her eyes softening. "Besides, if you'd stayed, you wouldn't have this amazing career that also gave me a chance to break free. So I guess it all worked out in the end."

"Yet you ended up returning home when you left me." Hell, he should be honest now while he had the chance. He didn't want to waste an instant or risk the baby waking up and interrupting them. "When I stupidly pushed you away."

Her arm dropped away again. "I returned with a degree and the ability to support myself and my child. That's significant and I appreciate it." Her hands fisted at her sides. "I don't want to be your obligation."

"You want a life of your own, other than being my assistant. I understand that." He kept his voice low, which brought her closer to listen over the crash of waves below the boardwalk. He liked having her close again. "Let's talk it through, like we would have in the old days."

"You're being so—" she scowled "—so reasonable."

"You say that like it's a dirty word. Why is that a bad thing?" Because God help him, he was feeling anything but reasonable. If she wanted passion and emotion, he was more than willing to pour all of that into seducing her. He just had to be sure before he made a move.

A wrong step could set back his cause.

"Don't try to manipulate me with all the logical reasons why I should stay. I want you to be honest about what you're thinking. What you *want* for your future."

"When it comes to the future, I don't know what I want, Lucy Ann, beyond making sure you and Eli are safe, provided for, never afraid. I'm flying by the seat of my pants here, trying my best to figure out how to get through this being-a-father thing." Honesty was ripping a hole in him. He wanted to go back to logic.

Or passion.

Her chest rose and fell faster with emotion, a flush spreading across her skin in the moon's glow. "How would things have been different if I had come to you, back when I found out I was pregnant?"

"I would have proposed right away," he said without hesitation.

"I would have said no," she answered just as quickly.

He stepped closer. "I would have been persistent in trying to wear you down."

"How would you have managed that?"

The wind tore at her dress, whipping the skirt forward to tangle in his legs, all but binding them together with silken bands.

He angled his face closer to hers, his mouth so close he could claim her if he moved even a whisker closer. "I would have tried to romance you with flowers, candy and jewels." He watched the way her pupils widened with awareness as his words heated her cheek. "Then I would have realized you're unconventional and I would have changed tactics."

"Such as?" she whispered, the scent of fruit juice on her breath, dampening her lips. "Be honest."

"Hell, Lucy Ann, if you want honesty, here it is." His hand slid up her bare arm, along her shoulder, under her hair, to cup the back of her neck, and God, it felt good to touch her after so long apart. It felt right. "I just want to kiss you again."

Five

Lucy Ann gripped Elliot's shoulders, her fingers digging in deep by instinct even as her brain shouted "bad idea."

Her body melted into his, the hard planes of his muscular chest absorbing the curves of her, her breasts hypersensitive to the feel of him. And his hands… A sigh floated from her into him. His hands were gentle and warm and sure along her neck and into her hair, massaging her scalp. Her knees went weak, and he slid an arm down to band around her waist, securing her to him.

How could he crumble her defenses with just one touch of his mouth to hers? But she couldn't deny it. A moonlight stroll, a starlight kiss along the shore had her dreaming romantic notions. Made her want more.

Want him.

His tongue stroked along the seam of her mouth, and she opened without hesitation, taking him every bit as much as he took her. Stroking and tasting. There was a certain safety in the moment, out here in the open, since there was no way things could go further. Distant guest houses, the echoes of the reception carrying on the wind and of course the baby with them kept her from being totally swept away.

Her hands glided down his sides to tuck into his back pockets, to cup the taut muscles that she'd admired on more than one occasion. Hell, the whole female population had admired that butt thanks to a modeling gig he'd taken early in his career to help fund his racing. She'd ribbed him about those underwear ads, even knowing he was blindingly hot. She'd deluded herself into believing she was objective, immune to his sensuality, which went beyond mere good looks.

The man had a rugged charisma that oozed machismo.

Heaven help her, she wanted to dive right in and swim around, luxuriating in the sensations. The tingling in her breasts sparked through her, gathering lower with a familiar intensity she recognized too well after their night together.

This had to stop. Now. Because mistakes she'd made this time wouldn't just hurt her—or Elliot. They had a child to consider. A precious innocent life only a hand's reach away.

With more than a little regret, she ended the kiss, nipping his sensuous bottom lip one last time. His growl of frustration rumbled his chest against hers, but he didn't stop her. Her head fell to rest on his shoulder as she inhaled the scent of sea air tinged with the musk of his sweat. As Elliot cupped the back of her head in a broad palm, his ragged breaths reassured her he was every bit as affected by the kiss. An exciting and yet dangerous reality that confused her after the way they'd parted a year ago.

She needed space to think through this. Maybe watching the wedding and seeing all those happy couples had affected her more than she realized. Even just standing here in his arms with the feel of his arousal pressing against her stomach, she was in serious danger of making a bad choice if she stayed with him a moment longer.

Flattening her palms to his chest, Lucy Ann pushed, praying her legs would hold when he backed away.

She swayed for an instant before steeling her spine. "Elliot, this—" she gestured between them, then touched her kissed tender lips softly "—this wasn't part of our bargain when we left South Carolina. Or was it?"

The night breeze felt cooler now, the sea air chilly.

His eyes stayed inscrutable as he stuffed his hands in his tuxedo pockets, the harsh planes of his face shadowed by moonlight. "Are you accusing me of plotting a seduction?"

"*Plotting* is a harsh word," she conceded, her eyes flitting to the baby in his stroller as she scrambled to regain control of her thoughts, "but I think you're not above planning to do whatever it takes to get your way. That's who you are. Can you deny it?"

His eyes glinted with determination—and anger? "I won't deny wanting to sleep with you. The way you kissed me back gives me the impression you're on board with that notion."

Her heartbeat quickened with visions of how easy it would be to fall into bed with him. To pick up where they'd left off a year ago. If only she had any sense he wanted her for more than a connection to his son.

"That's the point, Elliot. It doesn't matter what *we* want. This month together is supposed to be about building a future for *Eli*. More of—" she gestured between them, her heart tripping over itself at just the mention of their kiss, their attraction "—playing with fire only risks an unstable future for our son. We need to recapture our friendship. Nothing more."

Her limbs felt weak at even the mention of *more*.

He arched an arrogant eyebrow. "I disagree that they're mutually exclusive."

"If you push me on this, I'll have to leave the tour and return to South Carolina." She'd seen too often how easily he seduced women. He was a charmer, without question, and she refused to be like her mother, swept away into reckless relationships again and again. She had a level head and she needed to keep it. "Elliot, do you hear me? I need to know we're on the same page about these next four weeks."

He studied her through narrowed eyes for the crash of four rolling waves before he shrugged. "I will respect your wishes, and I will keep my hands to myself." He smiled, pulling his hands from his pockets and holding them up. "Unless you change your mind, of course."

"I won't," she said quickly, almost too forcefully for her own peace of mind. That old Shakespeare quote came back to her, taunting her, *Methinks the lady doth protest too much.*

"Whoa, whoa, hold on now." Elliot patted the air. "I'm not trying to make you dig in your stubborn heels, so let's end this conversation and call it a day. We can talk more tomorrow, in the light of day."

"Less ambiance would be wise." Except she knew he looked hunky in any light, any situation.

Regardless of how much she wanted to go back, she realized that wasn't possible. They'd crossed a line the night they went too far celebrating his win and her completing her final exams.

It had never happened before she had a plan for her

own future. The catalyst had been completing her degree, feeling that for the first time since they were kids, she met him on an even footing. She'd allowed her walls to come down. She'd allowed herself to acknowledge what she'd been hiding all her adult life. She was every bit as attracted to Elliot Starc as his fawning groupies.

What if she was no different from her mother?

The thought alone had her staggering for steady ground. She grabbed the stroller just to be on the safe side. "I'm going back to the room now. It's time to settle Eli for the night. I need to catch up on some work before I go to sleep. And I do mean sleep."

"Understood," he said simply from beside her. "I'll walk back with you."

The heat of him reached her even though their bodies didn't touch. Just occupying the same space as him offered a hefty temptation right now.

She shook her head, the glide of her hair along her bared shoulders teasing her oversensitized skin. "I'd rather go alone. The palace is in sight and the area's safe."

"As you wish." He stepped back with a nod and a half bow. "We'll talk tomorrow on the way to Spain." He said it as a promise, not a request.

"Okay then," she conceded softly over her shoulder as she pushed the stroller, wheeling it toward the palace where they were staying in one of the many guest suites. Her body still hummed from the kiss, but her mind filled with questions and reservations.

She and Elliot had been platonic friends for years, comfortable with each other. As kids, they'd gone skinny-dipping, built forts in the woods, comforted each other during countless crises and disappointments. He'd been her best friend...right up to the moment he wasn't. Where had this crazy attraction between them come from?

The wheels of the stroller whirred along the walkway as fast as the memories spinning through her. That night eleven months ago when they'd been together had been spontaneous but amazing. She'd wondered if maybe there could be more between them. The whole friends-with-benefits had sounded appealing, taking it a day at a time until they sorted out the bombshell that had been dropped into their relationship: a sexual chemistry that still boggled her mind.

And yet Elliot's reaction the next day had made her realize there could be no future for them. Her euphoria had evaporated with the morning light.

She'd woken before him and gone to the kitchen to make coffee and pile some pastries on a plate. The front door to his suite had opened and she'd assumed it must be the maid. Anyone who entered the room had to have a key and a security code.

However, the woman who'd walked in hadn't been wearing a uniform. She—Gianna—had worn a trench coat and nothing else. If only it had been a crazed fan. But Lucy Ann had quickly deduced Gianna was the new female in Elliot's life. He hadn't even denied it. There was no misunderstanding.

God, it had been so damn cliché her stomach had roiled. Elliot came out of the bedroom and Gianna had turned paler than the towel around Elliot's waist.

He'd kept his calm. Apologized to Gianna for the awkward situation, but she'd burst into tears and run. He'd told Lucy Ann there was nothing between him and his girlfriend anymore, not after what happened the night before with Lucy Ann.

But she'd told him he should have let Gianna know that first, and she was a hundred percent right. He'd agreed and apologized.

That hadn't been enough for her. The fact that he could be seeing one woman, even superficially, and go to bed with another? No, no and hell, no. That was something she couldn't forgive. Not after how all those men had cheated on her mom with little regard for vows or promises. And her mother kept forgiving the first unfaithful jerk, and then the next.

If Elliot could behave this way now, how could she trust him later? What if he got "swept away" by someone else and figured he would clue her in later? She'd called him dishonorable.

And in an instant, with that one word, a lifetime friendship crumbled.

She'd thrown on her clothes and left. Elliot's engagement to Gianna a month later had only sealed Lucy Ann's resolve to stay away. They hadn't spoken again until the day he'd shown up in Carla's yard.

Now, after more impulsive kisses, she found herself wanting to crawl right back into bed with him. Lucy Ann powered the stroller closer to the party and their quarters, drawing in one deep breath of salty air after another, willing her pulse to steady. Wishing the urge to be with Elliot was as easily controlled.

With each step, she continued the chant in her brain, the vow not to repeat her mother's mistakes.

Wind tearing at his tuxedo jacket, Elliot watched Lucy Ann push the stroller down the planked walkway, then past the party. He didn't take his eyes off her or his son until he saw they'd safely reached the palace, even though he now had bodyguards watching his family 24/7. His family?

Hell, yes, his family.

Eli was his son. And Lucy Ann had been his only real

family for most of his life. No matter how angry he got at her for holding back on telling him about Eli, Elliot also couldn't forgive himself for staying away from her. He'd let her down in a major way more than once, from his teenage years up to now. She had reason not to trust him.

He needed to earn back her trust. He owed her that and so much more.

His shoulders heaving with a sigh, he started toward the wedding reception. The bride and groom had left, but the partying would go long into the night. It wasn't every day a princess got married. People would expect a celebration to end all celebrations.

A sole person peeled away from the festivities and ambled toward him. From the signature streamlined fedora, he recognized his old school pal Troy Donavan. Troy was one of the originals from their high school band, the Alpha Brotherhood, a group of misfits who found kindred spirits in one another and their need to push boundaries, to expose hypocrisy—the greatest of crimes in their eyes.

Troy pulled up alongside him, passing him a drink. "Reconciliation not going too well?"

"What makes you say that?" He took the thick cut glass filled with a locally brewed beer.

"She's returning to her room alone after a wedding." Troy tipped his glass as if in a toast toward the guests. "More people get lucky after weddings than any other event known to mankind. That's why you brought Lucy Ann here, isn't it? To get her in the romantic mood."

Had he? He'd told himself he wanted her to see his friends settling down. For her to understand he could do the same. But he wasn't sure how much he felt like sharing, especially when his thoughts were still jumbled.

"I brought Lucy Ann to the wedding because I couldn't

miss the event. The timing has more to do with how you all colluded to pull off that kidnapping stunt."

"You're still pissed off? Sorry, dude, truly," he said, wincing. "I thought you and Malcolm talked that all out."

"Blah, blah, blah, my good pals wanted to get an unguarded reaction. I heard." And it still didn't sit well. He'd trusted these guys since high school, over fifteen years, and hell, yeah, he felt like they'd let him down. "But I also heard that Lucy Ann contacted the Brotherhood over a week ago. That's a week I lost with my son. A week she was alone caring for him. Would you be okay with that?"

"Fair enough. You have reason to be angry with us." Troy nudged his fedora back on his head. "But don't forget to take some of the blame yourself. She was your friend all your life, and you just let her go. You're going to have a tough as hell time convincing her you've magically changed your mind now and you would have wanted her back even without the kid."

The truth pinched. "Tell me something I don't know."

"Okay then. Here's a bit of advice."

"Everyone seems full of it," Elliot responded, tongue in cheek.

Troy laughed softly, leaning back against a wrought-iron railing. "Fine. I'm full of it. Always have been. Now, on to my two cents."

"By all means." Elliot knocked back another swallow of the local beer.

"You're a father now." Troy rolled his glass between his palms. "Be that boy's father and let everything else fall into place."

A sigh rattled through Elliot. "You make it sound so simple."

Troy's smile faded, no joking in sight. "Think how different our lives would have been with different parents.

Things came together when Salvatore gave us direction. Be there for your son."

"Relationships aren't saved by having a child together." His parents had gotten married because he was on the way. His mother had eventually walked out and left him behind.

"True enough. But they sure as hell are broken up by fighting over the child. Be smart in how you work together when it comes to Eli and it might go a long way toward smoothing things out with Lucy Ann." Troy ran a finger along the collar of his tuxedo shirt, edging a little more air for himself around his tie. "If not, you've got a solid relationship with your kid, and that's the most important thing."

Was his focus all wrong by trying to make things right with Lucy Ann? Elliot had to admit Troy's plan made some sense. The stakes were too important to risk screwing up with his son. "When did you get to be such a relationship sage?"

"Hillary's a smart woman, and I'm smart enough to listen to her." His sober expression held only for a second longer before he returned to the more lighthearted Troy they were all accustomed to. "Now more than ever I need to listen to Hillary's needs since she's pregnant."

"Congratulations to you both." Elliot clapped Troy on the back, glad for his friend even as he wondered what it might have been like to be by Lucy Ann's side while she was expecting Eli. "Who'd have predicted all this home and hearth for us a few years ago?"

"Colonel Salvatore's going to have to find some new recruits."

"You're not pulling Interpol missions?" That surprised him. Elliot understood Hillary's stepping out of fieldwork while pregnant. But he wouldn't have thought Troy would ever back off the edge.

"There are other ways I can help with my tech work. Who knows, maybe I'll even take on the mentorship role like Salvatore someday. But I'm off the clock now and missing my wife." Troy walked backward, waving once before he sprinted toward the party.

Elliot knew his friend was right. The advice made sense. Focus on the baby. But that didn't stop him from wanting Lucy Ann in his bed again. The notion of just letting everything fall into place was completely alien to his nature. He'd never been the laid-back sort like Troy. Elliot needed to move, act, win.

He needed Lucy Ann back in his life.

For months he'd told himself the power of Lucy Ann's kiss, of the sex they'd shared nearly a year ago, had been a hazy memory distorted by alcohol. But now, with his body still throbbing from the kiss they'd just shared, his hair still mussed, the memory of their hands running frenetically—hungrily—over each other, he knew. Booze had nothing to do with the explosive chemistry between them. Although Gianna's arrival had sure as hell provided a splash of ice water on the morning-after moment.

He'd screwed up by not breaking things off with Gianna before he let anything happen between him and Lucy Ann. He still wasn't sure why he and Gianna had reconciled afterward. He hadn't been fair to either woman. The dishonor in that weighed on him every damn day.

At least he'd finally done right by Gianna when they'd broken up. Now, he had to make things right with Lucy Ann.

Their kiss ten minutes ago couldn't lead to anything more, not tonight. He accepted that. It was still too early in his campaign to win her over. But a kiss? He could have that much for now at least. A taste of her, a hint of what more they could have together.

A hint of Lucy Ann was so much more than everything with any other woman.

She was so much a part of his life. Why the hell had he let her go?

This didn't have to be complicated. Friendship. Sex. Travel the world and live an exciting life together. He had a fortune at his disposal. They could stay anywhere, hire teachers to travel with them. Eli would have the best of everything and an education gleaned from seeing the world rather than just reading about it. Surely Lucy Ann would see that positively.

How could she say no to a future so much more secure than what they'd grown up with? He'd been an idiot not to press his case with her last time. But when she'd left before, he'd thought to give her space. This time, he would be more persistent.

Besides, last time he'd been a jerk and tried to goad her into returning by making the news with moving on—a total jackass decision he never would have made if he'd thought for a second that Lucy Ann might be pregnant.

Now, he would be wiser. Smoother.

He would win her over. They'd been partners before. They could be partners again.

Lucy Ann peered out the window of the private jet as they left Africa behind.

Time for their real journey to begin. It had been challenging enough being together with his friends, celebrating the kind of happily ever after that wasn't in the cards for her. But now came the bigger challenge—finding a way to parent while Elliot competed in the Formula One circuit. A different country every week—Spain, Monaco, Canada, England. Parties and revelry and yes, decadence, too. She felt guilty for enjoying it all, but she couldn't deny that she'd missed the travel, experiencing different cultures without a concern for cost. Plus, his close-knit group of friends gave them a band of companionship no matter what corner of the earth he traveled to during racing season.

She sank deeper into the luxury of the leather sofa, the sleek chrome-and-white interior familiar from their countless trips in the past, with one tremendous exception. Their son was secured into his car seat beside her, sleeping in his new race car pj's with a lamb's wool blanket draped over his legs. She touched his impossibly soft cheek, stroking his chubby features with a soothing hand, cupping his head, the dusting of blond hair so like his father's.

Her eyes skated to Elliot standing in the open bulkhead, talking to the pilot. Her former best friend and boss grew hotter with each year that passed—not fair. That didn't stop her from taking in the sight of him in low-slung jeans and a black button-down shirt with the sleeves rolled up. Italian leather loafers. He looked every bit the world-famous race car driver and heartthrob.

How long would Elliot's resolution to build a family life for Eli last? Maybe that's what this trip was about. Proving to *him* it couldn't be done. She wouldn't keep his son from him, but she refused to expose her child to a chaotic life. Eli needed and deserved stability.

And what did she want?

She pressed a hand to her stomach, her belly full of butterflies that had nothing to do with a jolt of turbulence. Just the thought of kissing Elliot last night... She dug her fingers into the supple leather sofa to keep from reaching for him as he walked toward her.

"Would you like something to eat or drink?" he asked, pausing by the kitchenette. "Or something to read?"

She knew from prior trips that he kept a well-stocked library of the classics as well as the latest bestsellers loaded on ereaders for himself and fellow travelers. In school, he'd always won the class contest for most books read in a year. He told her once those stories offered him an escape from his day-to-day life.

"No, thank you. The brunch before we left was amazing."

True enough, although she hadn't actually eaten much. She'd been so caught up in replaying the night before. In watching his friends' happy marriages with their children and babies on the way until her heart ached from all she wanted for her son.

For herself, as well.

Elliot slid onto the sofa beside her, leaning over her to adjust the blanket covering Eli's legs. "Tell me about his routine."

She sat upright, not expecting that question at all. "You want to know about Eli's schedule? Why?"

"He's my son." His throat moved with a long swallow of emotion at the simple sentence. "I should know what he needs."

"He has a mom, and he even has a nanny now." The British nanny was currently in the sleeping quarters reading or napping or whatever nannies did when they realized mothers needed a breather from having them around all the time.

Elliot tapped Lucy Ann's chin until she looked at him again. "And he has a dad."

"Of course," she agreed, knowing it was best for Eli,

but unused to sharing him. "If you're asking for diaper duty, you're more than welcome to it."

Would he realize her halfhearted attempt at a joke was meant to ease this tenacious tension between them? They used to be so in tune with each other.

"Diaper duty? Um, I was thinking about feeding and naps, that kind of thing."

"He breastfeeds," she said bluntly.

His eyes fell to her chest. The stroke of his gaze made her body hum as tangibly as the airplane engines.

Elliot finally cleared his throat and said, "Well, that could be problematic for me. But I can bring him to you. I can burp him afterward. He still needs to be burped, right?"

"Unless you want to be covered in baby spit-up." She crossed her arms over her chest.

He pulled his eyes up to her face. "Does he bottle-feed, too? If so, I can help out that way."

Fine, he wanted to play this game, then she would meet him point for point. "You genuinely think you can wake up during the night and then race the next day?"

"If you can function on minimal sleep, then so can I. You need to accept that we're in this together now."

He sounded serious. But then other than his playboy ways, he was a good man. A good friend. A philanthropist who chose to stay anonymous with his donations. She knew about them only through her work as his assistant.

"That's why I agreed to come with you, for Eli and in honor of our friendship in the past."

"Good, good. I'm glad you haven't forgotten those years. That friendship is something we can build on. But I'm not going to deny the attraction, Lucy Ann." He slid his arm along the back of the sofa seat, stretching his legs out in front of him. "I can't. You've always been pretty, but you looked incredible last night. Motherhood suits you."

"Flattery?" She picked up his arm and moved it to his lap. "Like flowers and candy? An obvious arm along the back? Surely you've got better moves than that."

"Are you saying compliments are wasted on you?" He picked up a lock of her hair, teasing it between two fingers. "What if I'm telling the truth about how beautiful you are and how much I want to touch you?"

She rolled her eyes, even though she could swear electricity crackled up the strand of hair he held. "I've watched your moves on women for years, remember?"

"It's not a move." He released the lock and smoothed it into the rest before crossing his arms. "If I were planning a calculated seduction for you, I would have catered a dinner, with a violin."

She crinkled her nose. "A violin? Really?"

"No privacy. Right." His emerald eyes studied her, the wheels in his brain clearly churning. "Maybe I would kiss you on the cheek, distract you by nuzzling your ear while tucking concert tickets into your pocket."

"Concert tickets?" She lifted an eyebrow with interest. They'd gone to free concerts in the park when they were teenagers.

"We would fly out to a show in another country, France or Japan perhaps."

She shook her head. "You're going way overboard. Too obvious. Rein it in, be personal."

"Flowers…" He snapped his fingers. "No wait. A single flower, something different, like a sprig of jasmine because the scent reminds me of you."

That silenced her for a moment. "You know my perfume?"

He dipped his head toward her ever so slightly as if

catching a whiff of her fragrance even now. "I know you smell like home in all the good ways. And I have some very good memories of home. They all include you."

Damn him, he was getting to her. His words affected her but she refused to let him see that. She schooled her features, smiling slightly. "Your moves have improved."

"I'm only speaking the truth." His words rang with honesty, his eyes heated with attraction.

"I do appreciate that about you, how we used to be able to tell each other anything." Their friendship had given her more than support. He'd given her hope that they could leave their pasts behind in a cloud of dust. "If we can agree to be honest now, that will work best."

"And no more secrets."

She could swear a whisper of hurt smoked through his eyes.

Guilt stabbed through her all over again. She owed him and there was no escaping that. "I truly am sorry I held back about Eli. That was wrong of me. Can you forgive me?"

"I have to, don't I?"

"No." She swallowed hard. "You don't."

"If I want us to be at peace—" he reached out and took her hand, the calluses on his fingertips a sweet abrasion along her skin "—then yes, I do."

She wasn't sure how that honest answer settled within her because it implied he wasn't really okay with what she'd done. He was only moving past it out of necessity. The way he'd shrugged off all the wrongs his father had done because he had no choice.

Guilt hammered her harder with every heartbeat, and she didn't have a clue how to make this right with him. She had as little practice with forgiveness and restitution as he did.

So she simply said, "Peace is a very good thing."

"Peace doesn't have to be bland." His thumb stroked the inside of her wrist.

Her pulse kicked up under his gentle stroking. "I didn't say that."

"Your tone totally implied it. You all but said 'boring.'" His shoulder brushed hers as he settled in closer, seducing her with his words, his husky tones every bit as much as his touch. "A truce can give freedom for all sorts of things we never considered before."

"News flash, Elliot. The kissing part. We've considered that before."

"Nice." He clasped her wrist. "You're injecting some of your spunky nature into the peace. That's good. Exciting. As brilliantly shiny as your hair with those new streaks of honey added by the Carolina sun."

Ah, now she knew why he'd been playing with her hair. "Added by my hairdresser."

"Liar."

"How do you know?"

"Because I'm willing to bet you've been squirrelling away every penny you make. I can read you—most of the time." He skimmed his hand up her arm to stroke her hair back over her shoulder. "While I know that you want me, I can't gauge what you intend to do about that, because make no mistake, I want us to pursue that. I said before that motherhood agrees with you and I meant it. You drove me crazy last night in that evening gown."

He continued to stroke her arm, but she couldn't help but think if she moved even a little, his hand would brush her breast. Even the phantom notion of that touch had her tingling with need.

She worked to keep her voice dry—and to keep from grabbing him by the shirtfront and hauling him toward her. "You're taking charming to a new level. I'm impressed."

"Good. But are you seduced?"

"You're good, and I'm enticed," she said, figuring she might as well be honest. No use denying the obvious. "But Elliot, this isn't a fairy tale. Our future is not going to be some fairy tale."

He smiled slowly, his green eyes lighting with a promise as his hand slid away. "It can be."

Without another word, he leaned back and closed his eyes. Going to sleep? Her whole body was on fire from his touch, his words—his seduction. And he'd simply gone to sleep. She wanted to shout in frustration.

Worse yet, she wanted him to recline her back on the sofa and make love to her as thoroughly as he'd done eleven months ago.

Six

By nightfall in Spain, Elliot wondered how Lucy Ann would react to their lodgings for the night. The limousine wound deeper into the historic district, farther from the racetrack than they normally stayed. But he had new ideas for these next few weeks, based on what Lucy Ann had said on the plane.

After the fairy-tale discussion, inspiration had struck. He'd forced himself to make a tactical retreat so he could regroup. Best not to risk pushing her further and having her shut him down altogether before he could put his plan into action to persuade her to stay longer than the month.

Once she was tucked into the back room on the airplane to nurse Eli, Elliot had made a few calls and set the wheels in motion to change their accommodations along the way. A large bank account and a hefty dose of fame worked wonders for making things happen fast. He just hoped his new agenda would impress Lucy Ann. Winning her over was becoming more pressing by the second. Not just for Eli but because Elliot's life had been damn empty without her. He hadn't realized just how much until he had her back. The way her presence made everything around him more vibrant. Hell, even her organized nature, which he used to tease her about. She brought a focus, a grounding and a beauty to his world that he didn't want to lose again.

Failure was not an option.

He'd made himself a checklist, just like he kept for his work. People thought he was impulsive, reckless even, but there was a science to his job. Mathematics. Calculations. He studied all the details and contingencies until they became so deeply ingrained they were instinct.

Still, he refused to become complacent. He reviewed that checklist before every race as if he were a rookie driver. Now he needed to apply the same principles to winning back Lucy Ann's friendship...and more.

Their new "hotel" took shape on the top of the hill, the Spanish sunset adding the perfect dusky aura to their new accommodations.

In the seat across from him, Lucy Ann sat up straighter, looking from the window to him with confusion stamped on her lovely face.

"This isn't where you usually stay. This is...a castle."

"Exactly."

The restored medieval castle provided safety and space, privacy and romance. He could give her the fairy tale while making sure Lucy Ann and their son were protected. He could—and would—provide all the things a real partner and father provided. He would be everything his father wasn't.

"Change of plans for our stay."

"Because...?"

"We need more space and less chance of interruptions." He couldn't wait to have her all to himself. Damn, he'd missed her.

"But pandering to the paparazzi plays an important role in your PR." She hugged the diaper bag closer to her chest; the baby's bag, her camera and her computer had been the only things she'd insisted on bringing with her from home.

"Pandering?" He forced himself to focus on her words rather than the sound of her voice. Her lyrical Southern drawl was like honey along his starved senses. "That's not a word I'm particularly comfortable with. Playing along with them, perhaps. Regardless, they don't own me, and I absolutely will not allow them to have access to you and our son on anything other than our own terms."

"Wow, okay." Her eyes went wide before she grinned wryly. "But did you have to rent a castle?"

He wondered if he'd screwed up by going overboard, but her smile reassured him he'd struck gold by surprising her.

"It's a castle converted to a hotel, although yes, it's more secure and roomier." Safer, but also with romantic overtones he hoped would score points. "I thought in each place we stay, we could explore a different option for traveling with a child."

"This is…an interesting option," she conceded as the limousine cruised along the sweeping driveway leading up to the towering stone castle. Ivy scrolled up toward the turrets, the walls beneath baked brown with time. Only a few more minutes and the chauffeur would open the door.

Elliot chose his words wisely to set the stage before they went inside. "Remember how when we were kids, we hid in the woods and tossed blankets over branches? I called them forts, but you called them castles. I was cool with that as long as I got to be a knight rather than some pansy prince."

They'd climbed into those castle forts where he'd read for hours while she colored or drew pictures.

"Pansy prince?" She chuckled, tapping his chest. "You *are* anti-fairy-tale. What happened to the kid who used to lose himself in storybooks?"

He captured her finger and held on for a second before linking hands. "There are knights in fairy tales. And there are definitely castles."

"Is that what this is about?" She left her hand in his. "Showing me a fairy tale?"

"Think about coming here in the future with Eli." He stared at his son's sleeping face and images filled his head of their child walking, playing, a toddler with his hair and Lucy Ann's freckles. "Our son can pretend to be a knight or a prince, whatever he chooses, in a real castle. How freaking cool is that?"

"Very cool." A smile teased her kissable pink lips. "But this place is a long way from our tattered quilt forts in the woods."

His own smile faded. "Different from our childhood is a very good thing."

Her whole body swayed toward him, and she cupped his face. "Elliot, it's good that our child won't suffer the way we did, but what your father did to you…that had nothing to do with money."

Lucy Ann's sympathy, the pain for him that shone in her eyes, rocked the ground under him. He needed to regain control. He'd left that part of his life behind and he had no desire to revisit it even in his thoughts. So he deflected as he always did, keeping things light.

"I like it when you get prissy." He winked. "That's really sexy."

"Elliot, this isn't the time to joke around. We have some very serious decisions to make this month."

"I'm completely serious. Cross my heart." He pressed their clasped hands against his chest. "It makes me want to ruffle your feathers."

"Stop. It." She tugged free. "We're talking about Eli. Not us."

"That's why we're at a castle, for Eli," he insisted as the limousine stopped in front of the sprawling fortress. "Einstein said, 'The true sign of intelligence is not knowledge but imagination.' That's what we can offer our son with this unique lifestyle. The opportunity to explore his imagination around the world, to see those things that we only read about. You don't have to answer. Just think on it while we're here."

With the baby nursing, Lucy Ann curled up in her massive bed. She took comfort in the routine of feeding her child, the sweet softness of his precious cheek against her breast. With her life turning upside down so fast, she needed something familiar to hold on to.

The medieval decor wrapped her in a timeless fantasy she wasn't quite sure how to deal with. The castle had tapestries on the wall and sconces with bulbs that flickered like flames. Her four-poster bed had heavy drapes around it, the wooden pillars as thick as any warrior's chest. An arm's reach away waited a bassinet, a shiny reproduction of an antique wooden cradle for Eli.

Her eyes gravitated toward the tapestry across the room telling a love story about a knight romancing a maiden by a river. Elliot had chosen well. She couldn't help but be charmed by this place. Even her supper was served authentically in a trencher, with water in a goblet.

A plush, woven rug on the stone floor, along with

the low snap of the fire in the hearth, kept out the chilly spring night. The sound system piped madrigal music as if the group played in a courtyard below.

Through the slightly opened door, she saw the sitting room where Elliot was parked at a desk, his computer in front of him. Reviewing stats on his competitors? Or a million other details related to the racing season? She missed being a part of all that, but he had a new assistant, a guy who did his job so seamlessly he blended into the background.

And speaking of work, she had some of her own to complete. Once Eli finished nursing and went to bed there would be nothing for her to do but complete the two projects she hadn't been able to put on hold.

She'd expected Elliot to try to make a move on her once they got inside, but the suite had three bedrooms off the living area. One for her and one for him. The British nanny he'd hired had settled into the third, turning in after Lucy Ann made it clear Eli would stay with his mother tonight. While Mrs. Clayworth kept a professional face in place, the furrows along her forehead made it clear that she wondered at the lack of work on this job.

This whole setup delivered everything Elliot had promised, a unique luxury she could see her son enjoying someday. Any family would relish these fairy-tale accommodations. It was beyond tempting.

Elliot was beyond tempting.

Lucy Ann tore her eyes from her lifetime friend and onetime lover. This month was going to be a lot more difficult than she'd anticipated.

Desperate for some grounding in reality before she weakened, she reached for her phone, for the present, and called her aunt Carla.

* * *

She'd made it through the night, even if the covers on the bed behind her were a rumpled mess from her restless tossing and turning.

Lucy Ann sat at the desk at the tower window with her laptop, grateful to Carla for the bolstering. Too bad she couldn't come join them on this trip, but Carla was emphatic. She loved her home and her life. She was staying where she belonged.

Who could blame her? A sense of belonging was a rare gift Lucy Ann hadn't quite figured out how to capture yet. In South Carolina, she'd dreamed of getting out, and here she craved the familiarity of home.

Which made her feel like a total ingrate.

She was living the easy life, one any new mother would embrace. How ironic that at home she'd spent every day exhausted, feeling like Eli's naps were always a few minutes too short to accomplish what she needed to do. And now, she spent most of her time waiting for him to wake up.

She closed her laptop, caught up on work, dressed for the day, waiting to leave for Elliot's race. She still couldn't wrap her brain around how different this trip was from ones she'd shared with Elliot in the past. Staring out the window in their tower suite, she watched the sun cresting higher over the manicured grounds.

Last night, she'd actually slept in a castle. The restored structure was the epitome of luxury and history all rolled into one. She'd even pulled out her camera and snapped some photos to use for a client's web design. Her fingers already itched to get to the computer and play with the images, but Elliot was due back soon.

He'd gone to the track for prelim work, his race scheduled for tomorrow. Normally he arrived even earlier before an event, but the wedding had muddled his schedule. God, she hoped his concentration was rock solid. The thought of him in a wreck because she'd damaged his focus sent her stomach roiling. Why hadn't she considered this before? She should have told him about Eli earlier for so many reasons.

She was familiar with everything about his work world. She'd been his personal assistant for over a decade, in charge of every detail of his career, his life. And even in their time apart she'd kept up with him and the racing world online. Formula One racing in Spain alternated locations every year, Barcelona to Valencia and back again. She knew his preferences for routes like Valencia, with the street track bordering the harbor. She was used to being busy, in charge—not sitting around a castle twiddling her thumbs, eating fruit and cheese from medieval pottery.

Being waited on by staff, nannies and chauffeurs, being at loose ends, felt alien, to say the least. But she'd agreed to give him a chance this month. She would stick to her word.

As if conjured from her thoughts, Elliot appeared in the arched doorway between the living area and her bedroom. Jeans hugged his lean hips, his turtleneck shirt hugging a well-defined chest. Her mouth watered as she considered what he would do if she walked across the room, leaned against his chest to kiss him, tucked her hands in his back pockets and savored the chemistry simmering between them.

She swallowed hard. "Are you here for lunch?"

"I'm here for you and Eli." He held out a cashmere sweater of his. "In case you get chilly on our outing."

"Outing?" she asked to avoid taking the sweater until she could figure out what to do next.

She'd worn pieces of Elliot's clothes countless times over the years without a second thought, but the notion of wrapping his sweater around her now felt so intimate that desire pooled between her legs. However, to reject the sweater would make an issue of it, revealing feelings that made her too vulnerable, a passion she still didn't know how to control yet.

Gingerly, she took the sweater from him, the cashmere still warm from his touch. "Where are we going?"

He smiled mysteriously. "It's another surprise for you and Eli."

"Can't I even have a hint?" She hugged the sweater close, finding she was enjoying his game more than she should.

"We're going to play." He scooped his son up from the cradle in sure hands. "Right, Eli, buddy? We're going to take good care of your mama today. If she agrees to come with me, of course."

The sight of their son cradled in Elliot's broad hands brought her heart into her throat. She'd imagined moments like this, dreamed of how she would introduce him to their child. Day after day, her plan had altered as she delayed yet again.

And why? Truly, why? She still wasn't sure she understood why she'd made all the decisions she'd made these past months. She needed to use her time wisely to figure out the best way to navigate their future.

She tugged on the sweater. "Who am I to argue with such a tempting offer? Let's go play."

They left the suite and traveled down the sweeping stone stairway without a word, passing other guests as well as the staff dressed in period garb. The massive front doors even creaked as they swept open to reveal the waiting limousine.

Stepping out into the sunshine, she took in the incredible lawns. The modern-day buzz of cars and airplanes mixed with the historical landscaping that followed details down to the drawbridge over a moat.

The chauffeur opened the limo door for her. Lucy Ann slid inside, then extended her arms for her child. Elliot passed over Eli as easily as if they were a regular family.

Lucy Ann hugged her son close for a second, breathing in the baby-powder-fresh scent of him before securing Eli into his car seat. "Shouldn't you be preparing for race day?"

Getting his head together. Resting. Focusing.

"I know what I need to do," he answered as if reading her mind. He sat across from her, his long legs extended, his eyes holding hers. "That doesn't mean we can't have time together today."

"I don't want to be the cause of your exhaustion or lack of focus because you felt the need to entertain me." She'd been so hurt and angry for a year, she'd lost sight of other feelings. Race day was exciting and terrifying at the same time. "I've been a part of your world for too long to let you be reckless."

"Trust me. I have more reason than ever to be careful. You and Eli are my complete and total focus now."

There was no mistaking the certainty and resolve in his voice. Her fears eased somewhat, which made room for her questions about the day to come back to the fore. "At least tell me something about your plans for today. Starting with, where are we going?"

He leaned to open the minifridge and pulled out two water bottles. "Unless you object, we are going to the San Miguel de los Reyes Monastery."

She sat up straighter, surprised, intrigued. She took

the water bottle from him. "I'm not sure I understand your plan…."

"The monastery has been converted into a library. We've never had a chance to visit before on other trips." He twisted open his spring water. "In fact, as I look back, we both worked nonstop, all the time. As I reevaluate, I'm realizing now a little sightseeing won't set us behind."

"That's certainly a one-eighty from the past. You've always been a very driven man—no pun intended." She smiled at her halfhearted joke, feeling more than a little off balance by this change in Elliot. "I'll just say thank-you. This is a very thoughtful idea. Although I'm curious. What made you decide on this particular outing when there are so many more obvious tourist sites we haven't visited?"

"You sparked the idea when we were on the airplane, actually." He rolled the bottle between his palms. "You mentioned not believing in fairy tales anymore. That is why I chose the castle. Fairy tales are important for any kid…and I think we've both lost sight of that."

"We're adults." With adult wants and needs. Like the need to peel off his forest-green turtleneck and faded jeans.

"Even as kids, we were winging it with those fairy tales. Then we both grew jaded so young." He shrugged muscular shoulders. "So it's time for us to learn more about fairy tales so we can be good parents. Speaking of which, is Eli buckled in?"

"Of course."

"Good." He tapped on the window for the chauffeur to go. "Just in case you were wondering, I'm calling this the *Beauty and the Beast* plan."

They were honest-to-goodness going to a library. She sagged back, stunned and charmed all at once.

God, she thought she'd seen all his moves over the years—moves he'd used on other women. He'd always been more...boisterous. More obvious.

This was different. Subtle. Damn good.

"So I'm to be Belle to your beast."

"A Southern belle, yes, and you've called me a beast in the past. Besides, you know how much I enjoy books and history. I thought you might find some interesting photo opportunities along the way."

"You really are okay with a pedestrian stroll through a library." The Elliot she'd known all her life had always been on the go, scaling the tallest tree, racing down the steepest hill, looking for the edgiest challenge. But he did enjoy unwinding with a good book, too. She forgot about that side of him sometimes.

"I'm not a Cro-Magnon...even though I'm playing the beast. I do read. I even use a napkin at dinnertime." He waggled his eyebrows at her, his old playful nature more evident.

She wished she could have just slugged him on the shoulder as if they were thirteen again. Things had been simpler then on some levels—and yet not easy at all on others.

"You're right. I shouldn't have been surprised."

"Let's stop making assumptions about each other from now on about a lot of things. We've been friends for years, but even friends change, grow, even a man like me can mature when he's ready. Thanks to you and Eli, I'm ready now."

She wanted to believe him, to believe in him. She wanted to shake off a past where the people she cared about always let her down. Hundreds of times over the past eleven months she'd guessed at what his reaction would be if she told him about the baby.

She'd known he would come through for her. The part that kept haunting her, that kept her from trying… She could never figure out how she would know if he'd come through out of duty or something more.

The thought that she could yearn for more between the two of them scared her even now. She was much better off taking this one day at a time.

"Okay, Elliot—" she spread her arms wide "—I'm all-in…for our day at the monastery."

As she settled in for her date, she couldn't help wondering which was tougher: resisting the fairy-tale man who seemed content to ignore the past year or facing the reality of her lifelong friend who had every reason to be truly angry with her.

Regardless, at some point the past would catch up with both of them. They could only play games for so long before they had to deal with their shared parenthood.

Wearing a baseball cap with the brim tugged low, Elliot soaked in the sight of Lucy Ann's appreciation of the frescoes and ancient tomes as she filled a memory card with photos of the monastery turned library. He should have thought to do this for her sooner. The place was relatively deserted, a large facility with plenty of places for tourists to spread out. A school tour had passed earlier, but the echoes of giggles had faded thirty minutes ago. No one recognized him, and the bodyguards hung back unobtrusively. For all intents and purposes, he and Lucy Ann were just a regular family on vacation.

Why had he never thought to bring her to places like this before? He'd convinced himself he was taking care of her by offering her a job and a life following him around the world. But somehow he'd missed out on giving her so much more. He'd let her down when they were teenagers and he'd gotten arrested, leaving her alone to deal with her family. Now to find out he'd been selfish as an adult too. That didn't sit well with him.

So he had more to fix. He and Lucy Ann were bound by their child for life, but he didn't intend to take that part for granted. He would work his tail off to be more for her this time.

He set the brake on the stroller by a looming marble angel. "You're quiet. Anything I can get for you?"

She glanced away from her camera, looking back over her shoulder at him. "Everything's perfect. Thank you. I'm enjoying the peace. And the frescoes as well as the ornately bound books. This was a wonderful idea for how to spend the afternoon."

Yet all day long she'd kept that camera between them, snapping photos. For work? For pleasure?

Or to keep from looking at him?

Tired of the awkward silence, he pushed on, "If you're having fun, then why aren't you smiling?"

She lowered the camera slowly, pivoting to face him. Her eyes were wary. "I'm not sure what you mean."

"Lucy Ann, it's me here. Elliot. Can we pretend it's fifteen years ago and just be honest with each other?"

She nibbled her bottom lip for a moment before blurting out, "I appreciate what you're doing, that you're trying, but I keep waiting for the explosion."

He scratched over his closely shorn hair, which brought memories of sprinting away from a burning car. "I thought we cleared that up in the limo. I'm not going to wreck tomorrow."

"And I'm not talking about that now." She tucked the camera away slowly, pausing as an older couple meandered past looking at a brochure map of the museum. Once they cleared the small chapel area, she turned back to him and said softly, "I'm talking about an explosion of anger. You have to be mad at me for not telling you about Eli sooner. I accept that it was wrong of me not to try harder. I just keep wondering when the argument will happen."

God, was she really expecting him to go ballistic on her? He would never, never be like his father. He used his racing as an outlet for those aggressive feelings. He did what he needed to do to stay in control. Always.

Maybe he wasn't as focused as he claimed to be, because if he'd been thinking straight he would have realized that Lucy Ann would misunderstand. She'd spent her life on shaky ground growing up, her mother hooking up with a different boyfriend or husband every week. Beyond that, she'd always stepped in for others, a quiet warrior in her own right.

"You always did take the blame for things."

"What does that have to do with today?"

He gestured for her to sit on a pew, then joined her. "When we were kids, you took the blame for things I did—like breaking the aquarium and letting the snake loose in the school."

She smiled nostalgically. "And cutting off Sharilynn's braid. Not a nice thing to do at all, by the way."

"She was mean to you. She deserved it." He and Lucy Ann had been each other's champions in those days. "But you shouldn't have told the teacher you did it. You ended up cleaning the erasers for a week."

"I enjoyed staying after school. And my mom didn't do anything except laugh, then make me write an apology and do some extra chores." She looked down at her hands twisted in her lap. "Your father wouldn't have laughed if the school called him."

"You're right there." He scooped up her hand and held

on. It was getting easier and easier for them to be together again. As much as he hated revisiting the past, if it worked to bring her back into his life, he would walk over hot coals in hell for her. "You protected me every bit as much as I tried to protect you."

"But your risk was so much higher…with your dad." She squeezed his hand. "You did the knightly thing. That meant a lot to a scrawny girl no one noticed except to make fun of her clothes or her mom."

He looked up at Lucy Ann quickly. Somehow he'd forgotten that part of her past. He always saw her as quietly feisty. "What elementary school boy cares about someone's clothes?"

"True enough, I guess." She studied him through the sweep of long eyelashes. "I never quite understood why you decided we would be friends—before we started taking the blame for each other's transgressions."

Why? He thought back to that time, to the day he saw her sitting at the computer station, her legs swinging, too short to reach the ground. The rest of the class was running around their desks while the teacher stepped out to speak with a parent. "You were peaceful. I wasn't. We balanced each other out. We can have that again."

"You're pushing." She tugged her hand.

He held firm. "Less than a minute ago, you told me I have the right to be mad at you."

"And I have the right to apologize and walk away."

Her quick retort surprised him. The Lucy Ann of the past would have been passive rather than confrontational. Like leaving for a year and having his baby. "Yeah, you're good at that, avoiding."

"There." She looked up quickly. "Tell me off. Be angry. Do anything other than smile and pretend everything's okay between us while we tour around the world like some dream couple."

Her fire bemused him and mesmerized him. "You are the most confusing woman I have ever met."

"Good." She stood up quickly, tugging her camera bag back onto her shoulder. "Women have always fallen into your arms far too easily. Time to finish the tour."

Seven

Lucy Ann swaddled her son in a fluffy towel after his bath while the nanny, Mrs. Clayworth, placed a fresh diaper and sleeper on the changing table. After the full day touring, then dinner with the nanny so Lucy Ann could get to know her better, she felt more comfortable with the woman.

Elliot's thoughtfulness and care for their son's future touched her. He'd charmed Mrs. Clayworth, yet asked perceptive questions. The woman appeared soft and like someone out of a Disney movie, but over the hours it became clear she was more than a stereotype. More than a résumé as a pediatric nurse. She was an avid musician and a hiker who enjoyed the world travel that came with her job. She spent her days off trekking through different local sites or attending concerts.

Lucy Ann liked the woman more and more with every

minute that passed. "Mrs. Clayworth, so you really were a nanny for royalty? That had to have been exciting."

Her eyes twinkled as she held out her arms for Eli. "You have seen my list of references. But that's just about the parents." She tucked Eli against her shoulder with expert hands, patting his back. "A baby doesn't care anything about lineage or credentials. Only that he or she is dry, fed, cuddled and loved."

"I can see clearly enough that you have a gift with babies."

The nanny's patience had been admirable when, just after supper, Eli cried himself purple over a bout of gas.

"I had two of my own. The child care career started once they left for the university. I used to be a pediatric nurse and while the money was good, it wasn't enough. I had bills to pay because of my loser ex-husband, and thanks to my daughter's connections with a blue-blooded roommate, I lucked into a career I thoroughly enjoy."

Having lived the past months as a single mom, Lucy Ann sympathized. Except she had always had the safety net of calling Elliot. She'd had her aunt's help, as well. What if she'd had nowhere to go and no one's help? The thought made her stomach knot with apprehension. That didn't mean she would stay with Elliot just because of her bills—but she certainly needed to make more concrete plans.

"I want the best for my son, too."

"Well, as much as I like my job, you have to know the best can't always be bought with money."

So very true. Lucy Ann took Eli back to dress him in his teddy bear sleeper. "You remind me of my aunt."

"I hope that's a compliment." She tucked the towel into the laundry chute.

"It is. Aunt Carla is my favorite relative." Not that

there was a lot of stiff competition. She traced the appliquéd teddy bear on the pj's and thought of her aunt's closet full of themed clothes. "She always wears these chipper seasonal T-shirts and sweatshirts. She has a thick Southern accent and deep-fries everything, including pickles. I know on the outside it sounds like the two of you are nothing alike, but on the inside, there's a calming spirit about you both."

"Then I will most certainly take that as a compliment, love." She walked to the pitcher on the desk by the window and poured a glass of water. "I respect that you're taking your time to get to know me and to see how I handle your son. Not all parents are as careful with their wee ones."

Mrs. Clayworth placed the glass beside the ornately carved rocker thoughtfully, even though Lucy Ann hadn't mentioned how thirsty she got when she nursed Eli. Money couldn't buy happiness, but having extra hands sure made life easier. She snapped Eli's sleeper up to his neck.

"I do trust Elliot's judgment. I've known him all my life. We've relied on each other for so much." There had been a time when she thought there was nothing he could do that would drive a wedge between them. "Except now there's this new dynamic to adjust to with Eli. But then you probably see that all the time."

Lucy Ann scooped up her son and settled into the wooden rocker, hoping she wasn't the only new mother to have conflicted feelings about her role. As much as she loved nursing her baby, she couldn't deny the occasional twinge of sadness that the same body Elliot once touched with passion had been relegated to a far more utilitarian purpose.

"You're a new mum." Mrs. Clayworth passed a burp cloth. "That's a huge and blessed change."

"My own mother wasn't much of a role model." She adjusted her shirt, and Eli hungrily latched on.

"And this favorite aunt of yours?" The nanny adjusted the bedding in the cradle, draping a fresh blanket over the end, before taking on the many other countless details in wrapping up the day.

"She helped as much as she could, but my mother resented the connection sometimes." Especially when her mom was between boyfriends and lonely. Then suddenly it wasn't so convenient to have Lucy Ann hang out with Aunt Carla. "I've been reading everything I can find on parenting. I even took some classes at the hospital, but there are too many things to cover in books or courses."

"Amen, dear."

Having this woman to lean on was…incredible, to say the least. Elliot was clearly working the fairy tale–like life from all angles.

She would be pridefully foolish to ignore the resources this woman brought to the table. Isolating herself for the past eleven months had been a mistake. Lucy Ann needed to correct that tendency and find balance. She needed to learn to accept help and let others into her life. Starting now seemed like a good idea.

She couldn't deny that all this "playing house" with Elliot was beginning to chip away at her reservations and her resolve to keep her distance. Elliot had said they needed to use this time to figure out how to parent Eli. She knew now they also needed to use this time to learn how to be in the same room with each other without melting into a pool of hormones. Time to quit running from the attraction and face it. Deal with it.

"And that's where your experience comes in. I would

be foolish not to learn from you." Lucy Ann paused, patting Eli's pedaling feet. "Why do you look so surprised?"

"Mothers seek help from me, not advice. You are a unique one."

"Would you mind staying for a while so we can talk?"

"Of course. I don't mind at all."

Lucy Ann gestured to the wingback chair on the other side of the fireplace. "I'd like to ask you a few questions."

"About babies?" she asked, sitting.

"Nope, I'd like to ask your advice on men."

The winner's trophy always felt so good in his hands, but today…the victory felt hollow in comparison with what he really wanted. More time with Lucy Ann.

Elliot held the trophy high with one hand, his helmet tucked under his other arm.

His *Beauty and the Beast* plan had gone well. They'd spent a low-key day together. Her pensive expression gave him hope he was on the right path. If she was ready to check out and return to Columbia, there would have been decisiveness on her face. But he was making headway with her. He could see that. He just needed to keep pushing forward with his plans, steady on. And try like hell to ignore the urge to kiss her every second they were together.

A wiry reporter pushed a microphone forward through the throng of fans and press all shouting congratulations. "Mr. Starc, tell us about the new lady in your life."

"Is it true she was your former assistant?"

"Where has she been this year?"

"Did she quit or was she fired?"

"Lovers' spat?"

"Which designer deserves credit for her makeover?"

Makeover? What the hell were they talking about?

To him, she was Lucy Ann—always pretty and special. And even though she had come out of her shell some in the past year, that didn't change the core essence of her, the woman he'd always known and admired.

Sure, her new curves added a bombshell quality. And the clothes his new assistant had ordered were flashier. None of that mattered to him. He'd wanted her before. He wanted her still.

The wiry reporter shoved the mic closer. "Are you sure the baby is yours?"

That question pulled him up short in anger. "I understand that the press thinks the personal life of anyone with a little fame is fair game. But when it comes to my family, I will not tolerate slanderous statements. If you want access to me, you will respect my son and his mother. And now it's time for me to celebrate with my family. Interviews are over."

He heard his assistant hiss in protest over the way he'd handled the question. The paparazzi expected to be fed, not spanked.

Shouldering through the crowd, Elliot kept his eyes locked on Lucy Ann in his private box, watching. Had she heard the questions through the speaker box? He hoped not. He didn't want anything to mar the evening he had planned. She'd actually consented to let the nanny watch Eli. Elliot would have her all to himself.

He kept walking, pushing through the throng.

"Congratulations, Starc," another reporter persisted. "How are you planning to celebrate?"

"How long do you expect your winning streak to run?"

"Is the woman and your kid the reason your engagement broke off?"

He continued to "no comment" his way all the way up the steps, into a secure hallway and to the private viewing box in the grandstand where Lucy Ann waited with a couple of honored guests, local royalty and politicians he only just managed to acknowledge with a quick greeting and thanks for attending. His entire focus locked on Lucy Ann.

"You won," she squealed, her smile enveloping him every bit as much as if she'd hugged him. Her red wraparound dress clung to her body, outlining every curve.

He would give up his trophy in a heartbeat to tug that tie with his teeth until her dress fell open.

"I think we should go." Before he embarrassed them both in front of reporters and esteemed guests.

He couldn't wait to get her alone. All he'd been able to think about during the race was getting back to Lucy Ann so he could continue his campaign. Move things closer to the point where he could kiss her as he wanted.

"Right." She leaned to pluck her purse from her seat. "The after-parties."

"Not tonight," he said softly for her ears only. "I have other plans."

"You have responsibilities to your career. I understand that."

He pulled her closer, whispering, "The press is particularly ravenous today. We need to go through the private elevator."

Her eyebrows pinched together. "I'm not so sure that's the best idea."

Damn it, was she going to bail on him before he even had a chance to get started? He would just have to figure out a way around it. "What do you propose we do instead?"

She tugged his arm, the warmth of her touch reaching through his race jacket as she pulled him closer to the observation window. "You taught me long ago that the best way to get rid of the hungry press is to feed them tidbits."

The tip of her tongue touched her top lip briefly before she arched up on her toes to kiss him. He stood stock-still in shock for a second before—hell, yeah—he was all-in. His arms banded around her waist. She leaned into him, looping her arms his neck. He could almost imagine the cameras clicking as fast as his heartbeat, picking up speed with every moment he had Lucy Ann in his arms.

He didn't know what had changed her mind, but he was damn glad.

Her fingers played along his hair and he remembered the feel of her combing her hands through it the night they'd made love. He'd kept his hair longer then, before the accident.

Lucy Ann sighed into his mouth as she began to pull back with a smile. "That should keep the media vultures happy for a good long while." She nipped his bottom lip playfully before asking, "Are you ready to celebrate your win?"

Lucy Ann stepped out onto the castle balcony, the night air cool, the stone flooring under her feet even cooler but not cold enough to send her back inside. She walked to the half wall along the balcony and let the breeze lift her hair and ruffle through her dress before turning back to the table.

Elliot was showering off the scent of gasoline. He'd already ordered supper. The meal waited for them, savory Spanish spices drifting along the air.

There was no question that Elliot had ordered the dinner spread personally. The table was laden with her favorites, right down to a flan for dessert. Elliot remembered. She'd spent so much time as his assistant making sure to remember every detail of his life, she hadn't considered he'd been paying just as close attention to her.

She trailed her fingers along the edge of her water goblet. The sounds below—other guests coming and going, laughing and talking—mingled with the sound system wafting more madrigal tunes into the night. She didn't even have the nursery monitor with her for the first time since… She couldn't remember when. Mrs. Clayworth had already planned to watch Eli tonight since Lucy Ann had expected to go to an after-race party with Elliot.

Then she'd kissed him.

Halfway through that impulsive gesture, Lucy Ann realized that holding back was no longer an option. Sleeping with Elliot again was all but inevitable. The longer she waited, the more intense the fallout would be. They needed to figure out this crazy attraction now, while their son was still young enough not to know if things didn't work out.

Her stomach knotted with nerves. But the attraction was only getting stronger the longer she denied herself. It was only a matter of time—

As if conjured from that wish, Elliot stood in the balcony doorway, so fresh from the shower his short hair still held a hint of water. He'd changed into simple black pants and a white shirt with the sleeves rolled up. With the night shadows and flickering sconce lights he had a timeless air—the Elliot from the past mixing with the man he'd become.

She wanted them both.

Lucy Ann swallowed nervously and searched for something to say to break the crackling silence between them. "I can't believe the press actually left us alone after the race."

"We did slip away out a back entrance."

"That never stopped them before."

"I ordered extra security." He stalked toward her slowly. "I don't want anyone hassling you or Eli. Our lives are private now. I'm done playing the paparazzi game. At least we know this place is secure."

"As private as the woods we hid in as kids."

How many times had he made her feel safe? As if those quilted walls could hold out the world while they huddled inside reading books and coloring pictures like regular kids.

He stopped in front of her, his hand brushing back a stray lock of her hair. "Why did you kiss me after the race?"

"To keep the press content." To let other women know he was taken? "Because I wanted to."

He tugged the lock of hair lightly. "I meant why did you bite me?"

A laugh rolled free and rode the breeze. "Oh, that. Can't have everything going your way."

"You're more confident these days." His emerald eyes glinted with curiosity—and promise.

"Motherhood has given me purpose." Even now, the need to settle her life for her child pushed her to move faster with Elliot, to figure out one way or another.

To take what she could from this time together in case everything imploded later.

"I like seeing you more comfortable in your skin." He sat on the balcony half wall with unerring balance and confidence. "Letting the rest of the world see the woman you are."

As much as she feared trusting a man—trusting El-liot—she couldn't help but wonder if he would continue trying to spin a fairy-tale future for them long beyond tonight and ignore the fact that she had been the unno-

ticed Cinderella all her life. She wanted a man who noticed the real her—not the fairy tale. Not the fantasy. If
she was honest, she was still afraid his sexual interest
had come too late to feel authentic.

"You make me sound like I was a mouse before—
someone in need of a makeover, like that reporter said."

He cursed softly. "You heard their questions?"

"The TV system in the private box was piping in feed
from the winner's circle." She rolled her eyes. "It was a
backhanded compliment of sorts."

"Don't ever forget I saw the glow long before."

She couldn't help but ask, "If you saw my glow, then
why did it take you all those years to make a move on
me?"

"If I remember correctly, you made the first move."

She winced, some of her confidence fading at the
thought that they could have still been just friends if
she hadn't impulsively kissed him that night they'd been
drunk, celebrating and nostalgic. "Thanks for reminding
me how I made a fool of myself."

"You're misunderstanding." He linked fingers with
her, tugging her closer. "I've always found you attractive,
but you were off-limits. Something much more valuable
than a lover—those are a dime a dozen. You were, you
are, my friend."

She wanted to believe him. "A dime a dozen. Nice."

"Lucy Ann, stop." He squeezed her hand. "I don't
want to fight with you. It doesn't have to be that way for
us this time. Trust me. I have a plan."

She'd planned to seduce him, keep things light, and he
was going serious on her. She tried to lighten the mood
again. "What fairy tale does this night come from?"

"It could be reality."

"You disappoint me." She leaned closer until their

chests just brushed. Her breasts beaded in response. "Tonight, I want the fairy tale."

He blinked in surprise. "Okay, fair enough." He stood, tugging her to the middle of the balcony. "We're in the middle of Cinderella's ball."

Appropriate, given her thoughts earlier. "Well, the clock is definitely ticking since Eli still wakes up in the middle of the night."

"Then we should make the most of this evening." The moonlight cast a glow around them, adding to the magical air of the night. "Are you ready for supper?"

"Honestly?" She swayed in time with the classical music.

"I wouldn't have asked if I hadn't wanted to know. I don't think you know how much I want to make you happy."

She stepped closer, lifting their hands. "Then let's dance."

"I can accommodate." He brought her hand to rest on his shoulder, his palm sliding warmly along her waist. "I owe you for homecoming our sophomore year in high school. You had that pretty dress your aunt made. She showed me so I could make sure the flowers on your wrist corsage matched just the right shade of blue."

"I can't believe you still remember about a high school dance." Or that he remembered the color of her dress.

"I got arrested for car theft and stood you up." He rested his chin on top of her head. "That tends to make a night particularly memorable."

"I knew it was really your friends that night, not you."

He angled back to look in her warm chocolate-brown eyes. "Why didn't you tell me you thought that?"

"You would have argued with me about some technical detail." She teased, all the while too aware of the freshly showered scent of him. "You were even more stubborn in those days."

"I *did* steal that car." He tugged her closer and stole her breath so she couldn't speak. "And it wasn't a technicality. I wanted to take you to the dance in decent wheels. I figured the used car dealership would never know as long as I returned it in the morning."

"I wouldn't have cared what kind of car we had that night."

"I know. But I cared. And ended up spending the night in jail before the car dealer dismissed the charges—God only knows why." He laughed darkly. "That night in jail was the best night's sleep I'd gotten in a long time, being out of my father's house."

God, he was breaking her heart. Their childhoods were so damaged, had they even stood a chance at a healthy adult relationship with each other? She rested her head on his shoulder and let him talk, taking in the steady beat of his pulse to help steady her own.

"I felt like such a bastard for sleeping, for being grateful for a night's break from my dad when I'd let you down."

Let her down? He'd been her port in the storm, her safe harbor. "Elliot," she said softly, "it was a silly dance. I was more worried about how your father would react to your arrest."

"I wanted to give you everything," he said, ignoring her comment about his dad. "But I let you down time after time."

This conversation was straying so far from her plans for seduction, her plans to work out the sensual ache inside her. "This isn't the sort of thing Prince Charming says to Cinderella at the ball."

"My point is that I'm trying to give you everything

now, if you'll just let me." He nuzzled her hair. "Just tell me what you want."

Every cell in her body shouted for her to say she wanted him to peel off her dress and make love to her against the castle wall. Instead, she found herself whispering, "All I want is for Eli to be happy and to lead a normal life."

"You think this isn't normal." His feet matched steps with hers as the music flowed into their every move.

A castle? A monastery library? "Well, this isn't your average trip to a bookstore or corner library, that's for sure."

"There are playgrounds here as well as libraries. We just have to find them for Eli."

Lucy Ann felt a stab of guilt. Elliot was thinking of their son and she'd been thinking about sex. "You make it sound so simple."

"It can be."

If only she could buy into his notion of keeping things simple long-term. "Except I never contacted you about being pregnant."

"And I didn't come after you like I should have. I let my pride get stung, and hurt another woman in the process."

She hadn't considered the fact that Gianna had been wronged in this situation. "What happens in the future if you find someone else…or if I do?"

"You want monogamy?" he asked. "I can do that."

"You say that so quickly, but you're also the one spinning fairy tales and games." She looked up at him. "I'm asking honest questions now."

She wondered why she was pushing so hard for answers to questions that could send him running. Was she on a self-destructive path in spite of her plans to be with him? Then again, this level of honesty between them had been a long time coming.

His feet stopped. He cupped her face until their eyes met. "Believe this. You're the only woman I want. You're sure as hell more woman than I can handle, so if you will stay with me, then monogamy is a piece of cake."

"Are you proposing?"

"I'm proposing we stay together, sleep together, be friends, lovers, parents."

He wasn't proposing. This wasn't Cinderella's ball after all. They were making an arrangement of convenience—to enjoy sex and friendship.

She didn't believe in fairy tales, damn it. So she should take exactly what he offered. But she intended to make sure he understood that convenience did not mean she would simply follow his lead.

Eight

Lucy Ann stepped out of his arms, and a protest roared inside Elliot. Damn it, was she leaving? Rejecting him in spite of everything they'd just said to each other? He set his jaw and stuffed his hands into his pockets to keep from turning into an idiot, a fool begging her to stay.

Except she didn't move any farther away. She locked eyes with him, her pupils wide—from the dark or from desire? He sure as hell hoped for the latter. Her hand went to the tie of her silky wraparound dress and she tugged.

His jaw dropped. "Um, Lucy Ann? Are you about to, uh—?"

"Yes, Elliot, I am." She pulled open the dress, revealing red satin underwear and an enticing expanse of creamy freckled skin.

His brain went on stun. All he could do was stare— and appreciate. Her bra cupped full breasts so perfectly his hands ached to hold and test their weight, to caress her until she sighed in arousal.

She shrugged and the dress started to slide down, down—

Out here.

In the open.

He bolted forward, a last scrap of sense telling him to shield her gorgeous body. He clasped her shoulders and pulled her to him, stopping the dress from falling away. "Lucy Ann, we're on a balcony. Outside."

A purr rippled up her throat as she wriggled against his throbbing erection. "I know."

Her fragrance beckoned, along with access to silky skin. His mouth watered. That last bit of his sense was going to give up the fight any second.

"We need to go back into our suite."

"I know that, too. So take me inside. Your room or mine. You choose as long as we're together and naked very soon." She leaned into him, her breasts pressing against his chest. "Unless you've changed your mind."

The need to possess tensed all his muscles, the adrenaline rush stronger than coming into a final turn neck and neck.

"Hell, no, I haven't changed my mind. We'll go to my room because there are condoms in my nightstand. And before you ask, yes, I've been wanting and planning to take you to bed again every minute of our journey." He scooped her up into his arms and shouldered the doors open into their suite. The sitting area loomed quiet and empty. "Thank God Mrs. Claymore isn't up looking for a midnight snack."

Her hair trailing loose over his shoulder, Lucy Ann kissed his neck in a series of nibbles up to his ear. "You're supposed to be the race car driver who lives on the edge, and yet you're the one being careful. That's actually quite romantic."

"For you. Always careful for you." Except he hadn't been. He'd left her alone as a teen, gotten her pregnant and stayed away for nearly a year. He refused to let her down again in any way. She deserved better from him.

Lucy Ann deserved the best. Period.

She slid her hand behind his head and brought him closer for a kiss. He took her mouth as fully as he ached to take her body. With every step closer to his bedroom, his body throbbed harder and faster for her. The last few steps to the king-size bed felt like a mile. The massive headboard took up nearly the whole wall, the four posters carved like trees reaching up to the canopy. He was glad now he'd brought her here, a place they'd never been, a fantasy locale for a woman who deserved to be pampered, adored.

Treasured.

He set her on her feet carefully, handling her like spun glass. She tossed the dress aside in a silky flutter of red.

Nibbling her bottom lip and releasing it slowly, seductively, Lucy Ann kicked her high heels off with a flick of each foot. "One of us is *very* overdressed."

"You don't say."

"I do." She hooked her finger in the collar of his shirt and tugged down. Hard. Popping the buttons free in a burst that scattered them along the floor.

Ooooo-kay. So much for spun glass. His libido ramped into high gear. "You seem to be taking charge so nicely I thought you might help me take care of that."

He looked forward to losing more buttons in her deft hands.

"Hmm," she hummed, backing toward the bed until her knees bumped the wooden steps. "If I'm taking charge, then I want you to take off the rest of your clothes while I watch."

"I believe I can comply with that request." Shrugging off his destroyed shirt, he couldn't take his eyes from her as she settled onto the middle of the gold comforter, surrounded by tapestry pillows and a faux-fur throw. He toed off his loafers, his bare feet sinking into the thick Persian rug.

She reclined on the bed, pushing her heels into the mattress to scoot farther up until she could lean against the headboard. "You could have continued your underwear model days and made a mint, you know."

His hands stopped on his belt buckle. "You're killing the mood for me, Lucy Ann. I prefer to forget that brief chapter of my life."

"Briefs?" She giggled at her own pun. "You're right. You're definitely more of a boxers kind of guy now."

Fine, then. She seemed to want to keep this light-hearted, avoiding the heavier subjects they'd touched on while dancing. Now that he thought of it, they'd never gotten around to dinner, either. Which gave him an idea, one he'd be better off starting while he still had his clothes on.

"Stay there, just like that," he said. "I'll be right back."

Belt buckle clanking and loose, he sprinted out to the balcony. He picked up the platter of fruit and cheese and tucked the two plates of flan on top. Balancing the make-shift feast, he padded toward their room, careful not to wake the nanny or Eli.

Backing inside, he elbowed the door closed carefully. Turning, he breathed a sigh of relief to find Lucy Ann waiting. He hadn't really expected her to leave...except for a hint of an instant he'd thought about how quickly she'd run from what they shared last time.

She tipped her head to the side, her honey-streaked brown hair gliding along her shoulder like melted caramel. "You want to eat dinner now?"

He gave her his best bad boy grin. "If you're my plate, then yes, ma'am, I think this is a fine time for us to have supper."

"Okay then. Wouldn't want to mess up our clothes." She tugged off her bra and shimmied out of her panties, her lush curves bared and… Wow.

He almost dropped the damn tray.

Regaining his footing, he set the food on the edge of the bed without once taking his eyes off the long lines of her legs leading up to her caramel curls. He was definitely overdressed for what he had in mind.

He tugged off his slacks along with his boxers. His erection sprang free.

She smiled, her eyes roving over him in an appreciative sweep that made him throb harder. "Elliot?"

"Yes?" He clasped her foot in his hand, lifting it and kissing the inside of her ankle where a delicate chain with a fairy charm surprised him on such a practical woman. What else had he missed about Lucy Ann in the year they'd been apart?

"Do you know what would make this perfect?"

He kissed the inside of her calf. "Name it. I'll make it happen."

"More lights."

He looked up from her leg to her confident eyes reflecting the bedside lamp. "Lights?"

"It's been quite a while since I saw you naked, and last time was rather hurried and with bad lighting."

She was a total and complete turn-on. Everything about her.

"Can do," he said.

He placed her leg back on the bed and turned on the massive cast-iron chandelier full of replica candles that supplemented the glow of the bedside lamp. The rich colors of the bed and the heavy curtains swept back on either side somehow made Lucy Ann seem all the more pale and naked, her creamy flesh as tempting as anything he'd ever seen. The feel of her gaze on him heated his blood to molten lava, his whole body on fire for her.

But no way in hell would he let himself lose control. He took the time to reach for the bedside table, past his vintage copy of *Don Quixote*. Dipping into the drawer, he pulled out a condom. He dropped it on the bed before hitching a knee on the edge and joining her on the mattress. Taking his time, even as urgency thrummed through him, he explored every curve, enjoying the way goose bumps rose along her bared flesh.

She met him stroke for stroke, caress for caress, until he couldn't tell for certain who was mirroring whom. Their hands moved in tandem, their sighs syncing up, until they both breathed faster. He lost track of how long they just enjoyed each other, touching and seeking their fill. At some point, she rolled the condom over him, but he only half registered it since pleasure pulsed through him at her touch—and at the feel of her slick desire on his fingertips as he traced and teased between her legs.

Holding himself in check grew tougher by the second so he angled away, reaching for the platter of food on the corner of the bed.

He pushed the tray along the bed to put it in better reach. Then he plucked a strawberry and placed the plump fruit between his teeth. He slid over her, blanketing her. He throbbed between her legs, nudging, wanting. He leaned closer and pressed the strawberry to her mouth. Her lips parted to close over the plump fruit until they met in a kiss.

She bit into the strawberry and he thrust inside her. The fruity flavor burst over his taste buds at the same time sensation sparked through him. Pleasure. The feel of her clamping around him, holding him deep inside her as a "yes" hissed between her teeth. Her head pressed back into the bolster, her eyes sliding closed.

He moved as her jaw worked, chewing the strawberry. Her head arched back, her throat gliding with a slow swallow. Her breasts pushed upward, beading tight and hard.

Inviting.

Leaning on one elbow, he reached for another berry. He squeezed the fruit in his fist, dribbling the juice over her nipple. She gasped in response. He flicked his tongue over her, tasting her, rolling the beaded tip in his mouth until she moaned for more. The taste of ripe fruit and a hint of something more had him ready to come apart inside her already.

Thrusting over and over, he pushed aside the need to finish, hard and fast. Aching to make this last, for her and for him.

How could he possibly have stayed away from her for so long? For any time at all? How could he have thought for even a second he could be with anyone other than her? They were linked together. They always had been, for as far back as he could remember.

She was his, damn it.

The thought rocketed through him, followed closely by her sighs and moans of completion. Her hands flung out, twisting in the comforter, her teeth sinking deep into her bottom lip as she bit back the cry that might wake others.

Seeing the flush of pleasure wash over her skin

snapped the reins on his restraint and he came, the hot pulse jetting from him into her. Deeper, and yet somehow not deep enough as he already wanted her again.

As his arms gave way and he sank to rest fully on top of her, he could only think, damn straight, she was his.

But he hadn't been able to keep Lucy Ann before. How in the hell was he going to manage to keep the new, more confident woman in his arms?

A woman who didn't need anything from him.

Tingling with anticipation, Lucy Ann angled toward Elliot. "I need another bite now or I am absolutely going to pass out."

She gripped his wrist and guided his spoonful of flan toward her mouth as he chuckled softly. She closed her lips over it and savored the creamy caramel pudding. All of her senses were on hyperalert since she and Elliot had made love—twice. The scent of strawberries still clung to the sheets even though they'd showered together, making love in the large stone spa before coming back to bed.

Eventually, she would have to sleep or she would be a completely ineffective mother. But for now, she wasn't ready to let go of this fantasy night, making love with Elliot in a castle.

The luxurious sheets teased her already-sensitive skin, and she gave herself a moment to soak in the gorgeous surroundings. Beyond Elliot. The man was temptation enough, but he'd brought her to this decadent haven where she could stare up at carvings of a Dionysian revel on the bedposts or lose herself in the images of a colorful, wall-sized tapestry depicting a medieval feast. The figures were almost life-size, gathered around a table, an elegant lord and lady in the middle and an array of characters all around from lecherous knight to teasing serving maid. Even the scent of dried herbs and flowers that emanated from the linens immersed her in a fantasy world.

One she never wanted to end.

She scooped her spoon through the flan and offered a bite to her own sexy knight. "I have to say our dance tonight ended much better than our sophomore homecoming ever could have."

"You're right about that." He dipped his spoon into the dessert for her, picking up the rhythm of feeding each other. "Lady, you are rocking the hell out of that sheet."

He filled her whole fairy-tale fantasy well with his broad shoulders and muscular chest, the sheet wrapped around his waist. There was a timeless quality about this place that she embraced. It kept her from looking into the future. She intended to make the absolute most of this chance to be together.

They'd had sex before. They knew each other's bodies intimately. Yet there was a newness about this moment. She looked different now that she'd had a baby. Her body had changed. *She* had changed in other ways, as well. She had a growing confidence now, personally and professionally.

Lucy Ann searched Elliot's eyes…and found nothing but desire. His gaze stroked over her with appreciation and yes, even possession—stoking the heat still simmering inside her.

"I have to confess something." She angled forward to accept the next bite he fed her.

His face went somber in a flash even as he took the spoonful of flan she brought to his mouth. He swallowed, then said, "Tell me whatever you need to. I'm not going anywhere."

She carefully set her utensil onto the platter by the last strawberry, her body humming with the memory of the moment they'd shared the fruit, the moment he'd thrust inside her. The intensity of it all threatened to overwhelm her. She desperately needed to lighten the moment before they waded into deeper waters.

"I may like simplicity in many parts of my life—" she paused for effect, then stretched out like a lazy cat until the sheet slithered away from her breasts "—but I am totally addicted to expensive linens."

"God, Lucy Ann." He hauled her against his side, her nipples beading tighter at the feel of his bare skin. "You scared the hell out of me with talk of confessions."

"I'm serious as a heart attack here." She rested her cheek on his chest, the warmth of him seeping into her. "Every night when I crawled into bed—and trust me, cheap mattresses also suck a lot more than I remembered—those itchy sheets made me long for Egyptian cotton."

"Ahhh, now I understand." He tugged the comforter over them. "The fairy tale here is *The Princess and the Pea*. I will be very sure you always have the best mattresses and sheets that money can buy." He patted her butt.

"My prince," she said, joking to keep talk of the future light for now, all the while knowing that inevitably they would have to steer the conversation in another direction. "I don't think I ever said congratulations on your win today. I'm sorry you missed out on the parties tonight."

"I'm not sorry at all." He stroked back her hair, extending the length with his fingers and letting damp strands glide free. "This is exactly where I wanted to be. Celebrating with you, without clothes—best party ever."

"You do deserve to celebrate your success though. You've come a long way through sheer determination." She hooked a leg over his, enjoying the way they fit.

"Although I have to say, I've always been surprised you chose Formula One over the NASCAR route, given your early days racing the dirt-track circuit."

Why had she never thought to question him about this before? She'd simply followed, accepting. He'd always taken the lead in life and on the track.

He'd begun racing with adults at fourteen years old, then picked it up again when he graduated from the military high school in North Carolina. He was a poster boy for the reformative success of the school even without people knowing he periodically helped out Interpol.

Elliot rested his chin on her head, his breath warm on her scalp. "I guess I have a confession of my own to make. I wanted to go to college and major in English. But I had to make a living. I went back to racing after school because my credit was shot."

English? It made sense given the way he'd always kept a book close at hand, and yet she couldn't believe he'd never mentioned that dream. A whole new side of Elliot emerged, making her wonder what else he'd kept secret.

"Because of your arrest history?"

His chest rose and fell with a heavy sigh. "Because my father took out credit cards in my name."

Her eyes closing, she hugged an arm tighter around him. "I'm so sorry. Nothing should surprise me when it comes to that man, but it still sucks to hear. I'm just so glad you got away from him."

"You should be mad at me for leaving you," he repeated, his voice hoarse. "I let you down."

"I don't agree." She kissed his chest before continuing. "You did what you needed to. I missed you when they sent you to North Carolina, but I understood."

"All the same, you were still hurt by what I did. I could see that then. I can even feel it now. Tell me the truth."

So much for keeping things light. They would always have to cycle around to the weightier stuff eventually. "I understand why you needed a way out, believe me, I do. I just wish you'd spoken to me, given me an opportunity to weigh in and figure out how we could both leave. That place was bearable with you around. Without you…"

She squeezed her eyes closed, burying her face in his chest, absorbing the vibrant strength of him to ward off the chill seeping into her bones.

"I like to think if I could go back and change the past that I would. Except I did the same thing all over again. I let you go. You deserve to be put first in someone's life, someone who won't let you down."

Where was he going with this? Where did she *want* him to go?

After that, he stayed silent so long she thought for a moment he had drifted off midthought, then his hand started to rove along her spine slowly. Not in a seductive way; more of a touch of connection.

He kissed the top of her head, whispering into her hair still damp from their shared shower, "I didn't want to leave you back in high school. You have to know that." His voice went ragged with emotion. "But I didn't have anything to offer you if we left together. And I couldn't stay any longer. I just couldn't see another way out except to get arrested."

She struggled to sift through his words, to understand what he was trying to tell her. "You stole cars on purpose, hoping the cops would catch you?"

"That pretty much sums it up." His hand slid to rest on her hip, his voice strangely calm in contrast to his racing heart. "After that first night in jail, I started stealing cars on a regular basis. I didn't expect to be so good at it. I thought I would get caught much earlier."

"Why did you want to get caught?" she repeated, needing to understand, wondering how she didn't know this about him. She'd thought they told each other everything.

"I figured jail was safer than home," he said simply. "I didn't worry so much about myself with my dad, but I worried what he would do to the people around me."

"You mean me and your mother?"

He nodded against her head. "Remember when we went on that trip to the beach and my old rebuilt truck broke down?"

"You mean when the tires fell off." Only his incredible reflexes had kept them from crashing into a ditch. It had been a near miss.

"Right. When the first one fell off, I thought what crappy luck. Then the second one came off, too...."

Her stomach lurched at the memory. "We were lucky we didn't get T-boned in traffic. You had fast instincts, even then."

His arms twitched around her, holding her too tightly. "I found out that my father had taken out a life insurance policy on me."

She gasped, rising up on her elbows to look him in the eyes. His expression was completely devoid of emotion, but she could see the horror that must be on her face reflected in his eyes.

"Elliot, do you really believe your father tried to kill you?"

"I'm sure of it," he said with certainty, pushing up to sit, the covers rustling and twisting around their legs.

"You had to have been so scared."

Why hadn't he told her? Although the second she finished that thought, she already knew the answer. He didn't want to put her at risk. Debating the fact now, insisting he should have told the police, seemed moot after so long. Better to just listen and figure out why he was telling her this now.

"I didn't have the money to strike out on my own. I knew the odds of teens on the street." His head fell back against the carved headboard. "I figured the kids in juvie couldn't be as bad as my old man."

"Except you were sent to military reform school instead."

Thank heavens, too, since his life had been turned around because of his time in that school, thanks to his friends and the headmaster. The system did work for the best sometimes. Someone somewhere had seen the good deep inside of Elliot.

"I finally caught a lucky break." He cupped the back of her head, his fingers massaging her scalp. "I'm just so damn sorry I had to leave you behind. I see now I should have figured out another way."

"It all worked out—"

"Did it?" he asked, his eyes haunted. "Your mom's boyfriends… We've talked about so much over the years but we've never discussed that time when I was away."

Slowly, she realized what he was asking, and the thought that he'd worried about her, about that, for all these years… Her heart broke for him and the worries he'd had. She wondered if that's why he'd been so protective, giving her a job, keeping her with him—out of guilt?

"Elliot, the guys my mom saw were jerks, yes, and a few of them even tried to cop a feel, but none of them were violent. Some may have been perverts but they weren't rapists. So I was able to take care of myself by avoiding them. I escaped to Aunt Carla's until things settled down or until Mom and her latest guy broke up."

"You shouldn't have had to handle it yourself, to hide from your own home." Anger and guilt weighted his words and tightened his jaw until the tendons flexed along his neck. "Your mother should have been there for you. *I* should have been there."

She didn't want him to feel guilty or to feel sorry for her. Angling up, she cupped his face in her hands. "I don't want you to feel obligated to be my protector."

"I don't know what else I can be for you." His voice was ragged with emotion, his eyes haunted.

They could have been teenagers again, the two of them clinging to each other because there was so little else for them. So much pain. So much betrayal by parents who should have valued them and kept them safe. Her shared past with Elliot wrapped around her so tightly she felt bound to him in a way she couldn't find words to explain but felt compelled to express, even if only physically.

Soaking in the feel of bare flesh meeting flesh, Lucy Ann kissed Elliot, fully, deeply. She savored the taste of flan and strawberries and *him*. A far more intoxicating combination than any alcohol.

And he was all hers, for tonight.

Nine

Their tongues met and tangled as Lucy Ann angled her mouth over Elliot's. They fit so seamlessly together as she tried to give him some sort of comfort, even if only in the form of distraction. Sex didn't solve problems, but it sure made the delaying a hell of a lot more pleasurable. Her mind filled with the sensation of him, the scents of them together.

His hands banded around her waist, and he urged her over him. She swung her leg over his lap, straddling him. His arousal pressed between her legs, nudging against the tight bundle of nerves at her core.

She writhed against him, her body on fire for him. "I need… I want…"

"Tell me, Lucy Ann," he said between kisses and nips, tasting along her neck, "tell me what you want."

She didn't even know what would settle out their lives or how to untangle the mess they'd made of their world.

Not to mention their emotions. "Right now, I just need you inside me."

"That's not what I meant." He held her with those mesmerizing green eyes, familiar eyes that had been a part of her life for as long as she could remember.

"Shh, don't ruin this." She pressed two fingers to his lips. She didn't want to risk their conversation leading down a dangerous path as it had eleven months ago.

Even thinking about their fight chilled her. That argument had led to the most painful time in her life, the time without the best friend she'd ever had. They couldn't go that route again. They had Eli to consider.

And as for their own feelings?

She shied away from those thoughts, determined to live in the moment. She shifted to reach in the bedside table drawer for another condom. He plucked it from between her fingers and sheathed himself quickly, efficiently, before positioning her over him again. Slowly, carefully—blissfully—she lowered herself onto him, taking the length of him inside her until he touched just… the right…spot.

Yessss.

Her eyelids grew heavy but the way he searched her face compelled her to keep her eyes open, to stare back at him as she rolled her hips to meet his thrusts. Every stroke sent ripples of pleasure tingling through her as they synced up into a perfect rhythm. Her palms flattened against his chest, her fingers digging into the bunched muscles twitching under her touch. A purr of feminine satisfaction whispered free as she reveled in the fact that she made him feel every bit as out of control as he made her feel.

His hands dug into her hips then eased, caressing up her sides then forward to cup her breasts. She sighed at the gentle rasp of his callused fingers touching her so instinctively, his thumbs gliding over nipples until she feared she would come apart now. Too soon. She ached for this to last, to hang on to the blissful forgetfulness they could find in each other's arms. She flowed forward to cover him, moving slower, holding back.

Elliot's arms slid around her, and he drew her earlobe between his teeth. Just an earlobe. Yet her whole body tensed up with that final bit of sensation that sent her hurtling into fulfillment. Her nails dug into his shoulders, and she cried out as her release crested.

He rolled her over, and she pushed back, tumbling them again until the silver tray went crashing to the floor, the twang of pewter plates clanking. He kissed her hard, taking her cries of completion into his mouth. As orgasm gripped her again and again, his arms twitched around her, his body pulsing, his groans mingling with hers until she melted in the aftermath.

Panting, she lay beside him, her leg hitched over his hip, an arm draped over him. Her whole body was limp from exhaustion. She barely registered him pulling the comforter over her again.

Maybe they could make this friendship work, friendship combined with amazing sex. Being apart hadn't made either of them happy.

Could this be enough? Friendship and sex? Could they learn to trust each other again as they once had?

They had the rest of the month together to figure out the details. If only they could have sex until they couldn't think about the future.

His breath settled into an even pattern with a soft snore. What a time to realize she'd never slept with him before. She'd seen him nap plenty of times, falling asleep with a book on his chest, but never once had she stayed through the night with him.

For now, it was best she keep it that way. No matter how tempted she was to indulge herself, she wouldn't make the mistakes of her past again. Not with Eli to think about.

Careful not to wake her generous, sexy lover, she eased from the bed, tiptoeing around the scattered cutlery and dishes that looked a lot like the disjointed parts of her life. Beautiful pieces, but such a jumbled mess there was no way to put everything back together.

"Lucy Ann?" Elliot called in a groggy voice. He reached out for her. "Come back to bed."

She pulled on her red wraparound dress and tied it quickly before gathering her underwear. "I need to go to Eli. I'll see you in the morning."

Her bra and panties in her hand, she raced from his room and tried to convince herself she wasn't making an even bigger mess of her life by running like a coward.

"Welcome to Monte Carlo, Eli," Elliot said to his son, carrying the baby in the crook of his arm, walking the floor with his cranky child while everyone else slept. He'd heard Eli squawk and managed to scoop him up before Lucy Ann woke.

But then she was sprawled out on her bed, looking dead to the world after their trip to Monte Carlo—with a colicky kid.

The day had been so busy with travel, he hadn't had a chance to speak to Lucy Ann alone. But then she hadn't gone out of her way to make that possible, either. If he hadn't known better, he would have thought she was hiding from him.

Only there was no reason for her to do so. The sex

last night had been awesome. They hadn't argued. Hell, he didn't know what was wrong, but her silence today couldn't be missed.

Compounding matters, Eli had become progressively irritable as the day passed. By the time his private plane had landed in Monte Carlo, Elliot was ready to call a doctor. Lucy Ann and the nanny had both reassured him that Eli was simply suffering from gas and exhaustion over having his routine disrupted.

Of course that only proved Lucy Ann's point that a child shouldn't be living on the road, but damn it all, Elliot wasn't ready to admit defeat. Especially not after last night. He and Lucy Ann were so close to connecting again.

He'd hoped Monte Carlo would go a long way toward scoring points in his campaign. He owned a place here. A home with friends who lived in the area. Sure it was a condominium and his friend owned a casino. But his friend was a dad already. And the flat was spacious, with a large garden terrace. He would have to add some kind of safety feature to the railing before Eli became mobile. He scanned the bachelor pad with new eyes and he saw a million details in a different light. Rather than fat leather sofas and heavy wooden antiques, he saw sharp edges and climbing hazards.

"What do you think, Eli?" he asked his son, staring down into the tiny features all scrunched up and angry. "Are you feeling any better? I'm thinking it may be time for you to eat, but I hate to wake your mama. What do you say I get you one of those bottles with expressed milk?"

Eli blinked back up at him with wide eyes, his fists and feet pumping.

He'd always thought babies all looked the same, like

tiny old men. Except now he knew he could pick out Eli from dozens of other babies in a heartbeat.

How strange to see parts of himself and Lucy Ann mixed together in that tiny face. Yet the longer he looked, the more that mixture became just Eli. The kid had only been in his life for a week. Yet now there didn't seem to be a pre-Eli time. Any thoughts prior to seeing him were now colored by the presence of him. As if he had somehow already existed on some plane just waiting to make an appearance.

Eli's face scrunched up tighter in that sign he was about to scream bloody murder. Elliot tucked his son against his shoulder and patted his back while walking to the fridge to get one of the bottles he'd seen Lucy Ann store there.

He pulled it out, started to give it to his son…then remembered something about cold bottles not being good. He hadn't paid a lot of attention when his friends took care of baby stuff, but something must have permeated his brain. Enough so that he tugged his cell phone from his pocket and thumbed speed dial for his buddy Conrad Hughes. He always stayed up late. Conrad had said once that life as a casino magnate had permanently adjusted his internal clock.

The phone rang only once. "This is Hughes. Speak to me, Elliot."

"I need advice."

"Sure, financial? Work? Name it."

"Um, babies." He stared at the baby and the bottle on the marble slab counter. Life had definitely changed. "Maybe you should put Jayne on the line."

"I'm insulted," Conrad joked, casino bells and music drifting over the airwaves. "Ask your question. Besides, Jayne's asleep. Worn out from the kiddo."

"The nanny's sick and Lucy Ann really needs to sleep in." He swayed from side to side. "She's been trying to keep up with her work, the baby, the traveling."

"And your question?"

"Oh, right. I forgot. Sleep deprivation's kicking in, I think," he admitted, not that he would say a word to Lucy Ann after the way she was freaking out over him having a wreck.

"Happens to the best of us, brother. You were just the last man to fall."

"Back to my question. When I give the baby a bottle of this breast milk from the refrigerator, do I heat it in the microwave? And I swear if you laugh, I'm going to kick your ass later."

"I'm only laughing on the inside. Never out loud." Conrad didn't have to laugh. Amusement drenched his words.

"I can live with that." As long as he got the advice.

"Run warm water over the bottle. No microwave. Do not heat it in water on the stove," Conrad rattled off like a pro. "If he doesn't eat it all, pour it out. You can't save and reuse it. Oh, and shake it up."

"You're too good at this," Elliot couldn't resist saying as he turned on the faucet.

"Practice."

"This has to be the strangest conversation of my life." He played his fingers through the water to test the temperature and found it was warming quickly. He tucked the bottled milk underneath the spewing faucet with one hand, still holding his son to his shoulder with the other.

"It'll be commonplace before you know it."

Would it? "I hope so."

The sound of casino bells softened, as if Conrad had

gone into another room. "What about you and Lucy Ann?"

Elliot weighed his answer carefully before saying simply, "We're together."

"Together-together?" Conrad asked.

Elliot glanced through the living area at the closed bedroom door and the baby in his arms. "I'm working on it."

"You've fallen for her." His friend made it more of a statement than a question.

So why couldn't he bring himself to simply agree? "Lucy Ann and I have been best friends all our lives. We have chemistry."

Best friends. His brothers all called themselves best friends, but now he realized he'd never quite paired up with a best bud the way they all had. He was a part of the group. But Lucy Ann was his best friend, always had been.

"You'd better come up with a smoother answer than that if you ever get around to proposing to her. Women expect more than 'you're a great friend and we're super together in the sack.'"

Proposing? The word *marriage* hadn't crossed his mind, and he realized now that it should have. He should have led with that from the start. He should have been an honorable, stand-up kind of guy and offered her a ring rather than a month-long sex fest.

"I'm not that much of an idiot."

He hoped.

"So you are thinking about proposing."

He was now. The notion fit neatly in his brain, like the missing piece to a puzzle he'd been trying to complete since Lucy Ann left a year ago.

"I want my son to have a family, and I want Lucy Ann to be happy." He turned off the water and felt the bottle. Seemed warm. He shook it as instructed. "I'm just not sure I know how to make that happen. Not many long-term role models for happily ever after on my family tree."

"Marriage is work, no question." Conrad whistled softly on a long exhale. "I screwed up my own pretty bad once, so maybe I'm not the right guy to ask for advice."

Conrad and Jayne had been separated for three years before reuniting.

"But you fixed your marriage. So you're probably the best person to ask." Elliot was getting into this whole mentor notion. Why hadn't he thought to seek out some help before? He took his son and the bottle back into the living room of his bachelor pad, now strewn with baby gear. "How do you make it right when you've messed up this bad? When you've let so much time pass?"

"Grovel," Conrad said simply.

"That's it?" Elliot asked incredulously, dropping into his favorite recliner. He settled his son in the crook of his arm and tucked the bottle in his mouth. "That's your advice? Grovel?"

"It's not just a word. You owe her for being a jackass this past year. Like I said before. Relationships are work, man. Hard work. Tougher than any Interpol assignment old headmaster Colonel Salvatore could ever give us. But the payoff is huge if you can get it right."

"I hope so."

"Hey, I gotta go. Text just came in. Kid's awake and Jayne doesn't believe in nighttime nannies. So we're in the walking dead stage of parenthood right now." He didn't sound at all unhappy about it. "Don't forget. Shake the milk and burp the kid if you want to keep your suit clean."

Shake. Burp. Grovel. "I won't forget."

Lucy Ann blinked at the morning sun piercing the slight part in her curtains. She'd slept in this room in Elliot's posh Monte Carlo digs more times than she could remember. He'd even had her choose her own decor since they spent a lot of off-season time here, too.

She'd chosen an über-feminine French toile in pinks and raspberries, complete with an ornate white bed—Renaissance antiques. And the best of the best mattresses. She stretched, luxuriating in the well-rested feeling, undoubtedly a by-product of the awesome bed and even more incredible sex. She couldn't remember how long it had been since she'd woken up refreshed rather than dragging, exhausted. Certainly not since Eli had been born—

Blinking, she took in the morning sun, then gasped. "Eli!"

She jumped from the bed and raced over to the portable crib Elliot had ordered set up in advance. Had her baby slept through the night? She looked in the crib and found it empty. Her heart lurched up to her throat.

Her bare feet slipping on the hardwood floor, she raced out to the living room and stopped short. Elliot sat in his favorite recliner, holding their son. He looked so at ease with the baby cradled in the crook of his arm. An empty bottle sat on the table beside them.

Elliot toyed with his son's foot. "I have plans for you, little man. There are so many books to read. *Gulliver's Travels* and *Lord of the Rings* were favorites of mine as a kid. And we'll play with Matchbox cars when you're older. Or maybe you'll like trains or airplanes? Your choice."

Relaxing, Lucy Ann sagged against the door frame in relief. "You're gender stereotyping our child."

Glancing up, Elliot smiled at her, so handsome with a five o'clock shadow peppering his jaw and baby spit-up dotting his shoulder it was all she could do not to kiss him.

"Good morning, beautiful," he said, his eyes sliding over her silky nightshirt with an appreciation that all but mentally pulled the gown right off her. "Eli can be a chef or whatever he wants, as long as he's happy."

"Glad to hear you say that." She padded barefoot across the room and sat on the massive tapestry ottoman between the sofa and chairs. "I can't believe I slept in so late this morning."

"Eli and I managed just fine. And if I ran into problems, I had plenty of backup."

"I concede you chose well with the nanny." She wasn't used to taking help with Eli, but she could get addicted to this kind of assistance quickly. "Mrs. Clayworth's amazing and a great help without being intrusive."

"You're not upset that I didn't wake you?"

She swept her tangled hair back over her shoulders. "I can't think any mother of an infant would be upset over an extra two hours of sleep."

"Glad you're happy, Sleeping Beauty." His heated gaze slid over the satin clinging to her breasts.

"Ah, your fairy-tale romancing theme."

He arched an eyebrow. "You catch on fast. If you were to stay with me for the whole racing season, we could play Aladdin and his lamp."

His talk of the future made her...uncomfortable. She was just getting used to the shift in their relationship, adding a sexual level on a day-to-day basis. So she ignored the part about staying longer and focused on the fairy tale. "You've been fantasizing about me as a belly dancer?"

"Now that you mention it…"

"Lucky for us both, I'm rested and ready." She curled her toes into the hand-knotted silk Persian rug that would one day be littered with toys. "You're going to be a wonderful father."

As the words fell from her mouth she knew them to be true, not a doubt in her mind. And somehow she'd slid into talking about the future anyway.

"Well, I sure as hell learned a lot from my father about how not to be a dad." His gaze fell away from her and back to their child. "And the things I didn't learn, I intend to find out, even if that means taking a class or reading every parenting book on the shelves since I never had much of a role model."

Clearly, he was worried about this. She leaned forward to touch his knee. "Does that mean I'm doomed to be a crummy mother?"

"Of course not." He covered her hand with his. "Okay, I see your point. And thanks for the vote of confidence."

"For what it's worth, I do think you've had a very good role model." She linked fingers with him. "The colonel. Your old headmaster has been there for you, the way my aunt has for me. Doing the best they could within a flawed system that sent them broken children to fix."

"I don't like to think of myself as broken." His jaw clenched.

"It's okay, you know—" she rubbed his knee "—to be sad or angry about the past."

"It's a lot easier to just speed around the track, even smash into walls, rather than rage at the world." His throat moved with a long swallow.

"I'm not so sure I like that coping mechanism. I would

be so sad if anything happened to you." And wasn't that the understatement of the year? She had to admit, though, she'd been worrying more about him lately, fearing the distractions she brought to his life, also fearing he might have beat the odds one time too many.

He squeezed her hand, his eyes as serious as she'd ever seen them. "I would quit racing. For you."

"And I would never ask you to do that. Not for me."

"So you would ask for Eli?"

She churned his question around in her mind, unable to come up with an answer that didn't involve a lengthy discussion of the future.

"I think this is entirely too serious a conversation before I've had breakfast."

Scooping up her son from Elliot's arms, she made tracks for the kitchen, unable to deny the truth. Even though she stayed in the condo, she was running from him now every bit as much as she'd run eleven months ago.

Ten

Steering through the narrow streets of Monte Carlo, Elliot drove his new Mercedes S65 AMG along the cliff road leading to the Hughes mansion. His Maserati wouldn't hold a baby seat, so he'd needed a sedan that combined space and safety with his love of finely tuned automobiles. He felt downright domesticated driving Lucy Ann and their son to a lunch with friends. She was meeting with Jayne Hughes and Jayne's baby girl while he went over to the track.

Last time he'd traveled this winding road, he'd been driving Jayne and Conrad to the hospital—Conrad had been too much of a mess to climb behind the wheel of his SUV. Jayne had been in labor. She'd delivered their baby girl seventeen minutes after they'd arrived at the hospital.

How strange to think he knew more about his friend's first kid coming into the world than he knew about the birth of his own son.

His fingers clenched around the steering wheel as they wound up a cliff-side road overlooking the sea. "Tell me about the day Eli was born."

"Are you asking me because you're angry or because you want to know?"

A good question. It wouldn't help to say both probably came into play, so he opted for, "I will always regret that I wasn't there when he came into this world, that I missed out on those first days of his life. But I understand that if we're going to move forward here, I can't let that eat at me. We both are going to have to give a little here. So the answer to your question is, I want to know because I'm curious about all things relating to Eli."

She touched his knee lightly. "Thank you for being honest."

"That's the only way we're going to get through this, don't you think?"

He glanced over at her quickly, taking in the beautiful lines of her face with the sunlight streaming through the window.

Why had it taken him so long to notice?

"Okay..." She inhaled a shaky breath. "I had an appointment the week of my due date. I really expected to go longer since so many first-time moms go overdue. But the doctor was concerned about Eli's heart rate. He did an ultrasound and saw the placenta was separating from the uterine wall— Am I getting too gross for you here?"

"Keep talking," he commanded, hating that he hadn't been there to make things easier, less frightening for her. If he hadn't been so pigheaded, he would have been there to protect her. Assure her.

"The doctor scheduled me for an immediate cesarean section. I didn't even get to go home for my toothbrush," she joked in an attempt to lighten the mood.

He wasn't laughing. "That had to be scary for you. I wish I could have been with you. We helped each other through a lot of tough times over the years."

"I did try to call you," she confessed softly, "right before I went in. But your phone went straight to voice mail. I tried after, too…I assumed you were off on an Interpol secret 'walkabout' for Colonel Salvatore."

"I was." He'd done the math in his head. Knew the case he'd been working at the time.

"I know I could have pushed harder and found you." She shook her head regretfully. "I didn't even leave a message. I'm so sorry for that. You may be able to move past it, but I'm not sure I'll ever forgive myself."

He stayed silent, not sure what to say to make this right for both of them.

"What would we have done if Malcolm and Conrad hadn't kidnapped you from the bachelor party?"

Damn good question. "I like to think I would have come to my senses and checked on you. I don't know how the hell I let eleven months pass."

"Or how you found a fiancée so fast," she blurted out. "You proposed to another woman barely three months after we slept together. Yes, that's a problem for me."

He weighed his words carefully. "This may sound strange, but Gianna was the one who got shortchanged. I obviously didn't care about her the way I should have. I wasn't fair to her."

Her smile was tight. "Excuse me if I'm not overly concerned about being fair to Gianna. And from what I read in the news, she broke things off with you. Not the other way around. If she hadn't left, would you have married her?"

Stunned, he downshifted around a corner. She'd read about his breakup? She'd left, but kept tabs on him. If only he'd done the same with her, he would have known about Eli. As much as Elliot wanted to blame a remote Interpol stint for keeping him out of touch, he knew he should have followed up with Lucy Ann.

Then why hadn't he? She'd been so good to him, always there for him, always forgiving him. Damn it, he didn't deserve her— Could that have been part of why he'd stayed away? Out of guilt for taking so much from her all their lives?

That she could think he still wanted Gianna, especially after what he and Lucy Ann had just shared... Incomprehensible.

"No. I didn't want to marry her. We broke off the engagement. I knew it was inevitable. She just spoke first."

She nodded tightly. "Fine, I appreciate your honesty. I'm still not totally okay with the fact that you raced right back to her after we... Well, I'm just not okay with it. But I'm working on it."

Conrad had told him to grovel. Elliot scrounged inside himself for a way to give her what she needed.

"Fair enough. At least I know where I stand with you." He stared at the road ahead, struggling. Groveling was tougher than he'd expected after the way his father had beaten him to his knees so many times. "That was the hardest part about growing up with my old man. The uncertainty. I'm not saying it would have been okay if he'd punched me on a regular basis. But the sick feeling in my gut as I tried to gauge his moods? That was a crappy way to live."

"I'm so sorry." Her hand fell to rest on his knee again. This time she didn't pull away.

"I know. You saved my sanity back then." He placed his hand over hers. "I always knew it was you who let the air out of my dad's tires that time in sixth grade."

She sat upright. "How did you know?"

"Because you did it while I was away on that science fair trip. So I couldn't be blamed or catch the brunt of his anger." He rubbed her hand along the spot on her finger where he should have put a ring already. "Do I have the details correct?"

"That was the idea. Couldn't have your father get away with everything."

"He didn't. Not in the end." There'd never been a chance to make peace with his bastard of an old man—never a chance to confront him, either.

"I guess there's a sad sort of poetic justice that he died in a bar fight while you were off at reform school."

Her words surprised him. "You're a bloodthirsty one."

"When it comes to protecting the people in my life? Absolutely."

She was freaking amazing. He couldn't deny the rush of admiration for the woman she'd become—that she'd always been, just hidden under the weight of her own problems.

And on the heels of that thought, more guilt piled on top of him for all the ways he'd let her down. Damn it all, he had to figure out how to make this right with her. He had to pull out all the stops as Conrad advised.

Full throttle.

He had to win her over to be his wife.

Lucy Ann sat on the terrace with Jayne Hughes, wondering how a woman who'd been separated for three years could now be such a happily contented wife and new mother. What was her secret? How had they overcome the odds?

There was no denying the peaceful air that radiated off the bombshell blonde with her baby girl cradled in a sling. The Hughes family split their time between their home in Monte Carlo and a home in Africa, where Jayne worked as a nurse at a free clinic her husband funded along with another Alpha Brother. She made it all look effortless whether she was serving up luncheon on fine china or cracking open a boxed lunch under a sprawling shea butter tree.

Lucy Ann patted her colicky son on his precious little back. He seemed to have settled to sleep draped over her knees, which wasn't particularly comfortable, but she wasn't budging an inch as long as he was happy.

Jayne paused in her lengthy ramble about the latest addition to the pediatrics wing at the clinic to tug something from under the plate of petits fours. "Oh, I almost forgot to give you this pamphlet for Elliot."

"For Elliot?" She took it from Jayne, the woman's short nails hinting at her more practical side. "On breast-feeding?"

"He called Conrad with questions the other night." She adjusted her daughter to the other breast in such a smooth transition the cloth baby sling covered all. "I don't know why he didn't just look it up on Google. Anyhow, this should tell him everything he needs to know."

"Thank you." She tucked the pamphlet in her purse, careful not to disturb her son. "He didn't tell me he called your husband for help."

"He was probably too embarrassed. Men can be proud that way." She sipped her ice water, sun glinting off the Waterford crystal that Lucy Ann recalled choosing for a wedding gift to the couple.

There'd been a time when tasks like that—picking out expensive trinkets for Elliot's wealthy friends—had made her nervous. As if the wrong crystal pattern could call her out as an interloper in Elliot Starc's elegant world.

But it had taken walking away from the glitz and glamour to help her see it for what it really was…superficial trappings that didn't mean a lot in the long run. Lucy Ann was far more impressed with Jayne's nursing capabilities and her motherhood savvy than with what kind of place setting graced her table.

"There's a lot to learn about parenting," Lucy Ann acknowledged. "Especially for someone who didn't grow up around other kids." She would have been overwhelmed without Aunt Carla's help.

And wasn't it funny to think that, even though she'd traveled the globe with Elliot for a decade, she'd still learned the most important things back home in South Carolina?

"I think it's wonderful that he's trying. A lot of men would just dump all the tough stuff onto a nanny." Jayne shot a glance over her shoulder through the open balcony doors, somehow knowing Conrad had arrived without even looking.

"I just suggested that it wouldn't hurt to let someone else change the diapers," said Mr. Tall, Dark and Brooding. "Who the hell wants to change a diaper? That doesn't make me a bad human being."

Lucy Ann had to admit, "He has a point."

Jayne set her glass down. "Don't encourage him."

Conrad chuckled as he reached for his daughter. "Lucy Ann, let me know when you're done. I promised Elliot I would drive you and the kidlet back to the condo. He said he's running late at the track. Have fun, ladies. The princess and I are going to read the *Wall Street Journal*."

Conrad disappeared back into the house with his daughter, words about stocks and short sales carrying on the wind spoken in a singsong tone as if telling her a nursery rhyme.

Lucy Ann leaned back in the chair and turned her water glass on the table, watching the sunlight refracting prisms off the cut crystal. "I envy your tight-knit support group. Elliot and I didn't have a lot of friends when we were growing up. He was the kid always in trouble so parents didn't invite him over. And I was too shy to make friends."

"You're not shy anymore," Jayne pointed out.

"Not that I let people see."

"We've known you for years. I would hope you could consider us your friends, too."

They'd known each other, but she'd been Elliot's employee. It wasn't that his friends had deliberately excluded her, but Conrad had been separated for years, and only recently had the rest of them started marrying. She knew it would be easier for all of them if she made the effort here.

"We'll certainly cross paths because of Eli," Lucy Ann said simply.

"And Elliot?"

The conversation was starting to get too personal for her comfort. "We're still working on that."

"But you're making progress."

"Have you been reading the tabloids?"

"I don't bother with those." Jayne waved dismissively. "I saw the way you two looked at each other when Elliot dropped you off."

In spite of herself, Lucy Ann found herself aching to talk to someone after all, and Jayne seemed the best candidate. "He's into the thrill of the chase right now. Things will go back to normal eventually."

"I'm not so sure I agree. He seems different to me." Jayne's pensive look faded into a grin. "They all have to grow up and settle down sometime."

"What about—" She didn't feel comfortable discussing the guys' Interpol work out in the open, so she simply said, "Working with the colonel after graduation and following a call to right bigger wrongs? How do they give that up to be regular family guys?"

"Good question." Jayne pinched the silver tongs to shuffle a petit four and fruit onto a dessert plate. "Some still take an active part once they're married, but once the children start coming, things do change. They shift to pulling the strings. They become more like Salvatore."

"Mine is a bit wilder than yours." When had she started thinking of Elliot as *hers*? Although on some level he'd been hers since they were children. "I mean, seriously, he crashes cars into walls for a living."

"You've known that about him from the start. So why are things different now?"

"I don't know how to reconcile our friendship with everything else that's happened." The whole "friends with benefits" thing was easier said than done.

"By 'everything else' you mean the smoking hot sex, of course." Jayne grinned impishly before popping a grape in her mouth.

"I had forgotten how outspoken you can be."

"Comes with the territory of loving men like these. They don't always perceive subtleties."

True enough. Lucy Ann speared a chocolate strawberry and willed herself not to blush at the heated memories the fruit evoked. "Outspoken or not, I'm still no closer to an answer."

Jayne nudged the gold-rimmed china plate aside and leaned her arms on the table. "You don't have to reconcile the two ways of being. It's already done—or it will be once you stop fighting."

Could Jayne be right? Maybe the time had come to

truly give him a chance. To see if he was right. To see if they could really have a fairy-tale life together.

Fear knotted her gut, but Lucy Ann wasn't the shy little girl anymore. She was a confident woman and she was all-in.

Elliot shrugged out of his black leather jacket with a wince as he stepped into the dark apartment. He'd done his prelim runs as always, checklists complete, car scrutinized to the last detail, and yet somehow he'd damn near wiped out on a practice run.

Every muscle in his body ached from reactionary tensing. Thank goodness Lucy Ann hadn't been there as she would have been in the past as his assistant. He didn't want her worrying. He didn't want to risk a confrontation.

He tossed the jacket over his arm, walking carefully so he wouldn't wake anyone up. His foot hooked on something in the dark. He bit back a curse and looked down to find…a book? He reached to pick up an ornately bound copy of *Hansel and Gretel*. He started to stand up again and looked ahead to find a trail of books, all leading toward his bedroom. He picked up one book after the other, each a different fairy tale, until he pushed open his door.

His room was empty.

Frowning, he scanned the space and… "Aha…"

More books led to the bathroom, and now that he listened, he could hear the shower running. He set the stack on the chest of drawers and gathered up the last few "crumbs" on his trail, a copy of *Rapunzel* and a Victorian version of *Rumpelstiltskin*. Pushing his way slowly into the bathroom, he smiled at the shadowy outline behind the foggy glass wall. The multiple showerheads shot spray over Lucy Ann as she hummed. She didn't seem to notice he'd arrived.

He peeled off his clothes without making a sound and padded barefoot into the slate-tiled space. He opened the door and stepped into the steam. Lucy Ann stopped singing, but she didn't turn around. The only acknowledgment she gave to his arrival was a hand reaching for him. He linked fingers with her and stepped under the warm jets. The heat melted away the stress from his muscles, allowing a new tension to take hold. He saw the condom packet in the soap dish and realized just how thoroughly she'd thought this through.

He pressed against her back, wrapping his arms around her. Already, his erection throbbed hard and ready, pressed between them.

He sipped water from just behind her ear. "I'm trying to think of what fairy tale you're fantasizing about, and for water, I can only come up with the *Frog Prince*."

Angling her head to give him better access to her neck, she combed her fingers over his damp hair. "We're writing our own fantasy tonight."

Growling his approval, he slicked his hands over her, taking in the feel of her breasts peaking against his palms. His blood fired hotter through his veins than the water sluicing over them. He slipped a hand between her thighs, stroking satin, finding that sweet bundle of nerves. Banding his arm tighter around her waist, he continued to circle and tease, feeling her arousal lubricate his touch. She sagged back against him, her legs parting to give him easier access.

With her bottom nestled against him, he held on to control by a thread. Each roll of her hips as she milked the most from her pleasure threatened to send him over the edge. But he held back his own release, giving her hers. He tucked two fingers inside her, his thumb still working along that pebbled tightness.

Her sighs and purrs filled the cubicle, the jasmine scent of her riding the steam. Every sound of her impending arousal shot a bolt of pleasure through him, his blood pounding thicker through his veins. Until, yes, she cried out, coming apart in his arms. Her fingernails dug deep into his thighs, cutting half-moons into his flesh as she arched into her orgasm.

He savored every shiver of bliss rippling her body until he couldn't wait any longer. He took the condom from the soap tray and sheathed himself. He pressed her against the shower stall wall, her palms flattened to the stone. Standing behind her, he nudged her legs apart and angled until… He slid home, deep inside her, clamped by damp silken walls as hot and moist as the shower.

Sensation engulfed him, threatened to shake the ground under him as he pushed inside her again and again. Things moved so damn fast… He was so close… Then he heard the sound of her unraveling in his arms. The echoes of her release sent him over the edge. Ecstasy rocked his balance. He flattened a hand against the warm wall to keep from falling over as his completion pulsed until his heartbeat pounded in his ears. Shifting, he pulled out of her, keeping one arm around her.

Slowly, his world expanded beyond just the two of them, and he became aware of the water sheeting over them. The patter of droplets hitting the door and floor.

Tucking her close again, he thought about his near miss at the track today and all the relationship advice from his friends. He'd waited too long these past eleven months to make sure she stayed with him. Permanently. He wouldn't let another minute pass without moving forward with their lives.

He nuzzled her ear. "What kind of house do you want?"

"House?" she asked, her knees buckling.

He steadied her. "I want to build a real house for us, Lucy Ann. Not just condos or rented places here and there."

"Umm…" She licked her lips. The beads on her temple mingled perspiration with water. "What city would you choose?"

He had penthouse suites around the world, but nowhere he stayed long enough to call home. And none of them had the room for a boy to run and play.

"I need a home. We need a home for our son."

"You keep assuming we'll stay together."

Already his proposal was going astray. Could be because most of the blood in his brain was surging south. "Where do you want to live? I'll build two houses next door if that's the way you want it." Living near each other would give him more time to win her over, because he was fast realizing he couldn't give her up. "I have connections with a friend who restores historic homes."

She turned in his arms, pressing her fingers to his lips. "Can we just keep making love instead?"

Banding her wrist in his hand, he kissed it, determined not to let this chance slip away, not to let *her* slip away again. "Let's get married."

She leaned into him, whispering against his mouth as she stroked down between them, molding her palm to the shape of him. "You may have missed the memo…" She caressed up and down, again and again. "But you don't have to propose to get me to sleep with you."

He angled away, staring straight in her eyes, her eyelashes spiky wet. "I'm not joking, so I would appreciate it if you took my proposal seriously."

"Really? Now?" She stepped back, the water showering between them. "You mean this. For Eli, of course."

"Of course Eli factors into the equation." He studied her carefully blank expression. "But it's also because you and I fit as a couple on so many levels. We've been friends forever, and our chemistry... Well, that speaks for itself. We just have to figure out how not to fight afterward and we'll have forever locked and loaded."

The more he talked, the more it felt right.

"Forever?" Her knees folded, and she sat on the stone seat in the corner, her hair dripping water. "Do you think that's even possible for people like you and me?"

"Why shouldn't it be?" He knelt in front of her.

"Because of our pasts." She stroked over his wet hair, cupping his neck, her eyes so bittersweet they tore him to bits. "Our parents. Our own histories. I refuse to spend the rest of my life wondering when the next Gianna is going to walk through the door."

Gianna? He hadn't even thought of her other than when Lucy Ann mentioned her. But looking back, he realized how bad his engagement would have looked to her, how that must have played a role in her keeping quiet about the pregnancy.

This was likely where the groveling came in. "I'm sorry."

"For which part? The engagement? Or the fact you didn't contact me— Hell, forget I said that." She leaned forward to kiss him.

If they kissed, the discussion would be over, opportunity missed. He scooped her up in his arms and pivoted, settling her into his lap as he sat on the stone seat in the corner.

She squawked in protest but he pressed on. "You expected me to follow you? Even after you said—and I quote—'I don't ever want to lay eyes on your irresponsible ass ever again'?"

"And you've never said anything in the heat of the moment that you regretted later?"

Groveling was all well and good, but he wasn't taking the full blame for what shook down these past months. "If you regretted those words, it sure would have been helpful if you'd let me know."

"This is my whole point. We're both so proud, neither one of us could take the steps needed to repair the damage we did. Yes, I am admitting that we both were hurt. Even though you seemed to recover fast with Gianna—" she gave him that tight smile again "—I acknowledge that losing our friendship hurt you, as well. But friendship isn't enough to build a marriage on. So can we please go back to the friends-with-benefits arrangement?"

"Damn it, Lucy Ann—"

She traced his face with her fingers. "Do you know what I think?" She didn't wait for him to answer. "I think you don't believe in fairy tales after all. The dates, the romance… It has actually been a game for you after all. A challenge, a competition. Something to win. Not Cinderella or Sleeping Beauty."

"I suspect I've been led into a trap." He'd thought he'd been following all the right signs and taking the steps to fix this, but he'd only seemed to dig a bigger hole for himself.

"Well, you followed my bread crumbs." Her joke fell flat between them, her eyes so much sadder than he'd ever dreamed he could make them.

"So you're sure you don't want to marry me?"

She hesitated, her pulse leaping in her neck. "I'm sure I don't want you to propose to me."

Her rejection stunned him. Somehow he'd expected her to say yes. He'd thought… Hell, he'd taken her for granted all over again and he didn't know how to fix this. Not now. He needed time to regroup. "If I agree to stop pressing for marriage, can we keep having incredible sex with each other?"

"'Til the end of the month."

"Sex for a few weeks? You're okay with sleeping together with an exit strategy already in place?"

"That's my offer." She slid from his lap, stepping back. Away. Putting distance between them on more than just one level. "Take it or leave it."

"Lucy Ann, I'm happy as hell to take you again and again until we're both too exhausted to argue." Although right now, he couldn't deny it. He wanted more from her. "But eventually we're going to have to talk."

Eleven

Lucy sprawled on top of Elliot in bed, satiated, groggy and almost dry from their shower, but not ready for their evening together to end. Elliot seemed content to let the proposal discussion go—for tonight. So this could well be the last uncomplicated chance she had to be with him.

The ceiling fan *click, click, clicked* away their precious remaining seconds together, the lights of Monaco glittering through the open French doors, the Cote d'Azur providing a breathtaking vista. Who wouldn't want to share this life with him? Why couldn't she just accept his proposal? She hated how his offer of marriage made her clench her gut in fear. She should be happy. Celebrating. This would be the easy answer to bringing up Eli together. They were best friends. Incredible lovers. Why not go with the flow? They could take a day to see Cannes with the baby, and she could snap pictures…savor the things she'd been too busy to notice in the early years of traveling with Elliot.

Yet something held her back. She couldn't push the word *yes* free. Every time she tried, her throat closed up. She trusted him…yet the thought of reliving the past eleven months again, of living without him…

Her fingers glided along his closely shorn hair. "You could have been killed that day your hair got singed."

"You're not going to get rid of me that easily," he said with a low chuckle and a stroke down her spine.

Ice chilled the blood in her veins at his words. "That wasn't funny."

"I'm just trying to lighten the mood." He angled back to kiss the tip of her nose, then look into her eyes. "I'm okay, Lucy Ann. Not a scratch on me that day."

She'd been in South Carolina when it had happened, her belly swelling with his child and her heart heavy with the decision of when to tell him about the baby. "That doesn't make it any less terrifying."

He grinned smugly. "You do care."

"Of course I care what happens to you. I always have. There's no denying our history, our friendship, how well we know each other." How could he doubt that, no matter what else they'd been through? "But I know something else. You're only interested in me now because I'm telling you no. You don't like being the one left behind."

Breathlessly, she finished her rant, stunned at herself. Her mouth had been ahead of her brain. She hadn't even realized she felt that way until the words came rolling out.

"That's not a very nice thing to say," he said tightly.

"But is it true?" She cupped his face.

He pulled her hands down gently and kissed both palms. "I already offered to stop racing. I meant it. I'm a father now and I understand that comes with responsibilities."

Responsibilities? Is that what they were to him? But then, in a way, that's what she'd always been since he got out of reform school, since he'd offered her a job as his assistant even though at the time she hadn't been qualified for the job. He'd given it to her out of friendship—and, yes, the sense of obligation they felt to look out for each other.

That had been enough for a long time, more than either of them had gotten from anyone else in their lives. But right now with her heart in her throat, obligation didn't feel like nearly enough to build a life on.

She slid off him, the cooling breeze from the fan chilling her bared flesh. "Do whatever you want."

"What did I say wrong? You want me to quit and I offer and now you're angry?"

"I didn't say I want you to quit." She opted for the simpler answer. "I understand how important your career is to you. You have a competitive nature and that's not a bad thing. It's made you an incredibly successful man."

"You mentioned my competitiveness earlier. Lucy Ann, that's not why I—"

She rolled to her side and pressed her fingers to his mouth before he could get back to the proposal subject again. "You've channeled your edginess and your drive to win. That's not a bad thing." She tapped his bottom lip. "Enough talk. You should rest up now so you're focused for the race."

And so she could escape to her room, away from the building temptation to take what he offered and worry about the consequences later. Except with Elliot's muscled arm draped over her waist, she couldn't quite bring herself to move out of his embrace. His hand moved along her back soothingly. Slowly, her body began to relax, melting into the fantastic mattress.

"Lucy Ann? You're right, you know." Elliot's words were so low she almost didn't hear him.

"Right about what?" she asked, groggy, almost asleep.

"I like to win— Wait. Scratch that. I *need* to win."

Opening her eyes, she didn't move, just stared at his chest and listened. There was no escaping this conversation. Wherever it led them.

"There are two kinds of people in the world. Ones who have known physical pain and those who never will. Being beaten…" He swallowed hard, his heart hammering so loudly she could feel her pulse sync up with his, racing, knowing just what that word *beating* meant to him growing up. "That does something to your soul. Changes you. You can heal. You can move on. But you're forever changed by that moment you finally break, crying for it to stop."

His voice stayed emotionless, but what he said sliced through her all the more because of the steely control he forced on himself.

Her hand fluttered to rest on his heart as she pressed a kiss to his shoulder. "Oh, God, Elliot—"

"Don't speak. Not yet." He linked his fingers with hers. "The thing is, we all like to think we're strong enough to hold out when that person brings on the belt, the shoe, the branch, or hell, even a hand used as a weapon. And there's a rush in holding out at first, deluding yourself into believing you can actually win."

She willed herself to stay completely still, barely breathing, while he poured out the truth she'd always known. She'd even seen the marks he'd refused to acknowledge. Hearing him talk about it, though, shredded her heart, every revelation making her ache for what he'd suffered growing up. She also knew he wouldn't accept her sympathy now any more than he had then. So she gave him the only thing she could—total silence while he spoke.

"The person with the weapon is after one thing," he shared, referring to his father in such a vague sense as if that gave him distance, protection. "It isn't actually about the pain. It's about submission."

She couldn't hold back the flinch or a whimper of sympathy.

Elliot tipped her chin until she looked at him. "But you see, it's okay now. When I'm out there racing, it's my chance to win. No one, not one damn soul, will ever beat me again."

She held her breath, wrestling with what to do next, how they could go forward. This wasn't the time to pledge futures, but it also wasn't the time to walk away. Growing up, she'd always known how to be there for him. At this moment, she didn't have a clue.

The squawk of their son over the nursery monitor jolted them both. And she wasn't sure who was more relieved.

Her or Elliot.

Elliot barely tasted the gourmet brunch catered privately at a crowded café near the race day venue. With two hundred thousand people pouring into the small principality for the circuit's most famous event, there were fans and media everywhere. At least his friends and mentor seemed to be enjoying themselves. He wanted to chalk up his lack of enthusiasm to sleep deprivation.

Race day in Monaco had always been one of Elliot's favorites, from the way the sun glinted just right off the streets to the energy of the crowds. The circuit was considered one of the most challenging Formula One routes—narrow roads, tight turns and changing elevations made it all the more exciting, edgy, demanding.

And just that fast, Lucy Ann's words haunted him, how she'd accused him of searching out challenges. How she'd accused him of seeing her as a challenge. Damn it all, he just wanted them to build a future together.

What would she be thinking, sitting in the stands today with his school friends and their wives?

He glanced at her across the table, strain showing in the creases along her forehead and the dark smudges under her eyes. He wanted to take Eli from her arms so she could rest, but wasn't sure if she would object. He didn't want to cause a scene or upset her more.

With a mumbled excuse, he scraped back his chair and left the table. He needed air. Space.

He angled his way out of the room—damn, he had too many curious friends these days—and into the deserted patio garden in the back. All the patrons had flocked out front to the street side to watch the crowds already claiming their places to watch the race. But back here, olive trees and rosebushes packed the small space so densely he almost didn't see his old high school headmaster— now an Interpol handler—sitting on a bench sending text messages.

Colonel Salvatore sat beside his preteen son, who was every bit as fixated on his Game Boy as his father was on his phone. A couple of empty plates rested between them.

How had he missed them leaving the table? Damn, his mind wasn't where it was supposed to be.

Colonel Salvatore stood, mumbled something to his son, then walked toward Elliot without once looking up from his phone. The guy always had been the master of multitasking. Very little slipped by him. Ever.

The older man finally tucked away his cell phone and nodded. "We couldn't sit still," he said diplomatically, "so we're out here playing 'Angry Monkeys' or something like that."

"I'm sure you both enjoyed the food more here where it's quieter," he said diplomatically. "I could sure use parenting advice if you've got some to offer up."

Salvatore straightened his standard red tie. He wore the same color gray suit as always, like a retirement uniform. "Why don't you ask the guys inside?"

"They only have babies. They're new parents." Like him. Treading water as fast as he could and still choking. "You have an older boy."

"A son I rarely see due to my work schedule." He winced. "So again I say, I'm not the one to help."

"Then your first piece of advice would be for me to spend time with him."

"I guess it would." He glanced over at his son, whose thumbs were flying over the buttons. "Gifts don't make up for absence. Although don't underestimate the power of a well-chosen video game."

"Thank God we have the inside scoop with Troy's latest inventions." Maybe that's who he needed to be talking to. Maybe Troy could invent a baby app. Elliot shoved a hand over his hair, realizing how ridiculous the thought sounded. He must be sleep-deprived. "I'm a little short on role models in the father department—other than you."

Salvatore's eyebrows went up at the unexpected compliment. "Um, uh, thank you," he stuttered uncharacteristically.

"Advice then?"

"Don't screw up."

"That's it?" Elliot barked. "Don't screw up?"

"Fine, I'll spell it out for you." Salvatore smiled as if

he'd been toying with him all along. Then the grin faded. "You've had to steal everything you've ever wanted in life. From food to cars to friends—to your freedom."

"I'm past that."

"Are you?" The savvy Interpol handler leaned against the centuries-old brick wall, an ivy trellis beside him. "It's difficult for me to see beyond the boy you were when you arrived at my school as a teenager hell-bent on self-destructing."

"Self-destructing?" he said defensively. "I'm not sure I follow." He was all about winning.

"You stole that car on purpose to escape your father, and you feel guilty as hell for leaving Lucy Ann behind," Salvatore said so damn perceptively he might as well have been listening in on Elliot's recent conversations. "You expected to go to jail as punishment and since that didn't happen, you've been trying to prove to the world just how bad you are. You pushed Lucy Ann away by getting engaged to Gianna."

"When did you find time to get your psychology degree between being a headmaster and an Interpol handler?"

"There you go again, trying to prove what a smartass you are."

Damn it. Didn't it suck to realize how well he played to type? He took a steadying breath and focused.

"I'm trying to do the right thing by Lucy Ann now. I want to live up to my obligations."

"The right thing." The colonel scratched a hand over gray hair buzzed as short of Elliot's. "What is that?"

"Provide for our son... Marry her... Damn it, colonel, clearly you think I'm tanking here. Is it fun watching me flounder?"

"If I tell you what to do, you won't learn a thing. A

mentor guides, steers. Think of it as a race," he said with a nod—which Elliot knew from years in the man's office meant this conversation was over. Colonel Salvatore fished out his phone and headed back to sit silently beside his son.

Elliot pinched the bridge of his nose and pivoted toward the iron gate that led to the back street. He needed to get his head on straight before the race. Hell, he needed to get his head back on straight, period. Because right now, he could have sworn he must be hallucinating.

Beyond the iron gate, he saw a curly-haired brunette who looked startlingly like his former fiancée. He narrowed his eyes, looking closer, shock knocking him back a step as Gianna crossed the street on the arm of a Brazilian Formula One champion.

Lucy Ann usually found race day exciting, but she couldn't shake the feeling of impending doom. The sense that she and Elliot weren't going to figure out how to make things work between them before the end of their time together. Thank goodness Mrs. Clayworth had taken the baby back to the condo to nap, because Lucy Ann was beyond distracted.

Sitting in the private viewing box with Elliot's friends and the relatives of other drivers, she tried to stifle her fears, to reassure herself that she and Elliot could find a way to parent together—possibly even learn to form a relationship as a couple. That she could figure out how to heal the wounds from his past, which still haunted everything he did.

The buzz of conversation increased behind her, a frenzy of whispers and mumbles in multiple languages. She turned away from the viewing window and monitors broadcasting prerace hubbub, newscasters speaking in French, English, Spanish and a couple of languages she didn't recognize. She looked past the catering staff carrying glasses of champagne to the entrance. A gasp caught in her throat.

Gianna? Here?

The other woman worked her way down the steps, her dark curls bouncing. Shock, followed by a burst of anger, rippled through Lucy Ann as she watched Gianna stride confidently closer. Her white dress clung to her teeny-tiny body. Clearly those hips had never given birth. And Lucy Ann was long past her days of wearing anything white thanks to baby spit-up. Not that she would trade her son for a size-zero figure and a closet full of white clothes.

Above all, she did not want a scene in front of the media. Gianna's eyes were locked on her, her path determined. If the woman thought she could intimidate, she was sorely mistaken.

Lucy Ann shot to her feet and marched up the stairs, her low heels clicking. She threw her arms wide and said loud enough for all to hear, "Gianna, so glad you could make it."

Stunned, the woman almost tripped over her own stilettos. "Um, I—"

Lucy Ann hugged her hard and whispered in her ear, "We're going to have a quick little private chat and, above all, we will not cause a scene before the race."

She knew how fast gossip spread and she didn't intend to let any negative energy ripple through the crowd. And she definitely didn't intend for anyone to see her lose her calm. She hauled the other woman down the hall and into a ladies' room, locking the door behind them.

Once she was sure no one else was in the small sitting area or in the stalls, she confronted Elliot's former fiancée. "Why are you here?"

Gianna shook her curls. "I'm here with a retired Brazilian racer. I was simply coming by to say hello."

"I'm not buying that." Lucy Ann stared back at the other woman and found she wasn't jealous so much as angry that someone was trying mess with her happiness—hers, Elliot's and Eli's.

The fake smile finally faded from Gianna's face. "I came back because now it's a fair fight."

At least the woman wasn't denying it. "I'm not sure I follow your logic."

"Before, when I found out about you and the baby—"

Lucy gasped. "You knew?"

"I found out by accident. I got nosy about you, looked into your life…" She shrugged. "I was devastated, but I broke off the engagement."

"Whoa, hold on." Lucy Ann held up a hand. "I don't understand. Elliot said you broke up because of his Interpol work. That you couldn't handle the danger."

She rolled her dramatic Italian eyes. "Men are so very easy to deceive. I broke the engagement because I couldn't be the one to tell him about your pregnancy. I couldn't be 'that' woman. The one who broke up true love. The evil one in the triangle. But I also couldn't marry him knowing he might still want you or his child."

"So you left." Lucy Ann's legs gave way and she sagged back against the steel door.

"I loved him enough to leave and let him figure this out on his own."

If she'd really loved him, Gianna would have told him about his child, but then Lucy Ann figured who was she to throw stones on that issue? "Do you still love Elliot?"

"Yes, I do."

She searched the woman's eyes and saw…genuine heartache. "You're not at all what I expected."

Gianna's pouty smile faltered. "And you're everything I feared."

So where did they go from here? That question hammered through Lucy Ann's mind so loudly it took her a moment to realize the noise was real. Feet drummed overhead with the sound of people running. People screaming?

She looked quickly at Gianna, whose eyes were already widening in confusion, as well. Lucy Ann turned on her heels, unlocked the door and found mass confusion. Spectators and security running. Reporters rushing with their cameras at the ready, shouting questions and directions in different languages.

Lucy Ann grabbed the arm of a passing guard. "What's going on?"

"Ma'am, there's been an accident in the lineup. Please return to your seat and let us do our jobs," the guard said hurriedly and pulled away, melting into the crowd.

"An accident?" Her stomach lurched with fear.

There were other drivers. Many other drivers. And an accident while lining up would be slow? Right? Unless someone was doing a preliminary warm-up lap.... So many horrifying scenarios played through her mind, all of them involving Elliot. She shoved into the crush, searching for a path through to her viewing area or to the nearest telecast screen. Finally, she spotted a wide-screen TV mounted in a corner, broadcasting images of flames.

The words scrolling across the bottom blared what she already knew deep in her terrified heart.

Elliot had crashed.

Twelve

Her heart in her throat, Lucy Ann pushed past Gianna and shouldered through the bustling crush of panicked observers. She reached into her tailored jacket and pulled out her pass giving her unlimited access. She couldn't just sit in the private viewing area and wait for someone to call her. What if Elliot needed her? She refused to accept the possibility that he could be dead. Even the word made her throat close up tight.

Her low pumps clicked on the stairs as she raced through various checkpoints, flashing the access pass every step of the way.

Finally, thank God, finally, she ran out onto the street level where security guards created an impenetrable wall. The wind whipped her yellow sundress around her legs as she sprinted. Her pulse pounding in her ears, she searched the lanes of race cars, looking for flames. But she found no signs of a major explosion.

A siren's wail sliced through her. An ambulance navigated past a throng of race personnel spraying down the street with fire extinguishers. The vehicle moved toward two race cars, one on its side, the other sideways as if it had spun out into a skid. As much as she wanted to deny what her eyes saw, the car on its side belonged to Elliot.

Emergency workers crawled all over the vehicle, prying open the door. Blinking back burning tears, Lucy Ann strained against an arm holding her back, desperate to see. Her shouts were swallowed up in the roar of activity until she couldn't even hear her own incoherent pleas.

The door flew open, and her breath lodged somewhere in her throat. She couldn't breathe, gasp or shout. Just wait.

Rescue workers reached inside, then hauled Elliot out. Alive.

She sagged against the person behind her. She glanced back to find Elliot's Interpol handler, Colonel Salvatore, at her side. He braced her reassuringly, his eyes locked on the battered race car. Elliot was moving, slowly but steadily. The rescue workers tried to keep his arms over their shoulders so they could walk him to a waiting ambulance. But he shook his head, easing them aside and standing on his own two feet. He pulled off his helmet and waved to the crowd, signaling that all was okay.

The crowd roared, a round of applause thundering, the reverberations shuddering through her along with her relief. His gaze homed in on her. Lucy Ann felt the impact all the way to her toes. Elliot was alive. Again and again, the thought echoed through her mind in a continual loop of reassurance, because heaven help her, she loved him. Truly loved him. That knowledge rolled through her, settled into her, in a fit that told her what she'd known all along.

They'd always loved each other.

At this moment, she didn't doubt that he loved her back. No matter what problems, disagreements or betrayals they might have weathered, the bond was there. She wished she could rejoice in that, but the fear was still rooted deep inside her, the inescapable sense of foreboding.

Elliot pushed past the emergency personnel and… heaven only knew who else because she couldn't bring herself to look at anyone except Elliot walking toward her, the scent of smoke tingling in her nose as the sea breeze blew in. The sun shone down on the man she loved, bright Mediterranean rays glinting off the silver trim on his racing gear with each bold step closer.

She vaguely registered the colonel flashing some kind of badge that had the security cop stepping aside and letting her stumble past. She regained her footing and sprinted toward Elliot.

"Thank God you're okay." Slamming into his chest, she wrapped her arms around him.

He kissed her once, firmly, reassuringly, then walked her away from the sidelines, the crowd parting, or maybe someone made the path for them. She couldn't think of anything but the man beside her, the warmth of him, the sound of his heartbeat, the scent of his aftershave and perspiration.

Tears of relief streaming down her face, she didn't bother asking where they were going. She trusted him, the father of her child, and honestly didn't care where they went as long as she could keep her hands on him, her cheek pressed to his chest, the fire-retardant material of his uniform bristly against her skin. He pushed through a door into a private office. She didn't care whose or how he'd chosen the stark space filled with only a wooden desk, a black leather sofa and framed racing photos.

Briskly, he closed and locked the door. "Lucy Ann, deep breaths or you're going to pass out. I'm okay." His voice soothed over her in waves. "It was just a minor accident. The other guy's axle broke and he slammed into me. Everyone's fine."

She swiped her wrists over her damp eyes, undoubtedly smearing mascara all over her face. "When there's smoke—possibly fire—involved, I wouldn't call that minor."

Elliot cradled her face in his gloved hands. "My hair didn't even get singed."

"I'm not in a joking mood." She sketched jerky hands over him, needing to touch him.

"Then help me out." He stalled one of her hands and kissed her palm. "What can I say to reassure you?"

"Nothing," she decided. "There's nothing to say right now."

It was a time for action.

She tugged her hand free and looped her arms around his neck again and drew his face down to hers. She kissed him. More than a kiss. A declaration and affirmation that he was alive. She needed to connect with him, even if only on a physical level.

"Lucy Ann," he muttered against her mouth, "are you sure you know what you're doing?"

"Are you planning to go back to the race?" she asked, gripping his shoulders.

"My car's in no shape to race. You know that. But are you cert—"

She kissed him quiet. She was so tired of doubts and questions and reservations. Most of all, she couldn't bear for this to be about the past anymore. To feel more pain

for him. For herself. For how damn awful their childhoods had been—his even worse than hers.

Hell, she'd lived through those years with him, doing
her best to protect him by taking the brunt of the blame
when she could. But when the adults wouldn't step up
and make things right, there was only so much a kid
could do.

They weren't children any longer, but she still couldn't
stand to think of him getting hurt in any way. She would
do anything to keep danger away, to make them both
forget everything.

At this moment, that "anything" involved mind-
blowing sex against the door. Fast and intense. No fun
games or pretty fairy tales. This was reality.

She tugged at his zipper, and he didn't protest this
time. He simply drew back long enough to tug his racing gloves off with his teeth. With her spine pressed
to the door, he bunched up her silky dress until a cool
breeze blew across her legs. A second later, he twisted
and snapped her panties free, the scrap of lace giving
way to him as fully as she did.

But she took as much as she gave. She nudged the
zipper wider, nudging his uniform aside until she released his erection, steely and hot in her hand. Then, he
was inside her.

Her head thunked against the metal panel, her eyes
sliding closed as she lost herself in sensation. She glided a
foot along his calf, up farther until her leg hitched around
him, drawing him deeper, deeper in a frenzied meeting
of their bodies.

All too soon, the pleasure built to a crescendo, a wave
swelling on the tide of emotions, fear and adrenaline. And
yes, love. She buried her face in his shoulder, trying to
hold back the shout rolling up her throat. His hoarse en-

couragement in her ear sent pleasure crashing over her. Feeling him tense in her arms, shudder with his own completion, sent a fresh tingle of aftershocks through her. Her body clamped around him in an instinctive need to keep him with her.

With each panting breath, she drew in the scent of them. His forehead fell to rest against the door, her fingers playing with the close-shorn hair at the base of his neck. Slowly, her senses allowed in the rest of the world, the dim echo outside reminding her they couldn't hide in here forever.

They couldn't hide from the truth any longer.

Even as she took him now, felt the familiar draw of this man she'd known for as long as she could remember, she also realized she didn't belong here in this world now. She couldn't keep him because she couldn't stay.

No matter how intrinsic the connection and attraction between them, this wasn't the life she'd dreamed of when they'd built those fairy-tale forts and castles. In her fantasies, they'd all just looked like a real home. A safe haven.

She loved him. She always had. But she'd spent most of her adult life following him. It was time to take charge of her life, for herself and for her son.

It was time to go home.

As Elliot angled back and started to smile at her, she captured his face in her hands and shook her head.

"Elliot, I can't do this anymore, trying to build a life on fairy tales. I need something more, a real life, and maybe that sounds boring to you, but I know who I am now. I know the life I want to live and it isn't here."

His eyes searched hers, confused and a little angry. "Lucy Ann—"

She pressed her fingers to his mouth. "I don't want

to argue with you. Not like last time. We can't do that to each other again—or to Eli."

He clasped her hand, a pulse throbbing double time in his neck. "Are you sure there's nothing I can do to change your mind?"

God, she wanted to believe he could, but right now with the scent of smoke clinging to his clothes and the adrenaline still crackling in the air, she couldn't see any other way. "No, Elliot. I'm afraid not."

Slowly, he released her hand. His face went somber, resigned. He understood her in that same perfect and tragic way she understood him. He already knew.

They'd just said goodbye.

The next day, Elliot didn't know how he was going to say goodbye. But the time had come. He sat on Aunt Carla's front porch swing while Lucy Ann fed Eli and put him down for a nap.

God, why couldn't he and Lucy Ann have had some massive argument that made it easier to walk away, like before?

Instead, there had been this quiet, painful realization that she was leaving him. No matter how many fairy-tale endings he tried to create for her, she'd seen through them all. After their crazy, out-of-control encounter against the door, they'd returned to the hotel. She'd packed. He'd arranged for his private jet to fly them home to South Carolina.

Lucy Ann had made a token offer to travel on her own, not to disrupt his schedule—not to distract him. The implication had been there. The accident had happened because his life was fracturing. He couldn't deny it.

But he'd damn well insisted on bringing them back here himself.

The front door creaked open, and he looked up sharply. Lucy Ann's aunt walked through. He sagged back in his swing, relieved to have the inevitable farewell delayed for a few more minutes. He knew Lucy Ann would let him be a part of his son's world, but this was not how he wanted their lives to play out.

Carla settled next to him on the swing, her T-shirt appliquéd with little spring chickens. "Glad to know you survived in one piece."

"It was a minor accident," he insisted again, the wind rustling the oak trees in time with the groan of the chains holding the swing. The scent of Carolina jasmine reminded him of Lucy Ann.

"I meant that kidnapping stunt your friends staged. Turning your whole life upside down."

Right now, it didn't feel like he'd walked away unscathed. The weight on his chest pressed heavier with every second, hadn't let up since he'd been pulled from his damaged car. "I'll provide for Lucy Ann and Eli."

"That was never in question." She patted his knee. "I'm glad you got out of here all those years ago."

"I thought you wanted Lucy Ann to stay? That's always been my impression over the years."

"I do believe she belongs here. But we're not talking about her." She folded her arms over the row of cheerful chickens. "I'm talking about what you needed as a teenager. You had to leave first before you could find any peace here. Although, perhaps it was important for Lucy Ann to leave for a while, as well."

There was something in her voice—a kindred spirit? An understanding? Her life hadn't been easy either, and he found himself saying, "You didn't go."

"I couldn't. Not when Lucy Ann needed me. She was my one shot at motherhood since I couldn't have kids of my own." She shrugged. "Once she left with you, I'd already settled in. I'm on my own now."

"I just assumed you didn't want kids." He was realizing how little time he'd spent talking to this woman who'd given him safe harbor, the woman who'd been there for Lucy Ann and Eli. He didn't have much in the way of positive experience with blood relatives, but it was undoubtedly time to figure that out.

"I would have adopted," Carla confided, "but my husband had a record. Some youthful indiscretions with breaking and entering. Years later it didn't seem like it should have mattered to the adoption agencies that he'd broken into the country club to dump a bunch of Tootsie Rolls in the pool."

Elliot grinned nostalgically. "Sounds like he would have made a great addition to the Alpha Brotherhood."

And might Elliot have found a mentor with Lucy Ann's uncle as well if he'd taken the time to try?

"I wish Lucy Ann could have had those kinds of friendships for herself. She was lost after you left," Carla said pointedly. "She didn't find her confidence until later."

What was she talking about? "Lucy Ann is the strongest, most confident person I've ever met. I wouldn't have made it without her."

He looked into those woods and thought about the dream world she'd given him as a kid, more effective an escape than even his favorite book.

"You protected her, but always saw her strengths. That's a wonderful thing." Carla pinned him with unrelenting brown eyes much like her stubborn niece's. "But you also never saw her vulnerabilities or insecurities. She's not perfect, Elliot. You need to stop expecting her to be your fairy-tale princess and just let her be human."

What the hell was she talking about? He didn't have time to ask because she pushed up from the swing and left him sitting there, alone. Nothing but the creak of the swing and the rustle of branches overhead kept him company. There was so much noise in this ends-of-the-earth place.

Carla's words floated around in his brain like dust searching for a place to land. Damn it all, he knew Lucy Ann better than anyone. He saw her strengths and yes, her flaws, too. Everyone had flaws. He didn't expect her to be perfect. He loved her just the way she—

He loved her.

The dust in his brain settled. The world clarified, taking shape around those three words. He loved her. It felt so simple to acknowledge, he wondered why he hadn't put the form to their relationship before. Why hadn't he just told her?

The trees swayed harder in the wind that predicted a storm. He couldn't remember when he'd ever told anyone he loved them. But he must have, a long time ago. Kids told their parents they loved them. Although now that he thought about it, right there likely laid the answer for why the word *love* had dried up inside him.

He'd told himself he wanted to be a better parent than his father—a better man than his father. Now he realized being a better man didn't have a thing to do with leaving this porch or this town. Running away didn't change him. This place had never been the problem.

He had been the problem. And the time had come to make some real changes in himself, changes that would make him the father Eli deserved. Changes that would make him the man Lucy Ann deserved.

Finally, he understood how to build their life together.

* * *

The time was rapidly approaching to say goodbye to Elliot.

Her mind full of regrets and second thoughts, Lucy Ann rocked in the old bentwood antique in her room at Carla's, Eli on her shoulder. She held him to comfort herself since he'd long since settled into a deep sleep. She planned to find a place of her own within the next two weeks, no leaning on her aunt this time.

The past day since they'd left Monte Carlo after the horrifying accident had zipped by in such a haze of pain and worry. Her heart still hadn't completely settled into a steady beat after Elliot's accident. Right up to the last second, she'd hoped he would come up with a Hail Mary plan for them to build a real life together for Eli. She loved Elliot with all her heart, but she couldn't deny her responsibilities to her son. He needed a stable life.

To be honest, so did she.

There was a time she'd dreamed of escaping simple roots like the cabin in the woods, and now she saw the value of the old brass bed that had given her a safe place to slip away. The Dutch doll quilt draped over the footboard had been made for her by her aunt for her eighth birthday. She soaked in the good memories and the love in this place now, appreciating them with new eyes—but still that didn't ease the unbearable pain in her breaking heart as she hoped against all hope for a last-minute solution.

Footsteps sounded in the hall—even, manly and familiar. She would recognize the sound of Elliot anywhere. She had only a second to blink back the sting of tears before the door opened.

Elliot filled the frame, his broad-shouldered body that of a mature man, although in faded jeans and a simple gray T-shirt, he looked more like *her* Elliot. As if this weren't already difficult enough.

She smoothed a hand along Eli's back, soaking in more comfort from his baby-powder-fresh scent. "Did you want to hold him before you go?"

"Actually, I thought you and I could go for a walk first and talk about our future," he said, his handsome face inscrutable.

What else could there be left to say? She wasn't sure her heart could take any more, although another part of her urged her to continue even through the ache, just to be with him for a few minutes longer.

"Sure," she answered, deciding he must want to discuss visitation with Eli. She wouldn't keep him from his son. She'd made a horrible mistake in delaying telling Elliot for even a day. She owed him her cooperation now. "Yes, we should talk about the future, but before we do that, I need to know where you stand with Gianna. She approached me at the stadium just before your wreck." The next part was tougher to share but had to be addressed. "She said she's still in love with you."

His forehead furrowed. "I'm sorry you had to go through that, but let's be very clear. I do *not* love Gianna and I never did, not really. I did her a grave injustice by rebounding into a relationship with her because I was hurting over our breakup." The carefully controlled expression faded and honest emotion stamped itself clearly in his eyes. "That's a mistake I will not repeat. She is completely in the past. My future is with you and Eli. Which is what I want to speak with you about. Now, can we walk?"

"Of course," she said, relief that one hurdle was past and that she wouldn't have to worry about Gianna popping up in their lives again.

Standing, Lucy Ann placed her snoozing son in his portable crib set up beside her bed. She felt Elliot behind her a second before he smoothed a hand over their son's head affectionately, then turned to leave.

Wordlessly, she followed Elliot past the Hummel collection and outside, striding beside him down the porch steps, toward a path leading into the woods. Funny how she knew without hesitation this was where they would walk, their same footpath and forest hideout from their childhood years. Oak trees created a tunnel arch over the dappled trail, jasmine vines climbing and blooming. Gray and orange shadows played hide-and-seek as the sunset pushed through the branches. Pine trees reached for the sky. She'd forgotten how peaceful this place was.

Of course she also knew she'd walked the same course over the past year searching for this peace. Elliot's presence brought the moment to shimmering life as he walked beside her, his hands in his pockets. She assumed he had a destination in mind since they still weren't talking. A dozen steps later they came around a bend and—

Four of her aunt's quilts were draped over the branches, creating a fort just like the ones they'd built in the past. Another blanket covered the floor of their forest castle.

Lucy Ann gasped, surprised. Enchanted. And so moved that fresh tears stung her eyes.

Elliot held out a hand and she took it. The warmth and familiarity of his touch wrapped around her, seeping into her veins. She wasn't sure where he was going with this planned conversation, but she knew she couldn't turn back. She needed to see it through and prayed that somehow he'd found a way for them all to be together.

He guided her to their fort, and she sat cross-legged, her body moving on instinct from hundreds of similar hideaways here. He took his place beside her, no fancy trappings but no less beautiful than the places they'd traveled.

"Elliot, I hope you know that I am so very sorry for not telling you about Eli sooner," she said softly, earnestly. "If I had it to do over again, I swear to you I would handle things differently. I know I can't prove that, but I mean it—"

He covered her hand with his, their fingers linking. "I believe you."

The honesty in his voice as he spoke those three words healed something inside her she hadn't realized was hurting until now. "Thank you, Elliot. Your forgiveness means more to me than I can say."

His chest rose and fell with a deep sigh. "I'm done with racing. There's no reason to continue putting my life at risk in the car—or with Interpol, for that matter."

The declaration made her selfishly want to grasp at what he offered. But she knew forcing him into the decision would backfire for both of them. "Thank you for offering again, but as I said before, I don't want you to make that sacrifice for me. I don't want you to do something that's going to make you unhappy, because in the end that's not going to work for either of us—"

"This isn't about you. It isn't even about Eli, although I would do anything for either of you." He squeezed her fingers until she looked into his eyes. "This decision is about me. Interpol has other freelancers to call upon. I mean it when I say I'm through with the racing circuit. I don't need the money, the notoriety. The risk or the chaos. I have everything I want with you and Eli."

"But please know I'm not asking that sacrifice from you." Although, oh, God, it meant so much to her that he'd offered.

He lifted her hand and kissed the inside of her wrist.

"Being with you isn't a sacrifice. Having you, I gain everything."

Seeing the forgiveness that flooded his eyes, so quickly, without hesitation, she realized for the first time how much more difficult her deception must have been for him, given his past. All his life he'd been let down by people who were supposed to love him and protect him. His father had beaten him and for years he'd taken it to shield his mother. His mother hadn't protected him. Beyond that, his mother had walked out, leaving him behind. On the most fundamental levels, he'd been betrayed. He'd spent most of his adult years choosing relationships with women that were destined to fail.

And when their friendship moved to a deeper level, he'd self-destructed again by staying away. He'd been just as scared as she was about believing in the connection they'd shared the night they'd made love.

She knew him so well, yet she'd turned off all her intuition about him and run.

"Life doesn't have to be about absolutes. Your world or my world, a castle or a fort. There are ways to compromise."

Hope flared in his green eyes. "What are you suggesting?"

"You can have me." She slid her arms around his neck. "Even if we're apart for some of the year, we can make that work. We don't have to follow you every day, but Eli and I can still travel."

"I know you didn't ask me to give it up," he interrupted. "But it's what I want—a solid base for our son and any other children we have. I'm done running away. It's time for us to build a home. We've been dreaming of this since we tossed blankets over branches in the forest as kids. Lucy Ann," he repeated, "it's time for me to come home and make that dream come true. I love you, Lucy Ann, and I want you to be my wife."

How could she do anything but embrace this beautiful future he'd just offered them both? Her heart's desire had come true. And now, she was ready, she'd found her strength and footing, to be partners with this man for life.

"I've loved you all my life, Elliot Starc. There is no other answer than yes. Yes, let's build our life together, a fairy tale on our own terms."

The sigh of relief that racked his body made her realize he'd been every bit as afraid of losing this chance. She pressed her lips to his and sealed their future together as best friends, lovers, soul mates.

He swept back her hair and said against her mouth, "Right here, on this spot, let's build that house."

"Here?" She appreciated the sacrifice he was making, returning here to a town with so many ghosts and working to find peace. "What if we take our blankets and explore the South Carolina coast together until we find the perfect spot—a place with a little bit of home, but a place that's also new to us where we can start fresh."

"I like the way you dream, Lucy Ann. Sounds perfect." He smiled with happiness and a newfound peace. "We'll build that home, a place for our son to play, and if we have other children, where they can all grow secure." He looked back at her, love as tangible in his eyes as those dreams for their future. "What do you think?"

"I believe you write the most amazing happily ever after ever."

Epilogue

Elliot Starc had faced danger his whole life. First at the hands of his heavy-fisted father. Later as a Formula One race car driver who used his world travels to feed information to Interpol.

But he'd never expected to be kidnapped. Especially not in the middle of his son's second birthday party.

Apparently, about thirty seconds ago, one of his friends had snuck up behind him and tied a bandanna over his eyes. He wasn't sure who since he could only hear a bunch of toddlers giggling.

Elliot lost his bearings as two of his buddies turned him around, his deck shoes digging into the sand, waves rolling along the shore of his beach house. "Are we playing blind man's bluff or pin the tail on the donkey?"

"Neither." The breeze carried Lucy Ann's voice along with her jasmine scent. "We're playing guess this object."

Something fuzzy and stuffed landed in his hands.

Some kind of toy maybe? He frowned, no clue what he held, which brought more laughter from his Alpha Brotherhood buddies who'd all gathered here with their families. Thank goodness he and Lucy Ann had plenty of room in their home and the guest house.

He'd bought beach property on a Low Country Carolina island, private enough to attract other celebrities who wanted normalcy in their lives. He and Lucy had built a house. Not as grand as he'd wanted to offer her, but he understood the place was a reflection of how they lived now. She'd scaled him back each step of the way on upgrades, reminding him of their new priorities. Their marriage and family topped the list—which meant no scrimping on space, even if he'd had to forgo a few extravagant extras.

As for upgrades, that money could be spent on other things. They'd started a scholarship foundation. Lucy Ann's organizational and promotional skills had the foundation running like clockwork, doubling in size. They'd kept to their plans to travel, working their schedule around his life, which had taken a surprising turn. Since he didn't have to worry about money, thanks to his investments, he'd started college, working toward a degree in English. He was studying the classics along with creative writing, and enjoying every minute of it. Lucy Ann had predicted he would one day be a college professor and novelist.

His wonderful wife was a smart woman and a big dreamer.

There was a lot to be said for focus. Although with each of the brothers focused on a different part of the world, they had a lot of ground covered. Colonel Salvatore had taught them well, giving them a firm foundation to build happy, productive lives even after their Interpol days were past.

Famous musician Malcolm Douglas and his wife were

currently sponsoring a charity tour with their children in tow, and if it went as well as they expected, it would be an annual affair. The Doctors Boothe had opened another clinic in Africa last month along with the Monte Carlo mega-rich Hughes family—their daughters along for the ribbon-cutting. Computer whiz Troy Donavan and his wife, Hillary, had a genius son who kept them both on their toes.

"Elliot." Lucy Ann's whisper caressed his ear. "You're not playing the game."

He peeled off his blindfold to find his beautiful wife standing in front of him. His eyes took in the sight of her in a yellow bikini with a crocheted cover-up. "I surrender."

She tucked her hand in his pocket and stole the toy from his hand, tucking it behind her back. "You're not getting off that easily."

Colonel Salvatore chuckled from a beach chair where he wore something other than his gray suit for once—gray swim trunks and T-shirt, but still. Not a suit. But they were all taking things easier these days. "You never did like to play by the rules."

Aunt Carla lifted a soda in toast from her towel under a beach umbrella. "I can attest to that."

Elliot reached toward Lucy Ann for the mysterious fuzzy toy. "Come on. Game over."

She backed up, laughing. "Catch me if you want it now."

She was light on her feet, and he still enjoyed the thrill of the chase when it came to his wife. Jogging a few yards before he caught her, Elliot swept her up into his arms and carried her behind a sand dune where he could kiss her properly as he'd been aching to do all day. Except his house was so full of friends and family.

With the waves crashing and sea grass rustling, Elliot kissed her as he'd done thousands of times and looked forward to doing thousands more until they drew their last breath. God, he loved this woman.

Slowly, he lowered her feet to the ground, and she molded her body to his. If there wasn't a party going on a few yards away, he would have taken this a lot further. Later, he promised himself, later he would bring her out to a cabana and make love to her with the sound of the ocean to serenade them—his studies in English and creative writing were making him downright poetic these days.

For now though, he had a mission. He caressed up her arm until he found her hand. With quick reflexes honed on the racetrack, he filched the mystery toy from her fingers. Although he had to admit, she didn't put up much of a fight.

He slid his hand back around, opened his fist and found…a baby toy. Specifically, a fuzzy yellow rabbit. "You're—"

"Pregnant," she finished the sentence with a shining smile. "Four weeks. I only just found out for sure."

They'd been trying for six months, and now their dream to give Eli a brother or a sister was coming true. He hugged her, lifting her feet off the ground and spinning her around.

Once her feet settled on the sand again, she said, "When we were kids, we dreamed of fairy tales. How funny that we didn't start believing them until we became adults."

His palm slid over her stomach. "Real life with you and our family beats any fairy tale, hands down."

* * * * *

COMING SOON!

We really hope you enjoyed reading this book.
If you're looking for more romance
be sure to head to the shops when
new books are available on

Thursday 15th January

To see which titles are coming soon, please visit
millsandboon.co.uk/nextmonth

MILLS & BOON

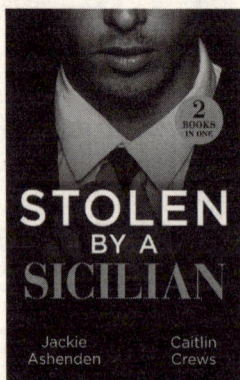

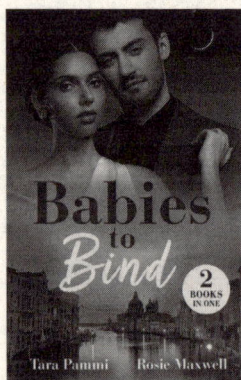

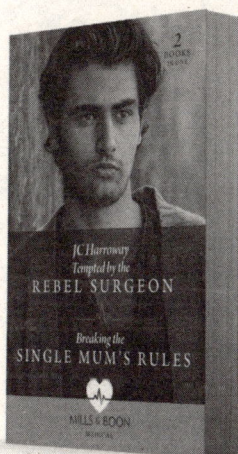

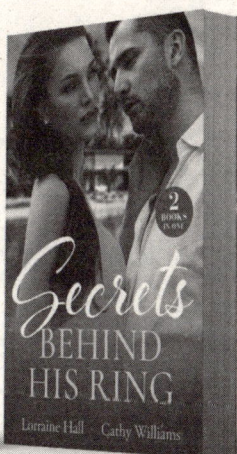

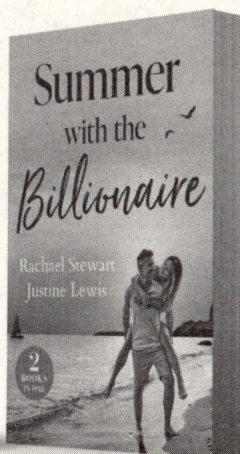

LET'S TALK
Romance

For exclusive extracts, competitions and special offers, find us online:

- **f** MillsandBoon
- **X** @MillsandBoon
- **◉** @MillsandBoonUK
- **♪** @MillsandBoonUK

Get in touch on 01413 063 232

For all the latest titles coming soon, visit
millsandboon.co.uk/nextmonth